HELEN FORRESTER

THE LEMON TREE

GUILD PUBLISHING
LONDON · NEW YORK · SYDNEY · TORONTO

This edition published 1990 by
Guild Publishing
by arrangement with William Collins Sons & Co. Ltd

First published in Great Britain by Collins 1990
Copyright © Helen Forrester 1990

CN 3454

Printed and bound in Great Britain by
Mackays of Chatham PLC, Chatham, Kent

AUTHOR'S NOTE

The author would like to thank sincerely Mr C. L. Bibby for his encouragement in the writing of this book and for the loan of much useful material, and also Mrs Lydia Hrabi for her descriptions of pioneer life.

The book is a novel, not a history. The Harding homestead, the Lady Lavender Soap Works and the people who lived or worked in them are all imaginary; whatever similarity there may be of name, no reference is made or intended to any person living or dead, except for a few well-known historical figures forming part of the background of the book.

Chapter One

'He's a woman,' Mr George Tasker announced lugubriously to Sarah, his wife of thirty years. He pushed the dog off the easy chair by the fire and sat down to take off his boots; they were very wet and were covered with wavy lines of white sediment. He put them neatly in the hearth to dry, as he continued, 'I'm workin' for a *woman*.' His thick Liverpool accent made him sound as if he had a heavy cold in the head.

'George, you know better than to walk on me new coconut matting with your dirty boots,' Sarah scolded. 'And what do you mean – he's a woman?'

'Wallace H. Harding is a woman!'

'Never!'

'He is – that is, *she* is. The Ould Fella's *niece* – not a nephew, like we imagined. She come into our department this morning, large as life, with the lawyer, Mr Benson, and Mr Turner, the chemist.' He stood up and rubbed his cold hands before the glowing fire. 'She stopped and shook hands with me, seeing as I'm the Soap Master,' he added with obvious satisfaction.

Sarah Tasker paused in the act of getting a casserole of tripe and onions out of the oven. She looked up at him through a burst of steam. 'Well, I'm blowed! How queer!'

She turned and laid the casserole on a white-scrubbed deal table. On a wooden board lay a loaf of bread with several slices ready cut; beside it, sat a small dish of butter. She said mechanically, 'Come and have your tea, luv.' She picked up a brown teapot from the hob of the kitchen range and put it on the table, beside two heavy pint mugs and a pitcher of milk. Then, from a built-in shelf, she lifted down the pride of her kitchen, a green glass sugar basin won at a fair. She put it by the teapot.

In anticipation of George's return from his job in the Lady Lavender Soap Works, she had laid his slippers on the fender to warm. George now put them on. He rose and stretched himself, a big, corpulent man, with a ruddy, kindly face boasting three generous chins. He sat himself at the table, surveyed the dish of tripe with approbation, and then said to Sarah, 'Nobody makes tripe better'n you do, luv. I can always savour a bit of tripe.'

He invariably made a similar remark, no matter what she cooked for this main meal of the day, and, equally invariably, she beamed as if she had never heard it before. It was what made George so nice to live with, she reflected. He always appreciated what you did.

'What's she like?' Sarah asked him, as she ladled generous dollops of tripe onto his plate.

Before answering, he considered the question carefully. Then he said, as he stuffed a forkful of tripe into his mouth, 'She's furrin – she's almost yellow. She int a lady like we understand one – and yet she is, if you know what I mean. And she's smart, no doubt about that.'

Sarah did not understand what he meant. She served herself, however, and commenced her meal, despite the flutter of worry in her stomach. This woman, whoever she was, could make or ruin their lives, she considered anxiously. When old Mr James Al-Khoury had died suddenly in November, 1885, they had heard that he had bequeathed the whole soap works, in which George had toiled for nearly twenty-five years, to his brother in the United States. Then Mr Benson, the lawyer, had discovered that the brother had also died, leaving everything he possessed to his wife. It had taken him some time to find out that she had moved to Canada, where she, too, had died, leaving as her sole legatee, Wallace H. Harding.

When George Tasker heard the name, whispered to him by Mr Helliwell, old James Al-Khoury's secretary, he had assumed that the new owner was a nephew of his late employer; Mr Helliwell, priding himself on his secretarial discretion, had not enlightened him further.

And now George was saying that it was a niece!

With a feeling that she was about to choke on her tripe, Sarah realized that this foreign woman from the Colonies, who wasn't a proper lady, would not, of course, be able to run the works, since she was a woman. Presumably she would sell it – and what happened to employees when a firm was sold over their heads, she dreaded to think. Too often, the older men found themselves out on the street. And then what would happen to them, with George out of work at fifty years of age?

George himself was ruminating over the same threat, but it did not deter him from eating his way steadily through his supper. His silent wife leaned forward and filled a mug with tea. She handed it to him. 'Like some more tripe?' she asked mechanically.

George wiped his mouth with the back of his hand and said he would. Then, while Sarah served him, he confirmed her fears by saying heavily, 'Rumour is she'll sell the place 'cos she couldn't run it – being a woman, like.'

'Aye, that's what I were thinkin'.' Then she asked warily, 'Who'd buy it?'

'Well, it *has* gone down a bit, since the Ould Fella died,' George acknowledged. 'But there's some as would buy it, I think, though times are bad. There's that Mr Lever what has started up by Crosfield's in Warrington. Soap mad, he is. And there's Crosfield's themselves. They might like it, seeing as it's close to the Brunswick Dock and the Brunswick Goods Station – very handy, it is, for shipping and receiving.' He sipped his tea and moved uneasily in his straight wooden chair.

'Would you keep your job?'

'It all depends,' he answered gloomily. 'I'm the Soap Master and they can't make soap without someone like me. But they could buy it and then shut it down – to get rid of a competitor.'

'Well, we'll worry about it when we get to it,' Sarah responded, determined to be brave and not increase her spouse's misgivings.

She wondered how far their savings, hidden under the loose board in the bedroom above them, would stretch if he were unemployed. With jobs so hard to find, he would hardly be likely to get another at his age, even though his mates always said he had a wonderful *feel* for soap.

'What's she like to look at?' Sarah felt very curious about this strange woman who had come all the way from Canada. Since she was the Ould Fella's nearest relative – except for his illegitimate son, Mr Benjamin, who didn't count, poor lad – she must be an Arab, like he had been. George had told her that James Al-Khoury had come from Lebanon, the same Lebanon that she had read about in her Bible. Did that really make him an Arab, she wondered suddenly, and was Miss Harding, therefore, an Arab lady, for all that she had a Western name? She smiled gently. The Ould Fella had been more like a friend than an employer. Many were the times when he had sat in this very kitchen, talking about the soap works. Always talked to George, he did, before making any changes. George and him got on like two o'clock.

With a sigh she pushed her plate of tripe to one side; she would try to eat it later. Arab or not, Mr James Al-Khoury and George had been happy together. Tears welled inside her, but she crushed them back; she must not let George know how worried she was.

While he ruminated over Sarah's question about Miss Harding, George took another slice of bread and spread it thinly with butter.

Eventually, he replied, 'Well, she's tall; same height as me, I should say. Thin as a rake. But when she smiles she's got a lovely face – and great brown eyes like a young heifer. She don't smile much, though. She were talkin' quite sharp to Mr Turner, the chemist. I didn't hear what she said, but I could see Turner didn't like it. He can be a bit uppity, and he wouldn't like being put down by a woman.'

'What was she dressed like?'

'Oh, she were all in black, in mourning, with a black veil thrown back from her face. She'd great rings·on her fingers, all gold. No stones. She'd a ring on her marriage finger what looked roughly made; ugly, it was – not much polished. Never seen one like it before.' He picked up his mug of tea and held it between his great hands. 'She int married, though. I heard her correct old Bobsworth, when he called her Mrs Harding. She's got a proud, cold way with her and she said as tart as a lemon to old Bob, "Miss Harding, if you please, Mr Bobsworth."'

Sarah knew Mr Bobsworth quite well and she smiled, despite her forebodings. The strange lady rose in her estimation. Though she would not have hesitated to call Mr and Mrs Bobsworth her friends, they did tend to put on airs, because he was the firm's head bookkeeper and forwarding clerk. 'And her only the daughter of a stevedore,' thought Sarah sourly.

George was speaking again, his heavy, grey brows knitted in puzzlement.

'As I said, Miss Harding shook hands with me, and then with everyone – even Alfie. She asked Alfie if he were born in Liverpool.'

Alfie was the seventeen-year-old mulatto labourer who swept the soap-boiling area. He also fetched and carried for the temperamental soap boilers, who sometimes dared not leave their soap pans, for fear they might miss the moment when the soap must be *proved*, or brine added or the boiling mixture turned off and carefully left to cool. The soap boilers were like housewives producing fine sponge cakes – everything had to be done exactly right. Sarah knew that a few people still regarded Mr Tasker as a magician, because he said he could *feel* how his great cauldrons of soap were getting on. He *knew*, they said. What he knew they did not specify – it appeared to them to be magic.

'She told me she makes her own soap on her farm in Canada,' expanded Mr Tasker. He put down his mug, leaned back from the table and belched. 'She told me as the nearest soap works is hundreds of miles off and there's no proper roads to it. Proper surprised I was, when she said it.' His three chins wobbled, as if to indicate agreement with his remarks.

Sarah omitted to remind him that she never used any soap at all on her face, because she believed that soap spoiled her skin. As a country girl, she had always scrubbed her face with a rag dipped in water from the rain barrel at her father's cottage door, and the present velvety smoothness of her complexion, despite her age, indicated that the natural oils of her skin had never been removed. Her five married daughters thought she was terribly old-fashioned and said that she owed it to her husband to use the soap he made. But she stubbornly refused, and told them that if they followed her example, they would not have to put that new-fangled cold cream on their faces every night. Lucky, they were, she thought, to be married to men with regular jobs, who could afford falderals like an occasional pot of cold cream.

'It's terrible she int a man,' George said with feeling. 'The Ould Fella was a good master, though he never paid out a penny he didn't have to. Young Benji takes after him – pity the lad's illegitimate; he could have followed him very nicely.' He paused to get a bit of bread from between his stained front teeth with his finger. 'Now, if she were a man, she'd be the same – a real firm hand on the tiller, she'd have. Backbone, she's got, by the sound of her. But a woman? What can a woman do? In a soap works?'

He paused, as he contemplated in his mind's eye the woman who now held his future in her slender fingers. Though she was so thin, he thought, she'd a nice waistline – and breasts like it said in the Bible, like pomegranates. Her long black dress fitted so closely, it stirred thoughts in a man, it did, he chided himself ruefully.

'What about Mr Benji?' inquired Sarah, interrupting his contemplation of the new owner's charms.

'Well, I'm sure James Al-Khoury were training him up to take his place when the time came, as a son should. But he only made one Will in his life, according to Mr Helliwell, and that were before Benji were born – and he were born on the wrong side of the blanket, so he int entitled to anything by law, poor lad. His dad could have left him everything in a Will and he would've got it all right. His mam and him and the lawyer has hunted everywhere, looking for another Will; but Mr Benson told Mr Helliwell that he'd have known if there *was* another Will – the Ould Fella would have come to him about it, 'cos Mr Benson used to vet all the firm's legal papers, contracts and such – James Al-Khoury didn't trust 'is own knowledge of English, so anything major he were goin' to sign, he got Mr Benson, his lawyer, to check first.'

'I suppose Mr Al-Khoury thought he'd plenty of time before he'd die.'

'Oh, aye. He weren't yet fifty. He never thought of a heart

attack, that I'm sure; it come as an awful shock to all of us. Proper sad it is for Benji and his mam. And him a smart lad, too.'

That night, in many tiny homes round the Brunswick Dock, Wallace Helena Harding was the subject of anxious discussion; times were so bad that the very hint of the loss of a regular job was enough to cause panic. Even Alfie, the mulatto casual labourer, who slept in the back hallway of a nearby warehouse, courtesy of the nightwatchman of the building, and who had endured bitter hardship all his life, viewed with equal terror the possibility of starvation or, the only alternative, the workhouse.

The warehouse watchman was an old seaman with a wooden leg who had known Alfie and his slut of a mother all the young man's short life, but as he sat beside him on the bottom step of the stone stairs of the great warehouse, a candle guttering in a lantern beside them, he could offer the lad little comfort.

'She'll 'ave to sell the soapery,' he said finally. 'It don't mean, though, that the new master won't take you on. Master Tasker'll speak for you, I've no doubt.' He paused to repack his clay pipe and then pulled back the shutter of his lantern to light it from the candle. He puffed thoughtfully for a few minutes. Then he said shrewdly, 'A new master could buy it and then shut it down, to put an end to it. Sometimes happens when shipping companies is sold – every bleedin' seaman that worked for the old company is out on the street – and the company what's done the buying puts its own men in.'

Alfie, who at best was permanently hungry, sat numbly silent, and then nodded agreement. He foresaw a long vista of petty theft to keep himself alive, unless he was prepared to seek out the homosexuals who roamed the streets in search of entertainment; either way, he could land in gaol. He hung his head so that the nightwatchman could not see the despair on his face.

7

Chapter Two

Unaware of the stir she had caused in the heart of Mr Tasker, her soap master, or the depth of the fears she had raised in all her employees, the thin, yellow woman from the wilds of Western Canada sat at a cherry-wood desk in the bay window of her bedroom in a house in nearby Hill Street. She was in the process of writing a letter to Joe Black, her partner on her homestead in western Canada.

She stared dismally at the soaking July downpour pattering against the glass. The room smelled damp and was unexpectedly cold. What a grey and black city Liverpool was and, yet, how exciting it was with its glittering gas-lamps and heavy traffic. And how alien she felt in it.

This proud Lebanese lady, who carried a man's name and then the name of the patron saint of Beirut, St Helena, and who normally feared nobody, was, for once, feeling intimidated by men. 'If you can call them men,' she muttered. 'Self-complacent barrels of lard.'

She scolded herself that she must not prejudge. 'You're tired with the journey, and the confinement of the ship. And being indoors all day. You must be patient.'

She leaned back and began to tug the hairpins out of her tight bun. 'I don't feel patient,' she informed herself through gritted teeth.

'Come on, now,' encouraged her cooler self. 'If you can make friends with miserable and angry Blackfoot and Crees, and cope with rebellious Metis – not to speak of Oblate Fathers with the power of God behind them – you can cope with an indifferent chemist named Turner, a Benjamin Al-Khoury, head of Sales and Assistant Manager, rude enough not to be here when the

8

new owner of his company arrives – and a lawyer you don't trust too much.' She pressed a tanned fist hard onto the desk, as if to emphasize her thoughts.

Then she absently spread out her fingers to look at her gold, handmade rings. Her eyes gleamed, and she laughed sardonically.

What would these stuffy Englishmen think if they knew that she lived with Joe Black, the son of a freed Ontario black slave and a Cree woman? He would make two of any of them, she thought with quiet pleasure; a big man with a face filled with laughter lines, lines that could harden when he felt insulted, till his jaw looked like a rat trap and his huge black eyes with their back-curling lashes lost their gentleness completely. He rarely struck anybody with his great fists, but when he did it was with the punishing skill of a Cree guard warrior. He had a clear, uncluttered mind, well able to assess a situation, an ability to reason, to negotiate with patience, before he struck.

These latter gifts were invaluable, she reflected, in a country full of wrathful native people; the Hudson's Bay Company had frequently used him as peacemaker between the Indians and themselves – and even missionaries were not past using him as an interpreter.

With one finger, she touched tenderly her gold rings. When Joe had discovered that she valued jewellery, he had panned for gold in the North Saskatchewan River and had fashioned the rings for her. Lots of men had subsequently tried to find the mother lode of the river's gold, but no one had succeeded; it was the rich, black soil which held the real wealth of the Northwest Territories.

She laughed again. 'These pink Englishmen would have a fit,' she told the raindrops on the windowpanes. 'But I'll teach them to patronize a woman,' she promised herself. 'I will decide the future of the Lady Lavender Soap Works!' In which remark, she was a little too optimistic.

As she met the various people in the new world she had entered in Liverpool, she had become slowly aware that she was shabby

9

and out of date, almost a figure of fun – a small snigger from a messenger boy, hastily stifled, a raised eyebrow, a stare in the street. She found the crush of people round her difficult enough, after the emptiness of western Canada, and this added attention had bothered her; it was the first time since she had left Lebanon that she had thought of clothes as anything else but covering against the elements.

She was unaware that, despite her clothes, she had a formidable presence. She moved swiftly with a long effortless stride, and she had responded in cold, clear sentences to the explanations given her by her escorts through the soapery. When, later, she had asked for further explanation, she had surprised them by recalling exactly what had been said.

Most of the men in the soapery wore a head-covering of some kind; but only Mr Tasker, the Soap Master and key man in the whole soapery, had doffed his bowler hat, when she had been introduced to him by Mr Benson, the lawyer. He had answered her questions carefully, his blue eyes twinkling amid rolls of fat as he endeavoured to watch the great vats steaming and heaving, and occasionally said, between his answers to her queries, 'Excuse me, Miss', while he instructed one of his assistants in the delicate task of producing excellent soap.

After meeting Mr Tasker and his helpers, Mr Benson had handed her over to Mr Turner, the chemist, who was, in the lawyer's opinion, in the absence of Benjamin Al-Khoury, the most refined of her employees. He should, therefore, know how to treat a lady.

A shy, retiring man, who wanted to get back to his little laboratory, Mr Turner's conversation was strained and desultory and did not particularly impress Wallace Helena. She was interested, however, when he told her that Mr Tasker was probably the best soap man in south Lancashire and could probably have gone to a bigger company.

'You mean they would've paid him more?'

'Yes.'

'I wonder that he did not move.'

'He and Mr James Al-Khoury were great friends. I believe they were together from the first establishment of the soapery. And there's no doubt that he and Mr Benjamin get on very well.'

Wallace Helena murmured approbation.

They went into the Power House together, to meet Mr Ferguson, the Steam Engineer, a middle-aged man with a ruddy face and an air of great self-confidence and dignity. He was dressed in immaculate blue overalls. He was attentive and informative to his lady visitor, well aware that he belonged to a newly emerged class of employee able to cope with the mechanization of industry and was, therefore, a prized servant of the company. He was a trifle defensive with Mr Turner. Wallace Helena noticed this and wondered why. She had yet to discover the subtleties of class in British society; Mr Ferguson was exceedingly proud of his abilities, but he remained a working man; Mr Turner was also a highly trained man – but he was middle-class – a man of privilege as well as ability.

As she walked slowly round the works, she had noted carefully the reactions of her employees to herself and also reactions between them. After watching for years the body language of the Indians who passed over her land, to judge whether they were hostile or friendly, she had learned to observe the slightest shrug, the curve of a lip, the smallest move of hip or hand. She had quickly picked up the general nervousness of the men to whom she was introduced and she had felt sorry for them. In return, she had tried to show herself as a confident, capable person, and she felt that some of them had liked her.

Only Mr Benjamin Al-Khoury had failed to turn up.

According to Mr Bobsworth, the bookkeeper and forwarding clerk, he was in Manchester and would return in a few days' time. 'Life has been very hectic for Mr Benjamin since Mr James passed away, him being Assistant Manager to Mr James, like. Everything fell on him.' Mr Bobsworth heaved a sigh deep enough to make every inch of his five feet quiver.

She had nodded, and remarked that Uncle James's death must have been a shock to everyone.

'Indeed, yes, Miss Harding.' His eyes blinked behind his small, gold-rimmed spectacles, and then he said, 'I should tell you, Ma'am, that Mr Benjamin asked me to convey his regrets to you at not being here today; he's investigating the unexpected refusal of a customer to renew his contract with us – in the cotton trade, they are.'

'I see,' she had replied noncommittally, and Mr Bobsworth had begun to worry that young Benji had offended the lady deeply by his absence.

Now, seated in her stuffy bedroom, she made a face as she recalled the conversation.

If, as she suspected, Mr Benjamin Al-Khoury was her illegitimate cousin, a product of Uncle James's love affair with an English woman, about which she had heard vaguely as a young girl when she was living in Chicago, he was probably suffering from an acute bout of jealousy because she had inherited his father's business.

She was fairly sure that, if he had been a legitimate child, he could have claimed, in law, at least a part of his father's Estate, no matter what his parent's Will had said about leaving all his property to his brother, Charles, her own father. Mr Benson had, however, assured her that there were no other claimants to the Estate, and she presumed that Mr Benson knew his law.

It was possible, of course, that Benjamin Al-Khoury was some very distant relative, whose parents had also managed to survive the massacre of Christians in 1860.

With a wry smile at the foibles of his own youth, Mr Benson had explained to her that, when he was first setting up his law practice and was badly in need of every penny he could earn, her Uncle James had consulted him about the exact meaning of a contract he was about to sign. Afterwards, in pursuit of a small additional fee, he had inquired if Uncle James had a Will and, since he had not, he had been persuaded to make one.

At that time, Uncle James had had no one else to whom to leave his modest possessions, so, at the age of twenty-three, he had left everything to his brother, Charles, in Chicago. And now, as the residual legatee of her father's and her mother's own Wills, Wallace Helena found herself inheriting a well-run soap manufactory.

12

'Why did't Uncle James make a more recent Will?' she had asked Mr Benson.

'Dear lady, I do not know. I did mention the matter to him once or twice; but he was a tremendously busy man – and, like all of us, he did not anticipate dying at forty-nine.' He had smiled indulgently at her. 'Do you have a Will, Miss Harding?'

'No, I don't,' she had admitted, a note of surprise in her voice; she had never thought of dying herself, despite the hazards she faced daily in her life as a settler. Mr Benson's question had made her suddenly aware of the problems Joe Black might face if, indeed, she did die. She smiled a little impishly at the lawyer, and then said gravely, 'I'll attend to it.'

She reverted to the matter of her uncle's Will. 'Perhaps Uncle James really didn't have anyone else to leave his money to, except Papa – or me?' In view of her surmises about Benjamin Al-Khoury, the question was a loaded one, and she watched carefully for her lawyer's reaction.

Mr Benson was not to be drawn, however, and he answered her noncommittally, 'Possibly not.' She was left to puzzle about her Uncle James's private life.

Now, as she took up her pen and dipped it into the ink, preparatory to continuing her letter to Joe Black, she decided philosophically that she would deal with Mr Benjamin whenever he decided to turn up.

She wrote in English, a language she had learned in Chicago and from her stepfather, Tom Harding: 'Dear Joe, how I wish you were with me! I need your brains – and I need your love to sustain me.'

Should she tell this man, whom she loved with a passion and depth which sometimes frightened her, how nervous she felt?

No. He would only worry, and worry never solved anything.

With deliberate cheerfulness, she continued, 'Thanks to Messrs Cunard, I arrived safely in Liverpool yesterday morning. At Montreal, Mr Nasrullah, Grandpapa Al-Khoury's friend – a very old man – saw me and my baggage safely transferred to the ship, as we arranged. He was worried that I was travelling steerage, alone; but everyone was very friendly to me, though it was not very comfortable. I gave Mr Nasrullah a hasty note to post to you, and I hope you received it safely. Now that the railway line has reached Calgary, it should make a vast difference to the speed with which we can send and receive letters, even from as far north as Edmonton. (I wonder if Edmonton and St Albert will *ever* be served by a railway line?)

'My dearest, it was good of you to accompany me in the stage all the way down to Calgary, to see me onto the train. I shall never forget the wonderful night we spent in that dreadfully noisy hotel! How I miss you now!

'When the train moved out and your dear figure receded into the distance, I wished I had never set out on such a wild adventure – and yet the English lawyers sounded so eager to sell Uncle's business that I smelled a rat; as I said to you, the works could be more valuable than they would have me know. Could the lawyers make a gain by selling to someone with whom they had made a private agreement?

'Today, I did a fairly thorough inspection of the plant. I have not yet seen the company's books, nor do I know enough to say how well it is doing. I am, however, uneasy that Mr Benjamin Al-Khoury, the Assistant Manager, was not here to greet me; I felt snubbed!

'He was left nothing in Uncle James's Will, and I suspect that he is his *illegitimate* son. No matter which side of the blanket he was born on, however, I am excited at the thought that I may actually have a blood relative. You know how shorn I feel because I have no family – and, without your support, I am sure I would have given up on life long ago – bless you, my dearest one.

'I must bear in mind, though, that this man may be very jealous that I, and not he, now own the Lady Lavender.

'Mr Benson, the lawyer, has found me two rooms near the works, in the house of Mrs Hughes, a widow – the address is at the top of this letter. The rooms are clean and her cooking is good, though I am feeling the sudden change in diet.

'I wish you were with me. The city is very lively. I confess that I doubt if you would enjoy the noise and confusion – or the heavy smoke in the air – near the works, the filth of it is overwhelming.

'The products of the soapery put our home-made efforts to shame. They are sweet-smelling tablets, light brown or blue-grey in colour. To scent them, they use lavender oil, caraway or cinnamon. They have, also, a fuller's earth soap for very delicate skins. They do make plain bars of soap for laundry and for the cotton industry, and these do not smell much better than the ones we make at home!

'The lavender oil is produced by a lady in the south of England. She also makes a perfume of it by diluting it with spirits of wine and bottling it. We act as her northern distributor for these little bottles of scent and they are sold side-by-side with our lavender soap. It is very pleasant to dab a little on my wrist and sniff it.

'The whole operation is so interesting that I am already questioning whether I should sell it. If it is financially sound, I could, perhaps, find a knowledgeable man to run it.'

She stopped writing, and chewed the end of her pen. She knew already what she would like to do, she considered longingly. She had been born and spent her childhood in a city, and she would like to settle in Liverpool, rain and dirty air notwithstanding, and run the business herself. After all, she ruminated, she knew the centre of Liverpool quite well; she and her parents, as refugees, had spent some weeks in it, waiting for an immigrant ship to the United States – and she remembered with pleasure the pool crowded with sailing vessels which had given Liverpool its name.

'With all that Papa taught me, I *could* learn to manage the Lady Lavender – it's obviously got some good employees,' she assured herself. 'I suspect that before I was ten I'd learned more than some of these fat Englishmen know. I don't know the detail of their work, but I can organize people – I can sell. But what on earth would Joe think of it – of coming to a city?'

She considered the question seriously; he wasn't getting any younger; it was possible that he might enjoy the sheer comfort of city life after the remorseless struggle they faced on their homestead.

Wishful thinking! she chided herself, and slowly dipped her pen into the ink.

'If we drew income from the soap works,' she continued, 'we could accumulate more riverside land, as it becomes available, and increase our grain crops – the minute a railway crosses the North Saskatchewan and reaches Edmonton, eastern markets would be opened up to us – and we might even have money to spend!'

She paused in her writing and wondered how many more terrible winters they would have to endure before they made enough to, perhaps, move south to a better climate. And it's not only winter, she considered sadly, it's clouds of merciless mosquitoes, forest fires, unsettled Indians and Metis, floods – and hunger – gnawing hunger – and the endless, endless physical work.

She bit her lips, and continued to write, asking him how the crops were doing. She hoped the cougars were not being a nuisance again this year – that was a huge pair he had shot last year.

Cougars? Bobcats? Wolves? They were a curse when one had livestock. She grinned suddenly at the idea of a cougar sniffing its way comfortably into the yard of the soap works, and then went on to give him a different piece of news.

'Yesterday, in the street, I heard Arabic being spoken, and, frankly, I was surprised that I still understood it – though it is my childhood tongue. Three men definitely from the East, probably seamen, were talking together at a street corner; they had lost their way, but being a stranger myself to this end of the city, I could not help them so I passed on. While I am here, I hope to get some accurate news of the present situation in the Lebanon.'

She put down her pen and slowly stretched herself. It had been good to hear the language of her family. She would give a great deal to walk the ancient streets of Beirut or sit quietly in her parents' courtyard, if it still existed, and listen to cheerful Arab voices.

But there were no familiar voices left, she reminded herself; she would have to sit by herself under the old lemon tree.

She shivered, and a sense of awful aloneness engulfed her, the ghastly loneliness of a sole survivor, with no one else alive to understand completely the horrors she had seen. For a moment she did not hear the horses' hooves in the street outside or the rain on the window or feel the chill of her room; she was lost in a misty ebb of consciousness, through which she heard the roar of a mob out of control and the screams of the dying.

She sat perfectly still in her stiff little chair, her white face covered with perspiration, until the moment passed. Then she got up and stumbled to the washstand, to pick up a damp face flannel and press it to her temples.

Chapter Three

Feeling a little better after the damp coldness of wiping her face with a flannel, Wallace Helena sat down on the edge of the bed and slowly unlaced her neat black boots. She hauled them off and thankfully flexed her toes. On the homestead she wore soft Indian moccasins and gaiters, for which she traded barley with a Cree woman each year. She kept her precious boots for formal occasions, like visiting Mr Ross's hotel in the settlement by Fort Edmonton. In the hotel, she was sometimes able to contact small groups of travellers in need of supplies, like flour, meat or, perhaps, a horse; they were also occasionally glad to buy well-salted butter or sour cream. The visitors were usually surveyors and miners passing through, but increasingly there were well-to-do British hunters, who had simply come to enjoy a new wilderness and hunt big game. Most of them dealt with the Hudson's Bay Company or one or two other suppliers, who could provide coffee, sugar and salt, tobacco, alcohol and other imports. Wallace Helena, however, kept her prices low and she could usually find someone with little money only too thankful to buy cheaply. They were surprised, and sometimes amused, to be approached by a woman, particularly one who did not fit the usual mould. With her tall, spare figure and her long, mannish stride, her carefully calculated prices and her ability to strike a bargain, she was a well-known local character round Fort Edmonton, particularly disliked by the other suppliers.

Now, she longed to rest on the feather bed, but she felt she must finish her letter to Joe; she had promised to write frequently; and, even with the new railway, a letter would take some time to reach him. She made herself return to the tiny desk in the window.

After the quietness of the bush, it felt strange to be back in the hurly-burly of a city and be immediately plunged into the complexities of a factory, the first modern one that she had ever seen; it was stranger still to realize that, as soon as her uncle's Will had been probated, she would actually own the soap works.

Pen in hand, she stared thoughtfully out of the bedroom window. Already, she had casually remarked to Mr Turner, the chemist, that it might be cheaper for the Lady Lavender to buy seed and themselves press the oil they used, rather than import it.

Mr Turner had replied superciliously that to make it pay, they would probably have to find a market for the residual solids.

It was probably the most sensible remark he had made to her that day, but she had snapped him up promptly. 'The solids can be used for winter food for steers. Don't your farmers know that?'

Mr Turner had gulped and failed to reply immediately; he knew little about farming. What did women know about cattle?

When he had recovered himself, he pointed out that a new venture like that would need capital. 'Presses,' he added vaguely, 'and – er – men who understand farming, to sell the residue.'

'Right.' She had stopped to take a small black notebook and pencil out of her reticule, and made a quick note. She might, she thought, cost it out in years to come, when she understood more about the business.

Playing at her father's feet in his large silk warehouse in Beirut or cuddled by her mother's side when the family was gathered together in the evening, she had absorbed a great deal of the discussions going on over her head. Amongst much else, she understood the importance of estimating cost and return – and the ever-present risks of undertaking something new. During her long tour of the soap works, she had felt, at times, as if her father were whispering to her, telling her what to look for, giving her quiet advice.

And then there was the glycerine, which, the chemist had informed her, was left over after the soap was made. He had mentioned that, when properly refined, it was a good base for salves for the skin and for certain medicines; he and Benjamin

19

Al-Khoury were working on a scented lotion for chapped hands, to market alongside the lavender perfume and toilet soaps. At present, he had informed her, the glycerine was sold to explosives manufacturers.

Explosives were used for war, she ruminated, as she enclosed her letter to Joe in an envelope and licked the flap; and she had had enough threat of that round her farm near Fort Edmonton, when the Metis had risen in defence of their land rights. It was only last year that their leader, Louis Riel, had been hanged for rebellion.

Her mind wandered to the problems of her life as a settler. The rebellion had been very frightening; and yet, she considered uneasily, Louis Riel had had a rightful cause. His people were descendants of early European settlers and their Indian wives, and they had been dispossessed of their land further east by the rush of new immigrants from Europe. In despair, they had moved westward to squat on the undeveloped lands of the Hudson's Bay Company. Unlike her stepfather, who had himself been a squatter on the Company's holdings, many of them had not succeeded in establishing their right to remain on the land. She thought smugly that it was thanks to her stepfather's and her own sagacity that she now owned the land she farmed.

A squatter's legal rights were tenuous, she knew; she herself had once not hesitated to try to overset a Metis squatter's right to a riverside homestead which she had coveted.

'But at least I finished up by paying him for it,' she had said defensively to one of the Oblate Fathers from St Albert, when he had dared to criticize her ruthless business methods. 'It cost me all I had at the time,' she had added, hatred in every inch of her. 'I could have hounded him off – like the Hudson's Bay tried to do to my stepfather.'

Her eyes, long, oriental, heavily fringed with thick black lashes, were half-closed and averted from him, as she had continued, 'When I first came to Fort Edmonton, a young innocent girl, that man shouted obscenities after me, because I'm sallow-skinned and he thought I was a Chinese – a man's plaything. And I would prefer not to repeat what he used to call my stockman, Joe Black. Why should I care about him, Father?' She had given a dry little laugh, and had turned and left the discomfited priest standing in the middle of the spring mud of the Fort's yard.

The priest had sighed. He had been warned by an older priest that this wilful, proud, strayed member of the Christian flock, a lone Maronite Christian survivor of the 1860 massacres in Lebanon, had endured a lot of sorrow. She was now in her late thirties, and, in her business affairs, she had the reputation of being as merciless as an Iroquois woman – and when he considered what Iroquois women had done to captured Jesuit priests in earlier times, a faint shudder went through his thin, bent frame, as if the devil had touched him on the shoulder.

Yet, as he trudged along the trail to his Mission in St Albert, he had to admit that during the Metis uprisings she had been one of the few to remain calm. She had prepared to defend her homestead with more common sense than other settlers, many of whom had panicked – even he and his fellow priests, who ministered to the Metis, had been very frightened.

'Nobody has to worry about Wallace Harding or Joe Black,' one of his parishioners in St Albert had assured him. 'They're the best shots in the district and she's got that cabin well defended; the rebels'll go for easier loot.'

Then, of course, there was Joe Black himself, the priest reflected; Joseph Black, the only negro in the district. Joe had a history, too.

According to Father Lacombe, who knew almost everything about everybody, he was the son of a Cree woman and a freed slave who had accompanied John Rowand on his exploration of the Bow River, further south.

He had been brought up in his maternal grandfather's lodge and had then gone to work on one of the early ranches. In consequence, he had a wonderful way with horses – with any animals, if it came to that. Later, he had trapped for a time, following the animals northward, and had finally met up with Tom Harding, an American miner. The young priest had never met Tom Harding, but the story was well known; Tom had been a squatter on undeveloped Hudson's Bay Company land a few miles east of Fort Edmonton.

Disregarding the splutters of rage from the Hudson's Bay

Factor at the Fort, who was rapidly becoming less and less able to enforce his company's rights to the immense territory they were supposed to control, Tom Harding and Joe Black had, with sporadic aid from Joe's Cree relatives and a couple of temporarily stranded miners, slowly opened up several square miles, much of it forest. Based on what he had observed in the United States, Tom Harding sowed grass and clover, as well as barley, oats and potatoes. It was backbreaking work and, in addition, they had had the difficult task of protecting their first few animals and hens, not only from predators but also from increasingly hungry parties of Indians.

Despite Joe's abilities as a hunter and trapper, game was scarce and in the early years they were often hungry themselves. Each year, when the ferocious winter descended on them, they would ask themselves why they bothered and would become irritable with each other. But the first sound of water dripping from the snow-covered roof would raise their spirits, and they would begin to plan the coming year. The Hudson's Bay Factor, aware of whispers from eastern Canada and from London about the Hudson's Bay mandate being withdrawn, gave up on them and was thankful, occasionally, to buy or trade for some of their crops, to feed the increasing number of people living in and around the Fort.

The trust between the two men became absolute.

As the early winter cold bit into the priest's own underfed body during his long walk back to the Mission, he secretly envied Joe Black's physical strength. Over six feet tall, Joe was, and built to it, with wiry grey hair, teeth discoloured by tobacco, and big black eyes surrounded by innumerable wrinkles; those eyes, thought the priest, could be cold and watchful, like those of a cougar he had once seen; at other times they could dance with amusement, and his deep rumbling laugh would roll across the room. An old clerk at the Fort had told him that Joe had been a fine, handsome man until he had caught the smallpox. The dreadful disease had left its marks on his cheeks and forehead, the priest reflected with compassion, and probably on his character as well.

To the priest, Joe seemed quieter than his general reputation at the Fort would indicate. Men always said that he and Tom Harding were formidable in a fight, but it did not seem to the young priest that he ever tried to *pick* a quarrel.

He's very astute – and he's older now – perhaps that's why, guessed the priest; he must be at least fifty. But whatever a hard life had done to him, he was alert and quick to grasp a concept; you never had to explain anything twice to the man. And his looks did not seem to bother Miss Harding, Tom's stepdaughter; it was said that she slept with Joe every night.

They were always together, riding their range, branding, setting traps in the autumn, sowing, reaping, or out shooting for the pot – not that there was much left to shoot these days. Sometimes they would be down at the Fort bargaining for sugar, coffee and tobacco, anything they could not grow or get from the Indians, the tall woman with the marks of suffering on her face and Joe with his wide grin like a steel trap.

Wallace and Joe were notorious for never parting with a penny, if they could do a deal any other way, ruminated the priest, though it was said they often gave food from their slender store to hungry Crees and Blackfoot. Tom Harding had owed his life to a Blackfoot; and his half-Cree partner, Joe, fed his own people.

Now, one of the subjects of the priest's idle thoughts undressed slowly in a damp, cold bedroom in faraway Liverpool. She thankfully unlaced the tight corset she had bought in Montreal on the advice of the daughter of Mr Nasrullah, with whom she had stayed whilst waiting for the boat to Britain to arrive. She shivered in the unaccustomed dampness as she slipped on a cotton shift. At the washstand, she poured cold water from a pink, flowered jug into a matching bowl and slowly washed her face and hands with a piece of Lady Lavender toilet soap.

Earlier, her Welsh landlady, Mrs Hughes, had kindly put a stone hot water bottle in the feather bed, and when she climbed into the bed it was still warm. The British summer was abominably chilly, Wallace thought irritably, and she pulled the hot water bottle up from her feet and clasped it against her stomach.

It was hard and uncomfortable. Fretfully, she pushed it away from her.

Without thinking, she turned over and opened her arms to the other side of the bed. But there was no one there; and again she felt encompassed by an overwhelming loneliness. What was she doing here? Her life was with Joe, she told herself.

Still shivering slightly under the linen sheets, her mind, nevertheless, wandered to the new world of the soapery and its all-male managers and workers.

From her father she had learned that employees were to be treated like family. You scolded them and kept them in line with threats of unemployment; but you looked after them, and they looked after your interests. In fact, most of her father's employees had been blood relations, distant ones, sometimes – but related all the same.

Were some of the men in the soapery related to her? Or, regardless of that, did they think of themselves as being equivalent to her family? To be protected and cared for by her through good times and bad? It was a formidable thought.

She felt fairly certain that Benjamin Al-Khoury was a blood relation. She remembered vaguely, when her family had been living in Chicago, her father tut-tutting that her Uncle James appeared to be living with an English woman, without benefit of marriage. Such a misalliance would cast a bad name on the Lebanese community, he felt. She believed that he had written to Uncle James, saying that he should marry the lady. Wallace Helena could not recall that her uncle had ever replied to that particular point.

When, after her father's death, Uncle James had offered her mother and herself a home, her mother had explained that he was not married to the lady who lived with him; and this could make life difficult for them, if they joined his household.

Benjamin Al-Khoury was an employee like any other employee. Yet, if he were her cousin, should she treat him differently? If he were highly resentful that she, instead of himself, had inherited his father's Estate, how could she placate him, without losing her status as employer?

As she lay amid the unaccustomed softness of the feather bed, she began to think very carefully about how she could retain her authority and yet convey to him that she understood his probable unhappiness.

To her knowledge, she had no other blood relative and that would make him unique to her, someone very special in her estimation. It would put him on a completely different level from everyone else connected with the soapery.

A tiny thrill of hope went through her. To have a real relation implied a reciprocal obligation. Here might be a person of whom one could ask help and reasonably expect assistance as a duty, as from a brother. One could hope for consideration and affection, given freely. It was a wonderful idea to a woman who had faced as bravely as she could her uprooting from her native soil. And, when she had put down tenuous new roots in alien Chicago, she had been uprooted again, to face a life in Canada so harsh that she had expected to die. But, somehow, she had lived, a lonely refugee, misunderstood and disliked.

'And why I should survive, God only knows,' she thought wearily, with an odd sense of having been left out.

Amid the turmoil of new impressions collected through the day, it did not strike her that she had been thinking of the Lady Lavender Soap Works as an enterprise she would run herself. She had simply been annoyed when her lawyer, Mr Benson, had suggested that she should leave the selling of the works to him; she had brushed the suggestion off as an insult to her as a helpless woman. The fact that the original reason for her visit had simply been to assess the value of the business had been pushed to the back of her mind by the thrilling possibilities she had immediately seen, as she walked soberly round the buildings.

The straggling collection of sheds, which made up her late uncle's factory, suggested to her not only a means of livelihood but also the chance to live in a city again, a place of fine new buildings, and homes full of lively enterprising people – literate people. They might even know where Lebanon is, she considered soberly – even have commercial ties with Beirut; Liverpool ships probably docked in Beirut sometimes.

Could one visit Beirut from Liverpool, she wondered suddenly. By this time the city might have settled down again and be safe for a Christian to visit.

As she lay staring at the moulded ceiling of the bedroom, a tightness from a long, sternly suppressed anguish seemed to grow in her chest. She breathed deeply in an effort to stop it engulfing her, and gradually, like some threatening shadow, it retreated.

She sat up and took a sip of water from a glass on the bedside table. Then she lay down again and curled herself up into a tight, foetal position, as if to protect herself from feelings too painful to be unleashed.

Chapter Four

She slept uneasily and suffered a familiar nightmare, though some of the hazy, sadistic faces which seemed to peer at her out of the darkness were, this time, reminiscent of the men she had met in the soapery.

She cried out frantically to them, 'I'm not Wallace Harding, I'm not! I'm Helena Al-Khoury – and I hate the Territories. I want to go home to Beirut. Let me go! I want to go home.'

It seemed as if she pulled herself away from restraining hands, and floated easily along a seashore; and then she was in her father's courtyard amid the perfume from the blossom of the lemon tree. Uncle James was picking her up and saying she was as sweet as the flowers on the tree. She laughed in his swarthy, cheerful face, and he was gone. Instead, her mother was there, her blenched face beaded with sweat, as she held Helena's hand and pulled her along. 'Hurry, my darling. Run!'

1860 and she was nearly twelve. As her terrified mother pulled her along behind her father, Charles Al-Khoury, she heard his startled exclamations at the hideous sights which each turn in the narrow streets revealed, the carnage left by a mob gone mad.

Before turning into a narrow alley leading down to the waterfront, they crouched close to the side of the blank wall of a warehouse, to catch their breath, while Charles Al-Khoury peered down the lane to make sure it was clear.

It was already darkened by the long shadows of the evening and the smoke from the ruins of old houses further down, but there was no sound, except for the crackle of fire; the looters had been thorough. The little family flitted silently down it. As they crossed another alley they heard men shouting in the distance, and Charles Al-Khoury increased his pace.

27

Almost numb with fear, his wife and daughter followed closely after him. Suddenly, he half-tripped over a dark shape lying on the ground. His women bumped into him and clung to him.

They stared down in horror. A woman had had her clothes torn off her. She had been butchered like a dead cow, and the child of her womb lay smashed against a house wall. A horribly mutilated, decapitated man lay near her, and further down the alley were other pitiful bundles, blood-soaked and still.

Leila Al-Khoury vomited, the vomit making her fluttering black head veil cling to her face. Young Helena began to scream in pure terror.

Her father clapped his hand over her mouth. 'Helena!' he whispered forcefully. 'Be quiet.'

She swallowed her fear and nearly choked with the effort.

As they continued to scurry down narrow lanes, leading seaward, her father held her close to him, so that she would see as little as possible of the carnage; dogs were already nosing cautiously at the corpses of the Maronite Christians and being challenged by venturesome birds. One or two dogs had entered little homes through smashed doorways and could be heard growling over the spoils inside.

Wallace Helena, the grown woman, stirred in her bed, and cried out to the only person left to assuage her nightmares. 'Joe, darling! Joe!' But she was not heard and plunged again into her scarifying dreams, her heart beating a frantic tattoo.

Much later on, when they had established themselves in Chicago, she had asked her mother how the massacre had come about. She had been sitting cross-legged on her parents' bed, watching her mother struggle into Western clothes.

Her mother had explained that the Muslim Turkish rulers of Lebanon did not like Christians very much; neither did another sect called Druze.

Egged on by the Turks, the Druze set out to eradicate their ancient enemies, the Maronite Christians, some of whom were enviably richer than they should be. In Beirut, they struck on July 9th, 1860.

'We had heard rumours of unrest amongst the Druze, for some time before,' her mother told her, 'but neither your father nor your grandfather – my father – believed that we should be disturbed.

'Our family had always lived in or near Beirut; it was such a pleasant little place – and you'll remember our visiting our kin nearby. Our courtyard wall was high and strongly built – quite enough, we believed, to protect the house. And we were well-to-do; we could always placate the tax collectors and the servants of the Sultan, Abdul Mejid – may he be eternally accursed!' She sounded vicious, as she lashed out at the hated Turkish ruler. Then she said more calmly, 'You know, it's usually the less powerful, and the poor who can't pay, who are attacked.'

In the hope of obliterating her sickening memories, Helena had screwed up her eyes and covered them with her hands; yet there was a morbid desire to know more.

'Well, why did we run away then?'

'The rabble – Druze and Turks alike – swept right into our neighbourhood – you heard them and saw them. And your respected father knew then that this uprising was much more serious than usual; he had not believed an earlier warning which his brother had had whispered to him by a kindly Turkish official – he had felt the warning was part of a campaign by the Turks to get the Maronites to move out of their own accord.

'So when the mob came in like a flight of angry bees – they were mad with hashish, I suspect – he knew in a flash that the warning had been a genuine act of kindness. He heard the screams and the gunshots, and he ran upstairs from his office to the roof, to confirm his fears.' She paused, her voice harsh from unshed tears. 'You and I'd been sitting under the lemon tree, by the well – so quiet and peaceful. But from the roof Papa could really see what was happening. Dear Grandpa's house was already a great bonfire and the shrieking crowd was pouring into the square at the bottom of our street; he said the menace of the swords and guns flashing in the evening sun was terrifying.'

Helena said hesitantly from behind her hands, 'I remember Papa leaning over the parapet and yelling to us to come up immediately. I'd never seen Papa really frightened before.'

It was the moment when my whole world fell apart, she thought wretchedly; I simply didn't understand how it could be so.

She watched her mother buttoning her shabby black blouse, getting ready to go to work as a menial in a foreign city, and apparently accepting with fortitude what the Turks had done to her.

Leila continued her story. 'We didn't know it then,' she said, 'but Christians were suffering all over the Turkish Empire.

'When our servants heard the noise, they rushed into the courtyard to ask what was happening. They heard your father shout, and they panicked. Instead of running up to the roof themselves, they followed Cook, who ran to the main gate and opened it! I suppose he thought they would be able to escape before the mob reached us. For a second, I couldn't believe what I was seeing – it was so stupid – our gate was very stout; it might have held.

'As I whipped you indoors, I could hear their screams.'

Helena shuddered. 'I heard them.'

Leila ignored the interjection, as she sat head bowed, her fingers on the top button of her blouse. 'Well, after I'd bundled you into the house, I slammed the front door and turned the beam which locked it. That, and the barred windows, halted the crowd when they rushed into the courtyard, just long enough to allow us to escape.'

Helena sighed deeply. 'I remember the smoke – the yells – men pounding on the door – and the smell of gunpowder – and blood.'

Her mother put her arm around her and held her close.

'We were lucky, child, that we had an indoor staircase, not an outside one like many people have; if it had run straight up from the courtyard, the mob would have come up after us and killed us on the roof.'

'Papa had a piece of rope on the roof, I remember. I was so scared we'd fall, when he lowered first you and then me down into the tiny alley at the back of the house.'

Her mother nodded. 'I think he'd stored the rope up there, in case we needed an escape from fire,' she said absently. Then she added, 'The alleyway saved our lives by giving us an exit to another street.'

'I wonder why we were saved, Mama? Was our neighbour's family at the back saved?'

'Not to my knowledge, dearest. I was told that by the time the Druze and the Turks had finished, the whole area was one big funeral pyre.'

'Why does God allow such terrible things, Mama?' the young girl asked piteously.

Her mother looked shocked. 'We're not here to question God's Will, child.' Her pretty lower lip trembled. 'I didn't ask that even when your brothers died.'

Helena laid her head on her mother's shoulder. 'Of course not, Mama,' she said contritely. 'It was a wrong question to ask.'

Leila looked down at the child cuddled beside her, and she sighed. Her husband had always said that Helena was too clever to be a woman. She hoped he was wrong; women were supposed to accept, not ask questions.

Helena fingered a small pendant embossed with the head of the Virgin Mary that hung on a fine gold chain from her mother's neck. 'Did you bring this from Beirut?' she asked.

'Oh, yes, dear. For months and months that year, Papa insisted that I wear *all* my jewellery all the time. He must've been more nervous about the situation than he allowed us to think.'

'It's important for a lady to have lots of jewellery, isn't it, Mama?'

'Yes, dear – and small gold coins, easily carried. You never know what life has in store for you – life is very precarious. Jewellery is easy to carry – you can trade it anywhere – though at a great loss, of course.'

Helena nodded, and her mother hugged her again.

Leila thought with apprehension of a clouded future; but the child digested the lesson that good jewellery can be an important financial reserve – and that a collection of small gold coins is probably even better.

After a few minutes, Helena lifted her head and said heavily, 'We must've run for ages; I was so puffed.' Her young face was grim, and she swallowed. 'I don't think I'll ever forget the ghastly

31

cruelty – how can men do such dreadful things?' She looked at her mother as if begging for some reasonable explanation of what she had seen.

Leila Al-Khoury had resumed easing herself clumsily into black woollen stockings, while sitting on the end of her bed. Now she turned again to her troubled little daughter and put her arms round her. She wished she had an answer to the child's question.

'My darling, I don't know. Sometimes men seem to go mad.' She stroked Helena's silky black hair. 'In time the memories will go away, my love. And life is not all cruelty. All kinds of nice things will happen to you in your life, you'll see.' She felt Helena give a shuddering sigh, and she added, 'I wish we had foreseen what would happen, so that you could have been spared what you saw. And we might have been able to clear the warehouse and transfer some money – so that we wouldn't be in quite such dire straits. But we lived in a good district; we'd never been disturbed before.'

Helena shut her eyes tightly and wanted to be sick, as she remembered a young boy lying sobbing in the dust, one arm severed, the rest of him terribly cut about as he had tried to protect himself from sword or bayonet. Her mother had paused instinctively, bent on helping him, but her husband caught her arm to propel her forward.

'You can't leave him! He's alive!' she had protested.

He did not answer her. Terrified of what the rampaging rabble would do to his lovely wife and little daughter if they were caught, he dragged her onwards.

The dying boy haunted Wallace Helena's dreams all her life, returning like some eternal ghost to cry out to her in his agony, telling her that even loving fathers could have hearts of stone.

She had clear memories of reaching her father's silk warehouse, as yet untouched by vandals, though deserted by its panic-stricken nightwatchmen, and of meeting a youth of about fifteen when they entered the wicket gate. He was the bookkeeper's son, set to unlock the gate for any members of the family who might not have a key.

In answer to Charles Al-Khoury's inquiry, the boy said that

nobody had come, except his own parents and younger brothers and Mr James Al-Khoury.

Charles Al-Khoury told him to continue to keep watch through the grating in the main door and to hurry to the boat if he heard or saw anything suspicious.

The whey-faced boy had nodded assent, and Charles hurried Helena and her mother between bales wrapped in cotton cloth and through the silk carpet section, which smelled of hemp and dust.

They had emerged onto a covered wharf on the seaward side of the building, where a small sailing boat with an Egyptian rig bobbed fretfully on the sunlit water.

Charles's brother, James, was already in the boat. He looked up at the new arrivals and exclaimed fervently, 'Thank God you've come! Nobody came to work this morning – I tried to get back to the house to warn you that something was up; but the whole town seemed to be rioting – and drunk. So I returned here to alert the boatman to be ready. I guessed you'd hear the racket in the town and be warned.' He gestured towards the bookkeeper, and added, 'Then Bachiro, here, brought his family.'

'We got out by a hair's breadth,' Charles responded sombrely, as he took the hand of the Nubian boatman and jumped into the little craft. He turned to help his wife into the boat, and went on, 'I'm afraid Leila's family is lost.'

As James stared unbelievingly up at him, Leila balked and held back, as she cried out in horror, 'Mama and Papa dead? Oh, no! And my sisters – and Auntie and my cousin?'

James said gently, 'We'll wait a while; they may have got out.' He hoped fervently that her women relations were burned in their house rather than thrown to the mob.

Petrified and exhausted, Leila allowed her husband to lift her down into the boat. Uncle James turned to a benumbed Helena. 'Come on, my little lemon blossom, you're safe now.'

Without a word, she sat down on the edge of the wharf and jumped into her uncle's arms. He caught and held her to him for a moment, while the boat bounced unhappily on the water. Then he put her down beside her weeping mother, who snatched her to her. Bachiro's wife began to wail and was hastily hushed by her husband.

'When I went to see him this morning,' Charles muttered to James, 'Leila's father said it wouldn't be the first riot he'd seen, nor would it be the last. I reminded him that I'd had this felucca standing by for a week, in case of emergency, and he as good as told me I was a craven fool.'

His back to Leila, James made a rueful face, while Charles berated himself that he had not transferred money abroad.

'With the Turks watching every move, it would have been almost impossible,' James comforted him.

The wind showed signs of changing, and the boatman said it would be dangerous to linger any longer; the Turks would undoubtedly soon arrive to sack the warehouses along the waterfront. Better to leave while the wind held.

'For Jesus' sake, make him wait,' Leila whispered urgently to her husband. 'Mama – Papa – somebody – may come.'

Charles agreed, and argued heatedly with the stolid black seaman until, encouraged by some silver coins, he agreed to wait until the sun had set.

They waited anxiously through the afterglow, until shouts from the landward side of the warehouse and the sound of heavy thuds on wood brought Bachiro's eldest son speeding to the wharf. 'They're coming,' he shouted breathlessly, as he leapt into the little craft, his eyes starting out of his head with fright.

The felucca slipped seaward, while Leila crouched on a coil of rope and wept unrestrainedly for parents and sisters she would never see again. Charles Al-Khoury stared dumbly landwards and was thankful that his parents had died peacefully some years before.

Seated on the end of her bed in a small apartment in a Chicago slum, putting on her garters over her black stockings, Leila had pointed out in defence of her husband that he had done quite a lot to protect his family. Her deep, vibrant voice shook as she told Helena, 'Papa arranged that a shipment of French silk he was expecting be redirected to our friend, Mr Ghanem, here in Chicago – and he began to wear his special moneybelt

34

with gold coins in it, as did Uncle James. I wore my jewellery all the time.'

Helena sighed, and then she asked wistfully, 'When will we be able to go home, Mama?'

Her mother stood up and shook down her long black skirt. 'Some day, perhaps, dear.' She did not tell her that there was nothing and nobody to go home to. Her courage faltered for a moment, as she said, 'It was a terrible massacre – it'll never be forgotten.'

Helena rubbed her face wearily, and remembered again how they had sailed all night, seasick and then hungry.

As they worked their way from Beirut to Cyprus, there to be sheltered by business friends of her father's, all the certainties of her life had vanished. She had been an ordinary middle-class young girl, happy in a gentle routine of lessons from her mother and social occasions shared with her uncle and grandparents. There had been books to read, festivals to keep, music to listen to and to learn to play, forays into the mountains and walks beside the sea; and, in her father's warehouse, fabulous fabrics and carpets to be admired and carefully caressed, until one could unerringly recognize quality and fine workmanship. And tentatively, beginning to be mentioned in her mother's conversation, was the excitement of deciding who she should marry in a couple of years' time.

Instead, she was being shifted nightly from one alien house to another, in an effort to stay hidden from the ruling Turks. Then, when she began to think she would go out of her mind, they sailed one night in a stinking fishing boat to Nice, where they were, at last, safely outside the Turkish Empire. From there, they had travelled by train across France to Hamburg, where a Jewish friend of her father obtained a passage to Liverpool for them.

They had waited several anxious weeks in Liverpool in a boarding house packed with other immigrants, while a passage for America was arranged. Charles and James Al-Khoury, with Helena pattering along behind them, had filled in the time by exploring the city. In the course of their walks, Uncle James had been most enthusiastic about the modern, gaslit city, and despite his elder brother's advice against it, he decided to remain in it. Partly because of the valuable consignment of silk awaiting him in Chicago, which would help him to start a new business there, and the fact that there were already Lebanese refugees in that city, Charles Al-Khoury stuck to his original plan of settling in the United States.

Leila had nearly died during the passage to America in the steerage section of the cramped immigrant ship. Their small funds had dwindled during their journeying and Charles dared not spend any more than he did. Tended by other Christians who had fled the Turkish Empire, Greeks, Cypriots and Armenians, as well as Lebanese, her mother had lain weeping helplessly and muttering with fever. Huddled together in an unventilated hold, on a straw palliasse spread on a shelflike fixture above another family, Helena was very seasick. She wanted despairingly to die herself, as she watched her father grow more haggard each day, and listened to the horrifying stories of other refugees, of wholesale murder all over the Middle East.

When her nausea eased, her father took her up on deck and they walked together, too exhausted to say much.

After that, there was the incredible noise and smell in the great immigration shed, while the United States Immigration authorities worked their way through the anxious, pressing crowd washed up on their shores. Leila kept a firm hold on Helena's hand, in case, by some awful misfortune, they should become separated, so Helena sat by the listless bundle in black which was her mother and listened to the jabber of a dozen languages round her, amid the maelstrom of noisy, smelly humanity.

The three of them had made an effort to learn a few words of English while in Liverpool. The immigration officials, though harried, were not unkind, and eventually a bewildered Helena was hustled onto the Chicago train by a father who, for the first time, seemed more relaxed. The bookkeeper had decided to stay in New York with another Lebanese family from the same immigrant ship. They said an impassioned farewell and vanished into the turbulence of the great port.

It was only towards the end of her time in Chicago, when her life was again about to change completely, that Helena realized that, to her parents, Chicago had been yet another nightmare. Being young, she had herself begun to adapt to her new life. As she went to the shops for her mother, and helped her father as he tried to establish a little business in wholesale dress materials, she began to pick up some English.

In contrast, her gently nurtured mother, though educated, was used to being much at home, secure in the knowledge that her parents had married her to a comfortably placed, kindly man. She had rarely been stared at by strangers, never been hungry, never done much except to order her servants and adapt herself to her husband. In Chicago, she was, at first, shattered, unable to make much effort.

Another refugee, arriving after them, confirmed the death of Leila's parents and sisters and, indeed, it seemed of everyone they had known. As she mourned her loss, the fever she had suffered aboard ship returned to her, and Charles Al-Khoury's face grew thinner and grimmer. Helena tried to comfort her mother and not to cry herself. She closed her mind off from any thought of Beirut, feeling that if she allowed herself to contemplate what had happened, she would go mad. In those early weeks in America, the child grew into a stony-faced young woman, physically hardly formed, but mentally aged beyond her years.

Not daring to part with so much as a garnet from his wife's jewellery, unless he was starving, Charles Al-Khoury used the remainder of his little store of gold coins to augment his bales of silk with some dress lengths in other good materials. He found a tiny niche of a store on a main street crowded with immigrants. The door was strong and the windows had good wooden shutters. He paid a week's rent on it to a Greek immigrant, who had been in Chicago rather longer than he had.

Before opening his precious purchases, he bargained for cleaning help from a young negress who lived nearby.

Sally earned her living as a daily cleaning lady, and she came for two successive evenings to give the store a thorough scouring. As Helena said to her, 'You can't sell material for clothes if it's got dusty.'

A quick grin flashed across the black woman's lined face, as she agreed. On her second evening, she brought a toffee apple with her for Helena, and she watched with pleasure when the grim little face lit up at the sight of the gift.

Sally enjoyed working for people who treated her politely. She became interested in the fortunes of the tiny store and continued to clean it, though sometimes Charles Al-Khoury had to defer paying her during bad weeks. She would tease him good-naturedly about his broken English, which he took in good part, being anxious to improve it. She drilled Helena in the English names of everything around her, and Helena became devoted to the strong, graceful woman.

Mr Ghanem, the Lebanese who had kept Charles's bales of silk for him, was very nearly as poor as Charles himself. He had been in the States for a number of years with his own small business as an importer. He had, however, speculated in land and had gone bankrupt. He now had a small fruit and vegetable shop. Because they had been at school together, he had kept in touch with Charles sporadically over the years, and it was his presence in Chicago that had first given Charles the idea of beginning life again in that city.

It was Mr Ghanem who had met them at the station and had taken them in a borrowed horse-drawn delivery van to a room he had obtained for them. When Charles's shop was ready, Mr Ghanem's half-grown sons helped the new immigrant move the consignment of silk from their family's basement onto the shelves of the new store. Mrs Ghanem had done her best to comfort poor Leila Al-Khoury, and she gradually emerged from her prostration, white and thin, but in her right mind.

Much later on, Leila told Helena, 'I thought I'd go mad. There we were, in this strange country; nobodies, lost in a sea of nobodies. God curse the Druze – and may the Turks burn in hell!' The words seemed extraordinary, coming from a beautiful seductive woman, once again restored to health; but Helena understood, and thought burning was too good for Turks.

Leila had continued sadly, 'Outside that tiny room in which we existed, so few spoke Arabic – and nobody seemed to have heard of French! And the noise of screaming women and howling children in the other rooms seemed unending.'

Helena nodded agreement. Watching immigrant children

struggle for existence had made her feel that the last thing she wanted in life was to be a mother.

'When Mrs Ghanem suggested that I go to work like she did, I was really shocked,' Leila confided. 'But we needed ready money so badly that finally I agreed. It distressed your father very much.' She giggled suddenly, at the memory of her hard-pressed husband's agitation at the suggestion.

She giggled again, and then added, 'I must've looked a sight. I wore a second-hand black skirt, a black blouse and second-hand boots. I wore a head veil, like I had done in Beirut, and I felt terrible. It seemed to me that every man I passed stared at me.

'The attic we worked in was so badly lit that I could hardly see how to thread my needles. There, Mrs Ghanem and I sat on a piece of sacking for ten hours a day, stitching on buttons and finishing the buttonholes on men's suits. I've worked harder since then, but never in such confinement; I had to watch that my tears didn't fall on the fine cloth. What a time!' She threw up her hands helplessly.

Helena put her arms round her mother's neck. 'Poor Mama,' she said.

'Well, I lived,' responded her mother philosophically. 'But I didn't want you to be confined like that, so your dear father took you to help him in the store.'

'And he taught me how to run a business,' Helena had remembered gratefully. 'How to organize it and be neat and methodical. Buy cheap; sell dear. Have the patience of Job. Have a first-class product for the money. Keep two sets of books – one for the tax collector, and one which tells you what's really happening. Make friends – which I haven't done very well. Do favours and collect on them when you need to. Never forget a name – and smile, child, smile.' He would grin at her from under his black moustache. 'And don't trust anybody, unless you have to,' he would reiterate pithily in Arabic.

She would laugh back at him. But she learned, and never quite trusted anyone – except Joe Black.

Afraid to trust a bank, afraid of his wife being attacked in the street if she wore it, Charles hid some of Leila's jewellery in various spots in his tiny shop, a necklace wrapped in a scrap of black silk under a beam in the ceiling, several rings under a floorboard, a pair of hair ornaments in a box stuck to the underside of his long counter. He instructed Helena that, if he were out, she was never to leave anyone alone in the shop for a single second, including Sally.

Leila sewed two gold chains into the waistband of her ugly serge skirt, and her best emerald necklace was carried in a linen moneybelt round her husband's waist. Spread out like this, they agreed, they were less likely to be robbed of all of it; it was capital, partly inherited and partly carefully bought since their marriage; it was not to be used, except in the expansion of the dress material business, if they had some success with it; or, if that failed, to keep them from starvation.

In the store, Helena was in her element. She watched with care how her father set about establishing his new business, learned how to set up the bookkeeping, how to find suppliers and, most important of all, how to find customers. She would sit unobtrusively in the background while he bargained for bankrupt stock from other businesses or cajoled a lady who wanted the price of a dress length reduced, and when his English failed him, she quietly translated – though her own grasp of the language was not very good. When they had a quiet hour, he would reminisce about the family business in Beirut, and, when he found she was interested, would go into detail about its organization, its employees, and its links with distant countries. He was astonished that she knew and understood much of its detailed running already. She laughed at his astonishment and reminded him how he used to take her down to the warehouses to give her a change. 'I used to listen to you talking to people – and when I grew bigger, I used to ask Bachiro to show me the papers that seemed to be like oil flowing to facilitate the movement of everything coming in and going out.'

Her father laughed. 'You did? You nosy little person!'

'I wasn't nosy,' she replied indignantly. 'I was really interested in what you and Uncle James and Grandpa were doing. I kept thinking that if I had been a boy, you would have begun to keep me by your side and teach me everything.'

'Well, you're a great help to me now, little flower. I don't know how I would manage without you.'

Her big eyes shone at the compliment, and he thought that he should get her married as soon as he could, before the harshness of their life in Chicago toughened her too much. Men liked gentle amenable women; a ruthless trader would not appeal to them.

But, without realizing that he was doing it, he had already inculcated in her the basic principles of organization, enterprise, forethought and quick decision-making which were to be her strength in times to come.

Chapter Five

The two rooms above Charles Al-Khoury's shop in Chicago were occupied by Polish immigrants. When they moved out, he again bargained with his Greek landlord and succeeded in renting the rooms for little more than he was already paying for the shop. Triumphantly, he got Sally to clean the rooms and then he installed his wife and daughter in them.

The tiny store and the flat above it became Helena's world. She carried samples of materials to the houses of well-to-do ladies, when requested; and in the shop she made tea for women who began to discover the fine quality of Charles's stock. They sat by his counter and talked haughtily to him, under the impression that they were bargaining successfully for a better price than others obtained; dressmakers, who also came, always got materials at a better price, but they always received a lower grade silk. As her father warned her, 'Dressmakers are always poor; you can't get more money out of them than they have. Remember that!'

Helena was allowed to handle swatches from the fat bales on the shelves, and she soon learned what constituted a good dress length. Her English rapidly became better than his, so he encouraged her to write his business letters for him and then to keep the accounts. Though she did not write her father's letters in Arabic to Uncle James, she sometimes saw them. It was apparent that her father felt that Uncle James was quite mad; he was boiling soap in his landlady's wash boiler and was selling it door-to-door in Liverpool.

The bales of material were heavy, and Charles lifted them himself. Helena watched with anxiety the sweat pour down his face, as he moved the cotton-swathed rolls from shelf to counter to show them to customers, and, later, lifted them back onto the shelf.

One day, when he had gone with swatches of material to see a particularly high-class dressmaker and Helena was watching the shop for him, Sally remarked to her, 'Your pa's doing too much.' She was polishing the old wooden counter to a fine sheen, as she spoke, and did not appear to expect a reply.

Helena's heart seemed to miss a beat, as the implied threat of illness sank in. From then on, she insisted that she be allowed to help with the tidying-up of the shop, but she was a skinny youngster without much power in her arms; and he would laugh and take the bundles from her to lay them on the shelves.

Apart from his stock, American women found the Lebanese shopkeeper charming and they recommended the store to their friends. The tiny business began to prosper. The Al-Khourys hoarded every cent they could.

At the end of six months, Charles insisted that his wife give up her job with the tailor and stay at home. 'If we are very, very careful, we can manage,' he assured her. 'I don't like you doing menial work.'

Helena took her mother for granted; she did not realize that she possessed unusual beauty, and that, as she learned to dress in Western clothes, her father felt jealous when other men looked at her. He wanted her at home, not veiled like a Muslim woman but decently bundled up like a good Maronite.

Leila Al-Khoury was thankful to be released from the tailor's stuffy attic, but she refused to wear her native dress or veil her hair. She had fallen in love with hats and bought herself a plain black straw which she trimmed with shreds of silk from her husband's shop.

With this imaginative concoction on her head, she pressed herself lovingly against her husband and assured him that he had nothing to worry about. He was partially mollified, though the flowerlike face framed by the hat's brim was, he felt uneasily, very attractive.

Helena had not inherited her mother's beauty. Though she was not ugly, she had her father's strong nose and wide mouth. She was sallower than Leila and there was no hint of pink in her cheeks; and her long oriental eyes with their secretive, sidelong glances were too foreign for Western taste. The tumbling black mass of her hair was restrained in a bun at the back of her head and gave little hint of its richness. Amid the babble of thousands of immigrants, as a skinny young girl she passed unremarked. Until she met Joe Black.

Curled up alone in a feather bed in Liverpool, her dream passed from the nightmares of the Lebanon and Chicago, to Joe.

She smiled in her sleep, as she seemed to hear herself saying to him cryptically, 'You never gave me toffee apples.' And his laughing back at her and saying, 'I never thought of them. Want one?'

Joe had his own ideas of gifts. In her dream, she saw him lounge into their living-room, the original log cabin in which her stepfather had first lived in Canada. Peeking out of his jacket was a tame grey fox, a birthday gift.

One Christmas, he had brought her a muff made from a marten fur he had trapped; his mother had cleaned and tanned the skin and he had then given it to another Cree woman who had fashioned it for him. Sometimes, when he had been south to see his grandfather, he brought her a little opium to smoke, bargained from a lonely Russian farmer who had established his own patch of poppies, or, at other times, a small packet of tobacco from Virginia, passed from hand to hand across a continent, in trade.

The rising sun began to push long fingers between the heavy velvet curtains of her bedroom in Liverpool, and she sleepily stretched out to touch him. But he was six thousand miles away, harvesting a hay crop.

Chapter Six

Leila Al-Khoury lamented bitterly that it was Mr and Mrs Ghanem who had brought the typhoid into their Chicago home. The infection had, in fact, sneaked through the tumble-down, crowded neighbourhood like a smouldering fire; but Mr Ghanem was the first person to die from it.

The local inhabitants were used to illnesses which ran their course, and the patients were nursed at home. Though guesses were made, no name was put to the sickness. Immigrants had little money, so doctors were rarely called.

Charles Al-Khoury, worked to a shadow of his former self, was in no state to withstand such a virulent infection. The Al-Khourys knew that Mr Ghanem was also ill. His wife told Leila that it was 'Something he's eaten.' It was assumed that in both cases the fever would go away and the diarrhoea would ease, if the patients were kept on a liquid diet. Meanwhile, Helena served in their tiny shop and Leila nursed her husband.

When Mr Ghanem died, leaving a widow with five sons to feed, Leila realized, in a panic, that this was no ordinary illness. She sent for a doctor, only to be scolded by him in English she barely understood for not calling him earlier. Charles died in her arms.

Once more, Leila tore her clothes, and the household rang to shrieks of mourning. Both she and a terrified Helena were devastated, as was Mrs Ghanem in her tiny home. Other neighbours, afraid of being infected themselves, left small gifts of food at the shop door, but refused to come in.

Only Sally walked briskly up the stairs to the Al-Khoury flat, to bring some common sense into their lives. Hiding her own sorrow for a man she secretly adored, she instructed a grief-stricken

45

Helena to get back to the store and mind it. 'I'll look after your ma.'

Helena had obeyed, but she quickly found herself in difficulties. Men delivering cotton and silk her father had ordered through middlemen refused to leave the goods without her father's signature. 'You're too young to sign for it. You can pay cash, if you like,' she was told.

'Could Mother sign for it?' she asked, afraid of parting with the small sum in the secret drawer of the old till.

A man delivering a roll of silk had hesitated at this suggestion, but finally said uneasily that he did not think his company would accept a woman's signature, and went away with the roll still on his shoulder.

Beating down her increasing terror, she served customers from the existing stock with her sweetest smile, as she struggled with the heavy rolls. She knew that, unless she could buy replacement materials, the business was doomed.

Oblivious of the impending end to their sole source of income, Leila sat cross-legged on her bed, allowing Sally and Helena to minister to her. Occasionally, she would fling herself down on the pillows in a fresh burst of weeping.

Between bouts, Helena asked her urgently, 'Couldn't you run the business, Mama? I believe if you took it in hand, the suppliers would accept you – or perhaps we could import some silk direct from China?' She sighed, and got up to pull back the closed curtains to let in the evening sun.

Leila put down the coffee her daughter had brought her, turned her blotched face away from the light, and began to cry again.

Helena went back to her, to sit beside her and put her arms round her. 'Mama, dear, listen to me, please. If you can't help me, we'll have to close the shop – we don't make anything like enough to employ a manager, even supposing we could find an honest one.'

Leila wept on.

As she patted her mother's back in an effort to comfort her, Helena said savagely, 'I know what to do – but nobody will trust me. The salesman from Smithson's chucked me under the chin this morning, as if I were a baby. He actually said, "Pity you're not a boy!" '

'Mama, could we sell something to get money, so that I can pay cash for stock?'

'I don't know anything about business,' her mother sobbed, and continued to moan into the pillows.

In despair, Helena held a big sale and then shut the shop. She made just sufficient to pay their debts, except for one.

'Sally, dear. I don't have any money left to pay you. Instead, I saved these for you.' She proffered a package containing several pretty ends of rolls that she had been unable to sell.

Sally bent and hugged her. She sniffed, and then said, 'You don't have to worry about me, hon. There was many a time when your pa couldn't pay me. You and your ma are welcome to anything I can do.'

Before letting her out of the door, Helena clung to her. 'Thank you, Sally. Thank you.'

Left alone, she searched the little shop to retrieve the remaining bits of jewellery hidden there. 'I'd better take a good look upstairs, as well,' she thought, as she wrapped the pieces up in a scrap of cotton. 'If we don't pay the rent we'll be thrown out fast.'

As she tucked the little parcel well down into her skirt pocket, she cried helplessly. She was nearly fourteen years old, tall for her age and very thin, with eyes that were sadly old for one so young and feet that seemed too big for her stature.

Since her mother was in no state to do it, Helena sat down at their rickety table in their tiny apartment and wrote to her only surviving blood relative, Uncle James in Liverpool, to tell him of his brother's death and the penury of his widow. Tears blotted her shaky unformed Arabic script.

By the time they received a reply six weeks later, the landlord, a kindly man, had grown tired of a tenant who was not paying him rent, even though she was a pretty widow, and told them they had another week in which to start paying again, plus something towards the arrears.

If it had not been for a large bag of rice, which her father had obtained shortly before his death, and the kindness of their neighbours, Helena and her mother would have starved.

In his reply, Uncle James wrote that, if they could manage to pay their fares to England, he would be happy to give both mother and daughter a home. Unfortunately, he was not yet earning enough to send them their fares; he had just leased a small factory building and installed his first soap boiler, and this had drained his reserve and his credit.

He did not know how to express his own grief at the loss of a well-loved brother, so contented himself with the usual polite phrases. Leila's troubles were great enough without his adding to them.

He did not mention that the home he offered would actually be in a house owned by his English mistress, Eleanor. As he wrote, she was sitting on a chair opposite him, nursing their year-old son, Benjamin.

It had taken a great deal of coaxing on his part to persuade this downright little Liverpudlian that he owed shelter to his sister-in-law, Leila, and her daughter, Helena. It was a duty he could not evade, he assured her, and he would have to find another place to live if Eleanor could not help him.

'She's foreign,' Eleanor had protested.

James had looked up from his letter and responded dryly, though with a twinkle in his eye, 'So am I.'

'You're different, luv,' she told him, and smiled at him.

James's eyes were bloodshot from private weeping on top of long hours of work. He looked so drained that she impulsively got up from her chair and leaned over the baby to kiss his cheek. 'Well, never mind. Don't you fret,' she said kindly. 'I suppose I could give 'em the second-floor back room to theirselves. I'd have to give Mr Tomlinson notice, though, so as he can find somewhere else.' Mr Tomlinson was one of her three gentlemen lodgers, other than James Al-Khoury himself. She sighed heavily, as she sat down and rearranged Benjamin on her lap. 'I'd have to ask you for a bit more housekeeping to help out, like, 'cos I'll have two more mouths to feed – and I won't have Mr T's rent.'

'Of course I'll give you more,' he assured her, without any idea of where he was going to get the extra money from. He put down his pen and got up to embrace both mother and child; Eleanor was a wonderful comfort to a lonely man, a real help – and she had given him a son. He prayed to God that his new venture with George Tasker, the Soap Master, would prosper.

Eleanor told herself she would do anything she could for him; she'd never again meet a man like him. Mr T must go; she could not imagine her despair if James left her. She wasn't getting any younger; and now there was little Benji to think about.

In Chicago, a surprised Leila read his kind letter. Puzzled, she looked up from her meagre lunch of boiled rice and weak coffee, and asked Helena, 'Did you write to Uncle James?'

Having seen the English stamp on the letter, Helena was tense with anxiety, as she said eagerly, 'Yes.'

Leila sighed. 'I should have done it.'

'I did ask you, Mama. But you didn't listen.'

In the seven weeks since her husband had died, Leila had grown quieter. Though she did not cry so much, she was very listless. Nothing that Helena could do or say seemed to rouse her to the realization that, unless they did something quickly, they would die of starvation.

Now, seeing the letter, a wild hope surged in Helena. 'May I read Uncle's letter, Mama?' she asked eagerly.

Leila handed it to her without comment.

As the girl read, a tremendous relief made her want to shout with joy, the first sense of wellbeing since her father had died. 'Isn't he good, Mama? And his wife, too. We'll have to sell your jewellery – or some of it, Mama?' A hint of doubt had crept into her voice. Despite their desperate position, Leila had sullenly refused to part with the last of her chains and brooches. Her husband's declaration that he would only sell them *in extremis* had meant, to her, only in the case of death. A Lebanese, longer established than the Al-Khourys, had accepted a gold chain from her and had arranged Charles's funeral. That to her had constituted a time to sell.

Leila did not immediately reply to her daughter; she sat fretfully toying with her coffee cup.

'To get the fares to go to England, Mama – we have to get the fares from somewhere.'

Leila felt morosely that fate had dealt her an unbearable blow in the loss of her husband. In these last seven weeks of prostration, she had been waiting for that same fate to compensate her in some way. Her brother-in-law's kindly letter did not appear to do that, and she said capriciously, 'I don't want to go.'

'But, Mama, what else can we do? Uncle James is a dear – you know that.'

'He's kind,' Leila admitted reluctantly. She was quiet for a moment, and then, as if to justify her refusal, she added, 'I simply can't change countries again. It would be too much; I couldn't bear it.' She buried her face in her hands.

Helena swallowed, and replied carefully, 'It wouldn't be much different from America, would it, Mama? I liked Liverpool when we passed through it.'

'It would be quite different,' her mother replied shortly. She rose from the table and, dragging her bare feet on the planks of the floor, she went to Helena's small bed at the back of the room. She lay down on it, her face towards the wall, as if to shut out a life which was a burden to her.

Helena went to sit at the foot of the bed and continue the argument.

Without looking at her, Leila protested, 'Helena, you can't imagine what it would be like to be penniless in Uncle James's house. No matter how kind he is, we would be dependent upon the whims of his – er – wife. She's bound to resent us – or she'd make use of us as servants. It would be insupportable.'

Helena took another tack. 'I always imagined that Uncle James wasn't married?' she queried.

Leila bit her lower lip. She was not sure how to explain Uncle James's domestic affairs. She said cautiously, 'Some men have a woman friend who lives with them. Uncle James's situation could make it harder for us.' She turned slightly, to look at the frightened girl. 'In the West, it's not quite honourable, though I'm sure your uncle has his reasons for not marrying her . . .'

'If she's not his wife, couldn't he send her away? Then we could look after him.'

'I doubt he wants to be rid of her. They've been together a long time.'

'I see,' Helena muttered. But all she really understood was that her mother seemed totally incapable of doing anything. It was to be a number of years before she became aware of the profound effect her uncle's lack of a marriage certificate was to have on her own life.

Chapter Seven

Helena continued to sit by her mother on her bed and to beg her to reconsider her uncle's offer. She got no response, except for peevish monosyllables. Hope died in the girl and was replaced by dread.

Finally, in search of comfort, she went out into the street and made her way, through crowds on their way home from work, to Mrs Ghanem's tiny home. Perhaps another widow would be able to help her rouse her mother.

Mrs Ghanem was still at work, her five-year-old told her solemnly. He was helping Mama by looking after his little brother. He pointed to a crawling child behind him.

The children were filthy and the house stank. Poor Mrs Ghanem, thought Helena compassionately; her children and her home had always been immaculate before Mr Ghanem's death.

She promised the child that she would come again another day, and, feeling suddenly very weak, she walked towards home.

As she turned into the familiar narrow street, she caught a glimpse of Sally coming towards her, and her depression lifted a little. She ran towards her.

Sally caught her in a bear hug. 'Where've you been?' she inquired. 'I was just dropping by to see how your ma is.'

'I went to see Mrs Ghanem – but she's still at work.' She turned back towards her home, arm-in-arm with the cleaning lady.

'Uh-ha. So what's new with you, hon?'

Helena hastily told her about her uncle's letter. Then she added uneasily, 'I'm scared, Sally. Mama won't *do* anything. And we haven't paid the rent for weeks – and in a few days there won't be even rice to eat. At least Uncle James would feed us, and perhaps I could find some work in Liverpool; it's a very busy city.'

Sally paused on the ragged doormat at the foot of the stairs leading up to Leila's living quarters. 'Want me to talk to her?' she asked.

'She'd never forgive me for telling you.'

'I guess you're right.'

As they came up the last step, they were both surprised to see that Leila was up. Her hair had been combed and pinned up; she had put on a clean white blouse and her black stockings and boots. She had lifted the nearly empty sack of rice onto the table and had spread some of the grains on a tray in order to pick out any small stones in it.

Helena was astonished. It looked as if Uncle James's letter had had an effect, she decided thankfully.

Sally said to Leila, 'My, you do look pretty! How're you doing?'

The pale, delicate mouth quivered and the eyes were full of pain, but she answered Sally quite firmly, 'I'm better, thank you. Sit down.' She pulled out a chair for her visitor. 'Coffee?'

Sally accepted the proffered chair. Knowing how short they were of everything, she said she did not need coffee. Leila, however, was suddenly aware of neglected social obligations, and she insisted on using the last of their coffee to make a decent cup for her friend.

Helena went quietly to the table and took over the cleaning of the rice. She was afraid that if she said anything she would upset Leila again. Let Sally do the talking.

Sally did talk. She brought in all the polite gambits of the state of the weather, the price of vegetables and the latest news of the war raging further south, while she gravely sipped her coffee and Leila sat with her hands clasped in her lap, barely attending to the rich musical voice.

Finally, Sally told her, with real excitement in her voice, that she had managed to get a full-time job as a waitress in a new coffee shop being opened by Italian immigrants. It was close to the Al-Khourys' old shop.

Leila was genuinely pleased, and congratulated her. Then she sat looking at her hands for a moment, before she went on to say determinedly, 'Tomorrow, Helena and I, we go to tailor to ask for sewing work. Helena sew as good as me.'

'Well, that would keep you going for a bit.' Sally smiled at her, and then said very gently, 'With your looks you could get a healthier job, a clerk in a store, say.'

Leila smiled wanly back. 'Later. Tailor give job now.' She shrugged. 'Nobody give me good job now. English so bad.'

'You're doing just fine,' Sally assured her robustly.

Helena looked up from the rice. She was dumbfounded at her mother's decisiveness. A quick warning glance from Sally told her to be careful what she said.

She deftly picked out a piece of chaff from the rice. 'I'd love to work with you, Mama,' she said softly.

Her mother turned and smiled at her. 'Would you? That's good. We'll manage, darling, won't we?'

Thankfully, Helena got up and went to her. Leila took her warmly in her arms, and Helena wanted to burst into tears with relief.

The Civil War had caused an insatiable demand for uniforms. The tailor was very glad to have two skilled sewers for finishing work, though he bargained the wages down to near-starvation levels, on the grounds that Leila's English was poor and that, at nearly fourteen, Helena was not yet entitled to a woman's wage.

The two clung to each other and managed to continue to exist, two tiny boats bobbing along in a sea of other immigrants, all competing for jobs, cheap rooms and cheap food, in a country where war had caused prices to skyrocket. Their Greek landlord was appeased, and the shop beneath their small nest was re-rented, to a locksmith and his family, who both worked and slept there. Because they had a side entrance, the two women were not disturbed by them.

Helena had never in her life felt so exhausted. Underfed, she also lacked sunlight, diversions, and exercise. One day, on their return from work, she fainted.

Leila bathed her daughter's pinched, white face, and decided desperately that she would sell her best gold chain. In that way, she could pay the landlord his arrears instead of having to give

54

him extra money each week. They could then spend more on food. She herself felt apathetic and intensely weary, and she thought, with real horror, of what might happen to her daughter if she herself should die.

She took the necklace to a jeweller in a better area of the city, and it was in the jeweller's shop that she met Tom Harding.

Tom was a widowed settler from Fort Edmonton, a Hudson's Bay Company Fort on the banks of the North Saskatchewan River in western Canada, an area as yet barely explored. Though Tom claimed to be a settler, he was, in fact, a squatter on land owned by the great fur-trading Company which had established the Fort. To the Company's annoyance, he also trapped, and, having once been a miner, was apt to dig Company coal out of the banks of the river and to pan small amounts of gold out of the river itself.

His younger brother owned a prosperous grocery shop in Chicago, and their acerbic old mother lived with him. Tom had received an urgent letter from his brother, via the Hudson's Bay Company, saying that the old lady was in very frail health. She had several times expressed a strong desire to see him before she died, and he should hurry.

When he received the letter, Tom thought wryly that his brother had obviously no idea of the distances involved or the difficulties of the journey. He was, however, extremely depressed himself. He had recently lost his Cree Indian wife and his infant son in childbirth. An Indian wife was an enormous asset, besides which he had been quite fond of her and had been looking forward to the child. He wondered if he should return to Chicago and settle there.

After discussing the matter with his friend, Joe Black, who worked with him on his illegally held piece of land, it was decided that Joe could manage to look after the farm, while Tom made the journey. 'And mind you come back!' Joe shouted after him, as he prepared to leave. 'We haven't built this place out of nothing, just to see it go back to forest again. You'll feel a lot better when you've had a change – and I know lots of Cree women who wouldn't mind being Mrs Harding Number Two.'

Tom grinned and saluted him, as he turned his horse onto the trail which led to the Fort, where he expected to join the Company's boats going down the river to Lake Winnipeg. Then another boat down to Fort Garry – about a thousand miles, he believed, and he'd still be in Canada.

As he rode, he chewed one end of his moustache and considered the fragile hold he had on the precious piece of land for which he had struggled so hard. It was certainly Company land, but he reckoned that Joe was far too useful to the Company for them to try to dislodge him from it while he himself was away.

Joe was half Cree, half negro, and he knew the languages of the area. Slow to anger and trusted by both sides, he was frequently used by the Chief Factor at the Fort as a negotiator between the Company and the recalcitrant Blackfoot and Cree Indians. Though he had been known to get involved in fights which occasionally broke out amongst the Company's employees, when all concerned had drunk more than usual, and was consequently sometimes out of favour with Company men ruefully rubbing bruises he had inflicted, he was a godsend to a company which was not always able to keep control in the land over which it was supposed to rule.

In his heart, Tom felt that he himself was tolerated on the Company's land solely because Joe worked for him, that Chief Factor Christie did not have him removed because, if he did, Joe would probably drift back south to rejoin his Indian grandfather, of whom it was said he was very fond; and the Company would lose its best defence against the resentment of the displaced Indians.

Tom did not consider that he, as well as Joe, had built up a friendship with a number of Blackfoot families, because he owed his life to one of them, and that Factor Christie was aware of this useful relationship between a white man and a very proud and angry group of native people.

Tom certainly did not enjoy the hardships of the long voyage in a York boat down the North Saskatchewan to Lake Winnipeg and through the lake to Fort Garry. He was expected to make himself useful on the voyage; and he decided that his own life might be hard, but, being a voyager faced with portages and little but pemmican to eat, he preferred the hardships of a squatter's life.

From Fort Garry, he sailed in a small American trading boat down the Red River, then went by stagecoach to La Crosse and, thankfully, the rest of the journey by train.

Now, he wanted to return home before the winter set in, though his frail ghost of a mother begged him to remain in Chicago. Despite her invalidism, her tongue was as malicious as ever; and she had made him feel a sense of guilt at his decision to desert her once again. To soften the blow of his departure, he had decided to buy her a present.

His finances were limited and, as he pushed open the door of the local jewellery store, he had scant hope of finding what he wanted at a reasonable price.

Instead of a present, he found Leila Al-Khoury bargaining with the jeweller over the sale of a fine gold chain which had originally belonged to her mother-in-law; it had been given to Leila on the birth of her first son, who had died of a fever when he was six. Leila firmly tried to remember the old lady's delight at the child and to forget the gentle woman's terrible death at the hands of the Beirut Muslims. She spoke to the jeweller in the firmest tone she could muster.

Her voice rose and fell, as, in broken English, she refused to reduce the price that she wanted. The jeweller had assayed the gold and knew that the price she asked was not unreasonable, but he was in no hurry, so he let her rattle on.

While Tom loitered behind her, Leila whined and begged and pointed out the flawless workmanship of the Beirut goldsmith, until the jeweller became fed up with her; if he turned her away today, she would probably return tomorrow willing to accept his offer.

Tom shifted his feet uneasily, as he looked idly over a case of brooches. At the slight noise, the lady turned her head to look at him. She wore a plain white summer dress she had made herself and her face was framed by a cheap straw hat. Tom found himself looking into a pair of enormous, sad brown eyes – like a little spaniel's, he thought. A cupid's bow of a mouth trembled, as if tears were near. Under the white dress, a generous bosom heaved slightly.

The whole stringy six feet of Tom Harding shook with desire. What was a woman like that doing on her own? Was she a whore?

As he stared into the eyes of the pretty Lebanese, the argument with the jeweller appeared to have reached an impasse. The jeweller huffily banged the drawers of his counter shut and locked them. Tears glistened on the long black lashes of the lady. The necklace, a handsomely worked heavy chain with several red stones pendant from it, lay on the counter.

The jeweller moved slightly towards Tom. 'Can I help you, Sir?' he inquired politely.

Uncomfortably aware that he was roughly dressed in riding boots, a plaid shirt and a big felt hat, in a city which was quite full of prosperous people more formally attired, Tom looked down at Leila and replied soberly, 'I got plenty of time. Finish with the lady.'

Still looking up at him, Leila scooped up the necklace and put it back into her reticule. 'It finish,' she told him tragically, the words coming out in softly accented English. She bowed her head and began to move slowly and despondently towards the door, her white skirt swaying gently round her.

Tom jerked to attention. Once she was outside that door, he would probably never see her again.

He took off his big felt hat and bowed to her. 'Excuse me, Ma'am.'

She looked doubtfully up at him with a slight frown.

He swallowed. 'I'm in the market for a necklace, Ma'am. Would that necklace be for sale privately?' He paused, waiting for some response, but she had not fully understood what he said and was mentally translating his remarks. He hastened to add, 'It's a mighty smart chain – I believe my mother would like it – if you'll forgive me for being so forward, Ma'am.'

The jeweller threw up his hands and went to tidy a cabinet. He knew when a man was hooked. Nevertheless, a woman should not show a stranger a necklace which was worth twice what he had offered for it; she could be robbed. Then he shrugged. If she were that foolish, it wasn't his business. He took up a feather duster and began to dust the clocks in the cabinet.

At the mention of his mother, Tom was treated to a smile so delicious that he never quite recovered from it. He handed Leila out of the door and down the steps as if she were made of glass and then into a coffee shop two doors down the street.

Between coffee and pieces of pie and regrets that the necklace was too expensive for him to buy, he learned who she was and about her widowhood, her life in Beirut and in Chicago, and that she had a fourteen-year-old daughter. She told him frankly that she and her daughter both worked ten hours a day in a tailor's garret; she had had to beg the afternoon off in order to see the jeweller.

In return, he told her that he had been a miner and had gone west from Chicago, to work in gold mines. Then he had heard a rumour of gold easily panned in the North Saskatchewan River, in Canada. Hoping to stake a claim, he had travelled north with four men also bent on instant wealth.

'We knew that there was at least one Hudson's Bay Fort on the North Saskatchewan, and we reckoned we could make that our jumping-off place. A few other Americans had travelled part of the route before us; they sold liquor to the Injuns for furs.

'The trail wasn't very clear, and it was rough going. We did O.K., though, and we were well north, when we had to make a detour round a huge slough. I was lagging behind because I had to – well, Ma'am, relieve myself.'

There was a hint of impishness in her understanding smile.

Encouraged, he continued, 'And I'd got my eyes to the ground, watching where I trod between the bulrushes on one side and a lot of willows on the other – I guess they were willows. One minute I could hear the others shouting at me – and the next minute I couldn't; and the next thing I know the darned horse got mired, and I called and called to 'em to come help me out. And no answer.

'I couldn't get the animal out – the more it struggled, the deeper it went. Finally, I had to watch it drown.'

'Terrible, terrible,' Leila sympathized.

'I called and called to the other men. I was scared, I can tell you. Finally, I picked my way round the slough, but I'd no idea where I was. I couldn't find a hint of the trail; and I'd nothing – gun, blanket, beans and tools, all went down with the horse. When I couldn't even find the track of the others' horses, I must've gone stark mad. When the Blackfoot found me, I was clean out of my mind.'

'Blackfoot?' queried Leila, wide-eyed, her mouth open.

'Yeah. Injuns. A hunting party. They fed me and put me on a horse. I don't remember much about it – I was too far gone, I guess. Next thing I know truly is I'm in bed in Fort Edmonton, with a Cree woman nursing me better. She told me the Blackfoot simply dumped me at the gate of the Fort and rode away. She was a medicine woman sent for by the Cree wife of one of the Hudson's Bay clerks. I tell you, that old woman had me on my feet and sane very quick. I owe a lot to the Injuns up there – and I never forget it.'

'What happened to your friends?'

'Dunno. When I inquired around the Fort, they'd never arrived. Never heard of one of them from that day to this. Maybe they struck another Fort – or joined up with a group of whisky-runners. Or maybe they got lost, as well – and died.'

Leila nodded her head from side to side in wonderment. 'Terrible,' she repeated, it being the one word she knew in English to describe his experiences.

'We were plumb crazy to go north without a guide. We were miners, not explorers or even trappers.'

'What happen next?'

'Well, to be honest, I was afraid of the bush for a long time. So I stayed put, worked on the farm belonging to the Fort for a while, and got to know the land around so I wouldn't get lost again. Then I found a piece of land upriver, which the Bay seemed to have forgotten they owned. Somebody'd been there before – there was an old cabin there and I reroofed it, made a place to live. And I started clearing the land round it. After a while, I met up with a guy called Joe Black – and we worked together. We've got quite a homestead now – he's looking after it while I'm down here.' He took out a pipe and, without asking whether she minded the smoke, he lit up.

'You find gold?' she asked.

'Nope. I pan a bit out of the river sometimes – but nobody's ever found the mother lode.'

'Mother lode?' she queried in puzzlement, her smooth brow wrinkling slightly.

'The main vein of ore – gold, Ma'am.' He watched her delicately sipping her coffee. What a beauty she was! He wondered if she could endure a wilderness home, and told himself not to be a fool. She must be able to pick and choose the men she would take up with.

He plunged into conversation again. 'I don't make much in cash,' he admitted. 'But one way and another we mostly eat O.K. The worst years are over. We've two other men helping us now – both Crees. And Joe Black's mother came from working at the Fort, to help in the house. She's Cree, too.'

She dimpled, and inquired coyly, 'You're not married?'

'I was, Ma'am. Married a Cree lady – a nice, intelligent woman. But about a year ago, she died giving birth.' He sighed heavily.

'And the baby?'

'Little Wallace? He died a month later; it was a bitter winter and a lot of kids died – and old folk round the Fort.'

Remembering her own dead sons, Leila felt an overwhelming compassion for the man before her. Impulsively, she put out her hand and touched his arm. 'You suffer much.'

'I think you have, too, Ma'am.'

She nodded sad agreement.

He called for more coffee, and then began to describe the country he lived in, its superb beauty, the summers hot and comforting; he omitted to mention the myriads of mosquitoes and blackfly in summer, the problems of getting water into the house during the harsh winter, the vast unexplored territory round the tiny settlement.

She listened in wonderment. It was obvious that the man loved his adopted home. She visualized it as country rather like that she had passed through on the train between New York and Chicago, which had seemed very empty to her in comparison with the Lebanon or even Britain. She watched his face which was leathery with exposure to the weather, and noted the grey in his

61

moustache. He was a fine man, she felt, and her sex-starved body cried out with need, though she was thirty years old – quite old, she told herself.

By the time the fresh coffee had been consumed, Tom was telling himself there was no way he was going to let her go. She could adapt, like other immigrant women to the United States had done. 'She can take one more step in her life,' he assured himself, hope overwhelming his doubts.

He accompanied her home and left her on her doorstep, after agreeing to meet the following evening. Leila went up the stairs in a dream. She slowly took off her hat and laid it on the table. Helena was not yet home from work, so she flung herself on her daughter's bed, spread out her arms as if to embrace the world, and for the first time since she had come to Chicago, she laughed with pure joy.

Chapter Eight

A week later, Leila broke it to her daughter that she was seriously considering remarriage. Since Leila had already mentioned that she had met a very nice man, a Canadian, and had gone out to meet him every evening for the past week, Helena received the confidence without too much surprise. It did, however, sadden her that her own beloved father was to be replaced.

'It hurts, Sally,' she confided to her old friend, as they sat together on the bottom step of the staircase leading to Leila's tiny flat. The weather was thundery and the rooms upstairs stifling. Leila was out with Tom.

Sally took a pull at the cigarette hidden in the palm of her hand and slowly blew out the smoke. 'Your mother is a very beautiful person; it's bound to happen. She must like this guy particularly, though, because I know one or two who've approached her and she's turned them down.'

'Really?'

'Sure. I don't suppose your mother told you, because she wouldn't want to disturb you.' She did not say that the indignant young widow had probably turned the men down because their offers did not include marriage. Mrs Al-Khoury had asked Sally if such offers were customary, and Sally had replied, with a grin, that they were common enough, but you didn't have to accept them. Now Sally put her arm round Helena and reminded her that, when she herself married, Leila would be alone. 'I suppose,' Helena had replied uneasily, and had tried to accept the possible change in her life.

Leila stitched her necklace back into her black skirt. Then she told Helena that she had accepted Tom's offer of marriage, and that they would all be moving to western Canada, probably within the month.

'But, Mama!' Helena gasped. 'You said before you couldn't move to another country! What are you thinking of? Couldn't Tom live here?'

Leila's agitation was immediately apparent. 'He says he can't, dear; he's too much at stake in Canada – and he loves the country.' She lifted her hands in a small helpless gesture and let them sink into her lap.

'Well, you don't have to marry *him*! There're other men in Chicago, surely, Mama? I've got used to Chicago now – and so have you.'

'I don't want to marry anyone else,' Leila replied, almost crossly. 'Marriage is very special, very personal.'

'I know that!' Helena's pinched little face was taut with suppressed fear of the unknown. 'If he wants you, he can stay here,' she said resentfully.

'I've asked him, dear. But he either won't or can't. And I can't let him go.'

'Why not?'

'Because I love him very, very much.'

This silenced Helena. Falling in love was something that occurred in books. It had never occurred to her that it might happen to her mother – or, possibly, to herself. In Lebanon, you accepted gratefully the husband chosen for you by wise parents and then hoped he would be kind to you.

Emboldened by her daughter's sudden quiet, Leila said, 'Consider, my darling, how very poor we are. Where will I get the chance again to meet a really nice man – and he is nice.'

Stifling a desire to cry, Helena nodded dumbly. Their current life was very hard and seemed to lack all hope of change, at least until her mother's command of English improved. She could understand that, to her mother, Tom Harding offered an escape from total penury. But to what?

'Has he told you about where he lives?' she asked dully.

'Yes, he has. And it sounds possible, with a good future for you.'

Three weeks later, a numbed Helena found herself in a Registrar's office, standing behind her mother and acting as her bridesmaid, while next to her was Glenn, a rotund version of Tom Harding, acting as his brother's best man. Behind them stood Sally and Mrs Ghanem and one or two friends of Tom and Glenn. Seated in a chair specially set for her was Tom's scary old mother, anxiously attended by plump, harassed Ada Harding, Glenn's wife.

Old Mrs Harding had already told her besotted son, in front of his new fiancée and her daughter, that he was a fool and always had been one; these women would be no use to him in a pioneer settlement. She had been a pioneer herself and knew what it was like.

Helena had listened to her with growing disillusionment. Leila had been as terrified as if she had been cursed by a witch, and it had taken all Tom's cajolement to assure her that his friend Joe's mother lived on the homestead and would come every day to help her. To beguile her, he said he had a little sleigh which she could learn to drive in winter, and that Helena could go to school, either in St Albert, where there was a Roman Catholic Mission, or in the Fort.

On the eve of the wedding, Helena had sat with her mother in their bare, tiny living-room, while Leila unpacked a beautiful, embroidered head shawl, delivered by Mrs Ghanem's eldest son, with the family's good wishes for the marriage. Helena, seeing the fine Lebanese handiwork of the shawl, had put her head down on the table and wept.

'Couldn't we go home to Beirut, Mama? Please, Mama.' She spoke, as usual when addressing Leila, in Arabic, and the words seemed all the more poignant because of the language used.

'Darling child, you know I've thought of that often, but the times are bad. Even if we weren't murdered by either the Druze or the Turks, a widow woman, with no family to protect her, wouldn't stand a chance.' She put down the shawl and moved round the table, to hold Helena in a warm embrace.

With her head resting on her child's thick black hair, she said frankly, 'I don't know what life holds for us, my love. But I feel Tom is honest and kind; and he has high hopes of giving you a better life. He says there is a great shortage of women round the

Fort, so you should be able to make a good marriage when the time comes.' Her voice trailed off, but she continued to hold the girl close to her. She was herself very nervous. She was also desperately in love – and she had no conception of wilderness barely touched by human hands.

Helena did not reply to her mother's assurances. She wept for her father. Through her tears, she looked down at her hands. Her left forefinger was raw from constant pricks from blunted pins and needles at the tailor's workroom, and she remembered the long, dreary days she spent penned up there. If she stayed in Chicago, would that go on forever?

She raised her head. 'How do we know he's even got a farm?' she asked, as she fumbled in her skirt pocket for her handkerchief.

'Well, I've done my best to confirm it. You know that young lawyer on Main Street? He's originally from Lebanon. I asked him if he could inquire for me.'

Surprised at her mother's temerity, Helena glanced up at her. 'What did he find out?'

'Well, he confirmed that Tom's brother has a good reputation – it's been known for years that he had a brother homesteading in Canada. There's nothing to prove it, of course, but a neighbour told him that a few years back Tom asked his mother to join him. She didn't go because her health's so bad. The neighbour also said that the old lady is all against the marriage, because she says I won't be able to work hard enough; I'll be a burden to him.'

A small smile curved Helena's mouth. 'I doubt that, Mama. I think you'll make him very happy.'

Her mother bent and kissed her. 'Thank you, dear.' She paused, and then said, 'The lawyer also advised that Tom should make a Will, to be signed at the end of the wedding ceremony, leaving everything to me, if he should die – which God forbid. Tom's going to do this, so at least we'd have a farm, dearest.'

Though Tom agreed to the Will, he omitted to tell her that he was, as yet, still a squatter and that the Hudson's Bay Company still owned the land; he hoped sincerely that he would gain ownership before he died.

Later on that evening, when Tom came to spend an hour or two with Leila, he tried to reassure the girl.

'The Fathers will teach you school,' he told her. 'And Joe Black or me – we'll teach you how to skate and ride. And you can have a pup if you'd like one.'

She replied heavily, 'I can already read and write in French and Arabic. English is coming. And Papa taught me arithmetic and how to keep accounts – some geography, as well. And how to buy and sell – and judge silk.'

'Then you're a very accomplished young lady,' responded Tom patiently. 'I could use your help, if you'd give it me.'

Though he had caught her interest, Helena looked at him with suspicion. 'Help you?'

'Sure. I can get folks to do all kinds of chores – but Joe and me – neither of us is good at accounts, keeping records and such. And, one of these days I reckon the British Government's going to reach out and take over from the Hudson's Bay Company, which rules us now – and we'll have a pack of Government officials on our backs – and we'll need everything down in pen and ink.'

Helena smiled involuntarily. 'Just like the Turks?' she asked with sudden interest.

Tom did not understand what she was referring to and turned to Leila for enlightenment. Leila told him about the avaricious tax collectors of the Turkish Emperor, and he laughed. 'You've hit it right on,' he told Helena, which made her smile again.

Realizing that much of his and Leila's happiness depended upon Helena being reasonably content, he spent until midnight telling her about the Fort and his homestead. He also told her that he had married a Cree wife, and that the loss of her and of his son had been hard to bear. 'Cree women know how to preserve meat, and how to make clothes out of skins – and how to cure sickness,' he said. 'Joe's Ma is a Cree, and she came to help us when my wife died – and she'll help your Mama, so that it won't be too hard for you.' In the back of his mind, he fretted that two more mouths to feed that winter could be a problem, and he hoped the pig had produced a good litter.

Watching the man as he spoke, Helena felt a sense of pity

creep into her. He, also, had lost people he loved, she realized, and she felt a hint of kinship.

He was saying to her, 'I can't make up to you for your pa – I wouldn't presume to. But I'll take care of you as much as I can. You *could* be the only youngster your mama and I'll have.'

The inference that her mother could have more children shocked Helena. She looked up at her mother, who smiled quietly back. It could happen, she realized. She turned to Tom. His expression was quite sad. He said suddenly, 'I'd like to give you an extra name, in memory of my little boy. Then you'd be real special to me. I'd like to call you Wallace Helena.'

She was immediately offended. 'That's a boy's name.'

'It's a boy's or a girl's. We called the baby after my mother – she's Wallace Harding.'

'I don't need another name.' The wide mouth compressed in disapproval.

'Aw, come on, now. Indulge an old man's fancy.'

Helena looked up at her mother again. 'Do I have to, Mama?'

Her mother's mouth began to tremble, as it always did when she was in doubt. Helena saw it and remembered suddenly how close her mother had come to a complete breakdown after her father's death. She considered warily what might happen if she refused Tom's absurd idea. For a moment, she thought that if she raised a tremendous fuss about it, the whole engagement might be broken off, something she had been praying for for the last four weeks.

The silence between the three of them became tense. Helena's hands were clenched, her mother's eyes wide and despairing.

She understood her mother's passion for this man, and that if the couple married she herself would be dependent upon Tom's goodwill – not something she desired at all. But if she succeeded in breaking the liaison, what else was there? A dreadful servitude, unless she herself could marry decently – and she, like her mother, had discovered that in Chicago she ranked as a coloured girl, not suitable for marriage to a white man. She bit her lips as she bitterly considered this fact, and that there were few boys of her age within the Lebanese community and probably none who would want a penniless girl. She was poor and

68

plain and yellow, she told herself, and without any alternative future worth having.

She took a big breath, and said unsmilingly, 'I don't suppose it makes much difference.'

'Well, that's nice of you,' Tom told her, thankful that he had not alienated her; he had regretted his impulsive request the moment he had made it. Leila had, however, been strangely silent when he had casually mentioned the children they would have.

When pressed, she had said, with a faint smile, 'Let's not worry - see what God sends.'

He wanted another son, but it seemed suddenly possible to him that he would not have one. At the thought, he had urgently wanted to perpetuate the memory of the small brown innocent buried with his mother in the black earth of the north pasture. It had occurred to him that he could give the child's name to his stepdaughter and make her Wallace Helena.

When he was leaving, he shook the girl's hand, then held it for a moment, as he looked down at her. 'You won't regret it, honey,' he said warmly.

Wallace Helena smiled up at him wanly. He seemed to her a simple, honest man - but she wanted to cry.

Chapter Nine

Glenn and Ada Harding provided a modest wedding breakfast in their back garden. Since it was a second marriage, only a few neighbours had been invited over to join the party. All of them were curious to see the bride. The men thought she was very pretty and congratulated Tom; the women tended to side with old Mrs Harding in saying that she was not strong enough to be the wife of a homesteader – and they whispered disparagingly that she looked like a Jewess. Acutely embarrassed by their stares, Leila held the soft brim of her summer hat close to her face and stayed very close to Tom.

The bride's daughter sat, almost unnoticed, on a bench under a tree. Sally, who was herself totally ignored by the other guests, saw the forlorn young girl, and came over to join her. She saw tears on Wallace Helena's cheek and she immediately handed her the glass of wine she was carrying. 'Drink it down, hon. You'll feel better.'

As Wallace Helena silently drained the glass, Sally carefully arranged the skirts of her dress; she had made it out of the bits of black silk Wallace Helena had given her. She looked over at the bride, who was also wearing black silk. 'Gee, your mama looks pretty,' she exclaimed, as if she was seeing Leila for the first time.

'Yes,' agreed Wallace Helena, without enthusiasm. Far more astute than her mother, she foresaw problems arising like thunderclouds – and probably considerable hardship in an unexplored country like Canada. Yet, what could she do?

When she had suggested to Sally that perhaps she should remain by herself in Chicago, try to earn enough to keep herself, Sally had been very explicit about what was likely to happen to a fourteen-year-old left alone in a city.

Sally had added sharply, 'You be thankful your ma's found a decent man to take care of you both; I wish I could find someone like him. There isn't nothing to fear about Canada; slaves run away to it, so as to be free.'

'Do they? Could you come with us, Sally? Could you?' Her voice was suddenly wild with hope.

The black woman had laughed down at her. 'That Mr Harding don't need another mouth to feed, baby. And I got my mother to keep. I'm no slave – I'm free.' She had given Wallace Helena a playful shove with her elbow, as she said the last words. 'He's O.K. Be thankful he's willing to take you in.' She hesitated, and then said, 'He'll take care of you; he'll never touch you, I truly believe.'

Wallace Helena did not understand the import of Sally's last words; she was still overwhelmed at having to face another new country.

Old Mrs Harding did one very sensible thing for them. Realizing that she could not talk sense into Tom, as she put it, she persuaded Leila and Wallace Helena to buy a solid pair of flat-heeled boots each and enough veiling to attach to their hats, so that they were protected in some degree from blackfly and mosquitoes – and she ordered Tom to pay the bill.

In the course of their journey, which took weeks, both Leila and Wallace Helena had reason to be thankful to her: mosquitoes and blackfly plagued them most of the way. They went by train to La Crosse, then by stage to the Red River, and, despite the threat of yet another Sioux uprising, by paddle steamer to Fort Garry. There they rested for a couple of days, while Tom made inquiries. They were not very impressed by what they saw of their first Hudson's Bay Fort, and awaited with anxiety Tom's decision as to how they were to proceed. Their landlady, the wife of a miner who ran a small general store, was aghast when told where they were going; as far as she knew, only one white woman had ever travelled that far, and she was the wife of a Hudson's Bay man.

Leila wept, and Wallace Helena begged Tom to take them back to Chicago. Tom laughed, cheered them up and said they would travel by York boat. Several expeditions had gone out recently from Fort Garry to Fort Edmonton by land; but he was not going to chance such a dangerous journey.

The sail up Lake Winnipeg was not unpleasant. But the rest of the journey was done by York boat up the Saskatchewan River, a long dreary drag with little but pemmican to eat, cooped up in a tiny boat, one of a Company brigade returning to Fort Edmonton with stores.

To Leila's horror, the boats were from time to time dragged out of the river, their cargo unloaded and transported on the backs of the voyageurs, to bypass waterfalls or rapids. The boats themselves were hauled along rough tracks, sometimes made of tree trunks and sometimes a well-trodden path. During these portages, Leila and Wallace Helena stumbled along as best they could, following the crew for mile after mile. Despite the heavy veiling protecting their faces and necks, they were badly bitten by mosquitoes and blackfly, which rose like a fog around them at every step; Tom and the other men seemed to have a certain immunity – their bites did not swell so badly. The crew were Metis, short, tanned, muscular men who cursed in fluent French, as they waged their usual battle against the flow of the huge river.

Leila was not a heavy woman, but what fat she had fell off her. She looked so gaunt that both Wallace Helena and Tom began to wonder if she could survive the journey.

Wallace Helena had, at first, thought that she herself would not survive, but the arduous exercise and adequate rations of pemmican actually began to improve her health. She was filthy dirty and nearly insane from the incessant insect bites, and she longed for some privacy, if only to wash herself down in the cold river water. The men did try their best to provide a little privacy, inasmuch as they turned their backs when the women had to relieve themselves, but they had a tight, fixed schedule to follow, and very little time was spent ashore. No special allowance was made for the fact that they had women with them. The party was soaked through by rain and, on one occasion, by sleet. 'Lucky it hasn't hailed,' remarked one man to Wallace Helena. 'Sometimes it hails heavy enough to bruise you.'

When the wind was in the right quarter, sails were rigged to ease the amount of poling which the men had to do; it also temporarily scattered the mosquitoes. Wallace Helena thought that she had never seen men work so hard for a living; yet they remained fairly good-humoured with each other. They were surprised that both women spoke French, admittedly very different from their own patois, but nevertheless enough for both sides to make rueful jokes about their suffering.

Towards the end of the journey, Leila showed signs of having a fever, and Wallace Helena's heart sank. Wrapped in a blanket, she lay shivering beside her daughter, talking sometimes of the old days in Beirut or of her worries about Wallace Helena's future, her mind wandering so that she did not know where she was.

It seemed to Wallace Helena that she had been crammed in the hated boat for months and that the journey would never end. She felt furiously that Tom had embroiled them in an expedition that nobody should be expected to make.

'What if Mother dies?' she asked him desperately.

Dog-tired himself, Tom could not answer her. Although he knew the journey to be gruelling, he had not realized how profoundly different was the strength of his late Indian wife compared with that of city-bred women. He had expected his new wife to complain about the hardship, but he had not thought that it would be unbearable. Wallace Helena had only to see the anguish in his eyes to know that her dread of losing Leila was shared.

Then, when both women had nearly given up hope, it seemed that an air of cheerfulness went from man to man, an excited anticipation. The man in charge of their craft told Wallace Helena, 'Tomorrow, we'll land for a little while – get a chance to wash and stretch ourselves.' He looked at Leila, lying wrapped in a blanket in an acutely uncomfortable position towards the stern of the boat, and added kindly, 'We'll get a fire going when we're ashore, and I'll make a bit of broth for your mother.'

Wallace Helena smiled her gratitude; the man himself looked exhausted. 'Why are we stopping?'

'We have to make ourselves look decent – for when we arrive at the Fort!'

'You mean we're nearly there?' Her filthy face lit up.

'Be there tomorrow night, God willing.'

'Thank God!' Wallace Helena said, and meant it. 'Would you tell my stepfather?' she asked, pointing towards the rowers, where Tom had taken an oar and was rowing with a kind of deadly mechanical rhythm, his eyes half-shut; it was heavy work, and he was almost oblivious of what was going on around him.

He nodded, and she turned round and carefully eased herself closer to the tiny moribund bundle which was her mother, to tell her the good news.

As promised, the voyageur made a soup for Leila. While Tom built a fire, the man cut up some pemmican and put it into an iron pot with water and some bits of chopped-up greenery which he had hastily gathered. A tripod was rigged over the fire and the pot hung on it. When he considered it ready, he added a little rum; and Wallace Helena spooned the resultant soup into her barely coherent mother lying by the fire.

There was much scrubbing of faces and hands in the chilly waters of the river; one or two men sharpened their knives and roughly shaved themselves. Then, fortified with rum, they poled the last few miles. Several canoes came out to greet them, and there was a small crowd waiting for them when they landed at the foot of an escarpment.

The crowd was dumbfounded when Wallace Helena stepped ashore, followed by Tom carrying her mother.

The Factor was furious when he heard that he had two women from Chicago resting for the night in *his* fort; didn't his boatmen know that settlers were not to be encouraged? Tom Harding had been a big enough nuisance, an American carving out a piece of Hudson's Bay land to farm. Now he'd brought a white wife – and her daughter. Other women would follow them; there was already a rumour that a missionary's wife would be arriving in the district one of these days. Settlers would clear the land, ruin the fur trade. What were his men about?

Leila was put to bed in a comfortable cabin by the Indian wife of an acquaintance of Tom's, and, afterwards, she brought Wallace Helena a bucket of hot water in which to wash herself.

74

Tom was sent for immediately to attend the Factor at the Big House.

Tall and silent, an exhausted, worried Tom was harangued in the man's office. Both men were aware, however, that it was largely bombast; the British Government had left the renewal of the Hudson's Bay Company's Charter up in the air, when it had been discussed in 1858; and already Government survey parties were beginning to penetrate the Bay's kingdom; a few people, some American, had begun to settle.

Despite the hardships of his life, Tom loved his land and dreaded being driven off it by the Company; so, when the Factor had finished what he had to say, Tom politely told him that he missed his dead wife and son, and now sought to rebuild his family. He would be transferring his wife to his cabin in the morning – he carefully did not use the word *homestead* which would have implied his ownership of a piece of land claimed by the Company as their own.

The Factor had kept Tom standing and had offered him no hospitality, so Tom felt free to turn on his heel and walk out.

Chapter Ten

Word of the arrival of the brigade was brought to Joe while he was bringing the small herd of cattle he and Tom possessed closer in to the homestead. He had heard a rumour of a party of Blackfoot roaming the area, and he assumed that they had penetrated so far into Cree country because buffalo were getting scarce and they were hungry. He had no desire to have his precious beasts eaten by them.

The boy who brought the message was a Metis, the son of a friend of Joe's working as a cooper in the Fort. While he got his breath after jogging most of the way, he hung on to Joe's stirrup. Then he burst out, 'Mr Harding's with them. Brought a new wife, a white woman, and her daughter. Says to ask your mother to have the place neat and prepare some food. One woman's sick.'

'You're kidding?' exclaimed Joe, well aware of the Crees' sense of humour – and this youngster was half-Cree.

The lad was offended. 'I'm not,' he responded crossly. 'I saw them. They'll be at your place about midday tomorrow.'

Joe sat on his horse and stared down at him. 'I'll be damned!' he muttered.

He roused himself, and drew out a wad of chewing tobacco from his top pocket. He took out his knife and cut a generous piece of it which he handed down to the boy, with his thanks. 'Like to go down to the cabin and have something to eat?' he asked.

'No. Dad wants me back.' The boy let go of the stirrup. 'Mr Harding says not to send horses; he's borrowing two – and a cart – from Mr Ermineskin.'

Joe nodded, and handed the boy his water bottle so that he could take a swig. After he had drunk, the young messenger said he would sit under a nearby tree for a few minutes to rest and then go home.

Joe finished the job of persuading his steers into the home pasture, and then rode down to the cabin to break the astonishing news to his mother, Agnes Black. The bachelor home had a very fast tidying up.

Late the following morning, when Joe cantered down the narrow trail towards Edmonton to meet his friend, he could hear the ear-splitting shriek of the ungreased wheels of the Red River cart accompanying Tom, long before he saw him.

The wind was quite brisk and the mosquitoes were few. The breeze was whipping the leaves off the trees, and it was through a sudden storm of them that he caught his first glimpse of Leila, barely visible amid shawls and veils. Tom was riding a heavy, black horse and held her in the crook of his arm in front of him.

Behind him, clutching the reins of a smaller animal, rode a scarecrow of a young girl. She had thrown back the veil of the hat perched on the back of her head, to reveal a sallow face so thin that it seemed to consist of two enormous brown eyes surrounded by masses of newly washed black hair; soft strands of it blew across her hollow cheeks.

For a second, Joe ignored his grinning friend. As Wallace Helena approached and caught sight of him, he saw the desolation in the girl's wonderful eyes suddenly replaced by intense fear. It seemed to him that, on seeing him, she reined in her horse instinctively, and half-glanced back along the trail as if to escape.

Uncertain himself, Joe stopped his own horse and dismounted, to wait until Tom reached him. The infernal shriek of the cart behind slowed and ceased.

'Hullo, there,' said Joe carefully to the party. 'Glad to see you.'

A small hand emerged from the shawls in front of Tom, and Leila smiled shyly at him. Although she looked very wan, Joe understood immediately what had captured Tom. She was a beauty. He turned to look at Tom, whose lined, suntanned visage went suddenly bright red with embarrassment. He managed to say, 'Hi, Joe. Good to see you again.' Then he looked down at Leila and said, 'This is my wife.'

Joe raised his hand in salute to her, and said to Tom, 'Congrat-ulations! Du Pont's son told me the news.'

He turned towards Wallace Helena, who was regarding him cautiously from under her long fringe of lashes. He grinned up at her, and asked Tom, 'And this lady?'

'My stepdaughter, Wallace Helena.'

Joe's eyebrows lifted slightly at the familiar first name. He then raised his hand again to salute her. His eyes twinkled cheerfully, and he was glad to see her relax slightly, as he said, 'Nice to meet you, Miss. Hope you and your ma'll be happy here.'

She nodded, and replied in a shy whisper, 'Thank you.'

Because the path was too narrow to ride abreast, Joe remounted his horse to lead them back to the cabin. The cart resumed its terrible shriek, making any communication impos-sible. News would have to wait.

Thanks to Jeanette, her hostess of the previous night, a bathed and tidy Leila managed to walk across the threshold of the cabin which was to be her home for the rest of her life.

As she entered on her husband's arm, she paused. The room seemed quite large to her and, except for the hunting and trapping gear hanging on the walls, looked more comfortable than the miserable apartment they had left in Chicago.

During the night just past, her mind had cleared of the fever, and she had come to the conclusion that, whatever awaited her here, it could not be worse than the traumatic journey she had barely survived. Here were four solid walls to protect her from the jungle outside.

With timid determination, she surveyed the cabin's interior. If she could regain her strength, she would make it into a real home for the husband of her choice.

She looked up at Tom and smiled shyly. 'You have a nice home,' she lied.

Very thankfully, he squeezed her arm, as Agnes Black, another shy person, came out of the lean-to summer kitchen. She was a heavily built, short woman, garbed in a full, printed cotton skirt and a black blouse. On her feet, she wore shabby skin slippers. As she waited for Leila to speak to her, she pushed wisps of grey hair away from a face like a raisin. Her black eyes gleamed in the firelight.

Leila had not forgotten old Mrs Harding's remark that she would be no use as a pioneer's wife, and she realized that she would be dependent upon this quiet, foreign woman to show her how to do practically everything. She smiled at her and said slowly to her, in poor English, 'I am glad you here.'

The genuine relief expressed in the words touched the Indian woman. She made a small gesture towards the hearth where a pot of coffee was keeping warm before the fire. 'I've made coffee for you,' she said simply.

Leila nodded and smiled again, and Tom propelled her towards a roughly made wooden chair. She sat down thankfully and closed her eyes; tears of weakness eased out from under the lids.

She wondered how Tom could expose her to such a terrible journey. Yet, when he held a mug of coffee to her lips and she opened her eyes, to see him peering anxiously at her, a warmth coursed through her feeble frame. She drank the coffee slowly, allowing him to continue to hold the mug.

Wallace Helena and Joe Black had followed Leila and Tom into the cabin. Joe took his boots off at the door, so Wallace Helena did the same. Her eyes were wide with apprehension as she looked round her new home. She felt at a loss, almost unable to cope with anything more that was new to her.

Joe's mother poured cups of coffee for them and they sat down, side by side, on a bench to drink it. Most of the attention was focused on Leila, resting in the curve of her husband's arm.

Joe said something in Cree to his mother. She nodded, and asked Tom in the same language if his wife would like to lie down. What was her sickness?

Tom explained about the fever, and Agnes asked if she would like to have a draught which she could concoct; it would help her to sleep and relieve any fever remaining.

Leila was a little reluctant to take a strange medicine, but Tom assured her that Agnes was known for her ability to heal. She was persuaded to lie on his bed to rest, in a tiny, doorless room at one side of the cabin, and after supper she sipped down the bitter mixture which Agnes brought to her. Covered by buffalo robes, she slept for fifteen hours.

Meanwhile, Agnes, apparently unruffled by the addition of two females to the household, showed Wallace Helena the summer kitchen and the clay oven outside, in which she baked rough barley bread.

They inspected an adjacent store house, which had a hole dug into its earthen floor. 'When the river has frozen, Joe cuts out blocks of ice and lines the hole with them – it lengthens the time we can store raw meat,' she explained in halting English. The hut also held smoked fish, pemmican and various boxes and barrels collected over the years to store vegetables in.

Outside the cabin itself, against one wall, was a pile of roughly hewn logs. A middle-aged Indian with long thin plaits on either side of his face was stolidly swinging an axe, as he reduced the trunk of a tree to logs. He paused, put down his axe and leaned on it, as they approached. 'Simon Wounded,' explained Agnes. She spoke in Cree to the man, and he nodded understanding. He did not look directly at Wallace Helena, but lifted his axe again and continued his work.

'He lives with Joe and me over there.' Agnes pointed to a shack on the other side of the muddy yard. She turned and pointed again to a bigger building. 'That's the barn.' They walked over to inspect it and disturbed a flurry of hens.

Agnes showed her the outhouse behind the cabin, and then they returned to the cabin.

While Agnes watched her with some amusement, Wallace Helena walked slowly round it to examine the amazing collection of implements, pieces of harness, lanterns, clothes and wraps on the walls. There were guns on a rack over the fireplace, and shelves at man-height were littered with caps, hats, old boots and shoes, tools, a shaving mug, what looked like folded skins, and a series of beautifully woven round baskets. From the beams hung what Wallace Helena imagined must be traps for small animals, side by side with bunches of herbs, several bunches of onions and two flitches of bacon. Agnes pointed to the latter, and said, 'I finished smoking them a while back.

Tomorrow, Tom'll probably find time to make a space in the store house for them.'

Wallace Helena nodded. Despite the clutter, the place had a sense of being a home, long-established and cosy.

As she helped Agnes prepare an evening meal, and Tom went round his domain with Joe, to hear all that had happened in his absence, Wallace Helena began to emerge from the desolation and fear which had gripped her for so long.

She did not like what she saw, but Agnes's quiet competence assured her that there was an organized way of life in the isolated homestead, probably a more dependable one than that they had endured in Chicago.

Sensing the girl's uncertainties, Agnes told her about life inside the Fort, and that there were other forts strung across the country, with which the Company kept in touch. The boats plying the river brought them news from Fort Garry and York House, on Hudson Bay. 'And from London, where they say the Great Queen lives,' she added.

Wallace Helena was impressed and comforted; they were not quite so alone as she had imagined. Good weather also helped her; the autumn skies were a flawless blue and the leaves on the deciduous trees and bushes flaunted their reds and yellows. There was little hint of the bitterness of the winter to come.

Leila stayed in bed for most of the first few days in her new home. Then, as her strength returned, she got up and slowly explored the immediate environs of the cabin. In her soft, poor English, she asked quiet questions of Agnes Black and Simon Wounded about their daily tasks and listened respectfully to their replies. She asked Tom details about what was required to prepare for the winter, which, she had gathered from Agnes, was very severe. Once it was apparent to Wallace Helena that her mother was beginning to take charge of her new domain, she thankfully left her in the stuffy cabin and went out with Joe and Tom. She had ridden once or twice in the mountains behind Beirut but it took her some time to control the pony on which Joe mounted her. With a good deal of laughter, she learned to stay on it and became devoted to it.

Being short of labour because of Tom's absence, they were

late in getting in the last of the oats and potatoes, so Wallace Helena fetched and carried for all three men, who worked from dawn to dusk. She also helped Agnes raise water from the well, a long, slow job of lowering a bucket on a rope and hauling it up again. Agnes assured her that it was easier than carrying bucketfuls on a yoke, from the river.

She slept in a bunk in the living-room, so tired that she was not even haunted by her usual nightmare about the little boy she had seen dying in a lane in Beirut.

Though almost overwhelmed by the length and harshness of the journey, Wallace Helena had, throughout, followed Sally's advice with regard to her new stepfather; she had set out to make a friend of him.

A kindly man, worried to death about his new wife's health, Tom Harding thankfully met her half way. It was not an easy adjustment; they sometimes found themselves at loggerheads. Wallace Helena was understandably resentful that she had been replaced by the quiet American as first in her mother's affections.

For his part, Tom remembered his own terror of the empty wilderness, when he had become lost en route to Fort Edmonton. He sympathized with Wallace Helena's obvious fear of the strange, primitive world in which she now found herself. To help her in adjusting, he asked Agnes and Joe Black to be particularly patient with her. Though Wallace Helena was largely unaware of their solicitude, she began to relax with them and to talk to them.

It dawned slowly on Wallace Helena that, though everybody in this untamed land was subject to the vagaries of weather, forest fires, angry Indians and clouds of insects, she was herself much more free than she would have been as the daughter of a Beirut silk merchant. When she considered what her life would have been like had she returned to Lebanon after living in Chicago, she knew she would have found it difficult to endure such a protective environment. Yet, like other immigrants, she often wept, and longed to hear her own language, her own music, have books in Arabic to read, and be able to wear her soft, light native dress. The extraordinary lack of people also bothered her, and she once asked Joe lightly, 'If all the people in all Rupert's Land met together, would they form a decent crowd?'

'Well,' he drawled softly, 'there's plenty of Indians – only they don't build forts or homesteads; they can pack up a camp and move on – and a few months later you wouldn't know they'd been here. You'll see some of them, when they come in to trade at the Fort.'

She asked him what they traded, and so began a long period of learning the background of Indians, Metis and Europeans, now face-to-face in the land which she had, at first, believed to be empty. It was also the beginning of a great friendship with the big, dark man.

Chapter Eleven

The outdoor work in pure cool air acted as an anodyne to Wallace Helena's sense of loss, yet again, of her roots. Being young, she had begun to be accustomed to Chicago; faces of fellow immigrants had become familiar to her and she had made a devoted friend in Sally. Her father's little shop had begun to prosper. Within their tiny apartment they ate Lebanese food and spoke Arabic. The day her father died her small hopes had shattered; yet there remained the familiarity of place and neighbours.

Now, she and her mother had to start again. Leila had Tom to console her. Wallace Helena mourned for her father, and wondered if she would ever know again a peaceful life such as they had enjoyed in Beirut until the day of the massacre.

After living in cities, the immensity of the empty land appalled and terrified her; even the mountains of Lebanon did not have the close-packed, silent forests that the Territories had. Her journey by York boat had given her an idea of the hugeness of the country, and, though Agnes had comforted her by telling her of other forts and other settlements further east, she could, for a long time, be suddenly seized by an unreasoning terror of the unknown. When, once or twice, she rode along the old trail following the river bank to the Fort and saw it from a short distance as they came to land that had been cleared, it looked too puny to survive, a tiny anthill liable to be blown out of existence by the merciless gales. Closer to the river, below the Fort, there were usually a few small boats drawn up on the beach, and when she considered the hundreds of miles of river she had seen, they looked like little cockleshells, too small to take her back to civilization, even if she had a place to go to.

The days became sharply colder; the mud of the yard froze to an uneven lumpiness; the breath of men and animals hung like a mist in the air and the snow drifted down on the roofs, first a skiff of it, then short flurries and then the occasional storm. It did not melt but piled high enough for it to be necessary to dig paths to the barn, to the windbreak where the steers huddled against the rough shelter to keep warm, to the privy and to Joe's and Agnes's shack.

Fearing that the roofs might collapse with the weight of the snow, Joe and Tom several times during the winter climbed up to shovel some of it off. They were watched by both Wallace Helena and Leila with some apprehension for fear they would fall; broken bones could spell disaster for all of them. As the cold increased, their world became the yard and the buildings round it and the steers nearby. Occasionally, Wallace Helena would struggle down the slope to look at the white expanse of the river. Sometimes, there were the marks of a sleigh in the snow covering the ice, and once she saw one and waved to the musher, thankful to greet another person. He raised his whip in salute and she stood and listened to the occasional yap of the dogs as they vanished upriver.

Though she tried to keep a bright face for her mother and Tom and Joe, her courage sometimes failed her. In the privacy of the barn, when she went to feed Peggy, her piebald pony, she would, now and then, lay her head against the animal's blanketed flanks and weep.

Joe found her there, one night, sobbing quietly as she shovelled manure away from the animal, in the light of a lantern flickering on a shelf. He took the shovel away from her and leaned it against the wall. Anxious to stem the passionate tears, he put his arm round her. She put her head against his wolfskin jacket and cried, innocently unaware of the feelings engendered in him, 'It's so lonely, Joe.'

He patted her back as he held her. 'It's not so lonely as you think,' he assured her. 'You've got your ma and Tom and me – and Agnes and Simon.' He rocked her gently from side to side, and his voice was a little thick, as he continued, 'This cold spell will pass and we'll get a chinook wind; that'll send the temperature up.' The sobs began to ease, and he lifted her chin with one hand to look at her face. 'Don't cry, honey. Christmas will soon be here, and if your ma's well enough, we'll get out the sleigh and go to the dancing at the Fort.'

She smiled wanly at him, and said, 'Sally used to call me Honey.'

She felt the great barrel of his chest shudder, as he laughed down at her. 'Did she? Who's she?'

He let her go as she began to tell him. While she spoke, he took up the shovel and finished the job of moving the manure.

'Well,' he said slowly, 'you could write to her, if you know her address. Mail goes in and outta here twice a year at least. Mebbe she'd write back to you.'

'Really? Could I write to Uncle James in Liverpool - in England?'

'I don't see why not. The Bay carries letters for Tom, down into the States.' He hung the shovel on its hook and prepared to help her across the yard.

He had caught her interest. She rubbed the tears out of her eyes, and her expression was suddenly animated.

'I'll ask Tom if he can spare a piece of paper to write on. Mama might like to write as well.'

'Sure. Tom'll spare you a sheet - he keeps some to write his ma.'

He opened the small side door of the barn, and they fought to shut it again after them, while the wind tore at it. The cold hit them, and he put his arm round her to steady her across the yard.

Wallace Helena had been quiet as they battled their way to the cabin door. Now with her hand on the latch, she turned to Joe, and asked him without preamble, 'Joe, could you teach me Cree? Then I could talk to the Indians. When that band came through in the autumn, you and Tom had a good laugh with them. But I couldn't understand a word.' She pulled her scarf up over her mouth against the cold, though they were standing in the lee of the cabin.

Surprised, he said, 'Sure. I'll try.'

'Thanks, Joe.'

The big eyes narrowed in a smile of gratitude, as she lifted the latch. 'Goodnight, Joe.'

He nodded and turned away. Heavy with uneasy thoughts, he went over to his mother's cabin by the barn. Up till then he had enjoyed his bachelorhood; when food had been in better supply, he had gone to parties and special celebrations given by local Crees and had sometimes roistered with young Metis down at the Fort. Though women were a little scarce, there was usually someone happy to lie with a handsome man for a small consideration. When Tom had married for the first time, it had stretched the resources of the fledgling homestead to its limits, and Joe had decided that since there was no one whom he particularly fancied he would stay single for a bit longer.

That evening, as he sat cross-legged making a pair of snowshoes for Wallace Helena, he began to think differently. As he carefully twisted and knotted the gut in the snowshoes, he sighed. He was twenty-seven years old – getting on – to her fourteen; and, though Tom Harding spoke of him as his partner, he knew that Tom regarded the homestead as his, and Joe got his keep and a small share of any cash that came along – as wages. Only the money he earned from his trapline was his own, and fur-bearing animals got scarcer every winter.

He told himself not to be a fool.

Chapter Twelve

A few days later, just before Christmas, Leila asked Tom if he would take her down to the Fort to see Jeanette, who had kindly put her up on the night of her arrival at Fort Edmonton. It seemed warmer outside and the snow was not too deep on the trail, so Tom amiably agreed. Joe had gone to tend his trapline.

Eager for a change, Wallace Helena begged to go with them, so the sleigh was got down from the wall of the barn and, with hot bricks to their feet and blankets and a buffalo robe tucked round them, the women were driven in style down to the Fort. It was a bumpy ride, but they enjoyed it.

Leila was consumed with anxiety about her abysmal lack of knowledge, and while she sat by Jeanette's fire and discussed the duties of a settler's wife, Tom went to have a drink with the blacksmith, and Wallace Helena wandered out into the yard of the Fort, to see what was happening. Both men and women stared at her; she had thrown her shawl back from her head and it gave them a chance to examine Tom Harding's new daughter. Some of the women smiled at her and spoke to her in Cree, but she did not understand. So she smiled back, and passed on. The gate of the Fort was open and a number of Metis were hanging around it, smoking and gossiping. She had to pass close to them to go out of the gate, and one of them said to another in French, 'They're Chinks, all right.' He sounded derogatory and presumably believed that Wallace Helena could not understand French. 'Bit of stuff for a cold night.'

Wallace Helena stopped in her tracks. Slowly she turned to face the speaker. She took a step towards him, and slapped him hard across the face. 'You dirty bastard,' she shouted, and told him in fluent French translation of Arabic phrases who his mother had probably been.

Shocked and then outraged, his face contorted, the man would have gone for her, but he was held back by his friends, whispering anxiously to him, 'Tom Harding will give you hell. Leave her alone.'

Restrained by his friends, he could do nothing but spit at the girl's feet, as she turned and went hastily back to Jeanette's quarters. Terribly shaken, she sat quietly by her mother for the rest of the visit. She never forgot or forgave this first insult and the others which subsequently came her way when the Scottish clerks in the Fort decided loftily that she and her mother were Jewish and that Tom Harding should never have been allowed to bring them into the district; it was doubtful, she thought, if any of them could have found Lebanon on a map.

Leila never went anywhere without Tom, so she was spared direct slurs on her origins. She was willing to go to the dance at the Fort at Christmas, feeling that her daughter would enjoy the gaiety of the season there. The place was packed with men, women and children of all ages, though there were no white women. Leila sat on a bench beside Agnes Black and her sister Theresa, who worked in the kitchen of the Fort. She refused to dance because she thought it was unseemly, but she was polite and charming to those women who spoke to her, speaking French when they understood and her broken English when they did not.

Though both Tom and Joe encouraged Wallace Helena to join them in the mixture of Indian dances, Scottish reels and French folk dances, she was apprehensive and shy and was glad to go back to her mother and stay close to her. The Scots passed her with a scornful look. None of the Metis came near her, having heard the story of how one of their number had been slapped in public by this forward little piece who, if she wasn't Chinese, was indubitably Jewish.

Defiant and insulted, Wallace Helena stonily refused to go down to the Fort again. Since she would not give either Joe or Tom a reason for this, it was some time before the men heard the story and identified the man concerned. Tom was furious and wanted to ride down to the Fort straight away to give him a sound beating. Joe, more cautious, pointed out that the man was a Company employee and that the Factor would probably take his part against a pair of illegal squatters like themselves. It was possible that if they created a fracas, the Factor would make a much greater effort to drive them off the land they occupied. Better to wait and if anybody else insulted either Leila or Wallace Helena to immediately file a complaint with the Company. Meanwhile, one of them should always be close beside them, and not let them out of sight.

A fuming Tom was finally persuaded to agree to this, and Leila continued to visit Jeanette whenever Tom had business at the Fort. Jeanette did not return the visits, mainly because her growing number of small children tied her to her home. It was months before Wallace Helena was persuaded to accompany her mother, and she stayed with Leila in Jeanette's quarters until Tom collected them.

Slowly, the young girl learned Cree from Joe and Agnes. It was learned verbally, because there were no books in Cree, and she often made amusing mistakes, so that the three of them laughed together over them. Tom had a smattering of it, but Leila felt she had enough to learn anyway, without wasting time on another language, and she never learned to speak it, though through constantly hearing it, she often understood what was being said. The language opened the door to communication with friends and relations of Joe's who sometimes arrived in the course of their seasonal migrations. It was another new world to Wallace Helena, and, because she was respectful and a good listener, some of them became fond of her in their undemonstrative way.

As the winter passed and the spring sent the men out on to the land again, Leila discussed with Agnes the tremendous list that Jeanette had given her of the duties of a homestead wife. Neither spoke English very well, but Agnes understood quickly enough Leila's doubts that she would be able to fulfil them all.

Agnes said comfortably that there were two of them, which cheered up Leila a little. The Lebanese proved to be a good organizer; she had been used to supervising servants in her Beirut home. She could cook, and learned from Agnes how to make the most of what food was available to them. Between the two of them, they looked after the all-important vegetable patch and the precious hens, milked the cows, scrubbed clothes and sewed garments for all of them, either out of trade cloth, bought from the Hudson's Bay Company, or from skins that Agnes cleaned and tanned.

Prompted by Jeanette, Leila discussed quantities with Tom and Joe. How much wood, how much meat, how much grain should be ground for the winter? How many hens should they kill in the autumn? How many pigs – how much bacon? They soon learned to be thankful for her forethought.

As her health was restored to her, she used her own experience in Lebanon and made better use of the milk they had by preserving it for a few days as yoghurt, then making butter of it. She got Joe to make a small churn to her design and, later, a rough copy of a cheese press that she had seen in Chicago, so that she could make cheese.

The men got used to her shrill voice scolding Simon Wounded or Joe, reminding Agnes, calling in Wallace Helena to do something. Her daughter grinned, as she heard the familiar tones of an Eastern lady asserting herself in her domestic sphere. Leila was, however, generous with praise, as if, at times, everyone was a miracle worker, and she would croon tenderly over those who suffered the inevitable knocks, cuts and burns of their hard life, learning from Agnes something of local cures and sedatives.

Agnes, Simon and Joe often laughed at her privately, and occasionally cursed at her insistence on jobs being finished when she said they were to be. She treated them, however, absolutely as friends and equals and she often took their proffered advice. When she found their friends hanging round her door, she would always find something in her storeroom to feed them with.

Not everything went perfectly. In the first years, there were often domestic disasters, like the awful day when Leila clapped her hands at a skunk when it came into the summer kitchen and the skunk sprayed everything. Leila would cry passionately on Tom's shoulder, venting her frustration for all to hear. Yet he never regretted his marriage.

Under the weight of work in a harsh climate, her beauty soon faded. They became dear friends and often laughed at secret jokes, which sometimes made Wallace Helena feel left out.

Wallace Helena not only inherited Tom Harding's son's name, she also learned to do the work that he would have done, had he lived. It was as well that, though not large-boned, she was lithe and, as she grew older, she acquired considerable physical strength.

Joe Black reluctantly decided that he was much too old for her and continued his bachelor ways, visiting the obliging women who lived in a shack not far from the Fort when he felt the need for feminine company. As they worked together, however, he did shyly share with her his profound knowledge of the wildlife round them and of the sorely distressed aboriginal people who were beginning to feel the pressure of the white settlements in the east. She learned to speak enough Cree to enjoy a joke with them, and one young man asked Tom for her in marriage. She turned him down.

Though so hard-worked that she had little time to think of herself as a person with needs of her own, she was not unaware of the stirring of desires in her that, as far as she could see, could not be met. She nursed a terrible resentment of the men in the Fort and it became a latent bitterness as she grew older.

She thought of Joe as being of the same generation as her stepfather, though in fact he was much younger, and considered him the equivalent of an uncle.

Often dressed in an Indian woman's moccasins and gaiters, she would ride alongside him and became nearly as adept as him in caring for the livestock. She left the slaughter of pigs and steers to him, but she soon got used to cutting the throats of chickens, snaring and skinning rabbits and catching fish and gutting them.

Leila was, at first, shaken at what her daughter was doing, but Agnes Black laughed and told Leila she was lucky not to have to do the butchering herself. Leila cheerfully cooked whatever the others brought in, learning from Agnes the art of reducing a beaver, a lynx or, once, a bear, to edible stews. The skins of the wild game were carefully cleaned by Agnes or Tom and were sold into the fur trade, providing either much-needed cash, or credit at the Hudson's Bay trading post.

As Wallace Helena grew into a tough independent young woman, rejecting the people in the Fort as ignorant and uncivilized, Agnes Black, quiet and observant, worried a little about her son. Sometimes, after shutting the yard gate after them, she would stand and watch Joe and Wallace Helena race out along the rough lane which strung Tom's and Joe's holdings together, the girl nearly as skittish as the mare under her.

Joe should have got married years ago to some decent Cree girl, she thought. But she had never persuaded him to do anything he did not want to do; and his grandfather was too distant to exert his influence. Now, she sensed Wallace Helena's attraction for him; she saw it in the careful way he always dealt with her, keeping just sufficient distance between them to discourage intimacy.

On summer evenings, before they all went to bed, they would sometimes sit outside to catch the evening breeze, Leila and herself on the cabin step, Tom, Joe and Wallace Helena on the nearby fence. The men and Wallace Helena would smoke. Joe had taught the girl how to use a little Indian pipe or roll a cigarette for herself if papers were available. When she first arrived, she had been so on edge that Joe had feared she would be ill, and he had suggested that she learn to smoke, to calm her. Now, she could not imagine being without tobacco, and she looked forward to this quiet half hour when sometimes they talked and at other times were glad simply to relax under the wide, darkening sky.

Once the afterglow had faded, Leila would call them in, because, ever since the brush with the skunk and a later encounter with a porcupine, she had been afraid of wild animals straying in after dark. Wallace Helena never demurred and went in with her mother, and Agnes saw her son's eyes follow her.

'If he wants her,' she thought fretfully sometimes, 'why doesn't he ask her?' And she answered herself by saying that Tom would not tolerate it.

Chapter Thirteen

Though Leila sustained a friendship with Jeanette, she never became close to anyone else. The Harding homestead was less than five miles from the little Fort, but it was too far for frequent contact, particularly when the narrow trail along the river was often very muddy or, in winter, choked with snow. Except for the Indians and a few trappers, most of the activity of the Fort was with its connections downriver; what small traffic there was went that way and did not pass the Harding place. Even with Jeanette, both Leila and Wallace Helena sometimes found themselves at a loss, because they had had some education – Jeanette could not even read – and, further, they had had the experience of living in two other countries. On Jeanette's part, she could not understand Leila's disinterest in children – or her lack of them.

When Tom first married his pretty Lebanese, he had hoped for another son, but when he saw Leila collapse during her journey to Fort Edmonton, he realized that, as his mother had warned him, she had not the strength a pioneer life required. He began to fear that he might lose her in childbirth, as he had done his first wife. So, as the months went by and his new wife did not become pregnant, he was relieved. He soon tumbled to the fact that the few days each month during which she refused to make love, on the grounds of religious observances, had a twenty-eight-day cycle, and probably had something to do with the avoidance of pregnancy. Haunted by the fate of his first wife, he humoured her and settled down to being cosseted by a wife trained, since the day she took her first tottering steps, to please a man.

He appreciated the tremendous effort she made to do her part in running the homestead as well as a Metis woman would have done, except that she did not give much help in the fields or garden. He knew he was fortunate in having three women on the place who got along very well together; they rarely quarrelled and soon made up again; and, as he said one day to Joe, 'Between the three of them, they shift a hell of a lot of work.'

Joe grinned. From the hill that sloped upwards behind the cabin, he could see how far they had extended their cleared land since the advent of Leila and Wallace Helena. 'Yeah,' he agreed, 'and you and I've shifted a lot, as a result of being freed up a bit by them!'

Tom nodded agreement. 'We'll fence this section before the fall,' he said.

'The Company's not going to like it – it's still their land.'

'The Company won't last forever. They can't hold the land, as it is. If they could, they would've tipped out every Metis who's built himself a cabin and dug a vegetable garden, not to speak of running me out of town.'

'Well, mebbe you'll have a son who'll own it.'

'Humph.' Tom flicked the reins of his horse and started it down towards the cabin. He had been married three years, and Joe must be wondering why he had no more family. Well, he could keep on wondering.

Wallace Helena was seventeen. She had fully expected that by this time she would have some small brothers and sisters, and one day after visiting Jeanette and her brood, she asked her mother why none had arrived.

Her mother smiled secretively, and said, 'I'll explain it next time the boys are out and Agnes has gone to visit her sister at the Fort.' It was time, she felt, that Wallace Helena should understand these things.

Seated by the fire, one cool autumn evening, some mending in her lap, she said frankly to her daughter that, once she had seen the lonely little Fort and the still more lonely cabin, she had decided that she did not want to bear infants in such a deserted place only to see them die.

'An awful lot of them do die round the Fort, I know,' Wallace Helena agreed, holding up the sock she was knitting to see how she was getting on.

'I lost both your little brothers and that was enough. Thank

95

goodness I have you, my darling, and that you are strong and healthy. And I have dear Tom, bless him.'

'I would hate to see my babies die,' Wallace Helena said. 'I felt awful when the boys died.'

'I know, dear.' She looked suddenly old, as she sat with needle poised over the patch she was sewing and stared into the fire, to visualize the world from which she had come, the warmth, the vivacity, the sophistication of it – and the two small graves.

She shook her head and forced herself to attend to what she wanted to say. Smiling gently, she said, 'One day, perhaps some nice Lebanese will find his way here – and he'll marry you and take you away to a more civilized place. Then you can give me some grandchildren.'

Wallace Helena smiled back at her mother, but said nothing; Mama was entitled to her little flights of fancy.

Bored with knitting, she got pen, ink and paper down from a shelf, to write a thank-you letter to Uncle James for the small box of Arabic books he had sent them. The wonderful present had taken nearly a year upon its journey, and Leila had cried when she had lifted out the works of her favourite poet.

After the letter was written, Wallace Helena went over to the fireside, to pick up her knitting again. Tom and Joe were in the barn dealing with a mare which was having difficulty in dropping its foal.

'Mama, how is it that you can avoid having children? Agnes says children simply come, whether you like it or not.'

Her mother was mending a rent in one of Tom's jackets. She broke the thread with her teeth, as she considered the question. 'It is a delicate matter. You have to watch the moon and your monthly show of blood – and you have to find an acceptable excuse to give your husband for not lying with him on certain days.'

Wallace Helena picked out another ball of the coarsely spun knitting wool with which she was making socks. 'The moon, Mama?' she asked, a little incredulously, a suspicion of laughter in her voice.

'Yes. The moon. I'm not teasing you. It's a system usually used to help women conceive – if they've had no luck in becoming pregnant. But it can be used in reverse, to avoid children.' And she went on to share with Wallace Helena the observations of generations of women, that there appeared to be certain days in the monthly cycle when a child might be conceived – and that these days were limited. By watching the moon's twenty-eight-day cycle or by consulting a calendar, one could relate a *woman's* twenty-eight-day cycle to it – and thus know that at the rising of the moon, say, one should try for a child – or avoid those days if you did not want one.

Wallace Helena sat spellbound. 'What do you tell Tom, to avoid him on the wrong days?'

'I tell him I have certain religious days when I must make special prayers each month,' she replied placidly. 'And he humours me.'

Wallace Helena had always understood the relationship between man and wife; there was little privacy in the crowded busy homes of Beirut, and women talked and complained endlessly about their menfolk. Now, however, finding the young woman was interested, Leila began to instruct her in how to please a man. 'When you are older, you will marry,' she said, 'and you'll keep a man faithful, if you give him pleasure.'

'Do women get pleasure?'

'Certainly, my dear. But sometimes men are stupid and ignorant – and then you have to teach them what pleases you.'

'Humph.' Wallace Helena found it impossible to relate what her mother said directly to Tom; it was as if the faded, knowledgeable woman was a teacher, not her mother, and the man about whom she spoke was not Tom, but some abstract man conjured up to use as an example.

When Leila fell silent, Wallace Helena did not know what to say. Her mother had opened up a weird world which she had always known existed but had never really considered; it made her feel very uneasy.

Finally, she said lightly, 'It's easier to make moccasins than to knit this awful wool.' She flung down her needles irritably.

Leila agreed, and no more was said about the art of sex. Wallace Helena began to look at men with new eyes, however. Black, white or brown, were they all the same? She began to speculate

97

whether women were as powerless as they often appeared; her mother seemed to believe that men could, through sex, be easily manipulated.

She got up briskly from her chair, and said, 'I'll go over to the barn.' Then she paused, and asked idly, 'Mama, do you feel it has been worthwhile – leaving Chicago, I mean?'

The unexpected question startled Leila. She looked puzzled for a moment, and then said slowly, 'I don't think about it very much. When I first came I thought I was going to die, and I wished I had sent you, at least, to your Uncle James.'

Wallace Helena bent to kiss her mother lightly on the top of her head. 'I'd never leave you, Mama.'

'Bless you, child,' Leila responded absently, and then reverted to Wallace Helena's question. 'Once I was here, I was sure I could never face the return journey – or any similar journey – so I have made the best of it. And Tom is very dear to me,' she added defensively. 'I didn't make any mistake about him. He works like a devil for our sake.'

'Yes, he does,' admitted Wallace Helena. She sighed. 'We all work very hard.'

Her mother spread her hands on her knees and looked at the broken nails, the ingrained soot and their redness. 'Yes, dear,' she agreed, and then her usual optimism reasserted itself, and she said, 'Tom's saving to get us a proper iron cooking stove.'

'Good heavens! Where would he get that from?'

'He's trying to find out – and see if he can get one sent overland, now the trail is better.' She got up from her chair and shook out the jacket she had been mending. 'Up to now, he's had to collect farm implements – tools of every kind. Now it's my turn to have something, he says.'

'Great,' responded Wallace Helena, with enthusiasm. 'A stove will be a godsend.' She took her shawl from a hook and wrapped it round herself. 'I'll go over to see if the foal's born yet.'

Ice crunched under her moccasins as she walked across the yard to the barn. Her mother had not really answered her question regarding her inner feelings about living in such a primitive place. Did she find the small world of the homestead and its six inhabitants satisfying? Was the battle to survive each year perhaps a challenge that she enjoyed meeting? Yet, she had cried when she saw the tattered anthology of Arab poems which Uncle James had sent.

She stood in the yard for a moment, looking up at a peerless night sky where every star seemed to twinkle with the clarity of a view of them from a desert. It was uncannily quiet, except for the muffled sound of the men's voices in the barn. The wind was chilly and she began to shiver as she gazed at the cold silver of the rising moon. Living in the Territories was as lonely as living on the moon, she thought. There was nothing comfortable in the thousands of miles of unexplored forest and prairie that surrounded her. The untouched land sat there like a mountain lion waiting for prey – and it could spring nasty surprises on you just as quickly, she thought bitterly. And no matter what happened, there was no extended family to call on for help; no community. Nothing. Just nothing. Did Adam and Eve feel like she did, when they were cast out of Eden to face just such a world?

She began to shake with helpless fear, just as she had when she first arrived. Perspiration rolled down her face, and she wanted to turn and run. But there was nowhere to run, except into the very land which scared her so much.

The side door of the barn opened and Joe was silhouetted against the light of the lantern inside. He was wiping his hands and arms with some straw. He did not see her at first, but when he did, he asked, in surprise, 'Hi, hon, what are you doing out there?'

She turned. Her blanched face gleamed in the lantern light. She looked at Joe for a moment as if she did not recognize him. Her mouth tightened and she seemed much older than her seventeen years, as she sought to control her terror. She said shakily, 'I came to see if the foal was born.'

Joe threw away the dirty straw, and grinned. 'Sure. He's fine. And Queen'll be all right.'

She tried to smile, but there was no rejoicing in her; Uncle James's little lemon flower felt as bitter as a lemon fruit.

Chapter Fourteen

Leila was not the only one marked by the remorseless round of work on a homestead: Agnes Black was feeling her years. After talking the matter over with Joe and Simon Wounded, she suggested to Tom and Leila that they might take in an orphan girl from amongst those cared for by the Grey Nuns in St Albert, a small Metis and Cree community founded by an Oblate priest, Father Lacombe, about ten miles away.

'The girl could help in the house – and I'd teach her,' she promised. 'We wouldn't have to pay her anything for a while.'

They debated the problem of another mouth to feed, but, though the harvest that year had been good, the men were uneasy; some years they felt as if they had their backs to the wall. Another person was another responsibility. Leila, however, jumped at the idea, particularly since the girl would not be coming straight from her tribe, but would have been taught by the famous Grey Nuns. She had never met the nuns; they tended to stay close to their work in St Albert, but she had heard from Jeanette that they were white and were educated, and might even know what a Lebanese Maronite was.

So, speechless and terrified, Emily, aged ten, was added to the motley family. She clung to Agnes like a small brown ghost.

At first, Wallace Helena did not take much notice of her. She herself worked with the men outside; Emily would work with Leila. Then she noticed casually that the child never smiled and did not seem to grow much, though she ate with the family and consumed a fair amount of food. When spoken to, the girl slid behind Agnes, who often answered for her. This bothered Wallace Helena and she mentioned it to Joe, while they sat on the fence having their usual evening smoke.

Joe carefully crumbed up some tobacco in the pink palm of his hand, before he answered. 'Maybe she don't understand anything but Cree,' he suggested. 'What do you talk to her in?'

'English. She must know English. I tried French one day, but she just looked at me as if I were insane. I took it for granted that being with the nuns all her life, she didn't know Cree.'

'Try Cree – slowly.'

Wallace Helena followed his advice, though her own Cree often made a gleam of amusement rise in the eyes of Indian visitors. And slowly she began to unravel the small, grubby, miserable person that was Emily.

She was startled to find a mirror image of herself, when she first came to Fort Edmonton, a child uprooted, its origins and forebears either ignored or disparaged. In addition, she was parentless. Agnes Black, though not unkind, was often short with her because, as Emily told Wallace Helena, 'I'm slow, because I don't know anything. And Mrs Harding – I can't understand what she says. So she gets cross.' She did not cry; she avoided looking directly at her questioner, her face expressionless.

Wallace Helena nodded, her own face suddenly grim. Poor Mama had declared that knowing three languages was enough – she was not about to start on Cree; she spoke English to Agnes.

Emily slept in the bunk in the living-room where Wallace Helena had herself wept through her first weeks in the homestead; Tom and Joe had since built on a little room for her which backed on to the living-room fireplace and was warmed by it. She sighed, and looked again at the child before her. It was late, and Agnes, Joe and Simon had long since gone to their shack. There was a faint murmur of voices from her parents' room, as they, too, prepared for bed. With a sudden surge of pity, Wallace Helena took both the youngster's hands in hers. 'I think I understand how you feel,' she said. 'It happened to me once, when I couldn't speak any English.'

Emily's eyes opened wide and, for the first time, she stared directly at Wallace Helena.

Wallace Helena continued. 'I'll explain to Mrs Harding, and

she will ask Agnes to translate for you. And you can speak Cree to Joe, Mr Harding and Simon Wounded.'

At the men's names the girl looked frightened.

'What's the matter?' asked Wallace Helena.

'The Reverend Mother said we must never, ever, speak to men; it's dangerous for us.'

Wallace Helena leaned back in the old wooden chair and laughed. Emily looked totally discomfited at her sudden mirth.

'I don't think any of the men here will hurt you; they are more likely to protect you from other men. If any one of them does touch you in a way you don't like, tell me immediately. I'll take care of you.'

The girl squirmed, and then smiled slightly. Wallace Helena got up and suggested cheerfully, 'Let's have some hot milk before we go to bed. And tomorrow I'll teach you how to milk a cow.'

The next morning, she rode out with Joe to look for a missing steer; their herd was small and any absence was noted almost immediately. Unlike further south, where cattle ranged on the hills, Tom kept his in fenced pasture land, which he had taken a lot of trouble to improve.

Joe's handsome, high-cheekboned face creased up with laughter when she told him of little Emily's woes and mentioned the Reverend Mother's warning. His black eyes flashed, as he rose in his saddle to squint across the country in search of the lost animal.

'Tell your ma about her; she'll spoil her to death, once she understands what's the matter.'

His assumption was correct, and Emily became another little daughter to train, always a quiet shadow in the house, but devoted to Wallace Helena and Leila.

They found enough remains of the steer to indicate that someone had slaughtered it and taken almost all of it away with them.

'Must've been a party of 'em, blast them,' he muttered. 'I sometimes think we were crazy to bring cattle up here. Nobody else did for a while. I guess we lost this one to Indians last night – but if it isn't them, it's cougars – or they go eat something they shouldn't and make themselves sick; they haven't got the brains of mice. I'll never forget the time I had bringing the first three up from Fort Benton.' He bridled as he continued, 'I got them here, though – a bull and two cows, as scrawny as they could be and still stand on their feet.' He chuckled again. 'The fellows down at the Fort laughed their heads off and said it was a lot cheaper to hunt; but we nursed 'em along and we got calves and had meat when they didn't.'

As they went back to the cabin, laughing and making jokes about the chickens he had also bought, on another occasion, from American settlers further south, Agnes Black looked up from the barrel in which she was doing some washing, outside the door, and she sighed. Again, that night, she suggested cautiously to Joe that he should take a Cree wife.

He told her dryly that he and Tom had enough mouths to feed, without his adding to them. 'Tom looked as black as Old Nick when I told him about the steer this morning,' he added, as if to confirm the difficulty of feeding everyone.

Chapter Fifteen

Over the years, Tom and Joe struggled on, through good harvests and bad ones. They increased their holding and the cattle on it by not asking anyone's permission to clear land; they felled trees and then ploughed, and argued afterwards with the Hudson's Bay Company. The Company's Chief Factor finally gave up and decided to ignore them.

Then, in 1879, came the smallpox, sweeping through the west like the Black Death once swept through Europe.

Tom was the first to catch the disease, probably from a family of Crees he had met casually on the trail, who were subsequently wiped out by it. Leila and Agnes Black nursed the stricken man and both of them became infected; regardless of contagion, Leila held her husband in her arms when his pain was greatest, whispering to him to hold on and that he would soon be better. Inwardly, she was torn with anguish, as she watched his well-loved features almost obliterated by the huge pustules the disease produced; they blocked his nasal passages and his mouth so that he could not swallow the sedatives that Agnes brought. He died in a wild delirium, held down by both women, so that he would not roll off the bed.

As his poor racked body relaxed in death, the elderly Indian woman and the suddenly bereft wife stared blankly at each other across the bed as if stupefied. Then Leila screamed and flung herself across Tom, beating his pillow with her fists.

Agnes hastened round the bed to lift her away, calling at the same time for Joe to come to help her. He heard her and came immediately from the yard. Together, they half-carried the frantic woman into the living-room. She fought them off, continuing to scream and then to tear her clothes in mourning.

'Stay with her,' Agnes ordered. 'I'll get Wallace Helena – and something to soothe her.'

Not attempting to stop her rending her garments, Joe spoke softly to her and gradually persuaded her to sit down. Wallace Helena came running from the vegetable garden, where she had gone for a few minutes to get vegetables to make a soup for the invalid, a soup he would not now need. She knelt by her mother and wept with her. Then she persuaded Leila to sip the cordial Agnes brought for her and this helped to calm her.

When symptoms suggested that Leila herself had caught the disease, she shuddered inwardly and quailed at the thought of the suffering she must undergo. Secure in the belief that Tom would be waiting for her, she was not afraid of dying; without her husband, she felt she had no reason to live. While her mind was clear, however, she gathered up her courage; Wallace Helena was a woman now, but she needed to be able to continue on the land that sustained them. She sent Joe post-haste to bring a priest to her.

Two Oblate Fathers came from a nearby Cree encampment, where they had been tending the sick as best they could. They were surprised to find a woman who did not want to confess or receive extreme unction; she wanted them to write a Will for her and witness her signature.

'I may die, Father. I want to make sure that everything that belongs to me – including anything my beloved husband has left me . . .' Her voice broke as she struggled through her increasing pain to convey her sense of urgency to the priests. 'He wrote a Will when we were married – I haven't had the heart to look at it yet – but it's probably in his cash box.' She stopped, to gather what strength she had, and then continued, 'Everything to go to my darling daughter, Helena – Wallace Helena.'

It was arranged before the disease engulfed her completely. The priests did not stay; they returned hurriedly to the stricken encampment, only to die of the same disease themselves a short time later.

As Wallace Helena tended her mother, she wept openly for her well-loved stepfather, and she faced, with terror, the prospect of losing Leila as well.

Joe dug Tom's grave, near that of his old friend's first wife, and himself carried the body wrapped in a blanket down to it, and laid him in it. After throwing the rich, black earth back over him, he stood alone in the starlight, grieving for his boon companion of so many years, while in the cabin his mother and Wallace Helena strove to alleviate the death pangs of Tom's second wife.

The following day, Joe's mother showed signs of having the disease and took to her bed in their little shack, to be nursed by Joe. He had to order a terrified Simon Wounded to dig a grave for Leila, though, to save Simon from being infected, he left his mother for a few minutes while he took Leila gently from the arms of a shocked Wallace Helena and laid her in her last resting place.

He would not allow Wallace Helena near Agnes; the girl had, as yet, shown no sign of illness, and he hoped to save her from it. So Wallace Helena, wide-eyed and unweeping, cooked and brought food to the door of the shack, while Emily, whimpering like a lost kitten with nowhere safe to run, fed horses and hens, milked the cows, and, somehow, kept things together.

The night before Agnes Black died, it was obvious to Joe that he had become the next victim. He shouted to Wallace Helena that she was not to come near him, just bring water to the door.

She shouted back, 'Don't be a bloody fool; we'll live or die together.'

She marched into the little cabin, clean sheets over her arm, and helped the almost incoherent man out of his clothes in the hope of easing the pain when it came. She bullied a quivering Simon Wounded into helping her move Agnes's body outside, and sent him off to dig yet another grave. She shouted to Emily to take the bedding off her mother's bed and burn it outside. She was to remake the bed with clean bedding. Then she was to wash herself and boil her own clothes.

Simon Wounded did not have to be asked to take Agnes Black to her grave; pale and shaken, he silently did it, and took himself off to bed in the hayloft over the barn, to mourn alone.

The next morning, he helped Wallace Helena move Joe into the main cabin. The man was burning with fever and understood little of what was being done. Between them they nursed him through it. Emily was not allowed near him, but she kept the four of them fed, and, with unexpected stoicism, faced the fact that she might get the disease.

Wallace Helena, Emily and Simon worked to the point of exhaustion to prepare for the winter, none of them wishing to suffer near-starvation during it.

It was a shadow of Joe who survived, and it was months before he was able to handle his chores.

When, one night, he thanked Simon and Emily for not deserting them, Simon responded dryly, 'There was nowhere to go – everybody'd got it, except the Fort – and they weren't going to let anybody in from a homestead that had had it!' And he exchanged a toothless grin with Emily.

The family had been fortunate in being able to bury their dead. Amongst the terrified Indians, whole groups had died, their bodies torn apart and eaten by wild animals, their only monument a teepee centre pole bent by the uncaring wind.

Nobody really knew why Wallace Helena, Simon and Emily had not caught the disease. Simon said he had been through a plague of smallpox before on the prairies, and perhaps he and Emily had gained some immunity from it. Wallace Helena remembered a number of unnamed fevers she had survived as a child in Beirut, where smallpox also existed, and wondered if she had had some milder form of the disease which gave her immunity.

Wallace Helena burned Agnes's and Joe's hut, and as soon as they could get some help to do it, a new one was built with room for three helpers on the homestead. Joe stayed with Wallace in the main cabin, their devotion to each other, as yet, not verbally acknowledged. Joe had seen his face in the mirror and was shocked by the sight. Wallace Helena, with so much unexpressed grief penned up within her, hardly knew how to continue; she blundered on from day to day, simply trying to keep the farmstead going.

When Joe was fit to sit on a bench outside the cabin door, she said dully, one early spring day, 'I'm almost out of fodder; it's more than time I put the cows out to pasture. If we don't get any more snow, they should be all right. I'll do it tomorrow – Simon must plough.'

'I'll come with you,' Joe said suddenly.

'You're too weak yet; you couldn't even mount.'

'I could – and I will. I'll never get right sitting here.'

The next morning, he got Simon to give him a heft onto his horse and he rode out with her, to move their small, lowing herd through the mud in the yard and into a fenced pasture, beyond the field that Simon was ploughing. They would move them further out on their land when the possibility of spring snowstorms lessened.

They were silent as they rode. Wallace Helena's tired brain was filled with lists of neglected tasks, and Joe was concentrating on staying on his horse.

Though they were not out for long, the fresh spring breeze did them good. Wallace Helena began to unwind a little and talk desultorily. As they approached the yard again, however, her conversational efforts petered out, and she suddenly burst into violent tears.

'What's up?' Joe forgot his own weakness in the shock of seeing her acute distress.

Wallace Helena made a small hopeless gesture towards the cabin. 'Mama – Tom – they're not there,' she wailed, bending over her saddle, as great sobs racked her.

Joe leaned over and took her horse's reins in his hands, as they entered the yard. 'Emily,' he shouted urgently, 'Emily!'

The young woman flung open the door almost immediately and peered out, quivering like a rabbit scenting danger.

'Come here and help Wallace Helena – and help get me off this damned horse – and shut the gate behind us.'

Wallace Helena sat her horse, her head bent, and cried as if her heart would break, while a shaken Emily steadied Joe as he laboriously descended.

She held his horse, while he moved to take hold of Wallace Helena's mount's bridle; he wondered how long he could stay on his feet.

'Come on! Down you come, girl,' he ordered her as firmly as he could.

Though her grief seemed beyond control, Wallace Helena dismounted obediently and Joe put his arm round her, as much to

108

steady himself as to comfort her. He said to Emily, 'Hitch the horses and then shut the gate. And go make some coffee.'

'I'm in the middle of making the bread,' Emily protested.

'To hell with the bread. Do as I say.'

He took the distraught young woman into the cabin and sat her down in a chair. She wept on. He pulled up another chair facing her, and sat in it, while he unlaced her boots and took them off. She made no move to stop him. He untied the scarf she was wearing round her head, and he realized, with a pang, how thin her face was, the sallow skin etched with new lines.

'You're tired out,' he told her very gently. 'Come and lie down.'

Still moaning, she allowed herself to be led to her room and onto her bed, a bed which Joe had hastily constructed for her soon after her arrival at Fort Edmonton. It had a bearskin over it, from an animal he had shot during an unexpected confrontation on their trapline. She lay down on it, her face to the wall.

Joe pulled a stool close to the bedside, and thankfully sat down on it. He understood very well her need to cry. In the privacy of the night, he had wept himself, at his own weakness, at the loss of his friends and, not the least, for the loss of his mother. He was surprised that she had not expressed her grief at her mother's death long before.

Emily brought in two mugs of coffee and hovered beside him, looking down at the tightly curled-up figure on the bed. 'Put the coffee on the floor by me, and give me that shawl off the hook over there. And get out!'

Shocked by his snarl, Emily did as she was bidden; and, over the bread dough, she burst into tears herself. Joe had never been so sharp with her before, and added to that was the fear engendered by Wallace Helena's sudden collapse. In a burst of self-pity, she felt, quite rightly, that nobody had considered what *she* had gone through during the smallpox epidemic.

Joe laid the shawl over Wallace Helena and sat, for a while, watching her, while he quickly drank one of the coffees which Emily had brought in. Then as the passionate sobs did not seem to be decreasing, he leaned over and tentatively put his hand on her heaving shoulder. To his surprise, one of her hands emerged from under the shawl and clasped his tightly.

A surging need to weep himself hit him. Still holding her hand, he eased himself off the stool and onto the bed. He lay down on his side and folded himself round the curve of her back, his face half-buried in the mass of her hair. She felt the comforting warmth of another human being and sensed his own despair. The sobs faltered as she turned over to face him.

'Oh, Joe, darling Joe,' she wept. 'It's been pure hell, hasn't it?'

He nodded, and folded her into his arms.

They lay together for a long time, two exhausted people who loved each other with the deep devotion of years, made humble by a load of trouble they could not bear alone.

When, finally, Wallace Helena ceased her crying, she said, 'I'm sorry to inflict this on you.'

He managed to grin at her. 'I'm not in much better shape myself,' he confessed.

There was silence between them for a while, and then Wallace Helena said, 'You know, Joe, I don't understand why some are taken and some are spared. Do you? Mama came through that terrible time in Beirut – and it was no fun in Chicago either – simply to die out here – in nowhere. Why her? Why not you and me?'

'That's the way life is.'

'It doesn't make sense.'

They heard Simon Wounded clump into the cabin and ask Emily where everybody was. Joe hastily swung off the bed and sat a little dizzily on the stool. 'We're here, Simon,' he shouted. 'Wallace Helena isn't too well. I'll be right out.' He got up.

'Now, you stay here. I'll get Emily to bring you some supper.' He bent down and kissed her. 'You'll be better tomorrow.'

'Somebody's got to milk the cows.'

'We'll manage.'

He left her, closing the door softly after him. The cabin smelled of the bread Emily had taken out of the oven. He said to her, 'She'll be all right now. She was crying for her mother.'

Seated in his favourite corner by the fire, Simon Wounded packed his pipe and nodded agreement. Emily gave a heavy sigh. She had been through weeks of fear of the smallpox and day upon day of overwork. She said, 'I cried when *my* mother died; I

110

thought Wallace Helena never would. She's never shed a tear that I know of, before this.'

'She'd everything to see to – including me,' he snapped. 'Tell me when supper's ready.' He staggered in to Tom and Leila's old room, where Simon and Wallace Helena had nursed him, and threw himself onto his bed. He thought about the woman on the bed in the next room, and wondered what he had started.

Much later, when Emily was snoring comfortably in her bunk in the corner of the living-room, behind a curtain made of sacking, and Simon had gone over to his cabin, Wallace Helena got out of bed. She was garbed in the old petticoat she used as a nightgown and, as she picked up her candle and went out of the room, she shivered slightly.

She slipped into Tom's room and eased herself quietly under the bedclothes beside the sleeping man. She never afterwards slept anywhere else and, once he had regained his strength, he saw that she never regretted it.

The few white women in Edmonton gossiped about misalliances. But Joe knew that he and Wallace Helena were like two halves of the same coin; they belonged completely to each other.

Chapter Sixteen

When it seemed that the smallpox had run its course, Joe's aunt, Theresa Black, who had for years worked in the kitchens of the Fort, came to Joe and Helena's cabin to take her sister Agnes's place; they were very glad to welcome her into their devastated home.

The Fort she left slowly spawned a hamlet, and the first small signs of federal government replacing the old Hudson's Bay Company rule became apparent. A few stores, a hotel, a telegraph office and a postal system of sorts made their appearance. The Roman Catholic priests of St Albert, who had served the early inhabitants of the Fort, were joined by Methodists and Anglicans. Government surveyors arrived to subdivide the Territories into districts. Instead of bartering, the inhabitants were tending to use money. Land ownership had to be registered.

When the Hudson's Bay Company finally handed over jurisdiction to the government in Ottawa, Wallace Helena claimed the land which she and Joe had continued to farm. Tom had left everything to Leila and Leila to Wallace Helena. Joe was still technically an employee.

Thanks to a first-class lawyer, her claim to have been resident on it since 1862 and her stepfather for many years before that, and that between them they had cleared and developed it, was accepted.

Once she was assured that even though she was a woman, the land had been truly registered in her name, she ordered the lawyer to re-register it in the joint names of Joe Black and herself, as being a married couple according to the customs of the country. If one of them died, the other automatically inherited the whole.

Wallace Helena met the lawyer when she rode over to St Albert to return some books to the Oblate Fathers. They had brought him in to help them establish the claims of Metis to land along the Sturgeon River, and Joe often laughed at the dislike she had expressed at their having to part with every cent of the cash they had hoarded in her mother's old trunk, in order to pay the man's bill. But it was the best bargain they had ever made.

He had been surprised and touched when she told him that she had arranged to share the ownership with him.

Now she had undertaken this tremendously long journey to the place where her Uncle James had lived, and Joe was missing her badly.

Back home after the 200-mile ride to Edmonton, after seeing her onto the train at Calgary, he had slept the clock round, and now he crawled out of bed in a cabin already overly hot. He peered out of the small, glazed window to look at the yard. Emily was already plodding across the well-trodden bareness of it, towards the barn. She was carrying two milk pails.

Good harvesting weather, he thought. Hope it holds.

He shaved himself with a cut-throat razor, in front of a small hanging mirror, much prized by Wallace Helena because it had been her mother's. The mug of hot water which Aunt Theresa had brought in to him a few minutes earlier was already cool and the home-made soap was not lathering very well. He succeeded in nicking himself with the razor. Cursing softly, he pressed a finger on the bleeding cut, and unexpectedly chuckled; the scar would hardly be noticed amid the pits left on his face by the smallpox. In the sixteen years since he had had the disease, the dreadful scars had not improved. He remembered clearly the moment when he was better and had wanted to shave, and Wallace Helena reluctantly handed him a mirror, as he sat up in bed. The appalling shock had been no joke, he considered more soberly; and still, people who didn't know you stared at you as if you might still be a source of contagion. 'It sure didn't improve your looks, Joe Black,' he said.

He was only one of many in the district who carried the marks of the dreaded disease, and all of them would have been thankful for a salve to remove the ugly scars.

He made a face at himself in the mirror. A lot of Indians looked worse than he did. Funny how few men in the Fort had caught it. Wallace Helena and Simon Wounded had nursed him through it, and neither of them had caught it. He remembered how they had tied his arms to his sides so that he could not scratch the horrible pustules on his face.

He leaned forward to peer at his teeth. Though he still had a full set, they were stained by tobacco and coffee. He made another wry face at himself. Then he poured water from a jug into a tin bowl to rinse his face and splash the water up over his grey, tightly curling hair. If there were time, he might go down to the river, later on, for a quick swim. He had a sudden memory of Wallace Helena's slim, pale body flashing through the water beside him on other occasions, and his spirits fell a little. God, how he missed her lively presence.

As he dried his face, he shouted, 'Hey, Aunt Theresa, what about some coffee?'

'Comin',' responded a muffled, cracked voice from the direction of the lean-to which still served as a summer kitchen, though Tom and Joe had added a third bedroom for Emily and Aunt Theresa.

His aunt shuffled slowly into the bedroom, carrying a coffee mug in one hand and a piece of bread in the other. Her face was as wrinkled as an apple held too long in store, and she grumbled that tomorrow he could come to the kitchen and get his coffee himself; she and young Emily had more things to do than wait on him. She said this to him most mornings.

The corners of his mouth twitched, as she put the mug down on the chest of drawers beside his razor. He knew very well that she would be put out by any alteration in this morning routine, so he didn't reply. He picked up a wide-toothed comb which he had carved for himself and ran it quickly through his bushy hair, while she retreated to the kitchen. He'd better hurry, he considered. Simon Wounded and the jinglers would be in for breakfast soon.

Later on, that hot summer morning, he rode over to survey the

114

barley crop. As the merciless sun beat down on him, he wished heartily that he could find a couple of reliable labourers to help him. Now that the railway had reached Calgary, some Metis from Manitoba and a few white families had felt it worthwhile to come the two hundred miles further north by wagon to Fort Edmonton to take up land for themselves; there were few who would work for someone else for long. Over the years, he had seen a lot of miners pass through on their way to search for gold. One or two of them would have been good employees, he thought; but the lure of gold was too great, and they passed on west or north, or, in a few cases, preferred to pan for gold in the nearby river, or to mine the coal in the valley.

There were the Indians, of course. Some of them would sometimes work a season with him to oblige a friend, or if they were hungry enough. They were, however, still largely nomadic; they did not take kindly to settling in one place. Further, their numbers had been pitifully depleted by the smallpox. Many of their usual lodges were overgrown by bush; there was no one left to use them. Other white men's diseases, like measles and diphtheria, picked off their children. The buffalo herds on which they had depended had been wiped out by over-hunting, leaving them famished and destitute, with all the apathy that hunger brings in its train.

Thank goodness for old Simon Wounded, thought Joe; he, at least, seemed to be happy to stay put. In addition to him, they were currently employing two drifters, who lived with Simon in the bunkhouse. They had come up from the States, single men who had tried mining, whisky-running and being cowhands on a ranch south of Calgary. Wallace Helena was not very satisfied with them and said sarcastically that they were probably wanted by various sheriffs south of the border. She would not have them in the house, and they cooked for themselves; it was obvious that they were not happy sharing the bunkhouse with an Indian and resented Simon's privileged position in the household. Joe hoped they would last until Wallace Helena returned.

Emily was scared of them and, at first, they teased her. Joe noticed, and told them that if they touched her, he'd see that they were not much use to a woman after it. Because he was bigger and tougher than they were, they sulkily heeded him; they also bore in mind that behind Joe stood a woman like a ruthless witch, noted in the district for her almost superhuman abilities to get her own way and to pay back an insult.

'She'll take her time,' a labourer in the village had told them, 'but sooner or later, if you cross her, you'll find yourself run out of the place on some excuse – if you're not struck dead.'

Though they laughed at the old man, they bore the information in mind.

Wallace Helena had never killed a person in her life. But, once, she had had such a fearsome row with a Metis, who had tried to settle on a corner of her land, that the man had had a stroke and had subsequently died. The incident had been more frightening to the British inhabitants, in that the row had taken place in fluent French on the main trail through the settlement. Finally, she had poked him in the chest with a long forefinger and had sworn at him in *Arabic*. He had stormed back at her, and then he had suddenly clutched his throat and fallen to the ground.

Burning with rage, Wallace Helena had remounted Peggy and had ridden away, leaving him lying in the dust of the trail.

Though the more educated people understood what had happened, many did not. They knew that Wallace Helena came from some strange Middle Eastern country, and nestled in the back of their minds there remained the idea that she might have mysterious powers on which she could call; such powers could account for Joe's and her success as mixed farmers.

Joe and Wallace Helena grinned at each other, when the latter rumour reached them. They both knew that their thriving farm was due largely to Joe's and Simon's profound knowledge of the country, of its weather, its animals and the customs of the Crees. To help them further, Uncle James had sent them a steady succession of books on animal husbandry and grain farming, particularly in cold climates, like Russia. Tom had loved his land and had broken the sod; Wallace Helena and Joe were devoted to making it blossom, come drought, come bitter winter.

Though Wallace Helena was a proud, fierce and tetchy woman, she had not been so proud that she could not face picking the brains of the Manager of the Hudson's Bay Company's own farm, in order to avoid repeating any mistakes they had made. She also talked to the Oblate Fathers, when they came south from Lac St Anne or St Albert. None of them liked her very much; she did not belong to their flock and she lived in sin with Joe Black. She had the advantage, though, that she spoke fluent, educated French, and in their work of settling the Metis, they were just as interested as she was in good farming; so they exchanged ideas with her like scientists, regardless of their personal feelings, and, with a similar sense of rivalry, watched each other's experiments.

After breakfast, Joe Black went out into the yard to inspect a sapling he had brought up from Calgary, after seeing Wallace Helena onto the train. He had been told that it was almost impossible to grow apples so far north – the cold spring wind blew the blossoms off before they had set; he had expected that the tree would die during the several days he had taken to ride the two hundred miles home from Calgary, with it tied to the back of a packhorse, beside a couple of new pickaxes. The tree, however, was looking quite healthy; it had retained its leaves, and its branches were stretching upwards. In the hope that rabbits would not be able to get at it, he had fenced it round with a precious piece of chicken wire.

He smiled grimly to himself. Wallace Helena never wanted anything to be planted that could not be either eaten or traded. He had noticed that some of the white women now settling round Edmonton had planted little flowerbeds near their cabins or clapboard houses. He had asked Wallace Helena if she would like him to bring in some wild flower seeds, to start such a garden.

She had looked up at him from her account book, and had asked in a bemused voice, 'Why?'

'Well, the white women seem to plant them. Would you like some?'

She had caught his great hand and squeezed it, while she laughed up at him. 'I'm not white – any Metis would be happy to tell you that I'm yellow.' Her lips met in a thin line. 'I'm Lebanese. Flowers might seed amongst the vegetables – and we've got enough weeds already.'

'O.K.' He turned to leave her, but she still held his hand firmly. She said suddenly and very wistfully, 'I wish I could get a lemon tree.'

He had never heard of or seen a lemon, so he asked, 'What's that?'

She shrugged her shoulders, and laughed. 'It's a fruit tree – the blossoms have a heavenly perfume. We used to have one in my father's courtyard, at home.'

As Joe digested this, he looked down at her. She rarely mentioned Lebanon and he had tended to forget that she came from anywhere else but Chicago. He wondered where he could possibly obtain such a tree.

She laughed, and pulled his hand playfully. 'The fruit's awfully sharp. But its flavour is delicious in drinks – and in cooking.' She sighed, and then smiled up at him. 'But it couldn't live in this harsh climate.' She tugged his hand again, and ordered, 'Bend over, so that I can reach you.'

Clumsily, he bent his head towards her, and she kissed him soundly on the lips. He had gone away laughing, wondering for the umpteenth time exactly where Lebanon was. Some time, he must ask the priest who taught school in the village to show him on a map. It was further away than England, Wallace Helena had assured him of that.

After he had gone, Wallace Helena had sat staring at the rough logs of the old cabin's wall, her face drawn and infinitely sad. She saw, in her mind's eye, a country of beautiful mountains and rushing rivers, and, tucked along the coast and on the plateaus, orchards, flowering orchards, of oranges, lemons and apricots with a perfume so sweet that it hurt to think about it.

Well, he'd done his best, Joe considered. He had brought her a Macintosh apple tree.

With a half-peeled potato in her hand, Aunt Theresa had come out to view the tree when it had been planted. She had assumed he was planting it for shade.

'What kind of tree is it?' she had asked.

'It's a fruit tree – an apple tree.'

Aunt Theresa had never seen an apple, and she fingered one of

118

the leaves with interest. Then she said circumspectly, 'It has always seemed to me that trees – and plants – need others exactly like them round about, before they'll propagate.'

'I never thought of it.' He looked glumly at the little sapling. 'Will it flower?'

'If it lives, it probably will.' Then, to cheer him up, she added, 'You could watch out for a chance to get another one or two. Then you might get some fruit.'

'God knows where I'd find them. This one came on the train from the east, in a pot.'

'Trains bring lots of settlers. They bring plants they like with them,' prophesied Aunt Theresa shrewdly.

Next time he was in the little village outside the Fort, he dropped in on a member of the Agricultural Society, and explained his first effort at planting a tree. 'Usually, I'm felling them, to get them out of the way or because I need timber. I never thought of planting one before.'

Pleased to be asked for advice, the man confirmed Aunt Theresa's information.

Joe's face fell, so the man kindly went on to suggest how the sapling might be kept alive through the winter, until Joe had the chance to buy some more. 'I doubt you'll get many apples,' he finished up. 'Our winter's so cold, and the wind'll strip the blossom off in no time.'

Joe shrugged, and thanked his adviser. 'I'll nurse it along,' he said. And as he got on his horse and rode away, he thought of the young girl he had nursed along through her early years at Fort Edmonton. She'd turned out strong enough, God knows. Maybe the tree would, too.

Chapter Seventeen

Wallace Helena ate without comment the third English breakfast provided for her by her landlady, Mrs Hughes. The breakfast consisted of oatmeal porridge followed by two boiled eggs served with thick slices of toast. Though she enjoyed the luxury of wheaten bread, she found she lacked her usual appetite, and she realized that she did not need so much food. After days of train travel and the confines of an immigrant ship returning to Liverpool, she was now penned up in the odiferous soapery all day. She politely refused Mrs Hughes's offer of more toast with some home-made marmalade.

Mrs Hughes was uncertain whether or not she approved of Wallace Helena. In repose, the visitor's face was almost forbidding, though she was gracious enough in a foreign kind of way. While the Lebanese ate her breakfast, the puzzled Liverpool lady fluttered round the dark, high-ceilinged dining-room, straightening ornaments and pictures and commenting on the raininess of the day. She hoped to overcome Wallace Helena's uncompromising reserve and learn a little more about her.

Mrs Hughes considered that, despite her stuck-up looks, Wallace Helena was no lady. In justification of this observation, she had already told her next-door neighbour that Wallace Helena licked the butter off her fingers after eating her toast. 'Mr Benson told me,' she added, 'that she's a colonial from Canada – but she looks *real* foreign to me.'

In an absent-minded way, Wallace Helena was aware of her landlady's reflections, though she did not know that, from being much outdoors, her skin was dark enough, and the sweep of her black eyebrows and eyelashes was great enough, to make Mrs

Hughes wonder if she were harbouring an East Indian, like the lascars she sometimes saw in the city.

Wallace Helena was used to being disliked – because of her dubious origins, as one Scottish clerk at the Fort had once put it – and also because, around Edmonton, few people got the better of her when bargaining. She had become stiffly proud, and particularly quick to take offence if anyone cast a slur on Joe Black. She accepted that the pair of them were outcasts, and, in consequence, they owed no special loyalty to anyone except each other and those who shared their home. They took tender care of each other, and minded their own business.

As she drained her last cup of tea, her thoughts strayed for a moment to Joe. Despite her fascination with the new world into which she had plunged, she would have given a lot, today, to skip going to the soap works and, instead, to ride out with him under hot sunshine to the boundaries of their land, to check that the fencing was still in place; they could do with another hand to give most of his attention to fencing, she felt, and she wondered if the Liverpool business could provide her with enough money to invest some of it in the homestead. If a railway finally came as far as Edmonton, she might be able to sell grain to Europe – or even steers; amid the turmoil of coping with a Liverpool soap works, it was a cheering thought.

Stiff from lack of exercise and fretful from weeks of sleeping alone, she rose awkwardly from the breakfast table, aware of her heavy black skirt and petticoats dragging at her. She longed for the soft, worked skins of her old Indian tunic and leggings. Even her boots, newly cleaned by Mrs Hughes's maid-of-all-work, hurt feet normally encased in moccasins. Ordinarily, she wore formal clothes only when going down to Edmonton or to visit the priests in St Albert.

'I'll walk down to the Brunswick Dock, Mrs Hughes,' she announced. 'I need the exercise. Would you kindly tell Mr Benson, when he arrives with his carriage, that I have gone on ahead. I'll meet him by the dock gates – I presume the dock will have a gate?'

'Yes, there's a gate, Miss. But it's no district for you to walk by yourself, Miss. I wouldn't advise it.'

Wallace Helena laughed shortly. 'Don't worry. I'm used to being alone in wild country. Mr Benson says that *he* has to take me into the dock, because otherwise they won't let a woman in. Ridiculous, isn't it?'

Mrs Hughes ran her tongue round her teeth before replying. Then she said carefully, 'I appreciate your comin' from Canada and being used to all kinds of strange things, Miss, but Mr Benson's right to escort you. You could get accosted, like. We got worse 'n Red Indians round them docks, believe me. It's no place for a lady by herself.'

'Mr Benson will probably catch up with me in his carriage long before I reach the dock.'

'Well, if you get there first, you tell the Customs Officer or the policeman at the gate who you are, and you stay close to him till Mr Benson comes.'

Wallace Helena promised, and went upstairs to put on the black straw gable-brimmed hat which she had bought in Montreal; it suited her much better than the beaded bonnet she had bought in Mr Johnstone Walker's newly opened store in Edmonton. She reflected with amusement that Mr Walker had not thought much of a woman who tried to beat down the price of his millinery, so painfully freighted up by ox-cart from the railway at Calgary.

Since it had been raining and the air felt clammy, she put a black woollen shawl round her shoulders, and, when she went downstairs again, she accepted the loan of a long black umbrella from Mrs Hughes.

Mrs Hughes followed her uncertainly towards the front door. 'Now, you be careful of yourself, Miss. Turn left at the bottom of the hill and keep walking. You can't miss it.'

'Thank you, Mrs Hughes. I do know the way. Mr Benson drove me past it yesterday.'

Thankful to be out in the air, temporarily washed clean by the early morning rain, Wallace Helena ran down the wide stone steps of the house. Sunlight was creeping through the lifting clouds and the damp pavement shone in its rays. Two little girls were skipping towards her. She smiled at them and they smiled shyly back at her. She passed a number of women dressed in black, carrying shopping baskets on their arms. They stared at her as she strode past them, her unfashionable gathered skirt swinging round her a couple of inches above her ankles. Even to a city accustomed to immigrants of all kinds passing through, Wallace Helena seemed eccentric; her rapid, masculine walk, her almost scornful expression and an aura of great energy, barely suppressed, aroused casual interest.

As she walked, Wallace Helena concentrated on the day before her. Though she had made a list and it was safely tucked into her reticule, she went over all that she had learned from the Canadian lawyer who had secured her homestead for her, all she knew from her father about contracts, bookkeeping and running a business in Beirut, and her own limited experience, as first Tom's Will had been laboriously proven and then her darling mother's. Lastly, she thought of all that her father had done to re-establish himself in Chicago. Surely, she considered, between the lot of it, together with running the farm, I have enough experience to cope with the Lady Lavender Soap Works; it's not that big, really.

She felt a nervous excitement at the challenge she had been presented with. She had come to check what was being done by Mr Benson, the Executor of her Uncle James's Will, to make sure that selling the business was in her best interests and that she was going to get the right price for it. Now, already in the back of her mind, she itched to get her hands on it, to run it herself. She had not yet faced all the implications of this sudden desire.

Though its owner had died, the works seemed to be functioning fairly well under the care of Mr Bobsworth, the bookkeeper, and Mr George Tasker, the Soap Master, who had been with the company almost from its inception. Despite their devotion to their duties, however, she had noticed in some sections a lackadaisical air, a lack of good housekeeping which she would not, for one moment, have tolerated on her homestead; she sensed that the general discipline of the place had slipped a little.

Even when she, as the new owner, walked in, there had not been that quick shuffle to appear busy, which she would have expected. 'Perhaps they reckon I'm not going to be their new employer, since I'm a woman,' she thought with a wry grin. Then she muttered to herself, 'Little do you realize what is going to descend on you, my boys.'

If Joe Black could have watched her during that brief walk, he would have grinned lazily and would have sat back and watched the carnage she would subsequently wreak amongst the slothful. And then, had he been there when, drained and hungry, she had returned home, he would have encouraged her to eat plenty and afterwards spread herself before a good log fire, while he rolled a cigarette for her and listened to the successes and failures of her day. In their intimate enjoyment of each other, they would have found much to laugh at in the soap works.

The tightly packed rows of town houses, each with its shining brass doorknob and letterbox, past which Wallace Helena strode, seemed to shut her in, enclose her like some long narrow box. They soon gave way to humbler, even more closely packed homes, and then to small works and warehouses.

Over the stone setts of the street, huge horses pulled drays loaded with bales, barrels, boxes, and sacks of coal, all the needs of a great industrial country. The horses' big hooves splashed through puddles left by the early morning rain, spattering the passersby. Sometimes, they stood patiently slavering by the pavement while being loaded or unloaded; and clog-shod men in flat caps and sackcloth aprons shouted upwards to others peering down at them from behind blocks and tackle used for hoisting goods to the upper floors of the warehouses.

Suddenly, a black shadow passed over Wallace Helena. She looked up quickly.

'Mind yourself, Queen!' a man shouted urgently and pushed her roughly aside. Uncomfortably close to her, a sacking-covered bale was lowered swiftly onto a stationary dray at the kerb. 'Aye, Missus, watch yourself. You could've bin killed.'

Though a little alarmed by the unexpected danger, she managed to smile at the labourer and thank him.

Before she continued on her way, she edged past the great flanks of the horses, to stand well in front of them, so that they could see her, despite the blinkers that they wore. They were chomping at their bits as they waited. Another labourer stood idly by them.

'Are you the carter?' she inquired.

The man touched his cap. 'Yes, Missus.' Though he was respectful, there was nothing humble about him. His interest was aroused by her foreign accent, and he turned a brown, foxlike face towards her. 'You visitin' here, Missus?'

'Yes.' Her eyes were on the Percherons before her. 'May I pet them?' she asked.

'For sure, Missus. They're real gentle.'

She spoke softly to the nearest animal and, after a moment, it stretched forward to nuzzle her. She stroked its nose and neck.

The carter warned her. 'Be a bit careful, Missus. Bobby, here, could be a bit jealous.' He need not have worried; Wallace Helena had already transferred her attention to the other horse. Then she stepped back. 'I've got horses at home – but nothing as good as these; I could use a pair of them, especially in winter.'

'Where are you from, Missus?'

'Canada.' She turned to look him in the face and smiled her wide, generous smile. To the man, it changed her from an austere, strange lady into a warm human being. Emboldened, he asked what Canada was like.

'Very cold – and very hot,' she told him, and then added thoughtfully, 'It's big – the distances are enormous.'

She remembered suddenly the lawyer she was supposed to meet, so she smiled again and turned away.

At the bottom of Hill Street, when she was about to cross the road, her eye was caught by a flutter of brown sail in a gap between black buildings. She stopped to get a better look.

Between the Coburg Dock and the Brunswick Dock lay a small quay. It was being approached by a fishing smack floating lightly on the silver river. A man was reefing sail. Near the quay was a muddle of low domestic buildings, half surrounding a cobbled square, in which fishing nets had been spread to dry. Ivy nearly smothered a particularly pleasant-looking cottage at one corner; in its clean, curtained window sat a canary in a cage. Two men in rough blue jerseys came out of the cottage and went down to the quay to watch the smack tie up. At their approach a cloud of gulls glided into the air and circled the boat. One of the men leisurely lit a clay pipe. Despite the threat of rain, nobody seemed in a hurry; it was a peaceful vignette, next to the maelstrom of activity in the main road.

Wallace Helena thought a little wistfully how pleasant it would be to walk into the quiet square. She had a feeling that its inhabitants might greet her in a friendly country way, as she had been greeted as a little girl when her family had gone up into the mountains to avoid the damp heat of Beirut's summer.

For a minute, she stood entranced, poised on the corner of Hill Street, the soapery forgotten. 'That's how Liverpool must have been long ago,' she guessed. Then she roused herself and crossed the road. She was accompanied by a band of small ragamuffins; they ran in and out of the traffic, followed by the scolding voices of the draymen, who were afraid the scurrying mob would make their horses rear.

Before crossing Sefton Street, she paused again. Further along, in another side street parallel to Hill Street, lay the soap works. Across the road before her lay the Brunswick Dock. She watched carefully, as at the dock gate the driver of a cart paused to speak to a uniformed man at the gate and was then allowed to drive in. She presumed that everything that came into the Brunswick Dock for the Lady Lavender Soap Works would have to be off-loaded onto just such a cart and be taken the very short distance to the works to be unloaded. She had the previous day overheard a brief conversation between Mr Bobsworth, the bookkeeper, and one of his underlings from which she had understood that goods left long in the dock warehouse were subject to high demurrage charges; everything must be removed quickly to its own warehouse or yard. She was as yet unaware that the soapery had its own spur railway line, along which its goods could be rolled straight from the dock to its yard. She retreated to a niche in a wall, while she fished out a small black notebook and pencil to make a note to remind herself to ask Mr Bobsworth more details of the movement of ingredients and finished goods; the notebook was already nearly full of observations and questions in her small, cramped handwriting. Accustomed to the acute shortage of good farm workers in and around Edmonton, she had been shocked at the mass of labourers involved with the soap works, and many of her queries were in connection with the cost of this; she had as yet little idea of the cheapness of labour in Liverpool.

As she returned the notebook to her reticule, she wondered where on earth she could get something to smoke. She had smoked her last cheroot aboard ship and she was feeling the acute lack of nicotine.

She saw an elegant, dark green carriage drawing up at the dock entrance and, recognizing it as that of Mr Benson, her uncle's lawyer, she hastened towards it. She was nearly struck by a bicycle as she stepped off the pavement. The black-suited rider swerved to a stop, surprised to see a lady in such a place. He assumed that she must have come down to the docks to distribute temperance pamphlets to dockers. As he regained his balance and cautiously circled behind her, Mr Benson saw her and sprang forward from the pavement.

'My dear Miss Harding,' he expostulated, as he took her elbow and guided her solicitously towards the gate. 'Really, you should have waited for me. Anything could happen to you down here.' In the back of his mind, he was appalled to think of the awful problem of probably having to trace yet another legatee, if she managed to get herself killed by a cyclist. The very idea made him nervous.

'Nothing happened to me,' Wallace Helena stiffly responded. 'It was a most interesting walk, I assure you.'

Several men were leaning against the dock wall, enjoying the weak sunshine, while they laughed and joked with each other. They were dressed in flat caps, stained trousers and striped shirts without collars; one wore a leather waistcoat and carried a curious metal hook. They stopped their conversation to watch the peculiar-looking woman passing by, and, for a moment, Wallace Helena hesitated and stared back with cold, brown eyes. Mr Benson's hand under her elbow compelled her forward again, as she asked, 'Who are those men, Mr Benson?'

'Those? Just casual labourers – dockers – they come down here twice a day in the hope of getting work.' His tone was uninterested.

'Humph. I wish I had three or four of them on my farm.'

Mr Benson raised his eyebrows slightly, but made no comment. Idle men were two a penny on the dock road.

After stating their business, they were allowed into the dock, and Mr Benson led her over to the Dock Master who was standing at the far end of the wharf on the west side. Mr Benson had met him once before in the course of his duties as Executor of James Al-Khoury's Will, and he now introduced him to Wallace Helena.

The heavy, bearded Dock Master received her courteously, though he wondered why she should trouble to come to see the Lady Lavender's raw materials coming in. He assumed that Mr Benson was simply entertaining her; it did not occur to him that he faced a woman intensely interested in following all the processes of the soap works from beginning to end.

Holding on to her hat against the capricious wind, Wallace Helena turned to survey the scene before her.

On the other side of the dock, two sailing vessels were being unloaded, derricks bent over them like pecking vultures. The shouts of the dockers attending them came clearly across the water. Nearer at hand, two men stood by an iron capstan, presumably waiting for a pair of barges being slowly towed through the dock entrance. Another group of men, shirt sleeves rolled up, red kerchiefs round their necks and blackened leather waistcoats protecting their humped backs, seemed also to be waiting for the same vessels. The sun glinted on the hooks they carried and on the fair hair covering their reddened arms. Wallace Helena stared at them unabashed. Used to dark Metis or Indians or to men so wrapped up against the cold that it was hard to discover what colour they were, the red and gold colouring of the English dockers was a rarity to her; she wondered idly if the rest of their bodies were equally red and gold.

Her thoughts were interrupted by Mr Benson saying, 'Mr Bobsworth informed me that a shipment of carbonate ash was expected this morning from the manufacturers – and a cargo of salt – the salt's shipped by canal from the Cheshire salt mines.'

Wallace Helena nodded her head in acknowledgment of this information; she presumed that the carbonate ash was similar to that used by Aunt Theresa and herself when, each spring, they boiled soap in the yard.

Anxious to show that he understood something of his late client's industry, Mr Benson went on to explain, 'I understand they make it liquid and caustic by putting it into vats with lime and water.'

'In other words, they make lye out of it?' suggested Wallace Helena.

'Yes,' responded the lawyer, a trifle surprised that a woman would be aware of such chemistry.

Between watching the progress of the barges, the Dock Master had been eyeing his female visitor with some interest. He now mentioned to her that the shipping agent's representative was at that moment in the dock office ready to attend to the paperwork in connection with the expected cargoes.

He was a little disconcerted to have a number of relevant questions shot at him. Who did the actual unloading? How many men did it take? How were the goods transferred to the Lady Lavender warehouse? How long did it take?

He hastily swallowed his amusement as his replies were entered in Wallace Helena's notebook. As she wrote, he examined with curiosity the woman's firm mouth with faint lines down either side, the long nose which added further strength to a face which gave a feeling of anything but womanliness. She snapped her notebook closed and looked up at him, her brown eyes twinkling as if she knew exactly what he was thinking. Embarrassed, he dropped his own bloodshot blue eyes. He was further surprised, when they went into the dock office to meet the shipping agent's representative, to find that she understood much of the paperwork connected with the movement of goods, both within a country and when importing.

The enthusiastic young shipping agent ventured to congratulate her on her grasp of the matter, and she told him honestly, 'My father dealt in silk for export and I was often with him. When we were in Chicago, I was frequently his interpreter and his clerk. I grew up amid imports and exports.'

This was news to Mr Benson, too. James Al-Khoury had never mentioned to him what his brother had done for a living, and that his niece should understand something of the world of business seemed very odd; he had always believed that oriental women lived in strict seclusion. Even English women did not concern themselves with the outside world; the home and family were their sphere.

When Wallace Helena moved to go outside again to see the actual unloading, the Dock Master asked her kindly, 'Would you like to stay in the office and watch through the window? It's chilly out there – and the dockers' language is sometimes not fit for a lady's ears.'

Wallace Helena laughed. 'I have one or two male employees – I am quite used to being among men. And I love the fresh air.'

After stuffy offices, the wind was a joy and though it whipped at her skirt and shawl and she had to hold on to her hat, despite its huge hatpins, she leaned happily against it while she watched the dockers do their work. Mr Benson resignedly shrugged himself deeper into his Melton overcoat, and consoled himself with the thought that the Al-Khoury Estate would have to pay him well for these hours with its heiress.

Once she had the general idea of what was happening, she turned to him, ready to continue her morning in the Lady Lavender Soap Works itself. Looking over his shoulder, she pointed suddenly towards a young man entering the dock gates. 'Isn't that a boy from our works? I think he does messages for Mr Tasker.'

Mr Benson did not know the lad, but the Dock Master asked, 'The coloured boy? He often comes over from the Lady Lavender for one reason or another. Name of Alfie.'

Carrying a white envelope, the youth jog-trotted into the office.

'I'd like to speak to Alfie,' Wallace Helena said, as the messenger reappeared and moved with them towards the gate. Mr Benson immediately called him over.

Alfie whipped off his cap to expose a head of brownish, tightly curly hair. He smiled nervously at Wallace Helena and ran his cap through long, brown fingers. 'Yes, Sir?' he inquired of Mr Benson.

'Miss Harding wishes to speak to you.'

Alfie turned fully towards her, a wary expression on his face. 'Miss?'

'Alfie, you smoke, don't you? I saw you outside the works yesterday, smoking something.'

The youngster's thick lips parted in surprise and she saw his body tense, as if he might take flight. He replied uneasily, 'Well, yes, Ma'am.' He fully expected a lecture on the evils of smoking.

'Can you buy tobacco and papers – or ready rolled cigarettes round here?'

The astonishment on Alfie's face caused Wallace Helena's grim mouth to relax slightly. 'Yes, Ma'am.'

'Well, get me some. How much will it cost?'

He shrugged slightly and told her. Then, realizing that she was serious in her request, he added, 'You can get cigarettes ready rolled, Ma'am, if you like.'

'I would prefer to roll my own,' she replied, as she opened her change purse.

'Allow me, Miss Harding.' Mr Benson took out a net purse from his inner pocket and loosened a ring at one end in order to get at a silver coin.

She looked at him, shocked. 'Oh, no,' she replied firmly. 'I mustn't put you to expense.' She handed Alfie a shilling and asked him to leave the purchase with her late uncle's secretary, Mr Helliwell. She said that he could keep the change.

Disconcerted, Mr Benson restored his purse to his pocket. Mrs Benson had instructed him to ask Miss Harding to dinner the following evening. What would she say if Miss Harding lit a cigarette in her drawing-room?

Wallace Helena again faced the wind, as she glanced back once more towards the gaily painted barges. Bright red, yellow and blue flower designs ran riot all over them, and a metal ewer standing on a ledge at the front of the first barge had the same colourful patterns on it. She had been surprised that the person throwing the rope ashore from the first barge had been a well-built, middle-aged woman. Now the woman was sitting on the edge of the dock, her legs dangling over the water. She had a baby at her breast.

Mr Benson saw Wallace Helena's bemused expression at the sight, and he explained as they approached the dock gate that

131

whole families lived permanently on the canal barges. 'There are probably more children inside,' he told her.

Outside the gate, Mr Benson instructed his groom to pick him up from the Lady Lavender Soap Works in one hour's time. Then he and his client did a quick tour of the Brunswick goods station from which another railway spur line sunk into the street ran into the soap works. Pointing to the spur line, Mr Benson told her, 'That'll be the way in which your company's goods travel from the Dispatch Department to the railway.'

She nodded. Mr Bobsworth, the bookkeeper and dispatch clerk, had already told her that the lavender oil to perfume their toilet soap was shipped in by rail from Kent and that tallow and oil from seed processors was sometimes similarly shipped. He had said, 'Though it's quicker by rail, it is more expensive, so much of our raw material comes in by barge. We distribute our finished goods by rail – or by delivery van.'

Wallace Helena was very thoughtful as they walked over to the soap works. The general pattern of manufacture and distribution was clarifying in her mind. This afternoon she would look over the books with Mr Bobsworth and see exactly how their finances stood. 'Do you know if the Lady Lavender makes anything else other than soap?' she asked casually of Mr Benson as they walked through the soapery's yard.

Mr Benson cleared his throat. 'Well, Mrs Benson uses a very delightful scent which they sell. You'll have to ask Mr Benjamin Al-Khoury about anything else.'

'I will,' she replied gravely, 'when he returns from his trip to Manchester.' Then she said, 'I think it is always better to deal in more than one commodity. At home, I produce barley and oats for the Government – and to feed ourselves. But some years the crop gets lost to hail or is simply poor. Then I'm thankful to have steers and a hay crop to feed them – and a vegetable garden. Or I can cut wood. I keep hens, too, mostly for our own eating and for eggs, of course; but nowadays there is even a market for these sometimes.'

'We have mixed farms in Britain.'

'Do you? My partner also runs a trapline for furs, though we do have a constant battle with the Hudson's Bay Company over it;

132

they seem to think they still run the Territories and are entitled to buy anything they fancy.'

'So your farm isn't being neglected while you are over here?'

She smiled. 'Far from it. Joe Black is a very capable man – he used to be my stepfather's stockman.'

'Indeed?' The lawyer was already beginning to wonder if she would sell the soapery. Her general understanding and quick grasp of detail made him sense that she might attempt to run it herself, especially if her farm had someone in charge of it. He was sure she would face a lot of prejudice; neither the firm's employees nor the business community were likely to accept a woman very willingly.

As he handed her over to anxious, obsequious Mr Bobsworth, he wondered what Benjamin Al-Khoury would feel about her; James Al-Khoury's son had been cruelly cut off from his anticipated inheritance by his father's unexpectedly early death and he was hardly likely to welcome his cousin.

Chapter Eighteen

When Wallace Helena arrived at the soapery, she found Mr Bobsworth very busy in the Shipping and Forwarding Department. He was in his shirt sleeves, and in his hand he held a brush dripping with black paint. He was in the midst of carefully marking boxes of soap with identifying numbers and with the addresses to which they were to be delivered.

Embarrassed at being found in his shirt sleeves by a lady, he hastily put down his brush and wiped his hand on a cloth exuding a strong smell of solvent. He then groped behind him for his jacket, while apologizing to Wallace Helena for his disarray.

'So sorry, Miss Harding. I've always supervised Shipping and Forwarding myself; it avoids errors and delays in delivery, you understand.' He shepherded her gently into his little office. 'The smell of paint must be overwhelming to you,' he suggested, as he pulled out a chair and his assistant, Mr Le Fleur, sprang respectfully to his feet. He turned to Le Fleur, and ordered him to go and finish marking the crates. The young man went reluctantly; he had no desire to get drips of paint on himself, and old Bobsworth had a great streak of it across his chin.

As diplomatically as she could, Wallace Helena informed the accountant of the streak. This sent him flying to a mottled mirror hanging over a tiny office sink in the corner, where he rubbed it ineffectually with his handkerchief. 'So sorry, Miss Harding,' he breathed anxiously.

'Don't worry, Mr Bobsworth. I think it's time I looked at the company's books and inventory; I think I would first like to see what we owe and what is owed to us – and what orders and commitments we presently have.'

Poor Mr Bobsworth hastily stuffed his hanky back into his

trouser pocket and felt around in his waistcoat for the key to his wooden book cupboard. He looked quite flustered, as he took out several account books and his ledger. 'I'm sure you'll find everything in order, Miss Harding. Mr Benson has, more or less, left the accounts to me while we are waiting for Probate, though his auditor has popped in from time to time to see that all is well. Would you like to sit at the table here?'

'I'm sure everything will be just fine, Mr Bobsworth. No doubt Mr Benson has informed you that you may show the books to me?'

Though he assented, the remark sent him into another flutter; he hoped she would find his handwriting easily readable.

In dire need of a smoke, Wallace Helena rose from the table clutching the heavy books to her and announced that she would work in her uncle's office.

Mr Bobsworth took the books from her and escorted her.

Mr Helliwell, her uncle's private secretary, received her with the calm assurance of a man who had always enjoyed his master's total confidence. He had studied Mr James Al-Khoury with the greatest attention and had understood his whims and foibles. As he often said to his wife, his lips were sealed. 'Not even to you, dear heart, would I say anything about Mr Al-Khoury's affairs.'

He was a pleasant, slightly pompous man around thirty years old. Wallace Helena thought him rather stupid, but Mr Benson had told her that, like Mr Bobsworth, he was as faithful as a bulldog. She did not hesitate to ask him if the tobacco had arrived and if he had any matches.

He nodded and pulled out the desk chair for her. She sat down mechanically in front of the books and absently tore open the packet of cigarette tobacco handed to her by the secretary. While he watched the quick deft movements of her fingers as she rolled a cigarette and licked the paper to seal it, she said to him, 'Mr Helliwell, we use olive oil and other kinds of oil in our soap, don't we?'

'Yes, Miss Harding.'

'Do you know if anyone has discovered an oil which will heal smallpox scars?'

Though the question was unexpected, Mr Helliwell answered immediately in the negative. 'I believe I would know if there were such an oil. My wife's eldest sister is badly scarred – we still get smallpox here, sometimes – and I'm sure that if such an oil existed, we would have tried to obtain it for her.' He leaned forward, struck a sulphur match and lit Wallace Helena's cigarette. She thankfully inhaled.

'Poor woman,' she said with feeling. She half closed her eyes, sickened by the sudden memory of her stepfather's and her mother's last hours. It appeared that Joe would be terribly marked for the rest of his life, and she sighed. Then she smiled faintly. He was still her irrepressible Joe, always optimistic that the next harvest would be better, the next winter milder or that the trapline would unexpectedly yield a wondrous collection of valuable furs.

As she took another puff at her cigarette, she said to Mr Helliwell, 'Mother and my stepfather both died of smallpox.' The heavy lids of her eyes were, for once, lifted towards him and he saw and understood some of the tragedy of her life reflected in them. 'It took a third of our population,' she went on a little heavily, 'and the living are scarred to this day – that's why I asked.'

Mr Helliwell blinked. 'Dear Miss Harding,' he exclaimed with genuine feeling, 'how very sad for you. I wish I could suggest something for those who are pocked . . . you might ask a doctor, while you are here. Just in case something has recently been discovered – one never knows what science may divulge.'

'Very true. I must ask.' She looked up at him and said a little stiffly, as though she regretted the confidence, 'I'm sure you must have work to do. I'll ring if I need you.'

Dismissed, Mr Helliwell went back to his own small cubbyhole. Poor lady! She must also have gone through the same travail in Beirut that Mr James had; he knew about that because, once a year, on its anniversary, the old man had taken a holiday. He had explained to Mr Helliwell that on that particular day he wanted to be by himself to remember his friends killed in Beirut. As far as Mr Helliwell knew, he simply spent the day walking in the country. And, on top of that massacre, this poor woman had

136

gone through a smallpox epidemic. He wondered how she had herself survived the latter unscathed, and decided that it was pure luck; God chose those He would take.

Now, she had lost her uncle, as well as her parents. He decided that she needed his complete support as much as he needed to keep his job.

Mr Helliwell's perception of her was in contrast to that of nervous Mr Bobsworth, who became more and more defensive, as, for several days, she waded through his beautifully kept account books and pried into all his other responsibilities. He was a portly little man, with the colourless face of someone who has little time in the fresh air. There was a permanent deep frown line between his thin eyebrows; and his old-fashioned side whiskers stuck up over his winged collar in an equally permanent, untidy bristle. As he trotted importantly through the works, his pen parked comfortably behind one ear, Wallace was often beside him. When he sat in his tiny office, amid a sea of invoices and bills, receiving constant interruptions from boys or men in big aprons, who came for instructions, Wallace Helena was often there, too, perched on a stool to watch what went on. As the days went by, he began to regard her as a female busybody, an interloper in a life already made difficult enough by the death of his old friend, James Al-Khoury.

'Mr Tasker and me – we've bin bere almost from the day Mr Al-Khoury started up. We all worked together to get the business going. You really don't have to worry.' He took off his gold-rimmed glasses and polished them on a spotless pocket handkerchief with quick impatient movements. 'And Mr Benjamin Al-Khoury – he's been keeping tabs on everything as much as he could, ever since Mr James died.'

'I'm sure you have all done very well,' she soothed. 'My uncle's passing must have been a personal loss to you, as well?'

Surprised, he glanced quickly at her. 'Indeed, Miss Harding, it was,' he replied a little huskily. 'We were very good friends, if I may presume to say so.'

She was kind, he admitted to Mr Tasker. But she was a pest. 'Forever at my shoulder, as if I can't be trusted,' he complained. He was further annoyed that Mr Tasker seemed to be entranced by her – and at his age he should know better. Why didn't she get on with the sale of the place, so at least they would all know the worst, he asked Mr Tasker.

'She's not got no Probate yet,' responded Mr Tasker. 'She can't do nothing till she gets that.'

Chapter Nineteen

Though, as a refugee, Wallace Helena had passed through Liverpool on her way to an immigrant ship to take her to the United States, she had not mixed with its inhabitants. Now, in the Lady Lavender soapery, she had come face to face with a society very different from anything else she had previously encountered. Unlike Chicago, the city had a long history and well-established customs. Her new employees were touchy about any suggestion of change. Dealing with them was stretching her quick intelligence to the utmost.

While she was going through the books, Wallace Helena sat late in her uncle's office long after everyone else, except the night-watchman, had gone home. She felt she needed uninterrupted quietness while she considered the ramifications of what she was looking at. Twice, on following mornings, she had ordered a spot check of a particular stock, which caused a lot of grumbling amongst employees in the particular department; they could not think why she bothered, since she was not likely to remain at the soapery; anyway, Mr Benjamin always did stocktaking.

Undeterred, she confirmed the accuracy of the records, and learned the exact duties of each employee.

She thought irritably that she could have acquired an overall view of the business much more quickly if Benjamin Al-Khoury had seen fit to be at the Lady Lavender when she arrived. As assistant manager, he could have told her much that she had had to deduce herself. On further consideration, she concluded that, as she did not know anything about him, a personal check of the books was not a bad idea. Mr Bobsworth had been quite helpful.

Like Mr Tasker and everybody else, Mr Bobsworth seemed to have all kinds of duties.

'With Mr James Al-Khoury no longer with us and Mr Benjamin on a special visit to Manchester, I'm hard-pressed,' he told her, hoping she would leave him alone to get on with his work.

Though her respect for the busy accountant grew daily, Wallace Helena had no intention of going away until she was certain that the two key employees in the business were absolutely trustworthy. Young Mr Benjamin was apparently assistant manager, but she felt that Bobsworth and Tasker were the two who set the standard for the other employees.

'Some of our customers seem to have very long credit,' she remarked one morning; she could almost hear her father advising to collect from debtors as fast as possible and pay one's own bills only at the last possible moment – it gave a firm a better flow of money for temporary use elsewhere. She picked up three files from the desk. 'These firms seem to be particularly favoured.'

Mr Bobsworth answered her patiently, though his head ached abominably. 'They're our biggest and best customers in the Manchester–Warrington area, Miss Harding. We can't do less for them than our competitors would. We're having a real fight with a Mr Lever, who is marketing a soap he calls *Sunlight* – a washing soap.'

This was the first time that Wallace Helena heard the name of this formidable man, who was in the process of revolutionizing the soap industry. It was his aggressive selling practices which had sent Benjamin Al-Khoury on a special visit to the firms with whom Lady Lavender dealt in Manchester, in the hope of persuading them that his company's soap was far superior to anything Mr Lever could produce.

Wallace Helena had already learned from Mr Tasker that the soap industry was very competitive, and she now said, 'Somebody mentioned that we advertise our soap and that, unlike many soap companies, we mention the name Lady Lavender, so that housewives ask for it by name.'

Mr Bobsworth's side whiskers seemed to bristle more than usual, as he responded to the mention of advertising. He did not believe that newspaper advertising could improve sales; he

140

thought it was a waste of money. *Women* bought soap, and how many working-class women could read? he was liable to ask.

He answered Wallace Helena primly, 'Lines of credit were always negotiated by Mr James – Mr Benjamin does it at present. As for advertising, that is something Mr Benjamin introduced. You'll have to ask him about it.'

Wallace Helena nodded. 'I have not, of course, met Mr Benjamin,' she said, and paused. Then she added slyly, to see what Mr Bobsworth's reaction would be, 'He must be a relation?'

Mr Bobsworth flushed. He slowly put down on her desk the purchase ledger which he had been holding. He was tired and wished Wallace Helena would invite him to be seated. Coming from a rough, frontier society, Wallace Helena had wrongly assumed that if he wanted to sit down he would do so.

His reply was careful. 'Well, Mr James brought him into the business when he was about fifteen – and he knows the trade very well. He keeps an eye on Mr Turner in the laboratory, and he's in charge of all sales.' He stopped, and ran his finger round the inside of his stiff, winged collar as if it were too tight. 'As to his being a relation, you would have to ask him.' He hastened on to explain, in the hope of diverting her attention, that the firm distributed a lot of unperfumed toilet and washing soap through middlemen, and washing soap directly to cotton mills. 'We've also got three representatives, working on commission. They travel all the time in their own districts, to sell our best line, Lady Lavender scented toilet soaps, to chemists' shops and hairdressers, even a little to haberdashers; likewise, our line of Lady Lavender perfume – Mr Benjamin wants to extend our scent sales – scent is quite a profitable sideline in some places.'

The rough gold rings on Wallace Helena's fingers caught the sunlight, as she slowly drew on a cigarello which Alfie had brought her as a possible alternative to cigarettes. Mr Bobsworth carefully kept his eyes averted; his head enveloped in smoke, he was afraid that his expression might betray his disapproval of a female smoker, particularly in a works full of oils and fats where *No Smoking* signs were prominently displayed.

Wallace Helena let the subject of Mr Benjamin rest, and said,

141

'Mr Turner mentioned, when I spoke to him in his laboratory, that a residue of soap manufacture is glycerine. He said he is experimenting with a view to producing a line of emollients for ladies' skins? Another idea was a cream to clean delicate skins instead of soap?'

Mr Bobsworth drooped; it looked as if this interview would go on into the evening. He pulled out a chair and defiantly sat on it; he *had* to sit down.

Wallace Helena made no comment. If he wanted to sit, he was welcome. She had come to the conclusion during the last few days that Englishmen must enjoy standing, since none of them sat in her presence.

'Is glycerine really good for skins?' she asked.

'I believe it can be, Miss Harding. Mr James Al-Khoury was beginning to feel that there is a market for modestly priced products to enhance women's skins. City life seems to ruin complexions.' He paused, to clear his throat, and then went on. 'The aristocracy has always used beauty aids, but he had in mind the lower classes, that he would pack creams in small tins to cost a few pence. I warned him – and I have since warned Mr Benjamin – that we have a lot of Nonconformists in Lancashire who would decry the use of emollients as vanity – some of them are against baths for the same reason. The market may not exist here, in the North.'

Wallace Helena remembered the ladies of Beirut and their proclivity for using scented unguents and she grinned. She saw in her mind Leila rubbing a mixture of flour and lard into her reddened hands, in a prairie land where everybody's hands were work-worn. Vanity? How extraordinary.

She was suddenly very tired herself. She had had to keep up a firm façade before the men in the works; they seemed to consider that they were indulging her in permitting her to inspect her own property – her own except for the technicality of Probate.

'Damn them,' she muttered, as she rose slowly from her chair and began to walk stiffly up and down the dark, narrow room, to loosen her muscles.

'You said something, Miss Harding?'

'No.' She blew out a cloud of smoke, and then said, 'I believe you mentioned that Mr Benjamin will be back tomorrow morning. I'd like to see him at two o'clock.'

'I'll ask Mr Helliwell to put a note on Mr Benjamin's desk to that effect, Miss Harding.' Let Helliwell do something for his living, he thought crossly.

Wallace Helena stretched herself, and then she leaned over the desk to butt out her cigarello in an ashtray. 'Mrs Hughes will be expecting me for supper.'

Mr Bobsworth rose, his lips even tighter. Stretching herself in front of a man! Really, the woman had no manners. He said politely, 'I'll escort you home, Ma'am.'

'No need,' she responded lightly, as she pinned on her hat. 'I can walk up the hill by myself.' She took up her shawl and wrapped it round her shoulders.

'It's not safe, Miss Harding.'

'I am used to lonely country, Mr Bobsworth. There are no cougars or bears on Hill Street!'

Mr Bobsworth argued politely that there were other, unspecified dangers. She countered that she had kept him so late that she now wanted him to go straight home.

The man was tired to the bone, so he suggested that Alfie might still be cleaning out the stables. 'He usually does this job after hours, to earn a bit more. He's very reliable. He'd take care of you.'

Resigned to the inevitable, Wallace Helena agreed to Alfie, if he could be found. She sat down again in her chair, while Mr Bobsworth went to collect his top hat and cane and then find the youngster.

Wallace Helena was interested in the patient mulatto, who bought tobacco and cigarellos for her from sailors' shops in the Goree Piazzas. If she had had a child, she considered, he would probably look very like Alfie – though not so crushed.

A very bewildered Alfie, cap in hand and smelling distinctly of horse manure, knocked at the office door.

Wallace Helena rose and picked up her reticule. 'Come in, Alfie,' she said gently.

Chapter Twenty

The following morning, Wallace Helena sent for a hansom cab and went to see her uncle's lawyer, Mr Benson, at his office. She was immediately seated in a leather chair by the window of his room. Mr Benson was holding a weighty tome on the laws of succession and this he placed on his desk, as he sat down before it. He assumed that she had come to see how the matter of Probate was proceeding. This had not been her intention, but she let him talk about it.

'The Court will not be long now,' he assured her. He thoughtfully twirled the end of his neat moustache, and then continued, 'I felt, as Executor, that such an excellent little business should not be wound up or sold, until you were consulted, though I always presume that you will put it up for sale.'

Wallace Helena ignored the question of selling, and asked a little absently, 'What exactly is Probate, Mr Benson? I am not at all clear. When Mama and her husband died of smallpox, I was fortunate in finding a lawyer who had come west to work with the Oblate Fathers in St Albert, on the subject of Metis land claims. Father Lacombe recommended him to me. I was so upset, as you can imagine, that I left everything to the lawyer, and I'm not sure what he did. But he worked so well that I ended up with thirty-six square miles of good farm land and timber.' She smiled at the lawyer, and added, 'I thought I would never manage to pay his bill – cash is in short supply out west!'

At the disclosure of the size of her land holding, Mr Benson looked surprised. She must already be a well-to-do woman, despite her remark about a lack of cash.

In reply to her question regarding Probate, he said, 'The Court has to be assured that the Will is genuine and that it is the last

Will made by the deceased. They then have to ensure that the Estate is handed over to the right person.'

'Was it difficult in my uncle's case?'

'It has not been simple, but, despite a lengthy search and much advertising, no other Will has come to light – in any case, it was likely that Mr Al-Khoury would have asked me, as his lawyer, to make it for him. I held only the Will made when he was a young man.'

'Then you had to find me?'

'That wasn't difficult. Mr Helliwell had your address; he said he had posted boxes of books to you from Mr James Al-Khoury. The problem was to prove that your dear mother was Mr *Charles* Al-Khoury's sole legatee; secondly, that her Will leaving everything to you was in order, and, thirdly, that you were indeed Helena Al-Khoury, and not, perhaps, a daughter of Mr Harding by an earlier marriage.'

He was surprised to see Wallace Helena's firm mouth trembling; she looked as if she might burst into tears. He went on hastily, 'You were able to provide me with all the necessary addresses, and, though you had no birth certificate, there were several people still in the Hudson's Bay trading post who were able to confirm that you had arrived with your mother, and that Mr Harding had no known daughters. We found other confirmation in letters from you and your mother, written at Fort Edmonton, amongst Mr James's correspondence.'

'Good,' Wallace Helena muttered, and blew her nose hard. Mama, Mama, her heart cried, why did you have to suffer so much?

'I must tell you that I did mention, once or twice, to Mr James that he should update his Will,' the lawyer added. 'But he always seemed in good health and said he would do it some time; we none of us expect to be taken suddenly in middle life.'

He realized that she was no longer listening and he coughed to draw her attention. She turned to him, her eyes so full of pain that he was shocked. Like Mr Helliwell, he began to realize that this rather irritating, forward woman had undergone some very harrowing experiences in her life, experiences still in the forefront of her mind. She looked haunted. He wondered if she had

145

known *any* happiness in her life; frontier life, such as she now led, was not, presumably, very easy.

In the hope of amusing her a little, he began to talk of her uncle's early days in Liverpool. 'Mr James was a very enterprising man, as you may know. He began boiling soap in his landlady's cellar wash boiler. What gave him the idea, I have no notion, except that the use of soap was becoming common. He peddled the soap from door to door. Then he found a tumble-down cottage with a similar boiler. He rented this, and was able to keep his store of fat and so on in it – I imagine much to his landlady's relief!' He smiled at his client and the haunted look began to fade from the enormous brown eyes. 'Then he met Mr Tasker, a real Liverpool character. Together, they found a large shed which is now a part of the present soapery, and it was at that point that he came to me, because he wanted to understand exactly the terms of the leasing of the property – and his English was not too good – and, for some time, I vetted every agreement he signed.'

Wallace Helena forced herself to pay attention. 'Is Mr Tasker a partner, then?'

'No, he has always been an employee – a very trusted one, I may say.' The lawyer smiled again at her, as he saw the sorrow fade from her face. 'I'll always remember Mr James and Mr Tasker as being so exuberant and cheerful. Mr Al-Khoury always said, however, that family were the most important people in a man's life; without family a man was lost. In the early days, he spoke several times of his hope that your father, Mr Charles, would join him, and he was greatly distressed when Mr Charles died – and even more so when he discovered that your mother had married again and had taken you to live in a part of Canada almost unexplored. He couldn't believe it.'

'Why didn't he get married himself?' inquired Wallace Helena, trying to turn the conversation towards her original reason for calling.

'I'm not sure. He mentioned once a desire to return to Lebanon, when it became more peaceful – he always said it was the most beautiful country in the world – and he missed the perfume of the fruit trees.'

146

'That's strange. I do, too. I sit and dream of the smell of lemon tree flowers, sometimes.'

'Do you really? He may have thought that an English wife would not want to live there – and there are few prospective Lebanese wives in this city.' He stopped abruptly, as if he had intended to say more and had then thought better of it.

'I don't suppose there are any Lebanese here, male or female,' Wallace Helena suggested.

Feeling that it was time to terminate the interview, Mr Benson got up from his desk and returned the book on succession to its shelf. Across his stout stomach, the seals on his watch chain tinkled. Then he considered that he should ask her precisely what her intentions were concerning the Lady Lavender, so he sat down again and put the question to her.

Wallace Helena's long eyes narrowed. 'I've not yet made a decision,' she replied cautiously.

Mr Benson nodded understandingly, but did not reply. He sensed that she had more to say.

She stared out of the window at the tiny cobblestone court and watched expressionlessly as a man relieved himself in a quiet corner of it. Then she said, 'It would be nice to live in a lively city, like Liverpool – to be able to buy books and listen to music – and wear pretty clothes.' She smiled ruefully at her feminine desire expressed in the last words. Then she said, 'And you cannot imagine how wonderful a water tap is, particularly one which produces *hot* water! We have a well, which is better than having to haul water up from the river – but it's still very inconvenient, particularly in our climate.'

'Indeed,' he agreed, and waited.

As if she had made up her mind to trust him, she went on, 'I believe I could run the Lady Lavender, with the aid of Mr Bobsworth and Mr Tasker. I have, however, a homestead – a large one – and obligations in the Territories. So I must consider carefully what I am to do.' She gave him a bright, artificial little smile.

She seemed to have finished her confidences, so he said diplomatically, 'Well, it is not essential that you make a decision until Probate is received. I think it would be wise to be ready to decide immediately after that. Businesses do not thrive on indecision.'

'Indeed, they do not,' she agreed.

He went on to warn her about taxes that would have to be paid in connection with the transfer of the company to her. 'You'll need cash,' he warned. 'Mr Al-Khoury did have a small personal bank account, and, as you know, the Lady Lavender account has funds in it – but these will be needed for the day-to-day workings.'

Wallace Helena mentally saw the last really fine necklace that her mother had left her vanishing into the hands of moneylenders or a purchasing jeweller to cover taxes, but she answered smartly. 'Perhaps the company would be allowed to pay in instalments?' she suggested.

'Possibly,' he agreed.

A sudden thought struck Wallace, and it brought her to the real point of her visit. 'Who paid Uncle's funeral expenses?'

Mr Benson hesitated. 'They were initially paid by one of Mr Al-Khoury's friends.' He shifted uneasily in his chair. 'I've since refunded the money from his Estate.'

Now, she thought, I can broach the subject of Benjamin Al-Khoury – at last. She took a cigarello out of her reticule, together with a box of matches, and lit up, while she looked shrewdly at her embarrassed lawyer.

She leaned back and blew a cloud of smoke into the air. 'A lady friend?' she asked finally.

Mr Benson rubbed his neat grey beard, and blinked as the smoke got in his eyes. A most peculiar young woman, he considered, before he answered, 'Yes. It was a friendship of long standing.'

'She's not mentioned in his Will. I would have thought he would have left her at least some small remembrance?'

'Well, his Will was old. He was a young man when he made it . . .'

'Father Lacombe's lawyer wanted me to make a Will, but I couldn't afford any more on his bill!' She laughed, and looked round for an ashtray. Mr Benson hastily offered her his. She smiled her thanks.

Mr Benson bent his head slightly in response and wondered

who her beneficiary would have been. 'Very wise to make a Will, Miss Harding. Very wise.'

Wallace Helena drew on her cigarello and her mind wandered for a moment. 'If I die,' she thought, 'will Joe get all I possess? If the new railway brings in a lot of immigrants and there is a real demand for land, he could be a very rich man.

'He wouldn't really care about that,' she considered dispiritedly. 'He's happy. As long as he has familiar people around him, a good horse under him and something to eat, he'd be content.' In this she underestimated Joe Black; he appreciated the power of money, but he wanted it to ease the life of his treasured Wallace Helena.

As her lawyer watched the play of expressions across her face, it suddenly lit up with a mischievous smile, as she imagined what he would do if he suddenly found himself with a soap works.

'What? Me?' he would splutter. '*Women* make soap!'

Mr Benson saw the smile fade. Again she looked tired and grim. He had heard from an irate Mr Bobsworth how hard she was working. 'She ignored Sunday!' he had complained. 'I never got to Mass at all and the wife was furious.'

Wallace Helena realized with a jolt that there had been silence in the book-lined room for at least a minute. She remembered the question she wished to ask.

As if preparing to get up and leave, she picked up her gloves with studied leisureliness, and then inquired casually, 'Has Benjamin Al-Khoury anything to do with Uncle's lady friend? When I tried to ask Mr Bobsworth where he fitted in, he evaded the question. I need to know, because he's coming to see me this afternoon.'

Mr Benson suddenly saw the reason for the protracted interview. It had taken her a long time to get down to the real reason for it. 'He's her son,' he replied uncomfortably.

'I see. And she is known, perhaps, as Mrs Al-Khoury?'

Mr Benson's face went suddenly pink above his beard, as he answered her frankly, 'Yes, Miss Harding.'

'But she's not Mrs Al-Khoury?'

'No.' He hesitated, and then explained, 'I went to see her to confirm it, because if she was married to Mr James, she would

149

have certain dower rights – and Mr Benjamin, also, could have claims against the Estate.'

At Mr Benson's obvious discomfiture over such a delicate subject, Wallace Helena repressed a smile, and inquired gravely, 'So like a good Lebanese, he saw that her son had a decent job?'

'Yes, Miss Harding. I understand that he was sent to a good grammar school – and when he was fifteen Mr Al-Khoury took him into the business. Mr Tasker and Mr Bobsworth think very highly of him. I've met him, and he is a pleasant young man. Business associates – and the employees – fully expected that he would inherit the Lady Lavender.' He looked down at his hand lying on his desk and then tapped his fingers gently along the wooden edge. 'Be patient with him, Miss Harding. Not only has he lost his father, but he has been sadly humiliated publicly.'

'Because he is illegitimate?' she asked baldly.

'Yes. He could only inherit if his father had specifically willed the business to him.'

'I see.' She rose to leave. 'I'm glad you have been frank with me; it has confirmed what I believed before I left Canada. But I had to be sure.' She pulled on her gloves and held out her hand to the lawyer. 'Leave the matter with me. I will be careful with him. I naturally want to meet my only blood relative.'

Mr Benson had not considered that she might welcome a relation, and he shook her hand warmly with relief. Her attitude might at least mitigate a clash between their very strong characters.

Chapter Twenty-One

Wallace Helena had expected to be away from home not more than two months. But July inched into August and she had still not mentioned a possible date of return. In August, a depressed and overworked Joe Black asked her in his letters to name a date. But he finally got a letter explaining that she was held up by some nonsense called Probate. The fact that their letters crossed constantly added a note of confusion to their communication with each other.

In one letter which Joe received in mid-August, she inquired, 'How would you feel about living in Liverpool? It's such a marvellous city – it has everything. I believe I could manage the soapery and that it would provide a good living.'

The very idea of being penned up in a white man's city made Joe shudder. Born in the Bow Valley when first it was explored, and brought up within his grandfather's usual hunting grounds, he had never been further than Fort Benton in Montana, to the south, or St Albert in the north. He had never seen a city. He had heard about the human swarms in such places and he had no desire to become a human ant. He told his beloved to come home.

In another letter, she mentioned that the previous night she had dreamed of Lebanon. 'For once it wasn't a nightmare,' she wrote. 'I was gazing up at the mountains, and I saw the anemones shedding their red petals in the wind – my nurse once told me they were drops of blood shed by a beautiful god called Adonis, who was killed in a fit of jealousy. Then I found myself floating along the narrow seashore and I listened to the singing of the water. It felt very strange.

'I am told that a number of refugees have returned to the

country. It reminded me that between the mountains of Lebanon and those of the Anti-Lebanon lies the Buka'a Valley, good farm land watered by two rivers – the air there is as pure as that of the prairies. If we could buy such land, darling . . . but it would mean that you would have to learn yet another language as well as accept another culture.'

Joe began to worry, and told her again to come home as soon as she could. They were beginning to do fine in Edmonton. Why go anywhere else?

Twice a week, he rode the five miles down to the post office in Edmonton village. Though the post office had not been established very long, collecting the mail from it had become a bi-weekly social event for the whole district; it was a chance to meet neighbours one did not otherwise see. Everybody stood patiently gossiping in the queue, while they waited for the mail to be sorted by the slow meticulous man behind the counter at the far end of the long narrow room.

For the most part, Joe would lean silently against the office wall, his empty pipe cradled in his hand, unlit out of courtesy to the few women present. He did not invite conversation and did not get beyond a remark about the weather or the state of the harvest. He was, as ever, regarded with respect by those who knew him well, because of his knowledge of livestock breeding and also for his ability to talk sense into angry, despairing Crees and Blackfoot; as settlers slowly increased, face-to-face confrontations were more common with Indians, who did not think much of their limited treaty rights.

Being half-Cree himself, Joe was often furious at the treatment of his relations by both Government and settlers. But he knew that on the homestead he had to live with whites around him who disliked a negro owning land, so he was extremely wary in what he said. Friendly overtures had always been treated by both Wallace Helena and himself with reserve; and he never forgot that Wallace Helena faced prejudice because of her race and was solidly hated for the contemptuous arrogance with which she had countered it from the day of her arrival.

As he waited for his letters, Joe sometimes thought how strange it was that both he and Wallace Helena had learned to love Tom Harding, an American of almost silvery fairness. There was nothing saintly about Tom, he ruminated with a grin, but the man had always played fair; if he promised something, he did his best to keep that promise. And he never seemed to see what colour a man was. He looked straight *into* you, as if judging what you were really like, and, if he liked what he found, he was generous and open. Joe missed him like he missed his Cree grandfather; both men had had in common an inner wisdom sadly lacking in others. The only time Tom had seemed unwise was when he had fallen in love with Leila and had brought the poor woman to the Fort. She had made him happy, though, and Joe hoped suddenly that she had known a little happiness. If she had not come, he would never have known the bundle of vitality that was her daughter.

Now, he was beginning to sweat with anxiety that he had lost Wallace Helena to a damned soap works.

He shifted his feet and wished the post office clerk would hurry up with his sorting.

If Wallace Helena could not be dissuaded from leaving Edmonton, Joe worried, he would be as lonely as he was when his grandfather died. Without her, he felt, the struggle to keep the farm going would be pointless; almost everything he did was for her sake.

It had been different when he and Tom first set out to establish the place. He had been young and adventurous and it had been a great joke to cock a snook at the heavy-handed Hudson's Bay Company.

At a New Year's Day party, he had found himself drinking with Tom Harding, and the white man had inquired if the negro had come up from the States. Joe had replied tartly that he was no American slave; he had been born free in Canada.

They had gone on to an amicable, though drunken, exchange of reminiscences, Tom about his not very successful trapline and his desire to put in a vegetable patch and, if possible, plant a crop of barley. Joe confided that he hated working on the Hudson's Bay's farm a few miles north. He said his father had also been a Company employee under Factor John Rowand.

It was the beginning of a lifelong friendship and a long, not

153

uninteresting, vendetta with the Hudson's Bay Company, the latter ending only when Wallace Helena got title to the land.

The two men might both have died the first winter they lived together in the old cabin, had it not been for Joe's mother and his Aunt Theresa, both of whom were working in the kitchens of the Chief Factor's house. They stole barley and oats for them, to eke out the rabbits the men snared and the fish they got by fishing through a hole in the ice of the river. Tom had the dream of owning his own farm to sustain him, and Joe found it a welcome relief to be treated as a friend and equal.

Joe brought his own small mare with him to the cabin, and, later, he stole two horses that appeared to have got loose from a Blackfoot encampment some distance away. He hoped that by leading them through the shallows of the river, the Blackfoot would not be able to track them down, and they never did.

'Our need's greater than theirs,' Joe affirmed stolidly. It was true that the partners were quite as thin as the hungry Indians. The horses, very unwillingly, pulled the plough they had persuaded a friendly blacksmith in the Fort to make for them.

When times got better, Tom acquired his first wife, a plain, amiable Cree, and discovered that she was a gem of a helpmate. When she died in childbirth, both men mourned her.

Two years later, Tom had brought home Leila and her daughter. They belonged to neither the white nor Metis world of the Fort, nor were they Indians. They were, like Joe, outsiders.

The Scots in the Fort publicly called them Chinks or Jews, as they jeered at them if Tom was not with them. Both women looked down at them with silent contempt. Tom had not expected such reciprocal dislike. He became truculent and defensive of his womenfolk, fearing that they might be raped by men who obviously regarded them with such odium. He knew he could not hope for protection for them from his longstanding antagonist, the Chief Factor.

Leila regarded the Fort's inhabitants as clodhoppers, peasants, men without origins or history. She loved her fair-haired American husband and respected Joe Black for his courtesy and knowledge. The ill-assorted little family turned in upon itself;

154

they were like bison anticipating an attack, forming a tight, protective knot.

When, many years later, Wallace Helena successfully acquired title to a piece of land much larger than others, and had then made Joe her equal partner, the locals again began to call her a bloody Chink. Their jealousy was very great. It did not help her to make friends.

Joe loved her with an intensity which sometimes scared him; it was the only part of his life over which he was not in complete control. 'Prickly as a porcupine,' he would warn himself – and then he would laugh.

When the postmaster finally handed him several letters from her, he grinned his thanks and stuffed them inside his old wolfskin jacket.

Without a further word to anyone, he pushed his way through the small group still waiting. His horse was hitched to a post outside. He absently undid it and mounted. With the stiff envelopes crackling against his chest, he rode the old trail along the river escarpment, splashing through a couple of creeks, regardless of the fact that by then part of the track ran over lots owned by others. Alder and scrub oaks brushed him, as he passed, and flies buzzed crossly round him, but it was the easiest route home and he wanted to read his letters. If Wallace Helena was right in her predictions and if the railway came to Edmonton, there would soon be roads criss-crossing the whole district. There would be hordes of people glad of land and space, and they would form a ready market for everything a mixed farm could produce. But then, she had always been a bit of a dreamer, he considered wryly. He hoped that she was wrong; there were too many white folk and Metis around already.

Aunt Theresa stood expectantly at the cabin door and Emily ran out to open the yard gate for him as he rode in. Simon Wounded, out in the fields, saw him from a distance and came running to hear any news of Wallace Helena. They crowded round the scrubbed table in the old cabin, regardless of the fact that it was August and there was an immense amount of work to do.

Joe had been taught to read by an Oblate priest, and he read the letters slowly and accurately, translating into Cree some phrases which were difficult for his listeners to understand. He omitted paragraphs that were personal to him. Some parts of the letters were almost incomprehensible to them; they were too far removed from city life.

As he put down the last page, he felt a little forlorn himself. As if she understood, Emily brought him a hot cup of coffee from the kitchen lean-to. He nodded, and then sent them back to their work. 'Barley'll be ready for cutting,' Simon warned him.

Joe nodded again. 'We'll start tonight – it'll be cooler. And start again at sun-up. I'll be out to have a look at it soon.' He picked up the letters again and turned them over. Simon sighed and went to look at the pigs. He felt suddenly very old and was not looking forward to the long, arduous days of harvest without Wallace Helena's help.

Joe read parts of the letters again while he drank his coffee. Wallace Helena sounded too damnably comfortable amongst her lawyers, soap masters and accountants. Unlike the men in Edmonton, these men seemed to be treating her with some respect, though she had admitted flatly that being a woman was a disadvantage to her. He felt a strong twinge of jealousy.

He leaned back in his chair and lit his pipe. Until he had begun to receive letters from her in Liverpool, he had never felt himself to be less than she was; he had his own wide areas of knowledge and experience – she had hers. He knew how to foretell the weather with some accuracy and he decided when they should sow and when they should reap. He could hunt and trap as well as his grandfather had. Ahead of the other settlers, he knew the movements of the dispossessed Cree and Blackfoot, understood the desperate frustration of the Metis – hadn't he foretold the Riel rebellion long before it happened and prepared himself for it as far as he could?

Mr Tasker in Liverpool might have a *feel* for soap, but I have a *feel* about this land, he argued. Wallace Helena may do the bargaining with agents buying food for the railway gangs building further south or for the Indians, poor devils; it's me – me – who delivers steers and grain safely to their camps – and that's no mean feat, lady, in a country riddled with rivers and creeks and bogs to be crossed.

Frustrated by distance, by the strangeness of the world she described in her letters, he was vexed and confused. She wrote with affection and consideration for him – but she appeared far too happy!

Feeling sullen and resentful, he went to join Simon Wounded in the fields.

That night, he wrote asking her to come home as soon as possible; he needed her. He gave her no news of the harvest or the excellent contact he had made with a railway surveyor nosing round Edmonton and in need of provisions. He continued to reply to her letters, giving no news but simply asking when she expected to return.

The replies he finally received in answer to his campaign of near silence were positively acerbic. He chuckled with satisfaction. The epistles were full of inquiries about the homestead and himself; not one of them mentioned soap. Had he arranged for the threshing crew? Was he reading the *Edmonton Bulletin* and keeping in touch with its editor, Frank Oliver? Mr Oliver was a ready source of news of surveying or other parties passing through, who might need to be victualled. And he should keep up his contacts with Mr Taylor, the telegraph operator, who was in a better position than anyone else to have early news which would help them sell the crop or the animals they did not want to winter over. How was the vegetable garden doing?

He felt better, and was able to write to her that he and Simon had got the barley crop into the barn, one day before a heavy rainstorm carrying hail in it had destroyed neighbours' fields. Yet, when he thought of Wallace Helena's new world, the sense of inadequacy resurfaced. Against the comforts of a city, he had little to offer her, except himself, and the continuation of a harsh, uncertain life in a climate which would test anybody's fortitude.

Chapter Twenty-Two

After her visit to Mr Benson, Wallace Helena asked the cabbie to put her down at the gates of the Lady Lavender. She walked slowly through the wicket gate. To her left was the carpenter's shop, and she glanced through its open doorway. The boxes in which the soap was transported were made here, and at one end a young wheelwright repaired the delivery vans and their wheels. Heaps of wood shavings and sawdust lay in every corner of the shed, and, seeing them, she realized what a fire hazard they represented.

Without hesitation, she walked in and told the elderly carpenter to sweep them up and dispose of them. 'They could cause a fire,' she said sharply.

The man had taken off his cap when she entered, and now he scratched his head, while he gaped at her. 'Never in me life have I bin told by a woman what to do in me own shop,' he told his wife that night. 'Who's she to tell me what to do?'

Wallace Helena scouted round the rest of the shop. The young, dark-haired wheelwright ignored her and gave earnest attention to a wheel he was refitting to a light van; he didn't want any trouble.

As it became apparent that she knew the names of most of the tools lying around the shop and what they were for, the carpenter began to recover himself, and when she returned to his side to remind him again to sweep up, he stammered, 'Mr Al-Khoury were goin' to get me an apprentice, Ma'am. Me last one's gone to be a journeyman in another place; done well for himself, he has. An apprentice'd clean up for me, like. I gotta lot of work here.'

'Which Mr Al-Khoury?'

'The ould fella – Mr James, Ma'am.'

'I see. I'll see what can be done. Meanwhile, perhaps Mr Tasker could spare his labourer, Alfie, to sweep up for you. I'll speak to him.'

He heard the note of authority in her voice and muttered, 'Yes, Ma'am.'

The stable was next door, and she realized that she had not yet visited it, though from the wage sheets she knew the names of the employees working there. The stableman was eating his lunchtime bread and cheese, while he leaned against the open doorway. A heavy, red-faced man, he straightened up as she swept in. Lifting up her skirts, she walked the length of the building and returned to storm at him. How could he expect the horses to be healthy with weeks of manure underfoot? It was enough to make employees ill, as well. She ordered an immediate clean-up and the establishment of a manure heap in a corner of the yard which did not seem to be used. Horse manure was valuable to farms; she would find a market for it and have it collected weekly. 'It's a wonder that the city has not complained at such a conglomeration,' she raged. 'How do you dispose of it at present – when it gets up to your knees?' she asked with heavy sarcasm.

The man hung his head sullenly and did not reply. In fact, he periodically sold it himself; he considered it a perk which went with his job. But he wasn't going to tell a bloody bitch like her.

There had been a solitary horse in the stable and Wallace Helena had taken a good look at it. Now, finding that the man was not going to reply to her, she said, 'And give that animal a hot bran mash. I'll take another look at him in the morning.'

The man lifted his head and looked her angrily in the eye. 'I done it,' he replied.

Wallace Helena pursed her lips into a thin line. 'Right. I'll come in the morning.'

'Sour as a bloody lemon, she is,' this man told *his* wife, and then added thoughtfully, 'Seems she knows somethin' about horses, though.'

Outside the stable, Wallace Helena paused to scrape some of the muck of the stable off her boots. She sighed, as she rubbed the sides of her boots against cobblestones which she noticed were heavy with grease, presumably from the barrels of fat and oil stored on the far side of the yard. Here was another fire hazard, she considered uneasily.

Before moving, she pulled the hatpins from her hat and took it off, to let the light breeze cool a face flushed with anger. Not only did she feel hot, she felt nauseated from the reek of the stable. She thought she might vomit, and she turned to the office intending to run over to the latrine behind it.

She almost knocked down a stocky, well-built young man in a black suit and bowler hat. Off balance, he stumbled and dropped the carpet bag he was carrying. He was saved from a fall by the vicelike grip of Wallace Helena's long fingers on his arm. As he steadied himself, she took a large breath in an effort to quell her nausea.

Though the collision was not his fault, the man apologized for bumping into her, as he mechanically bent down to pick up his bag again. She nodded acknowledgment, and hurried away to the privy. He was left with the vague impression of a very thin, plain woman with a sickly, sallow face, dressed in shabby black and carrying a small hat; he assumed that she was the wife of one of the workmen, bringing in his midday meal.

Only when Benjamin Al-Khoury was discussing a minor complaint with Mr Tasker, and Miss Harding's name came up, did the likely identity of the woman in the yard occur to him.

The bitterness that had haunted him since his father's death welled up once again. His father had failed both him and his mother; and he wondered for the hundredth time why his parents had never married. They were obviously devoted to each other and the home was a happy one. His own illegitimacy had been well known in the neighbourhood and he had suffered the usual snide remarks flung at such children; presumably his mother also had had her share of opprobrium. It didn't make sense.

And now this wretched woman had been dug up by the lawyers as the legal residual legatee of his father's Estate; his patrimony was going to a cousin he had never heard of, because she was the only legitimate descendant of the two brothers. And, to add to his sense of a world turned upside down, she was presumably his employer – unless she sold the business, as expected, in which case he could lose his job as the new owner moved in his own choice of men. It was not a pleasant prospect.

He left Mr Tasker amid his bubbling cauldrons and went to see Mr Bobsworth, with whom he intended to have lunch. He was met by the information that Miss Harding would see him at two o'clock.

'Blow her,' he muttered, though he realized he could not put off meeting her much longer.

As if reading his thoughts, Mr Bobsworth said, 'Better to get it over with, lad.'

'What's she like?'

'A Tartar,' replied Mr Bobsworth gloomily. 'Thinks she owns the place.'

'She does, old man. Let's go and eat. I'll leave the orders I've got with Le Fleur – he can send them to be made up.'

'I'll check them as soon as we return,' Mr Bobsworth promised. 'I always label everything myself, you know that. Want a job doing well? Do it yourself.'

It was old Bobsworth's usual remark, so Benjamin let it pass.

In the shabby dockside café, crowded with seamen, Customs men and men from the warehouses nearby, though no dockers – they had their own, even smaller, eating houses, where the stench of the cargoes they handled was more acceptable – Mr Bobsworth found his usual quiet corner table. They hung up their bowlers, undid their jackets and sat down. Unasked, a florid woman in a coloured apron put a pint of bitter in front of each of them. 'Like to order?' she asked, a stub of pencil poised over a grubby notebook.

They both ordered steak and kidney pudding, and, while they were waiting, Benjamin brought up the problem of the rabid competition in the Manchester area, where the cotton mills consumed a massive amount of soap.

'This man Lever's started to wrap his *bar* soap in bright yellow paper with *Sunlight* printed all over it. Even his delivery vans are plastered with sunrays and the same word. And he's advertising "Don't just ask for soap – ask for *Sunlight*." He's making a hole in our market, I can tell you.'

'We make better soap,' responded Mr Bobsworth uncompromisingly. 'Tasker makes better soap than anybody.'

'Yes, but we're not telling everybody that – and women seem to love having their washing soap wrapped.'

'We wrap our toilet soap.'

'In mouldy grey paper – beige for the cinnamon and fuller's earth! Anyway, it's plain bar soap that everything gets scrubbed with – it's our bread and butter. I'm sure Dad would have done something about it.'

'Your father had in mind to branch out into lotions and scents for working-class women. He'd even thought of a kind of paste to tint the skin – cream colour for pale skins, pink for rosy youth – packed in chemists' little bottles and boxes. Vanity! Nothing but vanity, that's what I say.'

'Girls in the mills have a bit of money to spend, a few pence here and there. Dad would've been selling them something better than gin.'

'He had a job persuading their mams to let them have a bath with scented soap – and get the mams themselves to put a bit of lavender on their Sunday handkerchiefs.' Mr Bobsworth was a Roman Catholic and did not think much of Methodist austerity. On the other hand, he did not like to think of his wife and daughters painting their faces like actresses or worse; so he was quick to condemn cosmetics.

Plates of steak and kidney pudding were thrust under their noses. Though the pudding looked as flaccid as chicken waiting to be cooked, the aroma was delicious, and both men were hungry. They were silent as they ate their way through the steaming mass.

Afterwards, Benjamin stretched himself over the back of his chair, and sighed. Reverting to the subject of their business, he said dejectedly, 'It's not much use our discussing what we should do about Lever. It's out of our hands. Whoever buys us out will have to decide. And we'll be lucky if we have jobs.'

Over his beer mug, Mr Bobsworth made a glum face, and Benjamin went on, 'I don't know why she bothered to come over. It'd have been a lot quicker if Benson had sent her all the papers and arranged the sale for her. Wish I could afford to buy it – I'd make something of it.'

Mr Bobsworth put down his mug. 'She's a rum type,' he said. 'She's queer enough to think she could run the place herself. She's bin lookin' over everything.'

'A woman? What a hope!'

'Well, she's not like any other woman I ever met. She's smart at figures, I can tell you. Tasker says she's got a huge farm in Canada and runs it. I'd say the question is, does she want to live here?'

'Maybe somebody'll marry her – and take over the works as well,' Benjamin offered. He drained his mug and stood up, while he felt in his pocket for a tip for the waitress. He tucked two copper coins under his empty plate.

Mr Bobsworth rose, too. He wondered suddenly if Benjamin had the idea of marrying Miss Harding, and so gain control of the soapery. Perhaps he should remind the boy that, only a few years back, a law had been passed to protect the property of married women; it wasn't so easy nowadays to take over their assets. In any case, he hoped that Benji would fancy one of his own daughters.

He said soberly, 'Frankly, Benji, she'll be lucky if she finds anybody who wants to marry her. She's as thin as a flagpole – no comfortable pillow for a man's head! And she can come over the acid like some spinster headmistress of a girls' seminary.'

'Well, I've got to see her this afternoon, so we'd better hurry.' His usually lively expression drooped; he was suddenly aware that he had not shaved well that morning, and he supposed that his usual blue-black bristle was already visible. If he wanted to make a good impression, he should have gone home first, to shave and change his suit, creased with a week's travelling. Then he decided that it did not really matter; the person to worry about and smarten up for was the man who would buy the soapery.

Chapter Twenty-Three

Before he had set out on his trip to Manchester, Benji's mother, Eleanor Al-Khoury, had told him that, during the night, she had remembered his father saying that Charles Al-Khoury had a *daughter*. She looked exhausted from much weeping, and she added, as she wiped her eyes with a sodden handkerchief, 'When your uncle died in Chicago, your dad wanted to bring his wife and child over here, to live with us. I was that upset about – about your dad's passing, that I forgot. Funny to think you could've bin brought up together, in this house.' Her nose was running and she sniffed.

He had looked down at her rather helplessly. 'It doesn't make any difference, Mum. It was my recollection, too. But I was put off by the name *Wallace*; I thought I'd been mistaken. Now, don't you cry any more. I'll look after you, you know that.' He hugged her, and in hope of comforting her a little, he went on, 'When I get back, we'll go and find a real nice memorial for Dad's grave.'

She rubbed the tears off her fair lashes, and said as bravely as she could, 'Oh, aye. We'll do that, luv.'

'I'll ask Mrs Tasker to step in, as I go down the street,' he promised, as he kissed her goodbye. 'I don't want you to be too lonely.'

'I'll be all right,' she told him, her face so sad he could have wept himself. She shut the door quietly after him and began to weep some more.

A few minutes later, a concerned Mrs Tasker arrived. She had a seed cake, freshly baked, balanced on her ungloved hand, and she trotted straight into the big kitchen and proceeded to provide tea and kindly sympathy, while the bereaved woman sat by the fire and sang the praises of her Jamie. Mrs Tasker had heard it all several times in the previous few weeks, but she felt that the more Eleanor wept the quicker she would recover. She made the tea very strong.

Mr Tasker had said that the Will held, no matter whether Eleanor was married to James Al-Khoury or not. But Eleanor knew that a wedding cancelled out earlier Wills; if she'd been married and there had been no other Will, Benji would have inherited; and she mentally belaboured herself for accepting the status quo for so long. She wept not only for James Al-Khoury but also for her sadly humiliated son.

While she sipped the tea made by her friend, she recounted to her the story of how the handsome, cheery young James Al-Khoury, who spoke English in a proper funny fashion, had come to her front door in search of a room to rent. 'He hadn't even the money to pay for a week in advance,' she said with a dim smile. 'But he looked that handsome, I took a chance on 'im. Put 'im in me best room – front ground floor. And, aye, he were lovely.'

Ten months later, little Benji had been born, as Mrs Tasker knew, though it was before she had come to live in the same street. Eleanor must've endured a fair amount of backhanded whispering over that, Mrs Tasker meditated, as Eleanor droned on. Why hadn't the stupid woman insisted on marriage if she loved the man so much? And he was lovable, there was no doubt. She wondered suddenly if James had left a wife in Lebanon, to whom he had intended to return in due course.

'He charmed the hearts of the women round about,' Eleanor reminisced tenderly, 'and they bought his soap, what he made in me cellar, without hesitation.' She stopped and then smiled at her friend, who had joined her by the kitchen fire. 'Then he met your George – and we never looked back, did we? And just when it seemed nothing could stop him, he goes and gets a heart attack.' Her face became ugly with grief and again the tears trickled down her lined face. 'You take care of your Georgie, Sarah. He int gettin' any younger.'

'Oh, aye. He's all right,' she replied with more certainty than she felt. George worked very hard and was on his feet all day.

'Our Benji's got his dad's charm. Not so fine looking, but a nice lad,' Eleanor said after drinking her tea down to the dregs. She put her cup down in the saucer, as a memory struck her of

Benji coming home from school with a bruised cheek and an oozing nose. He must've been about nine, she thought, and a couple of bullies had called him an Arab and a bastard. Lucky for Benji, he was a heavily built boy and he had fought back. After that, Jamie had shown him a few ways to defend himself which must have been shudderingly painful to the recipient of the blows. Gradually, the boys left him alone – too alone. His best friend had been George Tasker's eldest, Albert, who'd gone away to be a soldier. In India, now, he was.

Mrs Tasker was fond of Benji and agreed with his mother that he was a nice lad. She laughed unexpectedly, and added, 'Maybe he could charm Miss Harding into marrying him; then he'd get the soap works right into his hand.'

Eleanor forgot her grief for a moment. 'You're right. But you never can tell with young people, and I'm told she's quite old.' She put down her cup into the hearth and stood up. 'I must start tea for me gentlemen. They all like a hot tea.'

'How many have you got?'

'Three of 'em. All very respectable.'

Mrs Tasker sighed. Lodgers would be a lot of work for Eleanor and she nearly fifty years old. 'Lucky for you, you own the house,' she said. 'Though I'm sure Benji'll take care of you.'

'For sure he will,' Eleanor agreed. 'But me dad thought I'd be alone all me life, so he made sure I had the house. He left it in good order, too, just like his auntie left it to him. We always had lodgers; it kept him in his old age.' She began to take out her mixing bowl, rolling pin and wooden spoons. 'And he had a water closet put in the back yard,' she added proudly. 'I started looking for good lodgers the minute our Jamie was buried, in case Benji loses his job. Gives us a bit of independence, it does.' She took out her scales and began to weigh flour for pastry. Through the dust rising from the shaken-out flour, Sarah Tasker watched her friend's face. It was pitifully woebegone.

To cheer her up, Sarah said, 'Well, let's hope Miss Wallace Helena falls for Benji. Then you could live like a lady, like Jamie managed for you these last few years.'

Chapter Twenty-Four

Wallace Helena leaned back in her office chair and stretched herself. In front of her was the correspondence which had accumulated for Benjamin Al-Khoury's attention during his absence. She had already read it. Her mouth twisted in a grim little smile, as she congratulated herself on having hit on such a simple method of keeping track of much that was going on in the soapery.

There was a quiet tap on the door. Mr Helliwell entered to announce Benjamin's arrival with Mr Bobsworth. She told him to show them in, and pushed the correspondence to one side.

As they entered, she stared at the handsome, untidy man who followed Mr Bobsworth in. He's quite young, she thought in surprise, younger than Helliwell, and, despite his western dress, he looks like an Arab. He seemed more relaxed than an Englishman, though he had the same self-confident air as Mr Benson. Although he was stocky, she gained an impression of physical fitness – and mental alertness. Very much his father's son.

Her stare was merciless and it embarrassed Benjamin, who was already very irate at the news that she had taken the week's correspondence to read. Beneath his black moustache, his mouth was clamped as tightly as hers.

The woman had eyes like stones, he thought as he greeted her with the courtesy of an experienced sales representative. She leaned over the desk to shake his proffered hand, smiling slightly, her eyes expressionless.

'A bloody Mona Lisa,' Benjamin added to his first impression, as she indicated the visitor's chair and he sat down.

Wallace Helena turned her attention to Mr Bobsworth standing primly behind Benjamin.

'Thank you for bringing Mr Al-Khoury in, Mr Bobsworth. I mustn't keep you from your work any longer.'

Mr Bobsworth reluctantly retreated with Mr Helliwell. It was improper for a lady to receive a man alone in an office. He himself was nearly old enough to be her father, so he felt it did not matter if he were alone with her. But it was different when young Benji or even Mr Helliwell were closeted with her; things could happen. A woman who smoked was not quite what she should be – Benji should watch out.

As Benji loosed Wallace Helena's long cool hand, his heart sank. He had had, in the back of his mind, the same vague hope that his mother had, that *things* might, indeed, happen. What he had not inherited because of his illegitimacy, he could perhaps gain control of by marriage, despite the new law.

But the long, almond-shaped light brown eyes, so like his own, were as cold as rain-washed pebbles on a November morning. The firm, wide mouth seemed infinitely unkissable, and the thin, pliant body, which had stirred Mr Tasker to unseemly thoughts, appeared sticklike to a younger man used to the plumper women of his own generation. Had Joe Black been present and able to read Benjamin's thoughts, he would have cuffed him like an angry bear for being so uncomplimentary about such a fine woman.

Wallace Helena understood men well enough to be subtly aware that she had not aroused any admiration in him; she did not feel the instant rapport that she had felt when meeting George Tasker.

She could see the family likeness between herself and him; he was indeed his father's son. She had at one point, when thinking about him, wondered if he was a child conceived in an earlier liaison of his mother's and foisted upon her uncle. The man before her had, however, the broad, muscular build of a Maronite from the mountains, the deep chest of peoples used to high altitudes, and muscles adapted to hard physical work, though in Benji's case town life had made them tend towards fleshiness. His nose was not as prominent as her own and had a slight upward tilt at the end. His glossy black hair waved back from his face and his skin was a weather-beaten olive.

There was nothing about him to indicate that he had an English mother.

She broke the silence between them by saying, 'I'm very glad to meet you – at last. I understand you were in Manchester when I arrived?'

He took this as an implied reproof for his absence, and, pulling himself together, replied quickly, 'Yes. I must apologize for not meeting you off the ship, but we suddenly lost a good contract to a new company setting up in Warrington. The Manchester market is so valuable that I thought I must go to see the customer myself.' He did not say that he had spun out his absence, by going to pay courtesy calls on other customers, because he did not feel that he could face her until he had gained command of the anger and frustration he felt. He had wanted to beat his breast and tear his clothes, get away from his rightly distraught mother.

'What had happened in Manchester?' Her voice was cool and she sounded very alert.

'Lever offered them a better price – and supporting advertising.' He went on to explain that Lever had begun to wrap his common washing soap in gaily coloured paper, and to scent it with citronella to drown its normally unpleasant odour.

'Humph.' She shifted in her chair. 'We'll have a meeting with Mr Tasker and Mr Bobsworth – and perhaps Mr Turner – that's the name of the chemist, isn't it? We'll go into the matter thoroughly, so that the minute I have Probate we can take some action. How did you leave the matter?'

'I asked them to let us tender next time the contract came up – they're middlemen and buy in bulk.'

She nodded agreement, and then banged the bell on her desk. As soon as Mr Helliwell materialized in response to it she ordered tea. While it was being made, she began to ask Benji a little about himself and the position of Assistant Manager, which he held.

Tight-lipped Mr Helliwell brewed tea in a pot, paid for out of Petty Cash with much grumbling from Mr Bobsworth. He was glad he had a gas ring in his office and did not have to go down to put the kettle on the watchman's coke brazier, which was not always alight on summer days. It would be humiliating to let the yard know that he made tea like a parlour maid. Mr James had always asked young Le Fleur to make it.

Benji had learned from his father the gentle art of making a customer feel comfortable – and tea or coffee had always been one of his father's ploys, whether the visitor drank it or not. He had also passed to his son, brought up in an alien culture, something of his own quick-wittedness and business acumen passed down to him through generations of traders in Lebanon and Syria. This began to surface in the son as he explained his duties in the company to Wallace Helena. In the back of his mind he wondered why she bothered, if the business was to be sold.

He mentioned that the idea of selling a scented soap for the skin had been his. 'There's plenty of competition,' he told Wallace Helena. 'But we make our tablets small and hard, wrap them and sell them as cheaply as possible. It's been my opinion, for a long time, that there's more *cash* in working families nowadays and they can afford small luxuries. My mother says that, in the old days, the women hardly spent anything on themselves; it was a matter of survival only. Now, I sell them not only a bit of scented soap but a little bottle of scent as well, despite the old diehards who say it's vanity – of course, old people often think having a bath is vanity!'

Wallace Helena laughed. 'Good heavens!' she exclaimed.

Emboldened by her spontaneous laugh, he went on, 'Another thing I think I could sell is a cream for hands. All the cleaning they do – with soap – takes the oil out of their skins, and immediately the cold weather comes they chap and the skin splits very painfully. In the country, on the farms, there's always a bit of lard or goose grease they can rub into the sore spots, but it's very sticky – and women in cotton mills and suchlike can't afford to have sticky hands. We've glycerine left over after the soap-making; Turner's working on the refining of it, to use as a base for a cream. We know how to do it, but we want something very, very cheap that will have a small mark-up and a big turnover – I've been pricing small ointment tins and glass jars to pack it in.'

'That's another thing to talk about after Probate,' Wallace Helena replied. 'We've got to decide what we'll make in future, particularly since competition seems to be getting more intense. I can see that Mr Turner may be invaluable.'

He was heartened that she said *we*, as if taking for granted that, whatever was to happen to the company, he was, as far as she was concerned, to be included in the decision-making. He wondered if Bobsworth's idea that she wanted to run the firm herself was correct.

He nodded agreement with her remark about the chemist. Then he said, with an amused expression on his face, 'Mr Al-Khoury used to watch and listen for news of towns putting in waterworks; he'd go personally to any such place and sell our soap to every grocer or hardware store he could find. "Once a woman has a water tap in the house, she wants soap," he would say. "So we get ours in first." '

Benji's description of her uncle's impetuosity was so apt that it made her smile. She mentally saw him bursting into the office of the silk warehouse in Beirut, eager to suggest something new to his elder brother; or, in the house, snatching her up from her play to whiz round with her and tell her she was his little lemon flower.

Benji watched the passing expressions on her face and wondered what she was thinking of. He was surprised by her next question.

'Aren't there any rich ladies in England?' she inquired. 'You speak all the time of women who do their own work. I thought everybody in England had servants?'

'Well, not everybody has servants. We're going after working-class women, because they're a comparatively new market. Rich women have bought quite expensive soap from their hairdressers, for years. The competition in that kind of soap is *very* keen.' He chuckled a little ruefully. 'For a long time in the new cities, like the cotton towns, working people didn't have access to much water – they had to endure the filth around them. Now, many of them have a decent water supply, so Fath . . . Mr Al-Khoury set out to sell them cheap soap. A small mark-up, but, on the other hand, a huge market.'

He was beginning to feel more at home with Wallace Helena, and he leaned back in his chair and shoved his hands in his pockets. 'But now we're faced with a very innovative competitor, in the shape of Mr Lever, trying for the same market. We often undercut the older firms, because our overheads are low – but Lever is another kettle of fish. He's causing ripples throughout the industry.'

'We'll try to give him a run for his money,' Wallace Helena promised, intrigued at the chance to outwit a smart man.

'Well, I was trying to persuade Mr Al-Khoury to improve the presentation of our toilet soap, at least – a brighter wrapper, or something. But he passed away before we got down to it – and now we're in limbo.' The last words came out with a sigh.

Wallace Helena observed his change of expression, the sudden woodenness of his rugged face. She began to realize his personal uncertainty – in limbo, he was, personally, and he also shared the uncertainty of the other employees. She knew she must soon make up her mind whether she would stay in England to guide the company – or sell it. It was not fair to the employees to dither. But there was Joe to consider. Could she persuade him to settle in a city, and if she did, what would he do? It would be like caging a tiger.

She thought bitterly that, if Joe didn't exist, she would never return to the hardship of her life in Canada – she would stay in Liverpool, and even, perhaps, take a look at making a second move back to Lebanon. And what would you do there, without a family or at least a man to protect you? she asked herself. She suddenly hated her kind, generous uncle for facing her with such a dilemma.

In an effort to clarify Benji's position, she said, 'I remember Uncle James writing to Father and mentioning that he had a little boy. Was that you?'

'Yes, Miss Harding.' He fidgeted uncomfortably, taking his hands out of his pockets and then clasping them in front of him on the side of her desk. He said abruptly, 'I didn't know you existed – I never saw your father's letters, of course. Mr Benson told me about you.'

'My father was the eldest and he used to worry about Uncle James. I'm sure he must have often scolded him when he wrote

172

to him. That'll be why you never saw the letters!' There was a hint of humour in her voice, but it did not raise his spirits. 'Probably you were too small to be able to read, anyway.'

'Yes, Miss Harding.'

'Stop *Miss Harding* me. I'm your cousin – that's almost like a sister. Call me Wallace Helena, like a relation, can't you?' She got up from her chair and began to pace up and down impatiently. Then she stopped in front of him, and said contritely, when he didn't answer, 'You must miss your father dreadfully, and I'm truly sorry you've lost him.'

'Thank you. I do miss him.' He suddenly looked very exhausted, and she said gently, 'I understand why you did not get any of Uncle's Estate – and I'm sure it was not Uncle's intention that I get it. But I'm stuck with it – and it's causing me considerable heartache, believe it or not.'

'Is it?' He was surprised out of his depression. 'Father simply didn't expect to die, so he didn't prepare for it. Which of us ever does?'

'Not many,' Wallace Helena admitted glumly. Her full skirt swished, as she returned to her chair. She opened a heavy box on her desk. 'Like a smoke?' she asked.

'No, thanks. I smoke a pipe.'

'Well, get it out and smoke it,' she suggested, as she put a cigarello between her lips, and struck a match to light it.

There was a strict *No Smoking* rule in the works, but he did not think this was an appropriate moment to mention it, so he took out his pipe and tobacco pouch and proceeded to pack the pipe. She threw the box of matches to him across the desk. 'Your official designation is Assistant Manager, isn't it?'

'Yes.' He struck a match and lit his pipe.

'Well, you continue what you're doing for the moment, though I'll consult you all along the way. We can't make any changes until Probate is granted; but I'll do my best to make up my mind quickly. If I sell, I'll make sure you get a decent contract with the new owner, if you want it. How would that be?'

'It'd help,' he admitted, and pulled on his pipe. He had never before broken the *No Smoking* rule, for fear of fire. 'Supposing you don't sell?'

'I'll manage it myself,' she replied, without hesitation. 'I'll work very closely with the senior employees, as Uncle did.'

'As a woman, you'll have particular difficulties.'

'So I'm told,' she responded dryly. 'We shall see.'

He warned her further. 'You should be aware that a lot of changes are taking place in the industry. Mechanization on a big scale – it's already very advanced in the bigger firms. Some employ German scientists – they've brought in some profound changes.'

Wallace Helena whistled between her teeth, while she considered this. 'That means money, doesn't it?'

'Yes, capital.'

She grinned at him suddenly. 'We live in interesting times, don't we? I imagine that if we have our wits about us, we can cope as well as anybody?'

His mood lightened. It felt good to be included in the battles to come. She was obviously willing to face a challenge. But he agreed cautiously, 'Well, yes. Minnows can swim along quite well beneath bigger fish – and not all of 'em get eaten!'

She laughed, and he continued, 'Tasker, Bobsworth, Ferguson – the Steam Engineer – and Turner. We've got good, informed employees. They used to meet in our sitting-room in the evenings. They'd spend hours bickering with each other, working out how to run the place, while Mother dished out cake and beer.'

'Like family?'

'Exactly.' He drew on his pipe and settled back in his chair more comfortably. 'Frankly, Turner's a bit of an expense for a small firm like ours. But he'll be useful if we go into emollients. And Frank Ferguson – well, he's like all engineers, nowadays, he's a king. He can name his own price anywhere. He was fond of my father, though, and I think he'll stay with us, if we treat him properly. He's always at war with old Bobsworth over costs.'

Wallace Helena's eyes glinted with amusement. 'I know. When we were going over the books, Mr Bobsworth must've said a dozen times, "Mr Ferguson doesn't appreciate that we can't go rushing out to buy every bit of equipment that comes on the

174

market. When we started we managed it much more cheaply without anything fancy." '

She had mimicked Mr Bobsworth's petulant complaint exactly. They looked at each other and began to chuckle like a pair of disrespectful youngsters.

He was agreeably surprised at what laughter did to her. She suddenly became human, approachable. And she was obviously perceptive – she'd got old Bobsworth down to a T.

She was looking at him with kinder eyes now, though there was still a twinkle of amusement in them. She said, 'Don't worry too much. I shall be very careful in what I do.' She picked up the sheaf of letters and handed them to him. 'Meanwhile, there must be a lot of work which has accumulated in your absence – I guess you'd better get on with it.'

He put the letters down on the desk, while he dowsed his pipe by fitting a small tin cover over the bowl. Then he got up slowly, nodding acknowledgment of her remark about his work as he did so. Having talked to her, he felt easier in his mind, but he wished his father were still sitting in the chair she occupied.

'Thank you, Miss Harding.' He bowed and quietly left the room.

She wanted to get up and go after the young man to comfort him. He was cousin-brother to her and had been bereaved. But she felt that if she was to maintain her authority, she must keep her distance. It was a lonely feeling.

Chapter Twenty-Five

The next morning, when Benji arrived at the plant, he found the day's correspondence neatly piled on his desk. When asked, Mr Helliwell said that he had, as usual, opened the envelopes and, at Miss Harding's request, handed the letters to her to read. He saw Benji's lips tighten at this information, and hastened to add, 'She said it was the quickest way to find out what was happening in the works. She said you'd deal with everything.'

'Humph,' Benji grunted, as he shuffled quickly through the pile. Wallace Helena had scribbled her suggestions on one or two of the letters and he made a face when he saw her notes. He said to Helliwell, 'I'll give you some dictation to be going on with, and we'll do the rest when I've done my round of the works.' He supposed he ought to be thankful that she had left any decisions regarding the matters raised in the letters to him. At least it showed a little trust.

He met his cousin coming out of the small laboratory presided over by Mr Turner, a lanky man in his thirties. Wallace Helena's set face told Benji immediately that she had not got along very well with the chemist. He looked past her at Turner and raised an eyebrow in query.

Turner blinked back at him through his gold-rimmed spectacles and shrugged almost imperceptibly. She had asked him to show her round his small laboratory and he had politely obliged, though tending to talk down to her as if she were a small girl to whom he was explaining profound mysteries. He had been taken aback when she made it clear that she knew the principles of soap-making; she made her own every spring, she had informed him tartly.

When she saw Benji, she managed to smile and greet him.

Without stopping to thank Mr Turner, she fell into step beside him and accompanied him through the works, as he went to see Mr Tasker about one or two matters and then to Mr Bobsworth about some points raised in customers' letters. 'Going to see the various mandarins?' she remarked to him. He grinned at her, sensing that they would often share small jokes, treating each other like cousins, not employer and employee.

They talked about the overheads of the works, how much they must sell to cover the basic costs of keeping the soapery open.

As they left Mr Bobsworth's office, she said, 'I imagine that having a fox terrier like Mr Bobsworth barking at the heels of our mandarins saves a lot of waste?'

'It does,' he responded, though he did not sound very happy about it. 'It's also frustrating, because only Mr Benson can authorize any real change in expenditure. He's the Executor – and he tends to execute.' He waited for her to appreciate his pun, but she did not understand it, so he said, 'I think he simply wants the soapery to tick over until Probate is received.'

Or until I make up my mind, ruminated Wallace Helena fretfully. But what could a black man do in Liverpool? I've only to look at Alfie – the bottom of the pecking order here – to sense the prejudice. And I doubt if I could live in Liverpool without Joe.

Benji found it irritating to have her often at his heels; he was young enough to feel that she might criticize the orders he gave to the various employees, and it was certain that the men tended to stare at her when he was speaking, rather than attending to his instructions. He underestimated the enormous curiosity about her amongst them.

A couple of days after his first interview with her, he mentioned impatiently that old Bobsworth was, as usual, complaining because he, Benji, was about to run an advertisement for their toilet soaps in a number of local Lancashire newspapers. 'He says our female customers can't read, so what's the good of an advertisement? Let them tell each other how good our toilet soap is, he says. It's nonsense! A lot of women can spell out a newspaper. A sketch of a pretty woman and the words, "Your daughters need a perfect complexion. Use Lady Lavender toilet soaps" will draw their attention.'

Wallace Helena could not resist a small giggle. Then she suggested shrewdly, 'To keep the cost down, why not put it in two newspapers for several consecutive issues – you should be able to squeeze a better rate out of them for several advertisements. And see if sales improve in those particular districts. If they do, you could possibly persuade Mr *Benson* to agree to a wider series of advertisements, despite Mr Bobsworth's opposition. You're in charge of sales.'

'I know – but I'm only Assistant Manager. If Father were here, he'd tell him to stick to his bookkeeping. But with Father gone, Bobsworth tends to throw his weight around – though he means well.'

Wallace Helena gave one of her little whistles between her teeth. Then she said, 'Well, I'm not supposed to make any decisions until Mr Benson has finished probating the Will, but I'd back you, if you want to ask him to O.K. the expense of the advertisements. Make sure you've plenty of soap in the towns you choose, though.'

'Thanks. Advertising doesn't always have any sudden effect; it simply reminds customers of the name.'

'Well, I leave you to decide,' she said, and then brought up another subject. 'If I'm to sell soap and emollients, I should like to know more about English women. I really haven't met any since I've been here, except Mrs Hughes, my landlady.'

He turned to glance at her sallow, haggard face. Her remark brough home to him that she was not only struggling to understand his father's business, but a whole society which was alien to her. He put down the layout of his proposed advertisement, to give his full attention to her.

'Yes, of course. You don't know anybody, do you? Father had a lot of business friends and acquaintances. I doubt if he ever met their wives – who might have called on you. Mother's best friend is Sarah Tasker; they both know every woman living round them, but they're not the kind to make formal calls, any of them – though I think they'd make themselves known, if you were living in the same street.'

'Hmm. I've met Mrs Benson – but strictly between you and me,

I thought her dreadfully ignorant and stupid. And Mrs Hughes, who pries.'

He surveyed her carefully, a small twinkle in his eyes. 'I think you'd find most middle-class women total bores. I do.'

She looked relieved. 'It's nice of you to say that; probably I'm boring to them.'

'You're streets ahead of 'em,' he assured her firmly. 'Too much for them; they don't know how to cope with a woman as experienced as you are.'

Though he had, in his irritation at her constant presence, been rather short with her that day, she warmed to him. Her long lashes flickered, as she glanced obliquely at him.

He asked, 'Would you like to meet Mother?' His voice was uncertain, because, though she understood his mother's relationship to her uncle, she might strongly disapprove of it.

'Good God,' she exclaimed, and sat down suddenly on her chair. 'What have I been about?'

He was shaken by her unexpected response, and he said defensively, 'You don't have to, if you don't want to.'

She smiled at him. 'No. No. Of course I want to meet her. I'm so cross with myself that I did not consider her more. She must be feeling dreadful. Her loss is the greatest. And I've never thought about it.' She banged her closed fist on the desk and her rings flashed in the morning light. 'Mr Benson mentioned her in connection with the Will, but, if I thought of her at all, it was as a lady who would resent me so much that she would not *want* to meet me. Do you really think she would want to meet me?'

'Well, she's very curious about you, now she's got over the first shock of Father's death.' He sighed.

'Should I go to see her?'

He made a little face. 'I think it's usual for the resident lady to call on a newcomer.'

'Humph. Well, tell her I'd enjoy meeting her and ask her to let me know when it would be convenient for her to call. How's that?'

He grinned. 'I'll ask her,' he promised. It would be a much-needed diversion for his mother, even if the two women hated each other on sight.

Chapter Twenty-Six

Benji evidently went home to lunch that day, because in the afternoon he brought a pink envelope to her office.

As he waited expectantly while she ripped open the envelope, she smiled at him. Behind the smile, she was rather regretting the impetuosity of her behaviour that morning. Supposing the woman turned out to be a servile sycophant, bent on manipulating favours out of her for her son? And just how much could she trust Benji himself?

On pink notepaper decorated round the edges with improbable-looking small flowers, Eleanor Al-Khoury wrote in a large, irregular hand that she would be pleased to call at half past six that evening, after tea, and please to tell our Benjamin if that would be all right.

Feeling that she was already committed, she agreed to the visit, though she said, 'I've got a bad cold – I hope she doesn't mind.'

'We've all got them,' Benji reassured her, and, indeed, his own voice suggested a thick catarrh.

As he was about to leave the office, she asked him, 'Have you any brothers or sisters?' It had not occurred to her before that there might be a number of young Al-Khourys.

He shrugged. 'No. I don't think I've got any relations. Mother hasn't any – except she told me once that there were some cousins of hers in Wales; but I don't think she ever kept in touch with them. She was an only child, and her father left her the house we live in. And Father had no living relations, except your family.' He paused thoughtfully, and then said, 'So she must feel very lonely now – though I do my best for her.'

'I'm sure you do. You must've had a lonely childhood?'

'Well, I always had a few good friends. George Tasker's eldest son, for one – till he went into the army.' He fell silent, as he remembered the bullying of the local boys. They'd given him hell and called him Blackie, until he and Tom Tasker had grown big enough and ruthless enough to fight back to good effect.

Watching him, Wallace Helena guessed that the young man's passage had not been easy. She had been much despised herself, because she was thought, in her early days at Fort Edmonton, to be part Chinese and, when this was discounted, to be Jewish and, therefore, not someone anybody white wanted to know. Thank God for Joe and his Cree relations, she considered grimly. Without them, she would have been very lonely, too.

He was speaking again, asking a personal question suggested by her remark about his loneliness. 'Do you have help on your farm – someone you can leave it with? Bobsworth told me you had a big farm.'

She gazed at him thoughtfully, the long narrow eyes weighing him up once again. 'I've a partner,' she admitted cautiously.

'What will you do, if you want to stay here with us?'

'I don't know yet whether my partner would wish to continue managing it or would want to sell up. I'm awaiting his reactions to some suggestions I have made by letter.'

That accounted for her dilatoriness in making up her mind. He was relieved that there was a sensible reason for her slowness.

But in her heart Wallace Helena knew that if she was not in Edmonton and he did not want to come to England, Joe would take his horses and drift back to the south, perhaps into the United States, to peddle his expertise in warmer climates; he did not have Tom Harding's passionate love of the land; he loved only her.

And how could she desert him? Yet she was tired of the unequal struggle in the Territories, the hardship; her body had begun to crave the comfort of a civilized city. 'Tush, I must be getting old,' she muttered. 'Wait and see what Joe has to say. And, meantime, get on with the job here.'

Benji was turning to leave the office. She took a handkerchief from her sleeve and blew her nose hard, her goodbye somewhat muffled.

Chapter Twenty-Seven

Living in the same district, Mrs Hughes was well aware of the social standing of the self-styled Mrs Al-Khoury, and, when the unfortunate lady presented herself on Mrs Hughes's snow-white doorstep, she treated her with supercilious disregard, as if she had never seen her before.

Eleanor Al-Khoury was in full mourning. The opaque black veil of her widow's bonnet had been thrown forward, to shield her face from the gaze of the vulgar. In one black-gloved hand she held a black-edged handkerchief and in the other a worn black change purse. She told the landlady in a low voice that Miss Harding was expecting her.

Mrs Hughes kept the visitor standing in the hall, while she went to inquire of Wallace Helena whether she was at home this evening.

Rather startled, Wallace Helena replied in tones muffled by her cold that, as far as she knew, she was right here. Why?

'A woman wishes to see you.'

'Mrs Al-Khoury?'

'I believe she goes by that name.'

'Why didn't you bring her right in?' Wallace Helena demanded irritably, as she rose from her fireside chair. Mrs Hughes sniffed and, full of offended dignity, reopened the sitting-room door, and snapped, 'You can come in.'

Holding her handkerchief to her streaming nose with one hand, Wallace Helena held out her other hand to Eleanor and drew her towards the fire. 'Come in, Mrs Al-Khoury, close to the fire. You must be quite chilled – it is so damp outside.' She pushed her handkerchief into her waistband, and saw the visitor comfortably seated opposite to her own chair.

Immediately a little relieved by the fact that Wallace Helena had called her Mrs Al-Khoury, an indication, she felt, of acceptance as a member of the family, Mrs Al-Khoury sat down.

'Do take off your bonnet and gloves,' Wallace Helena urged, anxious to make the bereaved woman feel at home. 'Let me take them from you.'

At such kindness and condescension, Eleanor Al-Khoury felt she wanted to cry again. She carefully lifted the ugly bonnet off, and handed it to Wallace Helena.

A round, pleasant face was revealed, framed by puffs of light brown hair streaked with white. Deepset blue eyes looked red from weeping and lack of sleep. Though the round cheeks were a deep pink, the lines of the face spoke of exhaustion. When Eleanor peeled off her black cotton gloves, Wallace Helena noted that her hands had the same work-worn look as did her own, except that Eleanor's were bright red from frequent immersion in hot water and soda.

The visitor sat bolt upright in her chair, as a lady should. When Wallace Helena, smiling, sat down again, she returned her hostess's inquiring gaze without faltering. Then suddenly she bent her head and burst into tears.

In a moment, Wallace Helena was on her knees beside her. She put her arm round the bent shoulders and pleaded, 'Please don't cry. There's nothing to be afraid of.'

'I'm not afraid of you, luv,' the woman snuffled through her tears. 'It's 'cos everything's gone topsy-turvy, like – and I miss 'im so much.' She sobbed for a moment, while Wallace Helena held her and tried to soothe her. 'And it hurts so much that he never thought to leave me even a bit to live on.' Her voice rose to a wail.

'It was an accident, Mrs Al-Khoury; he simply did not expect to die for a long time yet. I'm told he appeared to be a very stalwart man.'

The straightforward use of the word *die* instead of a euphemism caused another paroxysm of grief, which Wallace Helena did her best to stem by suggesting a nice, hot cup of tea. She had been much amused by Mrs Hughes's prescribing tea for every ill; colds, aches, lack of appetite, headaches, all yielded to a nice cup of tea, according to the landlady. Nothing like it.

While Mrs Al-Khoury sobbed her thanks, Wallace Helena pulled the bell to call Violet May, Mrs Hughes's maid-of-all-work.

By the time Violet May had arrived and had been asked for tea and cake or biscuits, Eleanor Al-Khoury had begun to gain control of herself. To divert her, Wallace Helena asked her if she lived nearby.

'Oh, aye. I'm only a little ways away, round the corner. Me pa left me the house, and it's a godsend, it's bin. It's old-fashioned, but Jamie liked it 'cos it's close to the soap works.'

Wallace Helena asked how she had met Uncle James, and Eleanor told her the story of how, as a young immigrant, he had knocked on her door and asked if she had a room to let. 'And we went on from there,' she said more cheerfully. 'He were always so good to me – that's why I can't understand . . .' Her face crumpled again and she took out her handkerchief to hold it to her quivering mouth.

'He was good to me as well. When Mama and my stepfather died and I decided to go on farming, I asked if he could get me some books about agriculture in a cold climate. He sent me several very helpful books. He must have had to send for some of them from other countries – one was in French and two on botany were in Arabic.'

Eleanor stopped weeping and looked at Wallace Helena in great surprise. 'I didn't know that,' she said.

'I gathered from the lawyer that Mr Helliwell did the dispatching.'

'Oh, aye. He'd have all the boxes and wrapping paper he needed by him in the office. That'd be it.'

Wallace Helena nodded. She recalled with amusement that he had never mentioned either Eleanor or Benji in his covering letters to her. He had, however, given her the name of a friend of her grandfather, long established in Montreal. She had written to him to ask if he knew of any research being done on farming in Canada, and he, too, had been very kind. He had sent her two papers on sowing pasture and one on the problems of raising wheat in a short growing season.

As Eleanor droned on with the story of her life with Uncle James, Wallace Helena berated herself for not keeping in closer touch with her uncle. But the distance had been so immense that she was always amazed when a letter or a box actually did arrive from him. And often the daily life of herself and Joe had been so hard that it had left little time to think of anything except the next task to be done. But the books had been a wonderful help, especially one he had obtained on Russian farming.

Eleanor was saying, 'Me next-door neighbour told me I were mad to take in a foreigner what could hardly speak any English. But he sounded loovely.' She stopped, and then added with a shy smile, 'And he were loovely to look at, with the same nice smile our Benji has.' She clutched her handkerchief in her hand, and wondered how she could explain to this woman from the Colonies the particular, magical attraction of James Al-Khoury as a young man of twenty-two.

The stranger would have understood perfectly. Had she not fallen in love at the age of eighteen with a fine, six-foot-tall, black cowpuncher and horse-breaker, whose voice still held traces of the deep vibrance of his Zulu forefathers?

Without apology, Wallace Helena blew her reddened nose hard; she wondered if she had a temperature.

The tea was brought by Mrs Hughes herself. Though annoyed at having to provide it, she was not averse to intruding on the visit. It was disappointing that, apart from Wallace Helena's murmured thanks, the two women remained silent while the tray was arranged on a low tea table. Eleanor did not smile at Mrs Hughes, though she managed a stiff inclination of the head. Mrs Hughes acknowledged it with a slight nod, as she left the room disappointed at not being drawn into the conversation.

As Wallace Helena poured the tea and proffered biscuits, Eleanor continued her tale. 'Though 'is English never were that good, he could speak French and Arabic – and our Benji grew up with three languages. They'd talk away for hours in one lingo or the other, till I says, "Let's have a bit of English, so I can be included in."' She smiled at this reminiscence, and then sighed. 'Clever, he was – and so's our Benji. He insisted on bringing me buckets of coal up from the cellar, and it was there he saw me wash boiler, and got the idea of making soap – came to 'im out of the blue, it did. So I managed to keep 'im fed, while he got started.'

'So you really gave him his start?'

'I suppose. I haven't never thought of it. He were welcome.'

As Eleanor became more relaxed over her cups of tea, Wallace Helena listened and watched her carefully. She had learned in the hard world of Chicago, and had it confirmed in the Territories, that behind the most innocent face could lurk a convoluted mind capable of all kinds of perfidy. She wondered if mother and son had any plan to undermine her ownership of the Lady Lavender. She could not immediately think what benefit the Al-Khourys might get out of a scheme to unseat her, but she did not underestimate the power of angry, overlooked relatives.

Finally, Eleanor Al-Khoury became quiet. Then she broached a fresh subject.

'Our Benji says as how you would like to know how an English lady lives – bearing in mind soap, like?'

Wallace Helena nodded. 'I would indeed,' she responded. 'Canada is so very different.' She sighed, but did not elaborate. She dabbed her reddened nose, which was feeling very tender. 'I've been to Mr Benson's house – it was, of course, a formal visit. I didn't like to ask about their private use of soap!'

Eleanor laughed suddenly, her face crinkling up to show the merry person she usually was. 'Well, I don't mind showing you, as long as you'll take me as you find me. If you don't mind clouds of steam, you come along on Monday morning – I do me wash then. I'll have me boiler goin' long before you arrive, and we can sit a few minutes and have a cuppa tea before I start to scrub.' She paused to ruminate over this statement, and then went on, 'That's where most of the soap gets used. I use some of the soapy water, afterwards, to scrub the floors and the steps.'

'In summer we do *our* washing in the creek,' Wallace Helena confided, feeling on safer ground. 'We pound it on a smooth rock. In the winter, the creek's frozen over, so we have to do our best in a wash tub in the cabin – it gets put outside to dry, though, spread over the bushes. It freezes solid and yet it gets almost dry. Then we finish it off over a line inside.'

'It must be proper hard for you livin' out there amongst the savages,' responded Eleanor sympathetically, though, despite

186

her liaison with James Al-Khoury, her own life had been a hard one.

Feeling that she had stayed long enough, she rose to take her leave. She smiled down at Wallace Helena, and said, 'You've been proper kind to me tonight, and you so poorly with a cold. Would you like to come on Monday?'

'I would.' She rose slowly from her chair, as her visitor went over to the centre table to pick up her bonnet and then came back to the fireside to arrange it in front of the mirror over the mantelpiece. 'It's been very nice meeting you,' the Lebanese told her, remembering her manners, as she shepherded the visitor towards the door of the room.

In the hallway, before lowering her black veil over her face, Eleanor surprised Wallace Helena by standing on tiptoes and gently kissing her on her cheek, despite the likelihood of catching her cold. At the same time, she squeezed her hand tightly.

Then she turned and let down her veil, while Wallace Helena, smiling, opened the front door for her.

'See you Monday,' Eleanor said with false brightness.

'I'll look forward to it,' Wallace Helena promised, hiding her general unease.

After Eleanor had gone down the spotless front steps, the hem of her skirt making a soft plop on each step as she descended, Wallace Helena slowly shut the front door and, as quietly as possible, turned the key; she had no wish to bring Mrs Hughes from her back sitting-room to begin a speculative conversation in the chilly hall.

Back in her own sitting-room, she sat for a long time before the dying fire, reflecting on Benjamin and his mother. Would they, in their bitterness, become her most dangerous opponents? Eleanor was, according to Benjamin, a close friend of Mrs Tasker and Mrs Bobsworth, who could, in turn, influence their husbands. The two men and Benji could make it impossible for her to keep discipline in the works, though they probably would not go so far as to ruin the business – all three earned a living out of it.

She remembered, with a sardonic smile, that in Edmonton, nowadays, men were distantly civil to her, but when it came to business transactions, there were no holds barred. She wished Joe Black could have a look at the mother and son; like a dog, he would sense whether they were to be trusted or not.

Dear Joe. I want this soap works and I want you; *and* I need Benjamin Al-Khoury's managerial know-how. And I'm not too sure how to secure any of them permanently.

Chapter Twenty-Eight

Lying in bed that night, unable to sleep because of her cold, Wallace Helena began to feel once more the sense of desolation that had, from time to time, haunted her ever since her mother's death. It was born of the knowledge that, after Mama had gone, there was nobody left who understood what the massacre in Beirut had done to her, that her whole life had been ripped apart, her roots destroyed, all the kindly people that she had known in her childhood cruelly murdered, simply because they were a minority, a fairly prosperous Christian minority. She knew she should be thankful that she had escaped, not only the massacre but subsequent death from smallpox; yet, at moments like this, when other problems impinged and seemed insoluble, a sense of being punished for surviving hit her. Was she to be a foreigner, a strange one forever, like the Wandering Jew who had to live until Christ returned to earth, alone, unliked, distrustful of everybody and everything?

Usually, Joe could comfort her a little when such morbid fancies sent her to bed to lie shivering helplessly in a kind of Hades. Tonight, Joe was six thousand miles away, and she felt bereft of courage, deserted, left behind.

Towards the end of the night, she must have slept, because, when Violet May knocked on her door to say breakfast would be ready in half an hour, for a second she could not recollect where she was.

She answered the girl. Then she slowly dragged herself out of bed to bring in the ewer of hot water left outside the door for her by the servant. She ached all over, and her nose and throat seemed half-choked with the cold.

189

After washing in hot water, she felt better, and, scolding herself for being so self-pitying, she went down to breakfast.

When Mrs Hughes brought her meal in and saw her, she said immediately that Wallace Helena should on no account go out that day; the milkman had forecast more rain, and he was always right.

Feeling that she could not endure sitting all day in the gloomy, over-furnished house, Wallace Helena insisted on going to the Lady Lavender. She asked her landlady if, when she went shopping, she would buy her a couple of dozen more handkerchiefs, and she agreed to do this. Then, with unexpected solicitude, she ran upstairs to fetch four of her late husband's big handkerchiefs to use in the meantime.

Although she did not like Mrs Hughes much, Wallace Helena had to admit that she was being very kind, and she accepted the proffered hankies with gratitude. Though she was just as capable of blowing her nose through her fingers as the labourers in the soapery did, she had quickly learned, when she did it once in their presence and heard their subsequent amused remarks, that English women did not do this. She wondered how such women felt when faced with a lonely homestead, where every scrap of material was precious; she herself used her few handkerchiefs only when visiting Edmonton village.

That evening, she returned pallid and obviously worn out, her clothes soaked by a summer rainstorm which had swept up the river.

As Mrs Hughes relieved her of a dripping umbrella lent her by Mr Helliwell, she protested, 'Miss Harding, you *must* take care of yourself. You'll get tuberculosis, if you don't watch.' She took the umbrella from her and put it to drip in the basin in an adjoining wash room. Then she returned to help her lodger remove her sopping wet shawl. 'I'll dry it for you in front of the kitchen fire,' she promised. 'And you give me your wet boots as well.'

'Thank you, Mrs Hughes. I'll be all right. I'm used to rough weather.'

She was not all right; she felt dispirited and very tired. Though she was used to extremes of heat and cold, she was not accustomed to damp, the penetrating dampness of the gentle rains of

Lancashire. In her bedroom, she took out her hairpins and rubbed her hair dry; her hat, also, was wet, and she cursed, because she did not know how to hold an umbrella to best protect herself. She longed for hot sun and clear skies, and wondered if the sun ever shone properly in Liverpool.

When Mrs Hughes came up to assure her that the fire in her sitting-room was lit and blazing well, she asked her landlady if Liverpool ever had any fine days.

'Of course we do,' Mrs Hughes assured her. 'It's just not such a good summer this year.'

'Humph. My bad luck?'

Mrs Hughes looked amused, and said that if Wallace Helena liked to change her dress, she would get Violet May to press her present one dry. Although she was inquisitive and very snobbish, Mrs Hughes was not unkind, and she did not want her lodger to become seriously ill.

The younger woman hastily unhooked herself and handed the garment to her.

'You'd better change your petticoat as well,' the landlady advised, as she noticed the wet mud along its hem.

Dressed in a white blouse and a black skirt, Wallace Helena went down to her sitting-room and was grateful for the warmth of the fire in the wrought-iron fireplace.

Violet May knocked at the door and brought in a tea tray. 'The mistress says to have a cuppa, while you're waiting on dinner,' she announced, as she put it on a table by Wallace Helena's chair. She wiped her big red hands on her apron, and asked, 'Will I pour it for you, Miss?'

'Thank you, Violet May.'

Wallace Helena felt inside her placket pocket and brought out a packet of Turkish cigarettes. Alfie had brought them to her that morning, after she had complained that, with such a cold, she could not taste the cigarellos she had formed the habit of smoking. 'You might like to try 'em, Missus,' he said. 'They got a real, strong scent.'

Violet May watched, pop-eyed, as Wallace Helena put a cigarette in her mouth, took a spill from a brass container in the hearth and lit it from the fire. She put the light to the cigarette, then leaned back in her chair and exhaled a stream of smoke.

Suddenly remembering her duties, Violet May drained the contents óf the teapot into the flowered cup. As she leaned over to put the tea closer to Wallace Helena, she whispered conspiratorially, 'The Missus isn't goin' to like the smell of smoke, Miss; the Master always smoked 'is pipe in the back room. She sniffed around the other day, when she come in here. We thought as a heavy-smoking man might've called on yez from the works, and the smell of smoke on 'is clothes 'ad spread into the room. But I really knowed it was you, Miss, 'cos your clothes always smells of smoke when I irons them.'

With an amused glint in her eye, Wallace Helena turned to look at the girl. 'I never thought of it troubling Mrs Hughes, Violet May; I'm so used to smoking.' She looked careworn as she added, 'I simply have to have a cigarette tonight – I'm so tired. What shall I do, Violet May? She won't want me smoking upstairs in the bedroom.'

As Violet May handed Wallace Helena the sugar bowl, she swallowed uncomfortably. She knew the mistress needed the money from her lodger; she'd been proper hard up since the old man died. She rubbed her hands on her grubby white apron, and said hopefully, 'What if I open the window by you and then one of the bay windows? That'll make a cross-draught and clear some of it.' She looked anxiously round the room, and then added with a mischievous grin, 'I can shake up the bowl of pot-pourri on the table – real nice, it smells – it'd help to drown the smoke a bit.'

Wallace Helena laughed, and agreed. So she sat in the cool draught and enjoyed her cigarette with her tea.

'There's a letter for you,' Violet May told her, as she was going out of the door. 'It's on the hall stand. Will I bring it to yez?'

The weary woman in the chair sat up straight, flicked ash into the fire, and replied with alacrity, 'Please do.'

In his scrawling handwriting, the despair of the priest who had taught him, Joe reported the flattening of the oats in a brief hail-storm just before harvesting. The crop would be good only for animal feed. He had also lost a sheep, he thought to a cougar;

there were certainly cougar tracks near the fold. He had been trying to track it down. The sheep were more trouble than they were worth and, if she wanted to raise a big flock, she'd better bring a shepherd from Britain – and a trained dog. 'It's another mouth to feed,' he noted sourly. 'You should think about that.'

Though he signed the letter with love, the tone of it was unusually testy. She put this down to the loss of the oat crop; it did not occur to her that her letters to him had been full of the men she had met, the charms of the city, the money that might be made out of the soapery. Joe was feeling more than a twinge of jealousy and had already begun to worry that she might not return.

With the idea of raising money for more modern farm implements to take back to Canada, she had brought with her the last of her mother's necklaces and three rings to sell. She thought it highly likely that she could get a much better price for them in a sophisticated city, where they might be regarded as exquisite workmanship rather than so many ounces of gold and a number of stones.

Now, she began to fret that she and Joe might need any money she got for the jewellery, to supplement their living expenses the following winter; even if they agreed to sell the homestead, it would take time, and they would have to live through the winter.

The cost of her trip to England, with its concomitant need for respectable clothing, had drained the cash she had saved in her mother's trunk. Mr Benson had lent her funds against the Estate to cover her current living expenses. It was worrying, however, to draw money from the Estate, when the soapery would obviously need further investment in modern equipment, if the various staff she had talked to were to be believed.

Should she sell the Lady Lavender to help sustain the farm? Or persuade Joe that they should sell up in order to get investment funds for the soapery?

But would Joe even consider coming to England? She had asked him in a letter to which she had not yet had a reply.

The thought of Joe in a business suit and a top hat made her giggle. Yet you never knew with people. He sometimes complained that he was sick of winters; he might seriously consider her suggestion, particularly if they could buy some land near Liverpool – he might enjoy that. And she could run the soap works.

Round and round in her head went her longing to live in a civilized place – and have Joe, too. Alfie's sad face floated before her. Would Liverpool crush Joe like that? She thought not; Joe was much, much tougher – but it could be a fight.

She had another bad night.

Chapter Twenty-Nine

In comparison with Mr Benson's elegant home in Falkner Square, Eleanor Al-Khoury's house seemed small and dark. Dark green linoleum polished to a high gloss covered the narrow entrance, the hall and the stairs. Near the front door stood a branched wooden hatstand on which Eleanor hung Wallace Helena's shawl and hat.

Eleanor's sleeves were rolled up, to expose plump mottled arms, and she wore over her dress a large white bibbed pinafore. Over the pinafore was wrapped a thick striped cotton apron.

'Come in. Come in,' she cried hospitably to Wallace Helena. 'How's your cold?'

As she was ushered down the hall to the back of the house, Wallace Helena replied that the cold was not much better. 'It'll go away soon, no doubt.' In fact, her chest felt badly congested and she had coughed steadily during the night.

'This is me kitchen-living-room,' Eleanor told her, as they entered a pleasant, cosy room with a big window facing a back yard. Under the window was a yellow sink with two shining brass taps, and beside it a wooden drain board. A large iron stove took up most of one wall; it had two ovens at one side and the fire was big enough to hold two iron kettles side by side. From the ovens came a distinct odour of mutton being stewed. A steel fender protected the hearth.

Against another wall was a table covered by a dark red chenille cloth which reached to the floor. A vase filled with dried flowers stood in the middle of it. Three dining chairs were tucked round the sides of the table, and much of the rest of the room was taken up by two easy chairs on either side of the fireplace. Over the mantelpiece hung two large amateur watercolours in mahogany frames, which Wallace Helena supposed were portraits of Eleanor's parents. Two small photographs in metal frames stood on the mantelpiece and immediately drew Wallace Helena's attention. 'Why, that's Uncle James!' she exclaimed, touching the unsmiling face with her finger. 'And this must be Benji when he was a little boy – in a sailor suit!'

Eleanor came to stand by her. 'Oh, aye,' she agreed. 'I got a nicer one of Jamie in me bedroom. Took about four years ago. I told him I wanted one of him smiling for me birthday – 'cos it were natural to 'im to smile and laugh a lot. I must've had a feelin' he wouldn't be with me that long.' She gave a long sobbing sigh, and turned away without saying anything about Benji's picture. 'Come and sit down, luv.' She gestured to one of the easy chairs, and Wallace Helena obediently sank into the collection of patchwork cushions which nearly filled it. 'I were just goin' to slice me soap for the boiler when you come. If you don't mind, I'll finish it afore we have a cuppa.'

Wallace Helena said she should go ahead exactly as she usually would. She remarked that she thought the picture of Benji was delightful. They talked desultorily about the peccadilloes of little boys, while Eleanor spread a piece of newspaper on the table and proceeded to shred up a bar of soap.

'What are you going to do with that?' Wallace Helena asked.

'I'll put 'em in the hot water in me boiler downstairs, and they'll melt. Then I'll put the clothes in and boil 'em. Then I'll scrub the clothes on me washboard and rinse 'em. I'm hoping it won't rain today, so as I can hang 'em in the yard to dry.'

'A lot of work,' Wallace Helena said.

'Oh, aye. Me gentlemen keep me busy. I got three, and then there's Benji. It makes a lot of shirts and sheets. I'm ironin' most of Tuesday.'

'Gentlemen?' queried Wallace Helena.

'Yes. I do for three gents. One has a bedroom and the front parlour, and the other two is younger and they have a bed-sitter each. I make a bit on them to keep the house goin', like. Our Benji's real good. Ever since his dad died he give me housekeeping in addition to the bit he always gave me for his own food. But letting the rooms makes it easier to manage.'

196

'Do you cook for them?'

'Oh, yes. Bed, board and laundry is what they get.' She smiled suddenly. 'I look for decent young fellas, and they often stay with me till they get married. Of course, I gave up for a good many years, 'cos Jamie were doing well and there were no need. But I've bin real thankful these last few months that I had the house and could go back to takin' gentlemen.'

'I'm sure you have.' Wallace Helena's voice was sympathetic; looking at the worn face and roughened hands of the woman at the table, she felt a sense of guilt.

The sliced-up soap smelt awful, and Wallace Helena was reminded that Mr Lever was putting citronella into his bar soap to drown its natural odour. Two can play at that game, she considered grimly. Perhaps they should put a splash of lavender into the soap she was responsible for. She made a mental note to talk to Benji about it.

'Do you get free soap from the Lady Lavender, since Benji works for us?' she asked. It was a loaded question.

Eleanor answered innocently, 'Well, you know, there's lots of bars as don't get cut quite neat; or they get dropped on the floor, so they look dirty. But it's still decent soap. So the men take it home to their wives. Benji brings me a bit regular.'

'I see.' Wallace Helena sounded so noncommittal that Eleanor paused in her slicing to look up at her. 'It goes with the job,' she said a little defensively.

'I understand.' Wallace Helena made another mental note; this time to check on theft, which she had felt from her quick checks on the inventories might be more widespread than was tolerable. She would have to walk lightly, because she saw the common sense of allowing the men to have stuff which was definitely unsaleable. It was possible that the Cutting and Stamping Room was being deliberately careless. In slums even faulty soap could be sold; all kinds of goods had been available in the back streets of Chicago, she remembered grimly.

Eleanor was again giving her attention to the soap. She hoped uneasily that she had not told Wallace Helena something that Benji would have preferred to keep from her. 'There,' she said, and put down her knife while she carefully gathered up the soap

197

chips into the newspaper. 'The water in the boiler downstairs must be hot now. Would you like to come down with me?'

Wallace Helena smiled and followed her hostess down the worn stone steps to the cellar. It had been stiflingly hot in the living-room and she hoped that the cellar would be cooler.

She found herself in a dank, windowless room lit by a kerosene lamp hanging on the wall. It was half divided by a partial wall; the furthest section held coal which gleamed faintly in the light. Nearer them, in one corner in a whitewashed area, was a steaming copper built of brick and clay; under it lay an iron grate protected by a perforated iron door; through the perforations, Wallace Helena caught a glimpse of glowing coals. The copper itself had a loose wooden lid over it. Nearby were two rough wooden tables, obviously well scrubbed. On one table were several heaps of damp, wrung-out dirty clothes; through the steam Wallace Helena could smell the odour of men from them.

Eleanor took the lid off the copper and sprinkled her soap chips into the heaving water. 'I always add a bit of soda,' she said, as she picked up an old earthenware marmalade jar and poured a little of its contents into the water. She then stirred the water with a pair of wooden tongs. She picked up a pile of white shirts and dropped them in, stirring them around and lifting them up with the tongs until they were thoroughly wet.

'There, now,' she said cheerfully, 'we can leave that for a bit, and go and have a cup of tea.'

'Will they come out nice and white?' asked Wallace Helena, in an effort to make conversation.

'By the time I've finished, they will,' Eleanor assured her. 'I'll put bleach in the second rinse. Then I rinse 'em again with blueing. And finally I rinse that out. With me sheets and tablecloths, I don't scrub 'em; I put them in this tin bath and I dolly 'em, after I've boiled 'em. Give 'em a couple of rinses, dollying them again, and that's it. I put everything through the mangle in the yard, before I hang it out – gets rid of any dirty water in it, better'n hand-wringing.'

Since Wallace Helena had never seen a dolly or a mangle, she was gravely introduced to the dolly in the corner of the cellar. It looked to her like a three-legged stool attached to a spade handle, and Eleanor showed her how she lifted it up and down and half twisted it to pound dirt out of a bath of clothes. The mangle standing in the yard seemed quite new. It had two heavy wooden rollers, but the rest of it was iron and was beginning to rust. 'Benji keeps the wheels oiled for me, but I've got to watch I don't get the grease on me clothes. He sometimes turns the mangle for me, if he can get home for lunch on Mondays, 'cos it's heavy work – though not so hard as hand-wringing sheets.'

Wallace Helena thought of the fast, perfunctory wash done on her farm, and asked, 'Is it necessary to work so hard?'

Eleanor looked at her as if she had queried the existence of God. 'Oh, aye,' she affirmed without hesitation. 'The clothes get filthy in the town, and my gentlemen work in offices or shops, so they have to be well turned out. Mr Jenkins wot has the ground-floor front changes 'is collar twice a day – not that I do 'is collars – I send 'em out to a woman wot does nothin' else.'

'It must take you all day to do so much.'

Eleanor sighed, and then said with a wry grin, 'It does. I put everything to soak the night before, and I were up at half past five this mornin' to get the boiler lit and the first load in afore I started breakfast for me gentlemen. And afore I go to bed tonight I'll get Benji to help me pull and fold me sheets and tablecloths ready for ironing. And I'll use the nice soapy water from the copper to scrub the kitchen and the bathroom floors.'

Wallace Helena glanced down at the kitchen-living-room floor; it was made of stone flags and had rag rugs under the table and near the fireplace. She decided she preferred to have to work outside, despite bitter winters or broiling sun. Her respect for Eleanor grew, as she realized the appalling amount of work the woman did.

She was grateful for a strong cup of tea and a piece of pound cake before she left. 'I do me cakes and pies on Fridays,' Eleanor confided. 'I used to bake me own bread when Jamie was alive, but lately I haven't had the heart, so I buy it.'

As the two women were going down the passage to the front door, and Wallace Helena reached for her hat, Eleanor said, 'You should take a mangle and dolly back to Canada with you, when you go. They'd save you a lot of work.'

Wallace Helena nodded. It was possible that by now she could obtain such worksavers in western Canada; the railway had suddenly made everything possible. She answered Eleanor circumspectly, though with a smile. 'I haven't yet decided whether to go back to Canada or not. I may stay here.' She was anxious that any idea that she *must* sell the soapery be dispelled; such gossip would not improve the price she would get if she did have to part with it.

Eleanor looked taken aback. 'What you goin' to do with it? You couldn't run it yourself.'

'I believe I could.'

'But you're a woman!'

'Women can do anything they set their minds to.'

'Well, I nevaire!' Then Eleanor's eyes twinkled. 'Good thing your uncle can't hear you.' Then she looked sad. 'He didn't like women going to work.'

'I wonder if he believed they didn't work at home? You work crushingly hard.'

'I don't know, luv.' She picked up Wallace Helena's shawl and wrapped it round her shoulders. 'Now, you take care of yourself, luv, with that cold. You've coughed quite a bit this morning; you should stay home today.'

'Thank you very much, Eleanor,' Wallace Helena said with feeling. 'You take care of yourself.'

'I'm all right, for sure. Now I must go and start me coloureds and me woollens. I haven't done nothing about them yet.'

Chapter Thirty

Wallace Helena went back to Mrs Hughes's house for lunch, but, after Eleanor's pound cake, she only picked at the sausage, mashed potatoes and peas, followed by cold apple pie, which Mrs Hughes regarded as a light lunch.

As she drank a pot of tea, she reviewed carefully many of the things that Eleanor had mentioned. Cheap soap, she had said, had filler in it – fuller's earth or sand – and it was not much good if you wanted a clean wash. She had also told her that she kept her supply of soap on a shelf for weeks to harden it, because it then didn't melt so quickly and she got a better lather. Was the latter true? If so, how long did the Lady Lavender keep its soap in store? Did Mr Lever store his soap for long?

It seemed clear that the Lady Lavender would have to sell on quality and low price, to stay in business. She wondered if the patronizing Mr Turner had ever tried to deduce exactly what was in their various competitors' soap – it could be interesting to know. Mr Turner seemed a bit of a luxury for such a small firm, despite what Benji had said about him; she would put him to work.

That afternoon she discussed some of her ideas with Benji, and particularly asked him straightforwardly about theft.

He confirmed his mother's remark that the men were allowed to take soap that was, in some way, not fit for their customers. She suggested that the system be tightened up and that the handling of the finished soap should be more carefully supervised, so that it was not deliberately made unsaleable.

He chewed the end of a pencil, while he considered this, and then he said, 'I don't think it's out of hand yet. But it could be happening, if you say the inventories are not too accurate. The business has grown so much in the last three years that we need to look at the organization of the staff and the chain of responsibility. I haven't had time to do a thorough inventory for eighteen months.' He put his pencil into his top pocket and took out a handkerchief to mop the perspiration off his face. Though the stiff office window had been prized open by Mr Helliwell, on Wallace Helena's instructions, the room was still uncomfortably warm, and the smell of the fats and the oils and the boiling, together with that of manure, drifted unpleasantly round them.

Wallace Helena closed her eyes. Her head felt heavy and her chest hurt every time she coughed; for once, she was not smoking.

She said slowly, 'As soon as we get Probate – Mr Benson says it will be a few weeks yet – and we're free to really manage, we'll look at the whole staff situation in the light of what we intend to produce – and we'll look at the long term – new machinery, and so on.'

'So you'll stay here? Have you heard from Canada?'

'Not yet. But I intend that if we have to put this place up for sale, we get the best possible price for it – and the best arrangement we can for the employees. And we can only do that if it looks like an excellent purchase.'

'Of course.' She was talking sense, but he wished the uncertainty was over. He was tired of being asked persistently by worried men if he knew what was to happen.

She was feeling exactly the same. The tug-of-war between what she wanted to do and what was possible was getting her down; and now she was so full of cold that she felt downright ill.

As the days moved into weeks, Wallace Helena got impatient at the length of time Probate was taking. Mr Benson assured her that it always did take time; she was not to worry. During August, she began, bit by bit, to take control, regardless of the fact that she did not yet own the firm. Mr Benson seemed to be glad not to be bothered with day-to-day problems, and arranged that Mr Bobsworth and Benji could jointly sign cheques under a certain value. She was careful to consult Benji or Mr Bobsworth as she took her first steps in management; and the company began to function better.

The bad cold which she had had left her with a hacking cough, which was not improved by her smoking. She ignored it. She was feeling the change in her lifestyle very keenly. As the summer wore on, the damp heat and the polluted air seemed stifling. If she opened the office window, her desk and papers were rapidly covered with black dust, and the collar on her dress was grey before evening came. After the dryness of the Territories, the humidity of the Lancashire climate made clothing and bedding feel damp to her. To her surprise, she began to appreciate the pristine blue skies and the strong sunshine of her faraway homestead.

She also found the food unsatisfying. After years of eating her own beef and pork or wild ducks and moose brought in by Joe, she thought it tasteless. Even a plate of Aunt Theresa's beaver tails would have been welcome.

Yet both the city and the soapery fascinated her. Encouraged by a friendly Eleanor, Benji introduced her to the pleasures of the music hall and the theatre. Eleanor would not go herself; she said it was too soon after her husband's death to consider it. Anxious to foster the relationship between her son and Wallace Helena, she did, one Sunday, accompany them on the ferry boat, to New Brighton, where they walked along the shore and ate a picnic lunch; it was a relief to Wallace Helena to find brisk, clean breezes and an open space to walk.

Another time, Benji took her to a concert in St George's Hall and for the first time saw her overawed. 'It's so beautiful,' she cried, and she sat spellbound as the mighty organ was played by the City Organist, Mr W. T. Best. Nothing would please her until he took her again, and she wrote ecstatically to Joe about it.

'I've never heard such music,' she told Eleanor, her face alight.

In Benji's eyes, Wallace Helena improved on acquaintance. He reckoned she must be close to forty, but she could be so light-hearted and enthusiastic that you'd never know it, and it was street lore that an older woman was more interested in you, because she was grateful for a sex life. He began to think seriously of marrying her. He was aware that under a fairly recent law about married women's property the soap works would not automatically become his on marriage; nevertheless, he took it for granted that, in practice, he would be in charge of Lady Lavender if he married the owner – women always deferred to men.

His own sex life had been somewhat limited. His father kept a close hold on him, because he wanted him to marry a Lebanese. He had, however, met young women at church social events, and had been out on the town with young Tasker a sufficient number of times to be acquainted with the ladies of Lime Street.

On her part, Wallace Helena was amused by him. Though she was ignorant of English marriage laws, she knew it was not simply cousinly solicitude which had sparked so much attention, and she awaited events with detached interest. She was also very lonely in Liverpool. Not only did she miss Joe as her lover; she missed him as a close companion with whom she could freely discuss anything. Despite her growing trust of Benji, he was a poor substitute; he was too young, though indubitably very capable. She wondered idly what he would be like in bed; she had never slept with anyone but Joe. She decided the boy would probably be charming, like his father had apparently been, and she then dismissed the matter. She was not going to mix business with pleasure.

One close bond the couple had: after Eleanor's remark that he spoke both Arabic and French, Wallace Helena spoke to him daily in Arabic, and was delighted to find that he understood the subtlety of it, although he was not acquainted with any of its poets – or with Middle Eastern music. Wallace Helena's English, though adequate, was not nearly as good as her native tongue, and the bond of a common language grew between them.

When she was alone in the evening and the day was fine, she occasionally walked in the park or in the centre of the city. At other times, she sat in her high-ceilinged, gloomy sitting-room and read books culled from her uncle's office shelves on various aspects of soap-making, and one or two on factory planning and management. Without chemistry and without personal knowledge of other great industries in the north of England, she sometimes had difficulty in understanding what she had read. At such times, she would either consult Benji or seek out Mr Turner or Mr Tasker and ask them to clarify the text for her.

Mr Tasker was, by far, her favourite. 'Without a good product to sell, you can't do nothing,' he once said, mopping the perspiration from his face with a large, red-spotted handkerchief. 'And good soap begins with good ingredients. And that's me first task – to check on the incomings.'

'What about Mr Turner, the chemist?'

'Oh, aye. Mr Turner can analyse and tell you what he reckons is in a barrel of tallow. But he don't allow for fiddles.'

'Fiddles?'

'Aye. Like when there's a bit o'summat inferior at the bottom, and such. Pass something like that and you've clarified it before you know it int up to snuff. Meself, I go and stand over an open barrel and I smell it – careful, like. I can tell you right off, when they're tryin' to fob us off with somethin' inferior.'

He did not explain who *they* were and she presumed they were the butchers and farmers who sold their surplus fat to soap makers. She was amused when he finished his remarks by a long slow sniff, as if to demonstrate the power of his nose.

She also felt a sense of trust growing between her and dapper Mr Helliwell, who was already betting to himself that she would be his new employer, after Probate. She knew that he had been aware, before her arrival, that Wallace H. Harding was a woman. He knew, because he had packed up and posted the books sent to her by Uncle James. Yet, since Mr Benson had not seen fit to mention her sex, even to Benji, while he was checking that he had tracked down the right legatee, Mr Helliwell had apparently maintained absolute silence on the subject. As he had once said to her, Mr James's business was confidential; if anybody knew about it, Mr James had told them himself. 'And you, Miss Harding, may be sure of the same confidentiality.'

Wallace Helena intrigued him. Seeing her each day at her uncle's desk, sometimes at bad moments coping with the many problems which inevitably arose in a small business, he felt that she would deal fairly with him and the rest of the staff, possibly better than a man would. And, like old Mr James, she was interesting.

Like Mr James, she swore and bullied, and he was fairly certain that anybody wanting a rise in pay would have to ask for it more than once; she obviously knew the value of every penny.

Again, like her uncle, she showed signs of being quite human. He had, each year, treated the whole works to a picnic on New Brighton beach, and he had made himself pleasant to their wives and children. When Mr Helliwell had ventured to inform her that, owing to Mr James's untimely death, the picnic had been cancelled, she had sat thoughtfully, her chin cupped in her hand, and then suggested, 'Perhaps we could clear enough space in the factory, somewhere, and have a Christmas party – with dancing – instead.'

Mr Helliwell assured her that it was a splendid idea. She had, however, asked him not to mention it to the staff until a firm decision had been made about the future of the Lady Lavender, and he had bowed and again assured her of his complete discretion. He did, however, assure the wheelwright, when he wanted a day off to attend his father's funeral, that she was a very human lady, and the man should go into the office and ask her.

When the request was immediately granted with a few words of kindly sympathy, Mr Helliwell was secretly triumphant that his belief that she belonged to the human race had been confirmed.

When she dictated a note to Mr Bobsworth, carbon copy to Mr Benjamin, saying that the man's wages for the day of absence were to be paid, he ventured to remark that it was just what Mr James would have done. 'Mr Al-Khoury very rarely had any trouble with labour, Miss Harding. Like you, he was compassionate towards the men's genuine problems. Once a man had a tally from the company, he did his best to keep him in work – even when we weren't doing very well. He knew everybody he employed by name – more than many employers do.'

'What's a tally?' It was the first time she had heard the word.

'Oh, hasn't Mr Benjamin mentioned them? Perhaps the need for giving one out has not arisen since you arrived. It's a tin tag that a man can produce to show that he's worked for us before. A decent, sober man, once he's taken on, we like to keep him. If business is so slack that we have to lay him off, he'd be the first to be taken on again – before any stranger.'

Wallace Helena nodded. Her father's firm in Beirut had treated casual labour in the same way, most particularly in connection with those, however humble, who could be considered related to the family. She wondered irrelevantly, as she looked up at her hovering secretary, whether any had survived the massacre. From stories she had heard from one or two other refugees who had followed them to Chicago, it would seem unlikely; the massacre had been horrifyingly thorough.

She said, 'I noticed that most of the men had a small metal disc pinned to their jackets or overalls. Is that the tally?'

'Yes, Miss Harding. It's a quick way for the supervisors to spot an intruder. If he's not wearing a tally, he's immediately stopped and asked what his business is with the company.'

'Do you know if the men are worried about what is going to happen to them in the present situation?'

'Well, naturally they will be. Unemployment is rife in Liverpool.'

She stubbed out the cigarello she had been smoking and rose, preparatory to going back to her lodgings for lunch. 'Perhaps I should talk to them,' she said.

'They might appreciate it, Miss Harding.'

'Hmm. I'll speak to Mr Benjamin about it.'

Chapter Thirty-One

Bidden to an informal meeting with their new mistress, the foremen and department heads crowded towards the door of Wallace Helena's office. One or two of them made sly jokes about now owning a mistress, until Mr Tasker overheard them. Incensed, he reminded them that she owned them, because their jobs depended upon what she decided to do. Immediately sobered, they slid through the door of the office, to find the lady sitting at their old master's desk, enveloped in a cloud of tobacco smoke. At their entry, she quickly stubbed out her cigarello and rose to face them, looking tall, angular and forbidding in her high-necked black dress.

As the men came in, they took off their caps, and when they were all assembled, she surveyed them carefully. Most of them looked middle-aged or over, some of them almost purple from years of exposure to rough weather; others were pasty-faced from too long hours indoors. Many of them shuffled uneasily, and only Mr Tasker and the Steam Engineer looked self-assured, probably because of their highly marketable skills. At the last moment, Mr Bobsworth entered and shut the door behind him. He felt a little resentful that he had not been asked to stand by Wallace Helena at the meeting. Young Benji was there, just behind her. Why not himself?

She began to speak, reminding them that she had already met most of them when she first arrived, and that she had realized that the sad passing of Mr James Al-Khoury had caused a crisis in all their lives – and in her own. They must be worrying about their future.

The word *crisis* caught their attention and her understanding of their own uneasiness about their jobs impressed them favourably. She went on to explain the matter of Probate which was holding up a final decision on the future of the works. The Executor of the Will could have sold the soapery immediately, but he had consulted her and she had decided not to sell at the moment. She would use the time before the Court granted Probate to learn all she could about it and then make a decision when the Lady Lavender became her absolute property. Not all of them understood what Probate was, but they had seen Mr Benson about the place and knew he was a lawyer, so they assumed it had something to do with him. At least they now knew why there was such a lack of information about their future. The woman had not yet made up her mind; women never did know what they wanted.

Until then, not even Mr Bobsworth or Mr Tasker had been given an explanation as to why the Lady Lavender had not been sold; their questions to Benji and to Mr Benson had not been answered. Her lack of decision did not give them peace of mind, but at least they now knew that, once Probate was granted, a decision would be made.

Wallace Helena was continuing. She said, 'In the meantime, I want the soapery to proceed with its usual efficiency. There are a few matters which we can currently address, the main one being the neatness and cleanliness of the plant and the yards.'

The face of the Transport Manager darkened. The stables came under his jurisdiction and he had been reprimanded for the laziness of his staff. Alerted by Wallace Helena, Benji had delivered a very stiff lecture. The stables were now mucked out daily.

Wallace Helena went on to say that each of them was to look at his own area and see where the labourers had failed to clean up. 'Get rid of rubbish,' she ordered. 'I myself slipped and nearly fell in the tallow yard, for example. It is to be scraped and sanded and spills mopped up as they occur. You know very well that some of the materials we use are hazardous, lye, for instance; and grease can cause a disastrous fire if we get slack, which will put you all out of work.' She paused, and looked again at the faces before her; some appeared sullen.

She resumed her speech, her tone a little lighter. 'I cannot alter the circumstances under which you work until the legal process is complete and we can look at the final balance sheet. But I understand that you have no proper place to brew tea or eat your noon meal. If I decide to undertake the management, this is one of the first things I wish to provide: a clean, decent room where you can eat and make tea. I suspect, also, that there is need for better immediate care for any of you who have an accident here.

'I see from correspondence that Mr Al-Khoury had in mind to begin some form of contributory pension for his people. I hope that we shall, in future, have regular meetings together to discuss such matters. Meanwhile, it is important not only that the Lady Lavender continue to do business successfully, but it should *look* successful, and a works that is as neat as a pin gives a good impression. After all, we're selling cleanliness! I want it clean! If I have to sell it, a smart-looking outfit is less likely to be closed down by a competitor buying it out.'

Some of the men grinned at her little joke about selling cleanliness, but the yard foreman lifted his hand and said sulkily that he was short of a labourer and did not know who to ask about it. 'Mr Benjamin not always being here, like.'

Wallace Helena looked up at a silent Benji. He certainly was away from time to time, since he was supervising sales. She turned back to the foreman, and ordered him to call in a man holding a company's tally as a temporary labourer and to give his name to Mr Bobsworth for the wage sheet. 'I'll discuss with Mr Benjamin whether the position will be made permanent. Meantime, pay him the casual labourer's rate.'

Mr Ferguson, the Steam Engineer, ventured to ask if she expected to actually run the works herself, if she did not sell it.

'For the moment, Mr Benjamin will deal with the day-to-day problems, as usual. If he is away, come to me. In the longer term, you will be the first people to be told my final decision. Our lawyer tells me that Probate should be granted within a matter of weeks now.'

With a dawning feeling of confidence in her, as she stood in front of them with as much presence as any man, most of her employees smiled slightly. Nobody else ventured a remark, however, so she dismissed them politely, after reminding them to take their problems to Mr Benjamin as they arose.

As she sank into her chair again and reached for her cigarello, Mr Tasker lingered behind.

She looked up at him. 'Yes, Mr Tasker?'

'I wanted to say, Ma'am, that it's not surprising that the men get a bit confused. Mr Al-Khoury was his own Plant Manager, Mr Benjamin having his own areas of command, like. Since Mr James passed away, Mr Bobsworth, Mr Ferguson and even Mr Turner've got into the way of giving orders outside their departments, and the foremen don't know for sure that that is what you want or who they should obey – especially if the orders is conflicting.'

'Blast!' She drummed her fingers on the desk, and turned to Benji. 'I'll make it clear that you make the decisions and report to me later. On the days when you have to go somewhere, the men are to come to me and I will tell them who to go to or what to do. I presume that all the men who were here today know what decisions they can make themselves within their normal departmental duties?'

George Tasker answered immediately. 'I think so, Ma'am.'

'Then I'll talk to Mr Bobsworth, Mr Turner and Mr Ferguson. I'm sure they've simply been worried and tried to fill in for the late Mr Al-Khoury during the present hiatus. We'll soon get straightened out.'

Mr Tasker smiled down at her, touched his forelock and went back to work. Real chip off the old block, she was. And he was glad she was bringing forward young Benji. Could be worse things happen. He began to whistle.

Chapter Thirty-Two

When Mr Tasker had gone, Wallace Helena turned and grinned at Benji. 'Come and sit down,' she invited. 'We must do something about keeping Bobsworth, Ferguson and Turner in line – stop them interfering in other departments. Any ideas?'

Benji shrugged and sat down. 'It depends on how much Benson is agreeable to our doing. He's still the Executor.'

'Well, he's been in once or twice to see how I'm getting on. He seems content to leave me to it, now he knows me better. He's warned me not to be extravagant in anything I do personally or in connection with the Lady Lavender – there are taxes and legal fees yet to be paid which could be quite a burden, if I want to keep the soapery.'

Benji laughed. 'Old Bobsworth was moaning that you are almost too careful. I think you've been a revelation to him. You didn't even pass all my Manchester expenses without query!'

'Sorry.' She bit her lower lip and smiled roguishly at him. Then she said, 'The problem is that you're away some of the time, looking after sales, and I'm still feeling my way – besides which I don't want to be bothered by day-to-day decisions, as I am beginning to be.' She picked up a coffee cup from her desk, saw that it was empty and rang for Mr Helliwell to bring two fresh cups. While he went to get them, she continued, 'My feeling is that you should be here all the time and that we should try to find a top, full-time salesman to take your place, somebody we could also consult about wrappers and advertising, someone who knows the soap trade.'

'Even on commission, such a man could be expensive. I think you're right, though.'

'Would it suit you? Or do you want to be a representative full time?'

'I hate selling. Father gave it to me to gain experience, so that I would have some knowledge of every department. Now we've got to face much more intense competition, we need a first-class man like you suggest. I'd be much better in the office; I can keep a tight hand on the organization of the staff and the buying, and so forth.'

With fresh coffee in front of them, they went on to hammer out exactly how to proceed. They concluded that Benji should cost out roughly what a full-time sales manager could expect, with the idea of recruiting such a man as soon as Probate had been received and taxes paid.

'He could cost a fortune,' Wallace Helena said nervously. Then, more bravely, she admitted that the challenge of Mr Lever had to be met.

To bring the old employees into line and stop them giving orders where they had no business to give them, Wallace Helena said she would send out a memo to all supervisory staff confirming Benji in his position as Assistant Manager responsible for day-to-day management and that, in his absence, she herself was to be consulted. 'If Bobsworth and the others don't take note of the memo, I'm not past firing them,' she said fiercely. 'Only Mr Tasker is absolutely irreplaceable at present, as far as I can see.'

'It won't come to that,' he assured her. 'The foremen will tend to come to me.' He got up and strode to the end of the room and back, then he added frankly, 'They expected me to take over immediately Father died – and I didn't. Backed by your memo, it'll seem natural to them to come to me.'

Wallace Helena suddenly had what Benji called her Mona Lisa look. Watchful eyes and a tight small smile made him regret his frankness. Looking at her seated in his father's chair, resentment flared in him once again. Because of a narrow, old-fashioned quirk of law, she was queening it in an office which should have been his.

As he stood up and collected his papers, preparatory to going back to his own small niche of a room, he raged inwardly. He was not suffering because he had quarrelled with his father or because his father thought him incapable. On the contrary, everything pointed to the fact that he was being trained to take his father's place when the older man had had enough. He cursed his father's blithe belief in his own immortality.

She had not responded to his last remark. She simply sat waiting for him to go, her long, weather-beaten hands, with their heavy, ugly rings, spread out before her on the battered desk.

Before turning towards the door, he nodded farewell, and she looked up. 'Cheer up,' she told him, her mouth softening a little. 'We'll both do well out of the Lady Lavender before we've finished. It's a tight little ship, as Mr Bobsworth says.'

Startled, he stopped in mid-stride to the door. Was the damned woman a thought reader, as well?

She chuckled, but did not say anything more.

His face like a thundercloud, he did not answer. It took all his self-control not to slam the door after himself. She could laugh, if she wanted; he could not.

Chapter Thirty-Three

As a result of the meeting which Wallace Helena had called in her office, it now became public knowledge that their new, female employer smoked in the works, as Alfie, the labourer, had said she did. The graffiti on the enclosure round the rough earthen lavatories in the corner of the yard consisted largely of pictures, since most of the men could not write; the drawings now featured a bosomy female with a cigar in her mouth.

Because of the acute danger of fire amid fatty substances, an employee found smoking had traditionally been immediately dismissed. Now, the men began to resent the rule; if the Mistress could smoke, so could they.

While waiting for a delivery van to be loaded or unloaded, the carters began to light up their clay pipes. The yard foreman demanded that they knock them out, and, when they became impudent about it, he threatened them with dismissal. This had the desired result; they grouchily put them away.

The threat had no effect on a grizzled old labourer, Georgie Grant, who had been steadily employed by the company since its inception.

'Herself is smokin', int she?' he inquired loftily of the foreman. 'Why can't I?'

'You should know – because of fire, you stupid old bugger.'

Georgie lifted his chin, thick with snowy stubble. 'Don't you go callin' me names. If the Mistress can smoke here, I can,' he responded stubbornly, and heaved a wooden box into a waiting van, his pipe firmly between his few remaining teeth.

The foreman controlled his seething temper. 'Now look here, Georgie. I don't want to fire yez. You put that pipe out for now, and I'll ask Master Benji if the rule is the same as always.'

Georgie took his pipe from his mouth and turned to look at his superior. He grinned. 'Not the Mistress?'

The foreman wanted to hit him. 'Mr Benji'll do the talkin' to her,' he replied through clenched teeth.

Georgie looked down his bulbous red nose at the foreman. Then very slowly he took a tin lid from the pocket of his fustian trousers and held it over the bowl of his pipe to dowse it. A mere woman was not going to tell him when he could or could not smoke, unless she obeyed the rule, too. 'Aye, you ask him,' he said with patent satisfaction.

Feeling that the threat of dismissal would probably quench Georgie's thirst for equality, the foreman did nothing. Whiffs of tobacco continued to be easily detectable in the yard and the stables.

Caught between an old, respected employee and a new, untried employer, the foreman gave up and went to see Benji. Ould James's bastard *ought* to have been the new master; he'd give sound advice.

Benji was seated at a crowded, high desk in his office, a tiny room next to the laboratory. The office was walled with clear panes of glass through which he could supervise much that went on in the works. He was in the midst of dictating letters to Mr Helliwell, when the foreman knocked and came in, doffing his cap as Benji lifted his head from his work. Seeing the worry on the man's long, hatchet face, he asked, 'What's up, Will?'

The foreman explained the recalcitrance of Georgie Grant. He ignored the silent Mr Helliwell.

'You don't want to dismiss him, do you?'

'Georgie? 'Course not, Sir. He's makin' a point. First, he don't like workin' for a woman and, second, if there's a rule it's for everybody, includin' Miss Harding. He don't approve of a woman smokin', anyways.'

Benji badly wanted to grin. He could visualize the monkey face of the old labourer, who had been born and brought up on the Earl of Sefton's Estate and would not have been afraid to tell a belted earl what was acceptable in an earl's behaviour. A soap mistress would be small fry in comparison.

'I doubt if Miss Harding has realized the danger of fire. I'll talk to her about it. Tell Georgie from me that there'll be no more smoking in the yard. If he disobeys send him up here.'

'Yes, Sir. Thank you, Sir.'

Benji slowly took off the paper cuffs he used to protect his shirt wrist bands and put on his jacket, to go to see Wallace Helena. Fire was too serious a matter to delay action.

'She's down in the Crutching Department,' Mr Helliwell told him, as he resignedly closed his notebook.

'Blast!' exclaimed Benji, and Mr Helliwell looked at him with closely pursed lips.

He finally ran her to earth as she watched the stamping of Lady Lavender soap tablets with the company's name on one side and what was meant to depict a bunch of lavender on the other side. Behind her, two boys of about sixteen were busy wrapping the tablets in a rough, greyish paper which they closed with a bright, painted sticker showing a reasonable facsimile on it of a sprig of lavender surrounded by the name of the company.

She did not think much of the imprint on the soap, and, when Benji approached, looking rumpled and a trifle harassed, she addressed him before he could open his mouth.

'The soap looks messy,' she said, petulantly tossing a tablet up and down in one hand. 'I think we put too much colouring in it – and couldn't we make it look shinier? And the paper it's wrapped in is so dull. No wonder Mr Lever used bright yellow.'

Normally Benji would have agreed with her; new packaging and finish had been under discussion just before his father's death. Today, however, he resented her criticism, particularly when he had a much more basic problem, that of fire, to discuss with her.

'Leave this,' he ordered. 'I need to speak to you in the office.'

The young man in a white apron who was doing the stamping looked up and raised one eyebrow suggestively towards the other lads placidly wrapping tablets not far away. Ears pricked, they waited for the Mistress's response.

She looked coolly at her cousin. He had no right to speak to her like that in front of junior employees; it could destroy her authority. She replied with asperity, 'I'm busy. I want to see the next few bars go through the stamping machine – Dick, here, has just adjusted the machine slightly, to see if we get a clearer stamp. I'll see you in the office in about half an hour.'

Benji's face darkened. He was equally sensitive to a slight to his authority, and it was his job to see that the finished product was marketable. He said angrily, in Arabic, 'Let it wait. I'll check it later. This is a matter of safety, and we must act quickly on it – before the place goes up in smoke!'

'Smoke?' she queried in the same language.

'Yes. Fire!' he snapped back.

'Very well.' She turned and said, with a smile, to the three young men concerned, 'We'll look at it again, later. For the moment, continue as before.'

Head held high, she swept out of the department and towards her office, a fuming Benji having difficulty in keeping up with her. Mr Helliwell in his tiny office scampered from his wooden filing cabinet to open the door of her office. She went through without so much as a nod of acknowledgment and Benji, like a rolling thundercloud, straight after her. Very thoughtfully, Mr Helliwell went back to his filing, and listened to the rising voices in the inner sanctum. He wished they would speak English.

The fear of fire temporarily forgotten, Benji was raging. 'If I'm the Assistant Manager in charge of day-to-day matters, why can't you leave me to manage? I know we need new stamping machines – we're going to need new everything before long!' He hammered on her desk with his fist, while she stood waiting for him to finish. He straightened up and shouted, 'And it's your job to plan what we're going to do in future. Where we're going to raise money. How we're going to meet competition – rabid competition in a slumping market, in case you don't remember it!'

The moment he stopped for breath, her reply came out in a menacing hiss. 'I have not forgotten anything,' she said. 'But you seem to have forgotten that I own this soapery – or will in a week or two. And, therefore, I will decide what I need to know before I begin to plan. And who will manage!' The last words came out in a threatening snarl.

He was immediately sobered, feeling that his livelihood was in jeopardy, though suppressed mortification made him tremble.

He stepped back from the desk and stared across it at her. He'd get another job as soon as he could, he promised himself.

She glared back at him. Then cold common sense flooded back into her, as she realized his humiliation. She had gone too far. She needed this man; it would not be easy to replace him, because it seemed likely that her large competitors would be able to offer more to such an employee.

Unhesitatingly, she apologized. 'I'm sorry, Benji.' Then she smiled. 'We must learn never to be angry with each other in front of the men. My partner and I always fight it out privately.'

He was still hurt to the quick. She walked round the desk and laced her hand into his. He did not grasp her fingers, but he did not withdraw his hand either. She bent towards him and gently kissed his cheek. 'Come on, Benji. I'm cousin-sister, remember. We can say things honestly to each other – privately. Sit down and tell me what it was you wanted to see me about. You said something about fire? Have we had one?' She was still holding his hand and sensed that he had relaxed slightly. 'We need each other.'

He remained a picture of wounded dignity, though he sat down.

She was suddenly smitten with a spasm of coughing, convulsed with it, unable to get her breath. She leaned against the desk to steady herself, clutching her chest as if to ease a pain. Benji leaned forward and poured a glass of water from the carafe on the corner of the desk, but she could not steady herself sufficiently to take it from him.

Concerned, he got up and put his arm round her back and held the glass to her lips. She took a tiny sip, swallowed it and then another, which made her splutter. She got her breath and made a big effort to swallow more. Gradually the spasm reduced and he led her to her chair. She sat there silently, breathing deeply, until she was a little recovered. Meanwhile, Benji pressed the bell for Mr Helliwell and told him to bring a hot cup of tea with plenty of sugar in it.

Mr Helliwell had heard the frantic coughing and needed no explanation. He hurried out to his gas ring.

Benji remained standing by her. 'You must stop smoking until that cough's gone,' he told her. 'Mother said you coughed a lot last time you visited her – she thought you ought to see a doctor.'

'Mrs Hughes was lecturing me about seeing a doctor, but I'm moving from her house tomorrow to a more airy place. I hope it may settle the cough. The wind blows straight off the river and there should be less smuts to irritate my throat.'

'Where are you going?'

'It's called The Cockle Hole – it's like a village by the water, next to the Coburg Dock.'

'Oh, I know it. Do you need any help?'

'I'll give Alfie a tip to carry my bags down; I don't have much.'

He nodded. Her need for help while she coughed had deflected his thoughts from his own distress; it had put him momentarily in command and he felt better.

Mr Helliwell brought in a steaming mug of tea and smilingly put it in front of her. She thanked him and dismissed him.

While she slowly sipped the sickeningly sweet brew, Benji sat down opposite her and explained about Georgie Grant.

'I think you must, for safety's sake, stop smoking in the plant. And let it be known that you have. I don't want to fire people like Georgie. He's as honest as anyone I'll ever find. Besides, he's been here all my life, very nearly.'

She did not miss the point that he considered that he had the right to hire and fire men in her soapery, but she felt it unwise to say anything so soon after their bitter row.

She said wearily, 'I've smoked for years. Joe brought me the kind of tobacco the Indian women smoke – and it's different from this stuff.' She pointed to the wooden box in which her cigarellos lay.

'Whatever you smoke is going to cause trouble,' Benji said. 'I enjoy a pipe – but I never smoke here.'

Her hands clasped round the mug of tea, she considered his remarks and saw the wisdom of them. She smiled ruefully, and said, 'I'm not sure how I'm going to survive. I was aware of the fire hazard – you heard me demanding that the works be cleaned up, largely because grease and straw can catch so easily. And I've fought prairie fires in my time. I imagined the office was far enough away from everything – that it would be safe to smoke.'

Benji made a face. 'It probably is, but the men would resent you having the privilege.'

'Hmm. I'm their Mistress!'

There she was again, emphasizing that she had the last say. He was no longer angry with her; he felt instead a terrible sadness, a sense that his father had discarded him, leaving him at the mercy of an eccentric woman.

He made an effort to appear conciliatory. 'If you continued to smoke and the men could not, they might try to get back at you. Liverpool men can be very pig-headed when they're angry; they've got their own ideas of what's fair. Though times are hard and they wouldn't want to lose their jobs, they could be obstructive. You've no idea how stuff could be inexplicably lost; they can forget to deliver verbal messages; horses would cast a shoe in the middle of a busy morning; a spoke fall out of a wheel. Once or twice when Father fell foul of them, all this happened. They can send management nearly out of its mind!'

'Really?' She began to laugh, until her cough recommenced and she hastily stifled her amusement.

He smiled. 'You ask any ship's officer,' he said. 'They'll tell you.'

'All right,' she said. 'You can tell Georgie that I have stopped smoking – in the soapery.' At the same time, she wondered if Benjamin considered himself a Liverpool man and was warning her that he could bring down the soapery if he wanted to.

Chapter Thirty-Four

With Alfie's help, Wallace Helena moved to The Cockle Hole. Later that evening, encouraged by Eleanor Al-Khoury, Benji called on her to see if she was comfortable.

The door was answered by a young woman in the late stages of pregnancy. There was none of the formality of Mrs Hughes. The woman wiped her hands on her apron and said, 'Come in, Sir.' She opened a door to his right and called, 'You've got a visitor, Miss.'

When Benji entered, he found his cousin standing by an open window looking onto the river. White curtains billowed in the breeze.

'Would you like a fire made, Miss? John'd do it in a tick,' the woman asked Wallace Helena.

'No, I'm warm enough, thank you, Elsie.' She turned to Benji and said, 'This is Mrs Fitzpatrick. She cooked me a beautiful fish dinner.'

Benji bowed to the blushing young woman, who smiled, and said, 'It were nothing.' She closed the door softly, as she went out.

Benji looked round the austere little room. Its whitewashed walls and bare, scrubbed floor gave a sense of coolness and space. A rag rug by the empty fireplace and cretonne-covered cushions on a pair of rocking chairs gave a touch of colour. A plain wooden table and two chairs stood under the open casement window, through which he had a view of the river. Another table with a single chair tucked under it held Wallace Helena's books and papers, not yet put in order, and an unlit oil lamp. Additional light was promised by two big brass candlesticks sitting on the mantelpiece, each with a large, fresh candle in it.

Wallace Helena sat down in one of the rocking chairs and invited Benji to take the other one. As he sat down, he told her that his mother was very tired after a day's baking, and that he had persuaded her to go to bed early. She would come to see her on Sunday afternoon.

'I'm sure she needs the rest; she works very hard.' She wondered if Benji had told her about the row they had had, and whether she had sent him to mend his fences. She told him she would be delighted to see his mother, anytime, and then said, 'Elsie was going to bring me a tray of tea, so she'll probably bring an extra cup.'

He nodded. Because of the fight they had had, he was not sure what to talk about. Yet, for his own and his mother's sake, a truce must be declared. She had offered him the chance last time they had spoken, and on the surface they had parted amicably. Inwardly, he had still been boiling with rage, and he guessed that she had realized it.

Finally, he cleared his throat and, for want of anything better to say, inquired how many rooms she had.

'I've two. I've the bedroom above this room. It looks out on the river, and there's a window-seat to sit on to watch the ships going to and fro. It's got a washstand – and Elsie has promised me as much hot water as I want. There is a water closet in the yard. It's all very simple, but I like it – and it is very quiet.'

He nodded. It certainly was peaceful and the air was fresh.

'I think I shall enjoy Elsie and her husband, John. They're unpretentious – unlike Mrs Hughes.'

He did not know Mrs Hughes, but her address was enough to suggest the type of woman, and he could understand that Wallace Helena might find the atmosphere in her old rooms oppressive.

He had had an argument with Eleanor over the need for this visit. He simply did not want to face his cousin for a little while. His mother had said, however, that one of them should go down to The Cockle Hole to inquire if she were comfortably settled. In her anxiety to keep on good terms, she had said desperately and almost in tears because her feet were so swollen from long hours of standing, 'Well, if you won't go, I must.'

Because he knew how very tired she was and could see her feet bulging along the edges of her shoes, he had given in. She had said he ought to take some flowers; but the only flower shop was closed, so she had pressed upon him a bottle of lavender from the soap works, wrapped in crumpled tissue paper. He now presented the little parcel to his cousin with apologies for the lack of flowers.

She was pleased. She had handled the sample bottles in the soap works, but had not thought of taking one for herself. Now she unscrewed the bottle and shook a little of the scent onto her wrist. Immediately the small room was flooded with perfume.

She inhaled luxuriously. 'It smells sharp and sweet at the same time – like citrus fruit.' She glanced up from sniffing her wrist, and her voice became wistful. 'You know, I miss the smell of the orchards in Lebanon. Oranges, lemons, apricots – they all smelled so lovely.'

'I've never seen them, of course,' Benji replied a little stiffly. 'Mother's got a mock orange blossom in the back yard. It's got a nice smell. When girls we know get married, they beg bits of it to make wreaths to hold their wedding veils.'

'What a charming idea.' She put the stopper back into the scent bottle. 'You've never thought of getting married, Benji?'

She had rarely asked a personal question of him, and this one made him more uneasy than ever.

'No,' he said, and then, feeling that he should give some explanation of the single state of a man of twenty-five, he said, 'Father wanted to find a Lebanese girl for me, and I wasn't too keen.'

'He'd have a long search in England, I imagine?'

'There are a few, I suppose.'

The advent of Elsie with the tea tray saved him from further questioning; she had brought a dish of hot, buttered scones to eat with the tea.

Wallace Helena busied herself with serving him, and then sat down again herself. She began to cough, and hastily put her teacup down in the hearth, in case she spilled some of its contents. It was not such a violent spasm as the one she had suffered in the office. When it lessened, she dabbed her lips with her handkerchief and picked up her cup again.

Her mind had obviously continued to run on the subject of marriage, because she said chattily, 'I've never married myself, though once a Cree Indian asked my stepfather for me. Tom had to be very diplomatic about turning him down – because we live outside the Fort we could be attacked very easily by anyone feeling disgruntled! I have quite a number of Cree friends now.' She went on to tell him of the sufferings of the Indians round her. 'My partner is half-Cree, and his relations come to call from time to time.'

'Must be an interesting man,' responded Benji, feeling an unaccountable pang of jealousy, despite his resentment at Wallace Helena's treatment of him.

'He is,' replied Wallace Helena. Then she said thoughtfully, 'I've written to ask him what he feels about my taking over the Lady Lavender; whether he would like to buy my share of the homestead.' She was lying because she felt suddenly embarrassed at having brought up Joe in a conversation about marriage; she had, after all, only asked Joe whether he would like to come to Liverpool. If he came, then it would be possible to sell their holding and he could invest his share in an English farm, if he felt like it. She fumbled for her handkerchief.

'I don't think, really, that he would want to run the farm by himself – there is too much work. But it's cleared and yielding well most years, so we could probably sell it to an immigrant – a few of them have money to invest.' She stopped to dab her nose, which was threatening to run, and Benji tried to visualize her life in Canada and what kind of a man her partner was.

She tucked her hankie back into her waistband, and then said she thought that Joe might like to consider moving to England and buying a farm, because the winters would be much less severe.

She leaned back in her chair and closed her eyes. The letters she had written to Joe suggesting that he should move had been difficult to compose, and she was sure Joe would think she was quite mad.

Benji said thoughtfully, 'Good farm land is costly in Britain – in spite of the depression.'

'Well, Joe was with my stepfather when he first squatted on

Hudson's Bay land, so I mentioned it as another option he could consider.' She did not say that she had not mentioned the option of her return to the Territories; she wanted to live in a decent city or near one – with Joe by her side. In truth, there was little hope of his deciding to leave Canada; but she clung to that slender thread – he just might like to try something new.

Apprehensively, Benji asked if her partner would ever consider working in the soapery. He was relieved when she answered, 'Not him. He's an outdoors man, through and through.'

'Do you really like Liverpool?' Benji inquired.

Her face lit up. 'Yes, I do. I understand the kind of problems we face in the Lady Lavender – but, believe me, doing business here seems less trouble than in the Territories – despite Mr Lever!' She had opened her eyes, and she saw his astonishment at this remark.

She grinned, and then told him what a bitter struggle it had often been to stay alive and provide for themselves on Tom's land. Now that they had surpluses to dispose of, they constantly pursued Government contracts to feed the Indian tribes round about. 'We watch, like lynxes, for news of surveyors and other travellers passing through – they need supplies to continue north or west. I try to find out who is expected at the hotel or the Fort; I even made the acquaintance of the man who runs the telegraph office, because he often gets news first!'

For the first time in his visit, Benji relaxed a little and laughed. He could well imagine her striding in where other women would fear to tread. She had the same drive as his father and himself.

Wallace Helena picked up her teacup and drained it. 'You know, when I set out from Canada, I never expected to find you here. I knew Uncle had fathered a child – but since he never mentioned you or your mother in his letters to me, I assumed your mother had left him and taken her baby with her; I'm told it's common enough. I imagined him living alone, except for some kind of housekeeper.' She paused to reflect for a moment, and then said, 'Mr Benson didn't mention you either.'

'In the circumstances, I don't suppose they would.' He fidgeted uncomfortably.

'You mean because Uncle didn't marry your mama?'

'Yes.' There was a world of bitterness in the single word.

'Tush! People cohabit for all kinds of reasons,' she responded briskly, suddenly acutely aware of her position with regard to Joe. They'd never even discussed marriage. Isolated, and with no intention of having children, they had not thought it mattered.

Benjamin looked down at the painted wooden floor, his expression grim and disillusioned. His situation certainly mattered to him, Wallace Helena realized. She examined him curiously in the light of the setting sun glowing through the window.

His eyelids were darker than those of English people she had met, the eyebrows heavier and smoother. His newly clipped hair was like a black satin cap on his big head. His hands, loosely clasped between his spread knees, were wide and stubby-fingered, the hands of a heavy, powerful man. When she had seen him walking about the soapery, he had given every indication of self-assurance and incisive confidence. Only when she asked stupid questions, she told herself, did he show the hurt man beneath.

He did not reply to her last remark, and, when the silence began to be painful, he lifted his eyes to look at her. Though his face was more youthful than hers, she had, once more, a feeling of looking in a mirror and seeing herself slightly distorted; they both bore lines of suffering and had the same air of cynicism and disillusionment.

'You've had a rough time, haven't you?' she asked gently, as if trying to reach out to him. 'Was it because your parents weren't married?'

'Of course. Marriage is very important here,' he replied with sarcasm.

'I suppose it is,' she agreed reluctantly. She got up from her chair and went to the side table to get herself a cigarello. As she lit it, she turned and inquired, 'Have you ever asked Mrs Al-Khoury *why* she didn't marry Uncle James?'

He was shocked. 'You can't ask a parent a thing like that! You don't mention such things – at least, not in this society, you don't.' He spoke in English and, as a Liverpudlian, he muddled up his negatives in his confusion. 'Actually, I thought Father

227

must have a wife in Lebanon, perhaps an arranged marriage when he was very young?'

'No. He was not married in Lebanon. But I don't see why you could not ask your mother. You're obviously very fond of each other, and you're grown up. I could ask Mama anything.'

Benji gathered up his scattered wits, and said diplomatically, 'You must have been unusually close, being a daughter.'

'We were very close. We went through a lot of terrible things together, she and I. She was wonderful under the most appalling circumstances.' She took another puff at her cigarello, and said absently, 'I miss her very much.'

Benji's father had said to him once that his sister-in-law was one of the most charming women he had ever seen. He said, 'Father was upset when he heard how she had died – smallpox! Poor lady! A terrible death!'

Wallace Helena felt her eyes prickle, as if she were about to cry. She swallowed hard and tried to control herself.

Noting her struggle, Benji said with compassion, 'I'm sorry.'

A tear ran down his cousin's sallow cheek. She nodded her head as if in disbelief, as she told him, 'It was horrifying. Afterwards, I stopped believing in God! The God for whom we had endured persecution had abandoned us. Mama and my stepfather – and Joe – suffered such agony – and each of them had already endured so much hardship in their lives.' She sounded savage, as she went on, 'If God exists, He is infinitely cruel.'

Benji had never thought very much about a deity. As a child, his mother had taken him to an Anglican church which they still attended fairly regularly, though she had once let slip that she had been born a Catholic. Early in his life, he had noticed that she never took Communion and, later on, he learned that she could not, because, as a neighbour's son told him scornfully, 'She lives in sin, she does; and me mam says you're a bastard.'

He sighed. It had not occurred to him, until Wallace Helena had mentioned it, that his father had been hounded out of Lebanon solely because he was a Christian. God had not been very kind to him either. Perhaps that was why he had never been known to attend a place of worship; he had always occupied his

Sunday mornings by checking the Lady Lavender account books and entering any profits in his private book, which he kept at home.

Wallace Helena had seated herself again in her rocking chair, her head leaned back against the cretonne cushion. Her cigarello dangled in a listless hand as a second tear slowly ran down her cheek.

Benji watched it. She looked very different from the assertive woman who had offended him so badly that morning. Whether he could bring himself to marry her was doubtful. But she was his cousin-sister and they had both let down their guards tonight, as if they were, indeed, siblings who could talk frankly to each other. He got up clumsily and went to bend over her and put his hand on her shoulder. 'Would you like to walk a little in the fresh air?' he asked, not sure what to do to comfort her. 'You might feel better outside.'

She put up her hand to touch his. 'Yes,' she said.

Chapter Thirty-Five

As Wallace Helena and Benji paced slowly round the cobbled square outside the Fitzpatricks' cottage, they discussed frankly the future of the Lady Lavender. It was as if during their slow conversation in the cottage, in which they had said very little, they had succeeded in communicating a great deal on a different level.

Benji had not forgotten the arrogance she had displayed during their hectic day, but he knew now that he could offer her something more than good management of the soapery. He could offer her an understanding and tolerance of her aggressiveness and arrogance; her tears had brought home to him forcibly the overwhelming hurt of the loss of her homeland and the subsequent loss of her father and mother, who had, in the alien world of North America, given her some tie to the country of her birth. Her description of the hardships of the first years in Canada had secretly appalled him, and even now it did not seem too easy; no wonder she was enjoying Liverpool, despite the rainy summer they had had. He was glad, for her sake, that September had brought more sunshine.

He had, as he grew more aware of his father's origins, caught glimpses in the man of the same terrible sense of isolation that being a refugee engendered; he knew there had been days when even his patient, cheerful mother could not console him. When his father found himself at loggerheads with a businessman born and bred in Lancashire and, therefore, having a different approach to whatever they were trying to negotiate between them, he would go out and walk for miles in the streets of Liverpool. When his frustration eased, he would return, sometimes late at night, tired, but himself. Eleanor and Benji would not comment on his absence but would cosset him with warmed slippers and the particular coffee, thick as creosote, which he liked.

It was late and the moon rose, but still they walked together, and Wallace Helena was grateful for the gentleness in his voice and the warmth of his presence; it was different from the comfort that Joe gave her because it was less easily defined. It had something to do with the soft Arabic phrases that he used and with an occasional gesture he made which was evocative of his father, when she had known him as a young man.

He did not attempt to court her in any way, for which she was grateful. He stuck firmly to the subject of the business in which they were both involved.

'I've been stewing over what we should do,' he told her. 'I'd like to suggest that, once we're up and running again after Probate, we should concentrate, first, on retaining and extending our market for soap. It's our bread and butter. Keep up our quality and speed of delivery – and go for a narrow margin of profit.' He put his hand under her arm and guided her down the slipway until the water nearly lapped their feet. The moon laid a pathway across the river and anchored ships looked like dark hulks on either side of it. Then he said, 'This assumes you're not going to sell.'

'Yes?' she queried, sensing he had not finished.

'Turner reckons that he now knows exactly how George Tasker gets such good soap. The next job – a bit further down the road – would be to reproduce it mechanically with consistent quality. Not that we'd ever want to get rid of George. No matter how good machinery is, there's no substitute for a good soap master watching it.'

She looked up at him thoughtfully. 'Are you afraid he's getting old?' she asked.

'Yes. He's older than Father was, and we'd be in deep trouble if he were ever ill – or, worse still, passed on.'

She saw the danger immediately. 'Aren't the men under him any good?'

'They know their jobs. But it's George who has a feel for soap. Without him, they'd be lost. Lever has two of the best soap masters in the business, but I'm sure they wouldn't want to leave him; I'm told they rule the roost there. Crosfield's have some good ones – they're right next door to him.'

'Really next door?'

'Yes. That's why he can't expand where he is; there's no space. Mr Benson said someone representing him was sniffing round our place, to see what room there was for expansion if they offered for the Lady Lavender.'

'Is there room to expand, if we wanted to?'

'Not really. I'd like to keep the operation small; maybe make better use of the floor space, but not try to become very big. It's not easy to raise capital in these depressed times, and we're debt-free at the moment. The way we run the Lady Lavender, our over-heads are low, and we can go for a lower priced market, if we're not too extravagant when getting a sales representative.'

'Could we choose a new employee to follow Mr Tasker – say, let him choose somebody himself?' Wallace Helena asked, shaken by the idea that they could lose their most important employee.

'He wanted his son to follow him, but he went into the army instead. We've never tried for an apprentice since then.'

They forgot their inner sadnesses, as they tossed ideas backwards and forwards in rapid Arabic, with an occasional English sentence to express a technicality. Three fishermen sitting cross-legged near the slipway mending nets shrugged and laughed surreptitiously at the strange couple; middle-class people were not often seen in The Cockle Hole.

Wallace Helena saw the point of Benji's caution in not launching any new products for the moment, though her suggestion was that, when they did, they should offer emollients, based on glycerine, as the beginning of a line of very cheap cosmetics. 'So many women work, in Lancashire,' she argued, 'and you your-self said there's more money in working-class households nowa-days. If they've got a little money to spend, the young ones will want to make themselves pretty, like the ladies in the shows you've taken me to.'

'They'd be afraid of censure if they used paint; their fathers would probably beat them if they did!'

'I realize that. That's why I said we should begin with creams to soften or heal the skin.'

'In time, in time,' Benji assured her.

She coughed, holding her hand to her chest to ease the pain. Then, when it passed, she managed to chuckle. 'It's good that you're here to restrain me; Joe always says that I want to do everything at once. He's suffering with my efforts to raise sheep at present – my latest idea.'

'When do you expect to get an answer from him about what he wants to do?'

'Soon,' she replied. She did not say anything more. Once his reply was in her hand she would have to make a choice, and the thought made her heavy-hearted.

The fishermen spread their nets over an upturned rowing boat, and stood around lighting their pipes in the cool moonlight. Though Wallace Helena seemed to have retreated into herself, Benji had in the quietness become aware, from the warmth of her beside him, that he had a woman on his arm, a woman still young enough to be desirable. He turned to her, lifted her chin with his free hand and kissed her on the mouth. It was a longing kiss, his tongue searching to open her mouth.

She broke away from him, immediately alert and teasing. 'Benji, you scoundrel! That was not a cousinly kiss!'

Behind them, the fishermen laughed. A little mortified, Benji did not attempt to follow it up, and she caught his hand, and said, to his utter surprise, 'I'm spoken for. You go find yourself some pretty young thing. Now walk me to the door.'

Dumbfounded, he did so and answered her cheerful goodnight with a bewildered 'See you tomorrow.'

Chapter Thirty-Six

While she waited for a reply from Joe, Wallace Helena continued to probe into the soapery. She was careful not to spoil her newfound freedom with Benji by failing to consult him. Though intrigued by her as a woman, he made no further sexual approach, being cautious about touching her in any way. He reluctantly assumed that she was committed to her Canadian partner.

She again visited Eleanor, and was taken to a local stone-mason's yard, to see the marble cross which was being carved as a memorial to be put on her uncle's grave. Eleanor wept over it, and Wallace Helena tried to comfort her.

She had a long conversation with Mr Turner, who, this time, was less patronizing. She asked him particularly to describe to her any new technical advances in the soap industry of which he was aware. He confirmed the need for an experienced soap master, no matter what machinery was eventually installed. He was flattered when, after listening to him for an hour, she asked him to sit in on a meeting with Mr Tasker that she and Benji proposed to have, where, amongst other matters, they would discuss the need to train an understudy for the soap master.

He looked at her curiously. She appeared to have understood his explanations of the approaching changes in methods of manufacture, and, since he was, like everyone else, a little apprehensive about his position, he asked shyly, 'Do you propose to stay with us, Miss Harding, or will you sell out?'

She answered him as she had done when at the meeting of the staff in her office. 'I'm not sure yet, but you will be one of the first to know my decision. It should not be more than a few weeks at most.' She smiled, as she picked up her notebook. 'Be patient a little longer. If I sold, I would do so on condition that all my senior employees are accommodated with the new company.'

His anxiety somewhat relieved by her last words, he bowed her out of his laboratory. He had no real desire to be absorbed into a larger company, where he would probably be outshone by more brilliant German chemists, and he hoped the Lady Lavender would continue. He smiled as he put on his white laboratory jacket. No lady would ever run a company, so Benjamin Al-Khoury would run it – a capable, forward-looking man of his own generation with whom he got on well.

Wallace Helena had, quite early in her visit to the soapery, felt that a full-time chemist was rather a luxury in such a small soapery, and had wondered why Uncle James had recruited him. It did not occur to her that her uncle might have been a little dazzled by other soap merchants employing well-known German chemists. Not being able to afford such exotic creatures himself, he had found an intelligent man with a modest B.Sc., who, in a depressed economy, was thankful for a respectable job testing the ingredients and the end products of the Lady Lavender.

Though Turner was not a Ph.D., and was, therefore, not a true research man, he was quick to understand the research of others and he read everything he could find on soap technology. He liked and respected Mr Tasker and listened patiently to his explanations of the need for a sense of smell and the delicate interpretation of exactly what was happening in his great cauldrons, when the well-sniffed-over ingredients were put together. In between his routine duties and his experiments with glycerine, he had sketched a design for a mechanized line for soap production. A good working chemist, Turner felt, should be able to reduce Mr Tasker's magic *feel* for soap to an exact recipe. Quite soon, machinery would make possible a constant flow of evenly mixed and formed bars of soap; and he discussed these possibilities with Mr Ferguson, whose alert and inventive engineer's mind sometimes ranged much further than his precious boilers and steam pipes. Mr Ferguson had done his apprenticeship in Manchester and was still a member of a Mechanics' Institute there. As he often said, he knew what was going on, because he had friends with whom he kept in touch, remarks which would have gravely disturbed other soap-makers, who were doing their best to hide any of their advances in technology from their competitors.

The Steam Engineer always made himself a can of tea to drink with his sandwich lunch, which he ate at an old desk in a corner of the shed which housed his boilers. Sometimes, Mr Turner would drop in to share a mug of tea with him. Mr Ferguson always set great store by the visits.

When Mr Turner mentioned Wallace Helena's talk with him, Mr Ferguson said earnestly, 'Other soap companies are on to mechanization like you'd nevaire believe. If there's anything left of the Lady Lavender by the time the lawyers and Miss Harding are finished with it, you and I should get together with Mr Benji right away.'

Unaware that she had been mentally dismissed by two of her more important employees as a minor aberration in the life of the Lady Lavender, Wallace Helena walked along busy Sefton Street to her lodgings in The Cockle Hole, for lunch.

She felt tired, and her chest hurt when she coughed. As she walked, she wondered idly if Mr Turner could, some time in the future, make anything of her mother's beauty recipes. Her mother had had her own little mixtures for enhancing her looks, though, once she was married to Tom and had moved to Fort Edmonton, she had not had much time to use them. In Canada, she had used lamp black as kohl for her eyelids, instead of antimony. It had certainly made her eyes look enormous and had enhanced their glitter.

Wallace Helena wondered if she could ever sell kohl to Lancashire women, and decided regretfully that, from what she had been told about them, she probably could not.

Better to do as Benji advised, and stick to making soap. But not forever, she promised herself. Fashions could change; women were already converted to using soap. Why not cosmetics?

Her mother's recipes did not have expensive ingredients. Packaged in small enough quantities, they could be sold cheaply and yet make an excellent profit. 'Buy cheap and sell expensive,' her father had told her, and she grinned. She might do better to buy very cheaply and sell inexpensively.

As she washed her hands before lunch with a sliver of washing soap put in the soap dish for her by Elsie, she realized that Mr Lever's idea of scenting his soap with lemon was a good one. The piece of soap smelled very badly, and yet surrounded by the reek of stable and cowshed, of unwashed, sweating men and strong tobacco, she had, at home, never noticed that the soap she made did not smell good. She made a wry face at the discovery; she wondered if the smell bothered Eleanor – or Elsie – surrounded with Monday washing, boilers and dolly tubs.

When she went down to her sitting-room, she was surprised to find her meal served to her by a stranger, a flustered elderly woman, who carefully set a dish of scouse before her and ladled the mixture of lamb, onions and thin slices of potato onto her plate.

'I'm Mrs Barnes from next door,' she introduced herself. 'Elsie's beginnin' to feel 'er pains. It's too early yet to get the mid-wife, if you know what I mean. But it's her first, like, and she's nervous, so I come in to be with her for a while – and I'll be lookin' after yez while she's confined.'

Wallace Helena nodded and asked if she could be of help. 'I've never delivered a human baby, but I've helped cows calve and horses in foal – and I even managed a sheep that was in trouble last spring.'

'Really, Miss? Well I never.' She smiled down at the soap mistress, and said confidentially, 'I've helped a few into the world meself in me time, but I don't like doin' first births – sometimes they're difficult. Anyways, John Fitzpatrick's in regular work and he insisted Elsie have the midwife.'

'I hope she'll be all right,' Wallace Helena said, as she picked up her knife and fork.

Mrs Barnes heaved a sigh, 'Oh, aye, we all go through it – and she's a strong girl.' She went over to the mantelpiece and took down a letter which she handed to Wallace Helena. 'A Mrs Hughes sent this down for you by her maid.' It was from Joe, and Wallace Helena tore it open eagerly.

It was a month old and was full of the small problems of a

homesteading family looking towards the threat of winter. His short sentences made his letter sound petulant. She tossed the letter down on the table and picked up her fork again to eat a meal that she did not want.

She decided irritably that he had probably already dealt successfully with most of his troubles; surely he could manage without her for a few months. Then she chided herself that she was being unreasonable; he was carrying her work as well as doing his own, and harvest time stretched the capacity of all of them. Joe would ensure that all the outside work would be done, she thought uneasily; but it was she who drove Aunt Theresa and Emily to bottle enough fruits and vegetables, bury carrots in sand, make sauerkraut and pickles, even do another boiling of soap, so that the six people she had to feed during the winter kept well. And there were always hungry Indians passing along the trail – they had to be found a meal, somehow. She must remind Joe to chase Simon Wounded to urge him along to build up the woodpile ready for the cold weather; they had now cleared so much of their land that he had to log trees towards the edge of their holdings. Soon she would have to buy coal from the miners who dug the dirty stuff out of the river valley – and that meant they must pay out cash, an idea which made her feel even more irritable.

Tush! Here she was thinking as if it were certain that she would return to the Territories, and she did not want to. She rose, and put down her napkin on the table. The letter she slipped into her pocket. Hurry up, Joe, she muttered, and tell me you'll take a chance on a new country and come here.

The sudden movement of getting up set her coughing again. Mrs Barnes came in with a kettle of hot water to fill up her teapot, and said, 'Aye, Miss, that's a nasty cough you got. I can hear you wheezin' from here.' She whipped the tea cosy off the teapot and poured a little water into the pot. 'I'll give yez some tea to sip.'

The paroxysm was so intense that Wallace Helena could not protest and found the teacup held to her lips. She tried to control herself sufficiently to drink a little and slowly her throat cleared, and she sank down onto the chair again.

Mrs Barnes put down the teacup and, hands on hips, surveyed

the younger woman. 'You should see a doctor, Miss. You could get T.B.'

'Yes.' That was what Mrs Hughes had said. She asked, 'Is tuberculosis common here?'

'Oh, yes, Miss. Me little sister died of it – only eleven, she was.'

Wallace Helena sighed. 'I am so sorry,' she said.

'You could buy yourself some honey and lemons and mix 'em with hot water. It might ease it.'

Wallace Helena smiled and nodded. The coughing had tired her more than she liked to admit, so she promised to try Mrs Barnes's remedy. She inquired after Elsie and was surprised to learn that Mrs Barnes had sent her outside to walk up and down in front of the house. 'It'll help her later,' she informed Wallace Helena.

As Wallace left the house to return to work, she paused for a moment to wish Elsie a safe delivery.

Joe had mentioned in his letter that two families had come west on the train to Calgary and then felt it worthwhile to trek north to take up land only a couple of miles from their boundary. 'Fort Edmonton's going to be a town one of these days,' he wrote. Wallace Helena smiled to herself. Joe was not fond of new immigrants; every white family in the district put further pressure on the dispossessed Crees. The plight of his mother's people troubled him and he often shared his own expertise as a farmer with them, in the hope that it would make their reserves more productive.

On her arrival in her office, she found on her desk a slender volume of verses by Mr William Wordsworth, which she had asked Mr Helliwell to buy for her.

Apart from conversations directly concerning the soap works, she had sensed in the bustling city a great pride in a newly acquired literacy. Even Mr Tasker read the papers; and he could quote an appropriate biblical text in almost any answer he gave her. Mr Helliwell, a man in his thirties, was very fond of larding his discourse with poetical quotations, and she had even come across a Latin tag in one of Mr Bobsworth's letters to a debtor.

She had been brought up as a child amongst talented, cultivated people, and she found her employees' carefully inserted quotations endearing, and had asked Mr Helliwell to buy a few poetry books for her. She promised herself that that evening she would read Mr Wordsworth's book instead of one on oils and fats lent her by Turner. The more she saw of Liverpool, the more she realized what was lacking in her life in the Territories; there was more to existence than a battle for survival. There were other places, besides Beirut, where people had time for pleasure.

She slipped William Wordsworth into her reticule, and leaned over her desk to study a sheet of paper which was spread out on it. The scrawls on it looked like an untidy family tree descending from herself. Her name was written at the head of the paper and was joined by a line to that of Benjamin written immediately below. From him, lines arched out to the names of the senior employees. Beneath them, were the names of the men who reported to them. At the very bottom, were listed people like Alfie and the recalcitrant Georgie. By each name, in brackets, were a few words describing the man's duties.

She wanted now to ask Benji at what points in the structure she had depicted they could, perhaps, provide simple machinery to speed up their lines and their delivery process.

She rang for Mr Helliwell. He was busy making her two card indices, one of the name and address of every supplier from whom they had bought and another of every company who had ever made a purchase from the Lady Lavender. When she had first asked him if a proper record existed, he had replied simply, 'Mr James knew the names of everyone; he didn't need any more record than Mr Bobsworth's account books, occasionally.'

She now asked him to find Benji and see if he could spare her a few minutes. He bowed slightly and, with huge dignity, sailed into the works to find the man.

During the last week, as a result of Wallace Helena's memos, Benji's position as Assistant Manager had been clarified, and the men thankfully turned to him for their orders. Most of them would have agreed that a *woman* couldn't even run a kitchen properly, never mind a soap works.

When Benji entered, she said, 'Come and see what I've done.'

He went to stand close to her, while, with one beringed finger, she pointed out various employees' names and checked that she had correctly described their duties. As they talked to each other, he again began to be aware of her as a desirable woman. He flushed with embarrassment and tried to concentrate on what she was saying, but she was so close that he wanted to put his arm round the thin waist and forget about diagrams for a while. Perhaps his mother was right; she would make a good wife.

He carefully put his arm round her waist to see what would happen. Nothing did; she simply went on talking, her finger squarely on one man's name, waiting for his reply. She did not even look at him.

She was in fact acutely aware of him – Benji would not be a difficult man to fall in love with. The more she saw of him, the more she liked him.

But there was Joe. If he were here, she would not even think of anyone else.

Benji was disappointed. When she began to cough, he let his arm drop, as she moved to take her handkerchief out of her waistband.

They sat down and she began a discussion to explore whether their present staff and equipment were utilized in the best way. At first he answered her in monosyllables, but he soon became engrossed in what she was saying and began to put forward his own ideas.

She mentioned her first visit to his home to learn exactly how an English woman used soap. 'I saw your mother slice up the soap to put it in her boiler. Could we produce a ready-sliced soap?'

'I've a recollection that someone tried it, but that it did not catch on too well.'

'Perhaps it was too expensive? Or was it not sliced thin enough? Your mother said it must be sliced very thin, so that it melts and doesn't cling to the clothes.'

They were in the midst of a lively argument as to whether a line like she had suggested was a possibility for the Lady Lavender, when Mr Helliwell knocked at the door and brought in a written message for Miss Harding.

Mr Benson presented his compliments and would be obliged if Miss Harding could call upon him that afternoon. Probate had

241

been received and he needed her signature on a number of papers. He apologized for not calling on her, but he felt it advisable that she should come to his office, so that if she required clarification on any point of law or needed advice about how to proceed as the new owner, she could have the benefit not only of his counselling but that of his partner as well.

Wallace Helena raised her eyebrows at the formal missive and passed it to Benji, while she scribbled a note for the lawyer's office boy to take back to him, saying that she would be with him at half past three.

Benji read the letter. This was it, he thought bleakly. From this afternoon she would hold his future in her hand. He must now decide whether he should stay to serve her, whether he should try to court her or whether he should apply to other soaperies for a position. He looked round his father's office as if seeking an answer. He had, all his life, taken it for granted that from this little room he would preside over an expanding Lady Lavender, whenever it suited his father to step down. For that, he was sure he had been carefully groomed. And now the whole dream was gone, gone because of a crazy quirk of the law.

Chapter Thirty-Seven

After Mr Helliwell and the lawyer's messenger had gone from the room, Benji and Wallace Helena continued their discussion a little longer.

Benji said, 'Talking about new lines, I don't know the extent of father's Estate, but I do know that he was saving like mad to finance an expansion. He believed in ploughing money back into the business.' He glanced at Wallace Helena out of the corner of his eyes, and continued ruefully, 'You've probably realized that we lived very modestly – he didn't keep any kind of carriage, for instance.'

Wallace Helena nodded. She had realized, when seeing Eleanor's house with its shabby furniture, that either the soapery did not make very much or the family were very careful spenders. His remark about savings confirmed Mr Bobsworth's records that the soapery, after the first few anxious years, had produced a healthy profit – even the current quarter had showed a gain, despite the intrusion into the market of the redoubtable Mr Lever.

In the back of her mind, she had wondered what Uncle James had done with his money. Now she thought, with a flash of humour, that he probably stashed it into an old trunk, exactly as she did. She hoped Mr Benson had the trunk and that it had been sealed before witnesses. And there must be a private account book, somewhere, if he were anything like Father, she considered.

She said, in response to Benji's remark about their standard of living, 'I have every faith in Uncle James's business acumen. I'll know this afternoon exactly what the position is.' She did not want to appear too mercenary by expressing her inward relief that there might be some hard cash forthcoming, apart from the firm's working capital in the bank.

As she folded up the diagram she had made of the staff's positions, she asked her cousin if he would instruct Mr Helliwell to order a cab to take her down to Mr Benson's office.

He had had a faint hope that she would ask him to escort her. He would have liked to know the exact value of the Estate and what taxes would be levied; the sums could make all the difference between having to sell the works or not. In any case, the levy would be a burden for them to carry, at a time when they needed further investment.

Unfortunately, in her excitement, Wallace Helena had not considered the wisdom of including Benji in the interview, so he went off a little huffily to order the carriage.

While waiting for the hackney to arrive, Wallace Helena tried to rest by sitting in her chair, her gloved hands holding her reticule in her lap. She wished she dared to smoke; it was so comforting to smoke, and she supposed that was why a compassionate Joe Black had taught her to smoke like a Cree woman. It had certainly helped; or had it been the presence of Joe himself, a self-assured man showing her that there was nothing to be unduly afraid of, and saying, 'You've got to respect living things, but you've got to take enough to stay alive yourself – and this is how the Indians've always done it.'

She smiled wryly. By the time the Indians had discovered that their old ways would hardly keep them alive, in the face of the white invasion of their territory, Tom and Joe were managing to raise crops and a few precious animals. Smoking had helped her through the long and excruciatingly cold winters, when food became short and tempers even shorter.

And now, a surly old man called Georgie Grant made it impossible for her to smoke while working at her desk. He had done what even her mother had been unable to do – banished the cloud of smoke usually wreathed around her head. The thought made her want to giggle; the giggle became a laugh. When Benji came, she was in a high good humour and she surprised him by giving him a friendly peck on the cheek, as she stepped into the vehicle.

The kiss was noted by the men moving about in the yard, and they smirked at each other; Mr Benji seemed to be doing well for himself.

Because she and her parents had had to wait in Liverpool for an immigrant ship to take them to America, she knew the layout of the centre of the city, except where new construction had altered it. The family had taken lodgings in a hostel run for European emigrants. It had been crowded and dirty, so her father and her uncle had taken her for walks in the town, to try to distract the young girl from the hard facts of what had happened to them. Now as she looked through the window of the vehicle, she saw in her mind's eye the two brothers flapping along in clothes that made the local inhabitants stare, as they made jokes to keep her amused. They had tried so hard, she ruminated, to repair the ruin of their lives, and both had died comparatively young. Now, only she was left to carry the scars of their dreadful, shared experience. Once again, she wondered why she should have been spared.

It was a very sad, dignified lady who was led into Mr Benson's private office by an elderly solicitor's clerk.

Mr Benson had ready for her a number of papers requiring her signature, and he waited patiently while she read them through carefully. Sometimes she did not understand a sentence and had to ask him for an explanation.

She was shocked at the amount of tax, but Mr Benson assured her that he had arranged for it to be paid by instalments, rather than see the Estate drained to such an extent that the Lady Lavender would have to be sold.

The cost of Mr Benson's administration was not small, but he had paid himself, from time to time, so that most of it had already been met.

'If you decide to sell the soap works, the total tax assessed would be immediately payable,' he warned her. Then he explained that, as of that moment, he could no longer sign cheques on behalf of the Estate, and that she should see the firm's bankers immediately, to arrange for her signature to be honoured by them. She promised to visit the bank in the morning.

After the work had been done, she accepted a glass of sherry and they drank the health of the company together.

She leaned back in her chair, twisting her glass in her fingers. She felt more overwhelmed than she had expected, almost afraid. All the problems of the soapery were now hers. All its employees would turn to her for sustenance; and behind them were their families depending upon her to feed them, as surely as if they were impecunious blood relations. Though she did not doubt her ability to steer the little soapery quite competently, she was well aware that, as in Canada, a woman was regarded as an inferior being, put on earth to serve her masculine betters. She would have to compete with men in a system devised by them.

The sheer load of responsibility appeared very great, and she whistled softly under her breath, while her lawyer, a male, watched her with interest. 'It can't be worse than the Territories,' she said aloud.

'Pardon?'

She laughed, and made a deprecatory gesture with one hand. 'I meant to say that I don't think running the Lady Lavender will be any worse than running my farm in the Territories.'

'So you will manage it yourself?'

'Probably. I have written to consult my partner in Canada, because any decision I make will affect him – he owns half shares in the property. I expect to hear from him in a week or two. There are many ramifications in a move to England – and I've been giving them considerable thought over the last few weeks.'

'I'm sure. Please don't hesitate to consult me if I can be of help. Company law is quite complex, especially for a lady, who may not have come in contact with it before. I presume Mr Benjamin will be staying with the company?'

'Yes, indeed,' she answered automatically, and then hastily amended her statement, as she suddenly remembered the closed-off look on Benji's face when Mr Benson's note had been delivered. 'At least, I hope he'll stay,' she said a little anxiously.

Suddenly, the fear that he would not stay swept over her. Already very weary, her face went white, her glass fell from her fingers and she fainted.

Mr Benson half-rose from his chair. 'Miss Harding!' he exclaimed, and banged his bell frantically. When his clerk flew in, he demanded that his typewriting lady be sent to help his client.

In a few seconds, after a timid knock, a plain, small mouse of a woman, smelling salts in hand, slipped in.

'Oh, dear, dear,' she whispered, viewing Wallace Helena slumped in her chair. Blinking nervously behind her glasses, she put down the bottle of salts and very carefully removed Wallace Helena's hat. She put her arm round the unconscious woman's neck to raise her head a little, picked up the little bottle of *sal volatile* and waved it under her nose.

Wallace Helena did not stir. The typist turned a frightened face to her employer. 'Could we lie her down, Sir? I ought to loosen her lace collar – and, if you'll forgive me mentioning them – her stays – she probably laced them a bit tight.'

Mr Benson's expression had the slightly hunted look of a man suddenly enmeshed in a situation he wanted to get out of at all costs. He rang his bell again and sent for reinforcements. Two young clerks were instructed to lift the lady onto a straight-backed sofa on the other side of the room, a sofa usually sat upon by submissive wives, not directly included in a client's consultations with the lawyer.

Wallace Helena was rather tall for such a stiff narrow piece of furniture, but they tucked her feet up onto a chair hastily pushed close to it. The three men then stared uncertainly down at her, while the typist tried again to revive her with the smelling salts.

Fortunately, she began to stir, so the two clerks were dismissed, and Mr Benson went to his desk to find the bottle of brandy he kept there, for emergencies; sometimes, information he had to impart to clients was so shocking that they needed something to stiffen their resolve. It was the first time that a lady had actually fainted in his office, however, and he wondered, as he poured a little of the spirit into a sherry glass from the same cupboard, exactly what had caused Wallace Helena to lose consciousness. Al-Khoury had left her a good business and a reasonable bank account on which to draw for immediate needs, not to speak of a strong box holding a very nice sum in good golden sovereigns. What would make her faint?

He was not more puzzled than Wallace Helena. As she came round and was persuaded to drink the brandy, she was ashamed at her weakness.

'I've never fainted before, except once from hunger – one spring when we were down to porridge and very little of that.' She shrugged, as she handed her glass back to the typist and thanked her. 'It's probably the immense change from being out-of-doors all the time to spending most of my time at a desk.' She smiled up at her lawyer. 'I wonder if you could order a carriage for me?'

'Indeed, I will, and Miss Williams shall go with you.'

Mr Benson refused to accept Wallace Helena's protestations that she would be quite all right alone, and Miss Williams, armed with her return fare to the office by the clerk, was very happy to escape, though tomorrow she would have to finish the work left undone.

Though sapped of strength, Wallace Helena was still alert enough to notice a hoarding that they passed at the side of the dock road. It exhibited a large poster advertising Pear's Soap. 'Right on my doorstep!' she exclaimed to Miss Williams, with mock indignation. She immediately drew out her notebook and scribbled a reminder in it, to talk to Benji about a poster of their own.

Benji! He was the core of the whole ambitious enterprise she had in mind. And at a moment of intense pressure, the thought that he might leave the Lady Lavender, leave her stranded when she most needed him, had been the last straw. Already run down by the chill she could not shake off, she had fainted. Joe would never believe it!

Chapter Thirty-Eight

Joe never opened his letters at the post office, as many people did in their excitement; he waited until he reached the least travelled part of the track home. Then he would dismount, take the letters out of his shirt pocket and, leaning comfortably against his patient horse, would read them uninterrupted by Aunt Theresa or Simon Wounded who, at home, would clamour for news of her. Today, when he read her letter, he was glad of the solitude of the old pathway.

She had mentioned Benji a couple of times before and the reasons for his not inheriting his father's Estate. Now, she repeated how kind Benji and his mother had been to her, in spite of their disappointment at being left out of the Will; and a nagging fear in Joe's heart became a torrent of jealousy. He sensed that Benji was courting his precious lover. She had been away nearly three months, an extremely passionate woman, disdainful of church or state or custom, who had expressed that passion with him. He and Wallace Helena had established their own customs, he considered grimly.

But now she had this cousin, of whom she wrote with affection. A young man who spoke her own language! Who would probably enjoy bedding such a beautiful woman! He could barely read the whole missive.

He closed his eyes against the long slant of the late summer sunshine and to keep out the vision of Wallace Helena's slender legs curled round another man. He wanted to throw something, smash something, weep.

His horse turned to nuzzle him, as if she understood he was upset, and he leaned against her neck for comfort, until he had curbed his wild fury. Then he mounted her and rode slowly home, her reins loose in his hand and her hooves rustling sadly through the crisp, frozen leaves of autumn.

He unsaddled the horse and let it loose in the paddock, and then strode into the cabin. He flung his saddle into a corner, and shouted, 'Hey, Auntie! Got any coffee? Emily?' He pulled off his battered wolfskin jacket and flung it after the saddle, kicked off his boots, and went to stand by the small log fire that his aunt had made to cook a stew. 'Damn her! Damn her!' he swore under his breath.

'Shut the door,' shouted Aunt Theresa from the kitchen. 'It's getting chilly – I can feel the draught out here.'

Continuing to swear under his breath, he went to the heavy door and kicked it shut. Then he turned the beam across it to lock it; the beam thudded into its socket with a squeak of complaint.

Aunt Theresa shuffled in with a mug of coffee from the blue-enamelled pot on the back of her iron stove, where she had been preserving berries. Her soft moccasins made little noise.

She took one look at Joe's darkly flushed face, and asked in Cree, 'What's up? Did you get in a fight?'

'No.' He took the coffee from her and drank half the mugful, while she watched him, her anxiety hidden behind her blank, seamed face. She sensed a boiling distress which she had not seen since his mother had died of smallpox. 'A bit more, and he'll burst into tears,' she thought.

She moved round him and pushed a chair behind him. 'Sit down and tell me,' she ordered, as she lifted another chair close to him and sat down herself.

Joe ignored her, and continued to stand staring into the fire, his great fist clenched around the coffee mug, until the heaving of his chest under his check shirt became more normal.

Without taking his eyes from the fire, he sat down suddenly, as if the strength had gone out of him.

The old Cree sat patiently waiting.

At last he said slowly, his voice constricted, 'It doesn't seem as if Wallace Helena will ever come home.'

'Why not? Of course she will. You're here, aren't you? Who else has she got?'

In the flickering light of the fire, Joe's face had the frightening fixity of an African mask. Then, as if the information were being dragged out of him, he said, 'Remember she said in one of her letters she'd met a cousin, a white man, who works in the soap place?'

Almost imperceptibly, Aunt Theresa stiffened, like an old brown fox that suddenly smells something in the wind. She nodded.

'He keeps taking her out – walking with her – and, she says, planning with her.' He turned his eyes on his aunt, and said with anguish, 'I'm fifty-one, and my face is pocked – like the face of the moon. She's found this younger man – a city man – like she is.' He nodded his head helplessly. 'I've never seen a city. I don't know anything compared to her – I'm the son of a slave.'

Aunt Theresa thought this tirade over carefully, her face showing only her usual expression of resignation. She said quietly, 'I knew your father; he was a clever man. Don't put him down. He couldn't help it if he was taken as a slave. Mr Rowand who owned him thought a lot of him. And my father, Two Tailfeathers – your grandfather – taught you well. And you can read and write. You're as smart a man as she'd ever find in the Territories.'

'Yeah! In the Territories,' he repeated, with heavy sarcasm. He banged one fist on his knee and shifted himself angrily on his chair.

After a moment or two, Aunt Theresa went on, as if she had not heard the interjection.

'If it was looks that Wallace Helena wanted, you'd have been sent packing long ago!' She smiled faintly. 'She could have married Gagnon who used to hang around her, when she went down to the Fort. He was really handsome – and French-speaking.'

'A handsome fool!' retorted Joe.

'Right. And she knew it.' She chewed the end of one of her wispy white plaits. 'And you stop thinking wrong of her; she's clung to you like a burr ever since she was a girl, and she's been good to all of us – like her mother.'

Aunt Theresa rarely spoke her mind. When she did she was straightforward and without censure. Joe rubbed his eyes and his face, as if attempting to dispel his seething anger.

251

Aunt Theresa watched the play of emotion across his scarred face. She felt a great compassion for her big nephew, and had shared his mother's worries for him when they were young. He stood astride two nations, Cree and wherever his negro father had originally sprung from, and both peoples had suffered from white intrusion – were still suffering, she considered with a shiver, as she thought of the tattered, starving Crees, who occasionally knocked on their door to beg a little oatmeal or a bit of meat. Joe had been very lucky to have work with the Company and then to have made a good friend of Tom Harding, a simple man, she remembered, generous and outward-looking, who had taken a Cree as his first wife. After his death she had been glad to come to try to knit the shattered household together again; and seeing the affection between her nephew and Wallace Helena blossom had made her glad for both of them. Of course, the priest, who sometimes made the round of outlying homesteads, always said they should marry, but to Aunt Theresa it had not seemed a very important issue – until now.

At the moment, she thought that the added tie of marriage might have made Joe more confident that he would not be deserted, and would have eased the uncertainty within him. Privately, she could not imagine Wallace Helena being satisfied with some bleached-looking white man.

As she looked at Joe's bent head with its tight grey curls, she said firmly, 'Come on, boy. You must trust her. Read her letter to me, before Emily and Simon return – looks as if they're trying to lift all the turnips tonight. Where's the letter?'

Reluctantly he drew the offending missive from his pocket and, translating into Cree as he went along, tried to render it accurately. His jealousy lay within him like a dark, forbidding pool.

His aunt gestured helplessly with her hands. 'I don't know why you're making such a fuss,' she said. 'She's asking you to go to her. It's not you who've any worry. It's Simon and Emily and me who should be worried! What would we do, if you both moved?'

'I'm not moving. What would I do in a town?'

'She says what about a little farm? And she wouldn't be asking you to join her if she was thinking of marrying her cousin.'

He saw the sense in her remarks, but he was not comforted. He had many a time listened to Wallace Helena's longing for Beirut, heard her rail against the bitter winter, the lack of books, music, sometimes the lack of the basics of life when times had been bad. He judged rightly that, though Liverpool was probably different from Beirut, it might be a good substitute for her own city. And she had a relation to help her to settle there. He sat staring at the pot of stew plopping softly on the fire, folding and unfolding the letter with his long, splayed fingers, as he considered a future which seemed more hostile than the worst winter, the worst prairie fire, the worst invasion of grasshoppers.

He had believed that the soap works would yield some useful money with which she could buy good agricultural machinery, that she would be back home by this time. Instead it was creating a nightmare for him. Who, in the name of Jesus, wanted to live in a country other than his own?

Feeling that some of the tempest had passed over, Aunt Theresa heaved herself out of her chair and shook out her black skirt. 'You think carefully, boy, before you write back to her. She wants to stay there, I've no doubt. If you want her back here, you've got to tempt her, like you would a mare that's got loose and is running with a wild herd. Remind her of her warm stable and her bag of oats.' She allowed herself a small grin, and added, 'And the stallion in the paddock.' She unhooked a ladle hanging from the mantelshelf and bent down to stir the stew.

Chapter Thirty-Nine

Though Wallace Helena had noticed, when visiting Mr Benson on other occasions, that he had a typewriting lady at work in a corner of the general office, she had never spoken to her. When they were ensconced in the hackney together, however, she asked the woman how long she had been working for Mr Benson, and then leaned her head in a corner to rest, while she listened to the whispered flow of Miss Williams's confidences. She gathered from them that Miss Williams found herself the target of a great deal of hostility and misunderstanding, because she worked amongst men. 'But I felt that the shift-key typewriter was the coming thing, Miss Harding, and I have to keep my dear mother, so . . .'

Wallace Helena roused herself sufficiently to respond that she fully understood Miss Williams's difficulties, because she her-self was aware of similar attitudes to her ownership of the soap works. 'We shall have to teach men that we are to be respected, shall we not?'

Miss Williams agreed unhappily that they would have to be teachers. When they arrived at The Cockle Hole she refused an invitation to take tea, saying that she would like to go home to her mother as quickly as she could. 'Mother is an invalid, and she gets very lonely at times.'

Wallace Helena shook her hand and thanked her for her kind-ness, before descending carefully onto the cobblestones. She felt unusually weak.

She was surprised to find Elsie's front door open. To get out of the way of the hackney driver turning his horse around, she stepped quickly inside and found the house in turmoil. Sharp, short cries came from upstairs, as Mrs Barnes emerged from the kitchen-living-room at the end of the narrow entrance passage. Her hair hung in wisps from her bun and she seemed agitated. Two small boys were fighting over marbles in the hall, and a strange young woman was running up the stairs.

As Mrs Barnes saw Wallace Helena, she bent to slap one of the little boys and told him to be quiet or he'd have to play in the square. 'Our Elsie's in labour,' she told the Lebanese. 'I've got your tea ready, though.' She opened the door of Wallace Helena's living-room and bade her enter.

Wallace Helena went in and sat down thankfully. She took off her hat and laid it on another chair. Seeing her face, Mrs Barnes inquired kindly, 'Are you all right, Miss?'

Wallace Helena made a face. 'I fainted in my lawyer's office.'

'You're not well, Miss, I can see that. Elsie was sayin' as you've been coughing somethin' awful. You might like to walk up to see Dr Biggs, after you've had your tea. He has an evening surgery at seven o'clock. He's just round the corner, like. No distance, and he's proper kind. He'll see you all right – you might have to wait a bit.'

Wallace Helena nodded, and inquired how Elsie was.

'She'll be a while yet. It's her first and she's scared.'

'May I go up and visit her after I've had tea? It might take her mind off her pains.'

'For sure, Miss. The midwife's gone to have her tea – she reckons she'll have a long night of it. She'll be back in an hour. Don't make yourself too late, if you want to see the doctor, though. He shuts his door at nine o'clock.'

Aware that she had not eaten much lunch, Wallace Helena asked that her tea be brought in. She hoped that food might make her feel a little more energetic, though she felt more like taking to her bed than anything else.

Tea proved to be a filleted kipper on toast, followed by bread and butter and jam and a plain cake. It was tasty without being very fatty, and Wallace Helena ate all the kipper and then some bread and butter. She drank several cups of tea from the shiny brown pot. Feeling stronger, she found herself a cigarello and sat at the table smoking it with her last cup of tea. The smoke made her cough once or twice but she had no violent spasm.

She ground out the stub in a pottery ashtray liberally decorated with gold paint, and then went upstairs to wash her face and see Elsie.

When she knocked at Elsie's door, she was bidden to come in by her landlady, in a gasping, hoarse voice.

Elsie lay on the bed, her fair face flushed and perspiring. She was covered by a sheet and blanket, which had become tangled, as she heaved herself round in an effort to make herself more comfortable. Like the rest of the bare room, the bedding was spotless. On a table, the midwife had put a bowl, a pile of newspapers and some neatly folded clean rags. An empty bucket stood under the table and a flower-wreathed chamber pot was visible under the bed. A small fire had been laid in the fireplace; it had not yet been lit. A wooden chair stood by the bed.

Elsie smiled at her visitor and half rose, only to wince and fall back on her pillow. 'I'm sorry,' she gasped. 'Did Mrs B. give you your tea all right?'

'Oh, yes. Don't worry your head about things like that.' Wallace Helena approached the bed and sat down on the chair. 'I just came to sit with you for a few minutes, if you feel able to have a visitor. I believe the midwife will be back in a little while?'

Elsie agreed that she would, and added, 'Our John'll be home from work soon – and he'll sit with me a while later on. He's bin real good, helpin' me and having a real midwife and all.' She arched her back suddenly and cried out.

'Let me rub your back for you?' suggested Wallace Helena.

'Oh, I couldn't let you, Miss.'

'Why not? It's very comforting.'

''Cos you're a Miss, Miss.'

'Don't let that worry you,' Wallace Helena said with a laugh. 'I've helped many a cow calve. Turn on your side and we'll tuck the blanket under your stomach to support it. Now, then.'

Wide-eyed and doubtful, Elsie did as she was told, and long capable hands smoothed and soothed. After a minute or two, the girl was persuaded to sit up and Wallace Helena hitched her nightgown higher and eased and kneaded round the waist and down again. Elsie began to relax, and breathe more easily.

Wallace Helena kept it up until she herself was seized with a fit

256

of coughing, and had to stop. It was her turn to say, 'I'm sorry,' as she fumbled for her handkerchief. 'Mrs Barnes says there's a doctor near here. I think I'll go up and see if he can give me a cordial to ease this stupid cough.'

Elsie caught her lower lip between her teeth, as she lay back again on her pillows and pain shot round her waist. When it had passed, she confirmed that Wallace Helena should see the doctor. 'We're all afraid of coughs round here,' she said, ''cos of T.B.'

Mrs Barnes could be heard slowly climbing the stairs, so Wallace Helena took Elsie's hand and said goodbye. From Mrs Barnes she obtained exact directions to the doctor's house, and, with a quick smile to Elsie, she went to put on her hat and shawl.

As she was about to descend the stairs, she had a sudden thought, and she put her head round Elsie's door to ask, 'Can I get your mother or your mother-in-law for you – take a message to one of them?'

Elsie smiled sadly from the bed. 'Me ma lives in Dublin and she hasn't got the money to come – she sent me that lovely shawl hanging on the hook there – knitted from wool she got from the walls and hedgerows, where the sheep rub themselves; spun it, she did, and then knitted it. And our John's mam's crippled with the rheumatism – you should see her hands. She's comin' to live with us, once the baby's born.'

'My, you're going to be busy,' Wallace Helena said with a smile, as she pulled on her black cotton gloves.

'Oh, aye, but she's a real nice woman.' She winced, and Mrs Barnes leaned over to hold her hand.

Wallace Helena went slowly down the stairs, thinking soberly that wherever women lived, their lives were not easy.

The doctor's wife let her into the house and ushered her into what looked like a dining-room. A huge, polished oak table took up the centre of the room and matching chairs with seats covered in black oilcloth were ranged round the walls. At the door of the room, she said, 'He's nearly through. You won't have long to wait.'

'That's O.K.,' Wallace Helena responded.

The American phrase aroused the woman's attention. She had

realized that Wallace Helena was a foreigner, and now she inquired, quite politely, if she was from the United States.

Wallace Helena glanced at the pallid, lined face turned up towards her. 'No,' she replied, 'I'm from Canada.'

Two other people in the dining-room looked up, as Mrs Biggs said with forced cheerfulness, 'Well, now! Then you won't have been here before? It's as well you'll be his last – he likes to get the medical history of new patients, and he'll have time to do it without keeping anyone else waiting.' She smiled absently at the two other patients and softly closed the door behind Wallace Helena.

The room was made gloomy by heavy, dusty red curtains draped over lace ones. The dim light caught the mahogany features of a middle-aged working man in rough clothes and a battered bowler hat. He stared unsmilingly at the new arrival.

Wallace Helena sat down next to a heavy woman wrapped in a shawl. Her greasy black hair was caught up in a tight knot on the top of her head. Her hands were folded under her shawl. Her face was ashen and her lips compressed.

Despite her obvious pain, the woman looked sideways at Wallace Helena. Though Mrs Hughes might think Wallace Helena dowdy and old-fashioned, to residents close to the docks she seemed much better dressed than most of Dr Biggs's patients. As an opening gambit, the woman said to Wallace Helena, 'Doctor won't be long now; you're best off comin' late I always says.' She sighed.

'Yes?'

'Oh, aye. He's goin' to have to take 'is time on me finger. I got a whitlow, and he's goin' to have to cut into it, to get the pus out.'

'That sounds very painful.'

'Aye, it is, luv. Have you never had one?'

'No.'

'Well, they come if you get a splinter under your nail. Wood floors is the divil! I were scrubbin' the floor a couple o' weeks back and one went right under me nail. Proper mess it is. I won't show it to yez; you'd throw up if I did.'

Wallace Helena felt that she had dealt with enough sickness and injuries not to vomit. 'I hope it won't be as painful as you expect,' she said gently.

258

'Well, me hubby give me the money to come to Dr Biggs, rather than go down to the Infirmary or the Dispensary. Dr Biggs is proper kind. Does 'is best not to hurt you. He cares, he does.' Then she said, 'You're furrin, aren't you?'

For the second time, Wallace Helena said she was from Canada.

This caused an outpouring of information about the woman's nephew, who, she said, was working as a carpenter in Winnipeg. As she spoke, a distant bell rang and the man left the room. Distracted from thoughts of her painful finger, the woman seemed to gain a little colour, so Wallace Helena told her that she had actually been to Winnipeg, and this kept the conversation going.

When the bell rang again, the woman rose, bobbed gracefully to Wallace Helena, and said, 'It's bin a pleasure talkin' to you, Missus. I'll try not to be long.'

It was, however, almost ten o'clock by the black marble clock on the mantelpiece and the room was dark, before the little bell rang again.

Wallace Helena got up and went uncertainly into the hall. She paused, and then saw that the door opposite was marked *Surgery*. She knocked and a male voice told her to come in.

When she entered, she faced an unexpectedly long room. At the far end, between two long windows covered by the same type of dusty curtains she had seen in the waiting-room, a man sat facing her, at a desk. He was obviously elderly, and two sharp eyes peered at her over small, metal-rimmed spectacles, as she slowly crossed the room towards him. He gestured towards the chair set opposite to him, and said in a soft, melodious voice, 'Please sit down. We haven't met before, have we?'

She mechanically drew off her gloves, as she sat down. The doctor's shabby black suit and his bald head both shone in the light of lamps set on either side of his desk. He had a generous white moustache which emphasized a firm, but kindly, mouth. He continued to look at her, while he waited for her to reply.

Wallace Helena subjected the doctor to a slow, shrewd stare. Then, deciding that she liked what she saw, she told him about the cold and her subsequent coughing, and, a trifle reluctantly, that she had, that day, fainted in her lawyer's office.

In view of the fact that most of his patients hardly raised their eyes to him, he was rather amused at the weighing up of him that she had obviously done. He put her down as a lady coming to a slum doctor to whom she was unknown and where she was unlikely to meet an acquaintance, a lady who had something to hide.

'Well, well,' he said. 'Let us start from the beginning.' He went on to ask her name and address and what illnesses she had had in her life. Was she married or single?

She said she had enjoyed excellent health all her life, despite the harsh climate in which she had lived. He seemed interested, so she told him a little about her life as a homesteader and that she was now the new owner of the Lady Lavender Soap Works. She said she wanted to run the firm herself, and, therefore, particularly did not want to be ill at this moment.

He caught in her words the mispronunciation of the letter p and one or two other small slips amid her American accent, and he asked if she had been born in Canada.

'No, I was born in Beirut, in the Lebanon,' she told him with a hint of pride.

His wife brought in a glass of hot milk and put it silently on his desk for him. He accepted it with an absent nod; he was very tired. But the woman in front of him was most unusually interesting, so he carefully drew out of her the story of the massacre, of which he made a special note, of the flight to the United States, the awful journey to western Canada, and the subsequent loss of her mother and her stepfather.

'You have had a most eventful life, Miss Harding. And now you expect to begin yet another life in England?'

'All being well, I do.'

'May I ask whether your lawyer had something stressful to impart to you, that you should faint?'

'On the contrary, it was all good news. But I am very tired, as you can imagine, with such a long journey and profound change in life; in fact, I feel it may have precipitated the change of life in me.'

'What made you think the latter?'

'Well – er – my flowers have not come these past three months.'

'I see. And you are thirty-eight years old?'

'Yes.'

'It is possible.' He considered her for a moment, and then he said, 'I would like to listen to your chest and look down your throat, to see what is causing the cough. And, if you are agreeable, I would like to check you generally. Sometimes a cough is only a symptom of a deeper disorder.'

'Certainly. I am anxious not to be ill.'

'Well, well. We'll ask Mrs Biggs to come in.' He got up slowly and shuffled to a side door to call, 'Sarah, my dear. Could you spare a minute?'

Mrs Biggs put down her knitting and rose from her favourite basket chair. As she came into the surgery, she looked towards Wallace Helena, and inquired, 'Yes, dear?' of her husband.

Dr Biggs explained the examination he wanted to do, and Mrs Biggs turned briskly towards Wallace Helena, to help her remove her bodice. She was surprised to find that Wallace Helena wore no stays under it; only a chemise and a camisole. Wallace Helena unbuttoned the fronts of both garments and slipped them down to her waist, to reveal a creamy body and firm small breasts with dark nipples. The doctor knocked with his knuckles, first down her back and then her front. When he had finished, he continued to look at her breasts through tired eyes, half-closed. Then, as she lifted her camisole to cover herself a little, he asked, 'Have you noticed any other symptom of ill-health – a change in your normal weight, for example – during the last few months?'

'Not really. The change to city life, after being outdoors all the time, has been quite profound. I don't seem to be quite as energetic as I usually am. I've not lost weight; I've gained – probably because I'm confined – not out on horseback all day!'

He lifted one of the small lamps from his desk and handed it to his wife to hold, while he depressed Wallace Helena's tongue and looked down her throat. 'A little sore,' he told her, 'probably from coughing. It's not putrid in any way.' He stepped back and put down the spoon. He smiled gently down at his patient, and then said, 'Miss Harding, I would like to examine you thoroughly all over, if you wouldn't mind, to satisfy myself that all is well. I would not like you to walk out of here without help if you need it.'

Fear of the unknown shot into Wallace Helena's eyes. 'Are you looking for tuberculosis?'

'I doubt if you have such an infection.' He laughed quietly, and added, 'There are, however, so many woes that afflict the human race that I would like to make sure while you are here that everything is all right.'

Wallace Helena shrugged. 'O.K.,' she agreed reluctantly.

While the doctor went back to his desk and added some notes to his record of her, Mrs Biggs took her behind a screen where she divested herself of the remainder of her clothes. The doctor's wife wrapped a sheet round her, and then told her to lie on her back on a narrow, high bed against the wall. 'Nothing to be afraid of. Doctor is being thorough, that's all.'

Mrs Biggs hovered in the background, as the old physician went slowly and carefully down her body, uncovering only that part of her which he was immediately examining. He prodded round her stomach, turned her over and ran his fingers down her straight backbone, noting the firmness of her muscles. Then he turned her on her back again, and said, 'Spread your legs, please. This will feel a little odd to you, but it won't hurt.' He checked that she was not a virgin; then she felt his fingers probing carefully within. She lay perfectly still, gripped with fear. That was where cancers sometimes grew; she had heard about them. He said gravely, 'You may dress now,' and went to a washstand on the other side of the room, to wash his hands.

Mrs Biggs helped her off the bed and handed her garments to her, one by one. When she was dressed, she escorted her back to the chair in front of her husband's desk. Then, smiling sweetly, she slipped out of the room.

Dr Biggs did not look at her. He sat chewing his bone pen while he read his notes.

Then he looked up, and sighed, sharp eyes again peering at her over his glasses. Fiddling with his pen, he said, 'The cough is caused by a trickle of catarrh down your throat, made worse by the cold you have had. Such catarrh is common here and difficult to eradicate. I see from the stains on your fingers and teeth that you smoke, and this is making the catarrh worse. My first advice is to stop smoking. And I'll give you something to help to clear the catarrh.'

Wallace Helena smiled wryly. 'I'm not sure that I *can* stop smoking.'

'It's difficult, I know.' He paused, and then added, as if the words were being dragged out of him, 'I recommend that you stop for another reason.'

A fresh twinge of fear went through Wallace Helena. 'Why?' she almost snapped.

'Well, you must be aware that you are *enceinte*; it's not good for the child.'

'I'm what?'

'With child.' The doctor was obviously embarrassed, but he went on firmly, 'You have already mentioned that you've observed a cessation of your menses – discharges. During the last three or four months?'

Wallace Helena looked at him, speechless, as the colour ebbed from her face. Finally, she exclaimed, 'But I'm thirty-eight! I'm too old! It's surely the change of life?' She nodded her head unbelievingly. 'I've never been pregnant before – it's impossible.'

'I think you know that it is quite possible, Miss Harding.' The old man's voice seemed suddenly frigid.

Wallace Helena breathed slowly and shallowly, as the inference sank in. It seemed to her that all her hopes and dreams lay shattered round her feet. A spinster soap mistress, pregnant, facing her employees? Proud, scornful Wallace Harding riding down the main street of Edmonton, round with child? And Joe? What would he think, after all these years of never fathering a child? She shuddered to imagine it.

The doctor was saying, 'I'm quite sure, Miss Harding; I suspected it when you walked in.'

Wallace Helena licked her lips and stared at him dumbly, while with some bitterness, he added, 'Women sometimes consult a poor slum doctor, who does not know them, in the hope that he can abort a child for them. Otherwise, I do not often see middle-class women in my waiting-room. So I watched your walk – and looked at your skin – your complexion, as you came in.'

Wallace Helena was amazed. 'Is it that obvious?'

263

'Probably not – if you do not expect to observe it. People see what they expect to see.'

'I had no idea. I merely came about the cough and the fainting spell I had. With regard to – to my flowers, I simply thought I was getting old.'

'Can you expect that the father will marry you, Miss Harding?'

'He's in Canada – way out west. It would take months to arrange.'

'And you mentioned that you want to stay here to look after the Lady Lavender Soap Works?'

'Yes.'

'I see.' He sat considering the implications of all she had told him, and finally said, 'There's a nursing home in North Wales, an expensive but very discreet one – they could arrange matters for you, if you don't want to bear the child. It's a risky procedure – and time is running out for you; you should make up your mind immediately.'

Wallace Helena made an enormous effort to get a grip on herself again. She bit her white lips and clenched her hands in her lap. Joe's child. And Joe himself?

No words came to her.

Chapter Forty

In the distance the marble clock in the waiting-room chimed eleven. It reminded Dr Biggs that he had had a very long day and he might well be called out to a patient during the night. He got slowly up from his chair, and came round the desk to assist the frightened woman who had consulted him.

Realizing that she had kept him very late, Wallace Helena rose and thanked him stiffly. She promised to pick up tomorrow the cough medicine which he would make up for her.

He realized that his diagnosis had shocked her to the core, and his manner towards her softened; it was clear that she had not suspected that a pregnancy was the basis of her fatigue, and, in the back of his mind, he wondered why she had discounted this obvious result of coitus. At her age, surely she knew where babies came from!

She said, 'I will think about what you have told me, and I will come to see you again, if necessary.'

'Well, you're in good health,' he assured her. 'But remember that at your age you should have a doctor, preferably a specialist, in attendance when the child is born.'

Wallace Helena laughed shakily. 'If I go home to have it, there's only one doctor in the whole of the Territories and I doubt if he would want to come specially to Edmonton for the sake of a normal pregnancy.'

They were walking towards the door, and Dr Biggs suggested, 'Have the child here, and then go home.'

'I have yet to decide to have it,' she reminded him, her eyes large and sad.

He looked at her with pity, and said kindly, 'Well, come and see me again, if you need any further advice.'

Her pride in the dust, she walked slowly through the dark streets, empty except for a couple of cats growling at each other. She felt numb, unable to think clearly.

Though it was so late, the lights of the Fitzpatrick house still gleamed softly through the white curtains. She saw a woman's shadow flit across the window of the small upstairs hall. It jolted her. She had forgotten about Elsie's struggle to bring her baby into the world.

The panting cries of a mother giving birth and the mumble of other women's voices hit her ears the moment she opened the door. From the kitchen came the rumble of men's voices, and she presumed that John had a friend sitting with him to sustain him through the birth. He heard her entry and came out to meet her. Behind him she caught a glimpse of one of the older fishermen who also lived in The Cockle Hole.

Whether it was because he had company or had been drinking fender ale, John looked fairly cheerful as he greeted her.

'Elsie said as you was to have a fresh cup o' tea when you come in. Would you like one, Miss? It'd be no trouble – I'm up for the night, anyways.'

She stared at him, as if she had not taken in what he had said. She looked so desolate that he wondered if Ould Biggs had indeed found her tubercular – Elsie had told him where she had gone. She swallowed and responded with an effort, 'I would, John. I'd be most grateful.' She hesitated, and then inquired, 'Do you happen to have any rum? If you do, could I buy a thimbleful from you?'

'I don't, Miss. But I bet Ben here has. He can usually find a bit of brandy or rum for any as wants it.'

Even in her misery, Wallace Helena felt a quirk of humour, as she undertook to buy a small bottle of top-quality Jamaica rum from a smuggler. But she needed something to ease her sense of helpless shock. A few minutes of complete abandon had cost her her future. Even if she went home, would Joe believe the child to be his? She had not lain with anyone else, so it was his, conceived during a mad night in a noisy hotel in Calgary, while they waited for the train to take her to Montreal. For the first time, she had ignored the careful count she had always kept of the natural cycle of her menstruation. Like her mother, she had had no desire to bring children into her hard, relentless world. And no amount of importuning had made her break that rigid rule; not until she had been faced with parting from Joe for the first time since she was twelve, she thought. And she sensed again his anxiety at the long journey she was undertaking. Even then he had been afraid that she would not return, she remembered.

And she had promised that she would come back, that all she wanted to do in England was to see that she was not being cheated over the sale of the soap works.

Because of the slowness in obtaining Probate, she had remained in England much longer than she had intended, long enough to realize the comfort that life in Liverpool offered, long enough to make her want Joe to join her there. What a stupid hope! Every letter that Joe wrote asked her when she was coming back; and his jealousy, when she mentioned the men she had met, was clear in every word. He had ignored the letter in which she had first slyly mentioned the possibility of his coming to England; neither had she received a reply to her direct question in a later letter.

And now she feared she was caught in a trap. Would Joe believe the child was his?

As John pushed the door of her sitting-room with his foot, bringing in a tea tray which included a modest-sized bottle of rum, a gasping scream rent the air. John stopped, then hastened to put down the tray. He listened intently. Perhaps the child had come. It had not. Loud moans followed, and the twittering voices of women comforting.

'Who's up there?' asked Wallace Helena, pulling a chair to the table to sit down and pour the tea.

'Mrs Murphy, the midwife, and Mrs Barnes is helpin' her.' He gave a little laugh. 'Mrs Murphy says as all's well and not to worry – but you can't help being wishful that she didn't have to go through this so that we can have a family.'

John looked quite shaken, so Wallace Helena assured him that, once she had the baby, she would forget about the pain. It was a trite remark, but it seemed to comfort him.

'Yes, Miss. Thank you, Miss.' He withdrew, his expression still apprehensive. The baby could be safely born; yet, all too often, the mother could die of childbed fever within a week. He hoped he had been right in putting his faith in Mrs Murphy, the midwife.

Wallace Helena splashed rum into her tea and thought dejectedly that she would have to go through the same ordeal as Elsie, if she kept the child. Alternatively, an abortion often led to a painful death for the woman.

But, above all, she dreaded the calumny she would face, whether in Liverpool or in Edmonton, if she carried the child to fruition and Joe refused to marry her. And the child itself would suffer, like Benji had suffered.

Better to abort it, she decided grimly, as she poured another cup of tea and added rum to it.

Chapter Forty-One

Wallace Helena did not hear Elsie's triumphant shriek as John Patrick Fitzpatrick entered the world, nor the happy running up and down of the women attending to mother and child. She was sound asleep on top of the coverlet of her bed, still in her camisole and petticoat; the rum had done its work.

She slept until nine in the morning. Then Mrs Barnes knocked on her door, to inquire rather anxiously if she would like her breakfast. 'I've brought you a can of hot water,' she called through the door.

Dragged back from the dark oblivion in which she had spent the night, Wallace Helena responded sleepily. Then as consciousness returned, she swore. Oh, my God! The soapery! The bank! The child!

She stumbled out of bed and shouted that she would be down in a quarter of an hour. Her natural liking for Elsie asserted itself, so she opened the door and hissed down the stairs after Mrs Barnes, 'How's Elsie?'

Mrs Barnes turned her cumbersome body to slowly look up at her, her careworn face beatific. She whispered back, 'She's fine. She's sleepin' now, thanks be. It's a boy – and he's loovely. You must see 'im later on.'

Wallace Helena had to smile at the woman's pleasure. 'I will,' she promised, and shut her door.

Once she was washed and her hair brushed and neatly knotted at the nape of her neck, Wallace Helena's mind cleared and she went down to breakfast with some of her usual energy. The rum must have been excellent quality, she thought, as she tackled her breakfast bacon; she had not slept so well for weeks. She quelled the sense of panic that began to rise in her, at the thought of the

269

decisions she must make, and told herself that other women must have faced some of the same problems. Last night she had had a terrible shock; today, she would try to keep calm and deal with it.

No matter how she tried to gather up her courage, she still felt an appalling aloneness amid her difficulties. She longed to have her mother to talk to. She feared Joe's reactions, and, in any case, he was so far away; she must make a decision within a few days, at most.

Before she left for the office, she told Mrs Barnes not to bother to make lunch for her; she would eat at work. That, she thought, would ease the pressure in Elsie's house. She took a last pull at her after-breakfast cigarello and regretfully stubbed it out. She doubted if she could ever stop smoking.

It was easy to say to herself that she would analyse coldly the difficulties she was in; it was much harder to do it. The minute she allowed her thoughts to rest on any aspect of her predicament, such a turmoil of emotion rose in her that common sense was blotted out. Common sense said, 'Go quietly to North Wales for a holiday and be rid of the intolerable burden within you. You have enough problems already.' Sentiment whispered, 'It's Joe's child, an unexpected expression of years of devotion to each other. Remember, you may not be able to have another one. Remember!'

'If the pregnancy is aborted and you can live without Joe, you can stay in Liverpool – and never have to face a Canadian winter again. You can live a civilized, refined life – with every comfort.'

'And without Joe, it would be as empty as the food cupboard before the harvest,' prompted sentiment. 'He's all the family you've got – except for Benji, who in his deprivation of the Estate is another problem of family, blast him.'

Family? What is a child, if not the perpetuation of a family?

In the course of the morning, she and Mr Bobsworth discussed the satisfactory financial standing of the Lady Lavender with two greybeards at the bank. Specimens of their signatures were then put on file, so that cheques could be honoured by the bankers.

Wallace Helena gave only half her attention to these formalities. She kept thinking about her mother delightedly nursing a little grandson; Leila had nearly gone mad when her brothers had died as children in Beirut, Wallace Helena remembered; and here she was, ready to consign her own child to perdition. As one of the bankers tenderly blotted her signature, she wanted to cry.

Though respectful to her, the bank staff persistently addressed Mr Bobsworth and not herself, assuming that he would be in charge of the company's finances, and that Mr Al-Khoury, whose signature they would collect later, would be running it.

With a picture of her mother's grandchild dancing before her, Wallace Helena smartly disabused them of this idea with a polite snub. Responsibility for the soapery was not going to slip away from her like that; it would be passed down the family by her.

It was curious that the unthinking machismo of two old men in a bank should infuriate her so much that it drove her to an immediate decision. But it did. Sparked by bitter resentment, a mother instinct began to rise in a woman who had never wanted to be a parent, feeling that the world was too cruel a place into which to bring a child. Somehow, she swore, she and Benji would nurse the soapery along. It offered a way out from the slavery of a homestead, if not for her, for the baby. And her half share in the homestead might grow more valuable – might even now have a market value, since the railway had come to Calgary and opened it up to Europe.

As she and Mr Bobsworth, looking gravely important, sat quietly in a hackney carriage weaving its way slowly back to the Lady Lavender, she hoped that soon there would be a letter from Joe. She had given him the alternatives; he might feel old enough and tired enough to come to a more clement country and marry her – but there was so little time. She began to panic that some sharp-eyed employee, like old Georgie Grant, used to so many *enceinte* women in the packed streets in which he must live, would spot what Dr Biggs had – and make her name mud in the Lady Lavender. Pride made her clamp her lips together, till her face looked as if it had been hewn from rock. When, a little later, she sent Mr Helliwell out to get some lunch for her from a nearby café, he wondered anxiously what had happened to the charming lady who had asked him to buy a copy of William Wordsworth's work for her. She had given her orders to him as testily as her uncle would have done on a bad day. When he set a pile of beef sandwiches in front of her on her desk, however, she did say, 'Thank you,' and a few minutes later, when he brought a pot of tea for her that he had made himself, she was immersed in reading Mr Wordsworth's 'The Solitary Reaper'. Must've been hungry, he comforted himself, and thankfully went to have his own lunch.

Wallace Helena was unexpectedly very hungry, and she ate all the sandwiches; she did not have the same success in absorbing 'The Solitary Reaper'. No matter how hard she tried, the charming words danced in front of her eyes and made no sense. Eventually, she put the volume down. Crossly muttering, 'Damn Georgie Grant,' she took out a cigarello and smoked it.

It calmed her fretted nerves, but by the end of an afternoon spent in setting down her ideas for the immediate future of the Lady Lavender, for discussion, first with Benji and later with Mr Tasker and Mr Bobsworth, she was coughing badly.

She put down her pen, wiped her face with her handkerchief and looked at the somewhat disjointed jottings before her. It seemed suddenly pointless. If she kept the baby she would be out of circulation for some months, no matter what she planned.

She had gathered from one or two conversations with Elsie that most women did not go out more than was necessary, when they were breeding. Elsie said that middle-class ladies were penned up like chickens. 'If they go out in the street, they sometimes get jeered at,' she had added.

Wallace Helena mentally recoiled, both from the idea of being confined and of being humiliated in public. Her hands clenched in her lap, she stared out of the grubby office window at a sky promising perfect harvest weather. Frustration made her furious to the point of tears.

If the bloody Turks had had an ounce of compassion for their Christian subjects, she considered bitterly, she would probably now be living contentedly in Beirut, with full-grown sons, and summer holidays in Beit-Meri to look forward to; not a real worry in the world. Once one's roots were gone, the normal values by which one lived shattered, it was easy to trip up and be plunged into situations which would never have occurred, had the even tenor of one's life been left undisturbed.

She felt sickened, as she considered the attitude of the men round the Fort, if she had an obviously illegitimate child. She would be open to propositions as if she were a prostitute. They might call after a vinegary woman they believed to be a despised Jewess, but they would not touch her; with a bastard in her arms, it would be far, far worse. Unless Joe married her.

She closed her eyes. Her head throbbed, and she cursed that she had not realized, earlier, what the stopping of her menses spelled out. 'What you don't expect, you don't see,' she fumed helplessly.

She longed for Joe's slow, rich voice patiently sorting out the chaos in her mind for her, pointing out the options she had and the probable outcome of each of them. Between the two of them, they had always found ways out of situations that had left their neighbours decimated; snowstorms, grasshoppers, drought, Indian uprisings, epidemics – they had crawled through all of them to better days. But there was a real joker in the pack this time – a baby, which she was not prepared to plan away.

There was a knock at her office door, and she roused herself. Benji put his head round the door. 'All right if I come in?' he queried cheerfully.

She smiled as best she could and told him to enter. She had not seen him all day, because he had been across the river to Birkenhead, to see a middleman who distributed their products in Cheshire. Now, as he came in, he asked if all had gone well at the bank.

'Quite well,' she told him. She poured herself some water from a carafe on her desk and drank a little.

He stood looking down at her, hands in pockets, and she went on, 'I've arranged for you to see them tomorrow, to give them a new specimen signature. They've now got Bobsworth's and mine, and they'll honour cheques signed by any two of us.'

'Good,' he responded, and then, as she began to cough, he said, 'You *must* see a doctor.'

She was startled by the remark and glanced quickly up at him, her eyes wide, as if suddenly frightened. Then she looked down again at the sheaf of papers on her desk, and replied, 'I saw one last night – and I must remember to pick up the prescription he's making up for me, on my way home tonight.'

The last words came out slowly, as if her mind were elsewhere, and to Benji she looked extremely dejected. He wondered if the sudden absolute responsibility of the soapery was weighing on her. He had expected her to be bubbling with ideas and plans; dejection was not something he normally associated with her.

He had been on his feet all day, so he slowly pulled forward a chair and sat down beside her.

By degrees, he was realizing that the Lady Lavender had always been part of his life and that he did not want to leave it. This meant that he must resign himself to working with Wallace Helena, provided she stayed in England; and, though he often found her maddening, he liked her. She was family, and he felt a surprising warmth at having someone to whom he could speak frankly, without fear of serious censure. She barked and snapped like an irate terrier, but she rarely bit.

Wallace Helena put her elbows on her desk and rubbed her eyes with her fingers. Make up your mind, she ordered herself. You've either got to tell Benji everything and go on from there, or you have to say that you're tired and are going to take a week's holiday in North Wales.

Since she did not seem inclined to start a conversation, he told her about a successful arrangement he had made with the Birkenhead middleman to distribute posters with their washing soap; and he'd cut the wholesale price by a halfpenny to encourage him.

Though she nodded acquiescence to this agreement, she showed no enthusiasm; it was as if a light had gone out.

'What's to do?' he asked himself. Something was wrong. Had the company's finances proved to be in a worse state than anticipated? She had not yet told him the details of her visit to Benson.

'What's the matter?' he asked softly in Arabic.

The sound of her own language always drew her closer to him; it was the language of her childhood filled with nuances of love

274

and respect. His concern was obvious, and she put out her hand towards him in a hopeless gesture. She said with a break in her voice, 'I don't know how to tell you, Benji. How to explain. What to do.'

He went rigid. 'Is it to do with the Lady Lavender?' he asked tensely.

She made a wry mouth. 'Yes – insofar as what happens to me affects it.'

Oh, Lord! Something must have really blown up; she certainly looked a wreck. He swallowed and, filled with foreboding, said, 'You'd better tell me.'

'I'm going to have a baby.'

He looked at her in complete astonishment, and then burst out laughing. 'Well, I'm blessed! Congratulations! You always insisted that you were single and I accepted it. But I suppose you felt it would be better in business to be known as *Miss* Harding?'

'I am single; that's the trouble.'

His grin vanished. 'Are you engaged – or courting?' he asked.

'No.'

He looked at her in wonderment. This stick of a woman casually bedded? She wasn't the type. He couldn't believe it. Benson? Helliwell? Don't be funny, he told himself.

'You weren't attacked – in the street – or down in The Cockle Hole?'

'Raped? Far from it.'

Feeling he was sinking in deep water, he inquired, 'Will the father marry you?'

'I'm not sure. You see, the father is in the Territories, at Edmonton. If I write to him, it'll take months to get a reply – and my condition will be obvious pretty soon. And I'm not too sure that he'll believe it's his – because of the dates.' She gazed at the astonished man before her, the frank despair in her eyes communicating her distress to him.

This is how my mother must have looked, he realized uneasily, when first she knew I was coming. Pity welled up in him.

Wallace Helena was telling him about the obliging nursing home in North Wales, and he instinctively revolted against the idea. To his knowledge, he had not fathered any children himself, so this was the first of a new generation. 'You can't do that,' he protested, 'you could die yourself.'

'Oh, I don't want to lose it. I want it,' she said forcibly, as if to confirm her earlier decision at the bank. 'It's simply that I also want to stay here and see the soapery flourish – and Liverpool is such a beautiful place in which to live.' At the last words, her voice dropped wistfully.

She pursued a slightly different line of thought suddenly, and said, in the hope of conveying to him something of what she had been through, 'I'm so alone – not physically – but I am mentally. There's nobody left who knew me in Beirut, nobody who understands – or has, perhaps, a duty to try to understand, what it's like to be torn up by the roots and be tossed into an absolute wilderness.' She stopped, and he waited, feeling that there was more to come. Then she said, 'At least my own child is part of me, flesh of my flesh, as I was to my mother. It's probably the last chance I'll have to recreate a lost family.' She smiled a little grimly. 'At least I can teach it Arabic!'

Her cousin echoed her smile. He remembered how carefully his father had taught him Arabic; he must have felt like Wallace Helena.

'Would the father agree to settle in Liverpool?' he asked. Who was the man anyway? Her partner?

She sighed. 'I honestly don't know. I doubt if he would be happy here. But I have asked him.'

It must be her partner, Benji decided. His mind began to race. She had said once that the man might like to farm here. He hoped to high heaven that he would not want to poke his nose into the affairs of the soapery; if she didn't have a special marriage contract, the man might well manage to take over the Lady Lavender under some pretext or other.

Wallace Helena was looking at her hands tightly clasped on the desk. She loved Joe, would always love him – and it was his child; she had been completely faithful to him. It was all very well to say that the babe was flesh of her flesh; it was his, too. He was, however, clearly jealous of the people she had met in England, and this sudden pregnancy, after so many years with him without children, would look highly suspicious. She had been a fool,

276

she thought bitterly, to break an iron rule in Calgary. Her mother had always warned her that it took only one miscount and one could be pregnant. But her fear of the long journey, of doing everything alone, had been overwhelming, and she had given herself to her lover with the despairing feeling that, even on a train, the journey was so long and dangerous that she might not survive. A last fling, she considered wryly.

She laid her face on her clasped hands and closed her eyes. While she smiled at the memory, she cursed herself for being so stupid.

When he saw the gesture, Benji thought she was going to cry, and he leaned forward as if to touch her, but she turned her face towards him and said, 'How can I face the staff here, looking as round as a full moon? I can't. If I go home, what am I to do about the soapery? It takes time to sell anything at a decent price. I'd be as fat as butter before I could make a deal – I've already put on some weight.' She patted her waistline. 'And I don't want to sell,' she finished savagely.

'You could marry me,' Benji said softly. 'We'd get on all right.' And very practically added to himself, 'And you'd bring one hell of a dowry.'

He had the decency to feel a little ashamed at himself for considering that, as her husband, he, too, would indubitably try to gain complete control of the firm; against that, if her lover took it over, it could go out of the family as surely as if she'd sold it.

She straightened herself up, and smiled very sweetly at him. 'Bless you, my dear,' she said gently. 'I can't let you do that.'

He asked quite cheerfully, 'Why not?' He shrugged. 'I know there's a difference in age, but I don't mind – and I wouldn't mind betting that you could produce another little one a year after this one. Two's a nice family.'

She drew out her handkerchief and blew her nose hard. 'Benji, you're sweet. But it's more complicated than that. It would be obvious that the child isn't yours.'

'Who's to know?'

'Everybody who sees it will know. It'll be black – or at least as dark as Alfie at the works!'

Chapter Forty-Two

She saw Benji recoil in shock – and distaste. She hated him for it, and it immediately told her something about the unborn child.

Benji had had a father from the Middle East, but he had been moulded in the streets of Liverpool, a city built on the backs of slaves traded to the New World. To be black in such a city was to be a nobody – and she thought of Alfie, thin, sad, at the bottom of the pile. Not for my child, she thought proudly.

Benji had once or twice mentioned bullying he had endured as a child, not only because he was of mixed blood but because he was also illegitimate. How much worse would it be for a thoroughly brown boy who was illegitimate? How could Benji sit there looking so disgusted, when he had gone through so much himself?

In this she did Benji an injustice; it was precisely because he knew what Wallace Helena's baby would face in the back streets of Liverpool that he was so shaken. He didn't want to be a party to its happening. Better by far that she go back to Edmonton, where presumably there were lots of Red Indians who would look much the same.

Benji simply did not know what to say. Poor little bastard, he thought with compassion. To fill in the silence, he asked her to tell him about the child's father. 'Do you want to marry him?' he asked.

The answer was straightforward. 'Yes, I love him very much.' She lifted her head and stretched herself. 'You ask what he is? He's simply one of the finest men I've ever met.' She went on to tell him of Joe's origins, and he listened fascinated.

At the end, she said, 'He's like a bridge between the Crees and the Metis and white people. He grieves at what has happened to his mother's people. Like his Cree grandfather, he knows that the Crees don't stand a chance against the whites, now the buffalo herds are gone – the herds were a source of food. So he's spent his life trying to smooth out things where he could, trying to ease those he knows into farming. But these people have been cheated by the Government at every turn. So, when he had the chance he joined my stepfather, Tom Harding, in clearing a homestead – and trapping.'

She sighed. 'He and Tom went through some terrible times together – but they were great friends. Now the farm usually provides a surplus of one grain or another – and some meat. Up to now, it's been difficult to sell a surplus – but once the railway reaches us, we'll be able to sell it abroad. There's real hope now – for us – but the Crees, as a whole, are still in sorry straits.'

Her mind wandered from her own difficulties; and Benji saw the absolute fatigue and sorrow on her face, as she saw in her mind's eye the hungry people who often knocked at her door.

Benji roused himself. 'So your little one won't go hungry, if you take him back to Canada?'

'Not while I'm alive,' she replied with grim determination.

'What do you want to do?'

'I really don't know. My very first thought is to go to town and buy one or two nicely draped dresses to hide my condition in the next month or two – it's not really obvious yet, but it will be very soon. I'd noticed that my waistbands were tight, but I thought I was putting on weight from lack of exercise! Do you think a dress shop could help me in this?'

'I'm sure they could. Try Frisby, Dyke's on Lord Street.'

'Thanks. It may buy me a month or so, to get a reply from Joe – and think how best to keep the Lady Lavender going.'

'Well, I can manage it – as you know. So don't worry about it for a bit.'

'I know you can do it, Benji.' She smiled at him. 'And I must remember in all this that I have to take care of you and your dear mother.'

'What about talking to Mother about the baby?'

She considered this suggestion, and then said, 'I don't think I will, for the moment. Perhaps later. What I need is a couple of days, to collect my scattered wits. Then I'll find my way. At the moment I feel like a drunken seaman in a storm.'

She had spoken the last two sentences in English, and he laughed. 'You sound like an American seaman,' he told her.

'Not surprising – I learned my awful English in Chicago, remember – in a slum.'

He nodded. God, she'd been through it, he thought, as he rose. He went round to the back of her chair, and pulled it out for her. She turned, her face close to his. Very carefully, she kissed him on the cheek. 'Thanks, Benji,' she said.

'If all else fails,' he told her, with a quick grin, 'my offer of matrimony still holds. I'd protect the baby – and you – as best I could.'

'I really believe you would. Thank you, my dear.'

Chapter Forty-Three

Prejudice? The spectre raised its ugly head, in Wallace Helena's mind, as she walked swiftly up to Dr Biggs's house to collect her prescription.

Mrs Biggs opened the door to her and invited her into the hallway. A bottle of bright pink liquid, neatly labelled with her name, was waiting for her on a little table. Mrs Biggs handed it to her with a tiny slip of paper which proved to be her bill. She paid this by putting the coins down on the table, sensing that it might be rude to put the money straight into the hands of the doctor's wife.

Mrs Biggs thanked her and told her not to hesitate to return if the cough continued beyond another ten days. Wallace Helena smiled agreement, and wondered if Mrs Biggs knew she was pregnant. She wondered sardonically what the lady would think if she knew the child was coloured.

After the door closed on her, she hesitated on the pavement, and then she turned and walked up to Park Road, in the hope of finding a small shop that sold baby clothes. John Patrick Fitzpatrick had to have a present.

'Would it be for a boy or a girl, Ma'am?' the stout female behind the counter inquired.

'A boy.'

'Ah, then. It's blue you'll be wantin'?' She added coyly, 'Blue for boys; pink for girls.'

This was news to Wallace Helena, who had, for most of her life, seen only little papooses tucked into wood-backed bags on their mothers' backs. She accepted the word of the shopkeeper, however, and bought a blue knitted jacket. Then, feeling this was not enough, she bought a crocheted baby blanket, as well. Armed with these offerings, she went down to The Cockle Hole to have her dinner.

When she lifted the latch of the front door and entered, the house looked far from pristine; it did not even smell the same. An untidy woman met her in the hall. She had a bucket full of nappies in one hand.

'I'm Mrs Kelly,' she told Wallace Helena. 'I'm doin' a spell while Chrissie Barnes 'as gone to see to her hubby. I thought I'd do a fry-up for yez. It don't take long.'

'That sounds fine,' Wallace told her, though she was not certain what would arrive on her plate. 'May I go up to see Elsie?'

'For sure. She's learnin' the baby to suck, but she won't mind.'

The bedroom was stuffy and smelled of dried blood and another distinctive odour, which was, Wallace Helena supposed, a damp or dirty baby. The young mother was propped up in the muddled bed. She had opened her nightgown to expose perfect swelling breasts, and she was patiently trying to persuade the baby to accept her nipple.

At Wallace Helena's hesitant entrance, she hastily pulled the sheet up over the baby and her breasts, and greeted her with pleasure and apologies that her tea would be late.

Wallace Helena said it did not matter and sat down on the chair by the bed. 'How are you?' she asked, 'And how's the baby?'

Tenderly, Elsie slipped back the sheet, so that her lodger could admire the crumpled red face of her first-born. Large, blank eyes stared back at her between folds of fat, and tiny lips moved uncertainly. 'Would you like to hold 'im?' Elsie asked, and she lifted the tiny bundle and held it out to Wallace Helena.

Wallace Helena braced herself to take the weight without dropping the child – and was startled to find that it seemed to weigh almost nothing. She cradled the baby instinctively and looked down at the child's fuzzy head. In less than six months, she thought with wonderment, I'll be holding my own baby. And then a real fear that she would not know how to care for it struck her; she suddenly longed to ask Elsie to help her, show her what to do, prepare her for the advent of the child. And, if it's born in the Territories, it'll still be winter. What shall I do in that remorseless cold?

Elsie's voice broken in on her reverie. 'Shall I take 'im back, Miss? He might spoil yer frock.'

Wallace Helena forced a smile and handed the child back. She then proffered the parcels she had brought, and with one hand Elsie shook the presents out of their tissue paper. 'They're lovely, Miss. Proper kind of you – but you shouldn't have . . . you didn't have to.'

Wallace Helena told her it was a pleasure, and she was delighted to see mother and child so well. 'Oh, aye,' responded Elsie cheerfully, 'I'll be up and around a bit tomorrer, and the place won't be in such a mess.'

'Don't put yourself out for my sake. Mrs Barnes has been most kind, and I'm sure from the nice smell coming up the stairs that Mrs Kelly is making something good.'

'Oh, aye. I've wonderful neighbours. Most of them was in, some time or other, today; and they all brought a bite of food to help out – and some of their men's out of work, an' all.'

'I'm glad they're so kind.' Wallace Helena made her farewells, and went downstairs, wondering who would come to her aid when her child was born.

A perspiring Mrs Kelly was just coming out of the kitchen carrying a plateful of food, and Wallace Helena sat down to a dish of bacon and eggs, fried bread and fried cabbage, with a pile of bread on the side. Wallace Helena said it looked wonderful and ate the lot, while her brain searched for the best way to deal with her own child.

Dr Biggs had said she should have a specialist available, because she was older. This meant, though, that she would have to be delivered in England. On the other hand, if she went home, Joe would probably marry her – or would he? And there would be only Aunt Theresa to help the baby into the world – unless Aunt Theresa knew someone at the Fort who was knowledgeable and would come.

She had a bad night, and by morning she was still no further ahead. A crying baby did not help.

She rose early and washed herself in cold water from the ewer in her room. When she went downstairs, John Fitzpatrick opened the kitchen door and looked a little alarmed. She put her finger to her lips and then said quietly, 'I'm going for a little walk. Don't worry about me.'

John looked relieved. 'Thank you, Miss. I'm away to work in a minute, but Mrs Barnes'll come to make your breakfast and help Elsie.'

'Rough night?'

A grin spread over his face. 'A noisy one, Miss. I hope you weren't bothered.'

'Not at all,' she smiled.

She walked down to the slipway. Mist was clearing from the river and in places the sun dappled the water. People were already astir in the cottages, and a canary sang sweetly by an open window.

She wondered what these fisherfolk would think if a black man came to live amongst them – or a black child. She was not certain of the answer, so she posed the question the other way. What would Joe feel like, hemmed in by cottages, docks, warehouses and manufactories? She knew the answer immediately.

Unless he saw possibilities in it which she could not envisage, it would be like trying to cage an eagle from the Rocky Mountains; he would wilt and die. The baby as it grew up might make some sort of a place for itself. But not Joe.

She realized that he was too old to change much. And why should he? Apart from being part-owner of a fairly successful homestead, he was well regarded in and around the Fort and among his Indian relations; his knowledge of Indian languages and his negotiating abilities were prized by both sides. Apart from that, he and Wallace Helena herself had lived in the district far longer than most of the inhabitants and had acquired a degree of wisdom in handling both livestock and crops in such an inclement climate; Joe was often asked for his advice.

On the whole, she thought, Joe did not suffer too much from being black. She knew from the taunts she had received that it was his association with herself, a yellow woman, which put him at a disadvantage. Moreover, both she and her mother, being educated, considered themselves superior to ordinary folk; they weren't humble like the Chinese labourers who worked on building the railway, she thought sarcastically.

But, if she went home, what was she to do about the soapery? To sell it, she must somehow gain some time. And then she remembered Frisby, Dyke's – the shop which Benji had mentioned.

With sudden determination, she turned back towards her lodgings. Outside the house next door, two little girls had marked out the pavement ready for a game of hopscotch. She stopped, and asked if their mother would let them take a note to the Lady Lavender. Fingers in mouths, they said they didn't know – they would ask her.

A thin harridan in a dirty apron came out and said she didn't want the girls straying. Her son would take it on his way to work, if that would suit the lady. Wallace Helena took her notebook out of her pocket and hastily scribbled a note to Mr Helliwell to say that she would not be in until ten-thirty. She tore out the page and addressed it. She gave it to the woman, together with a threepenny piece for the boy.

After breakfast, she tidied herself and walked up to Park Road, where she caught a horse tram to town.

She found Messrs Frisby, Dyke and Company at 58 Lord Street. She had never been inside such a large shop, and she paused before entering to look at a pretty display of dress materials in the window. Then, summoning up her courage, she approached the door. It was courteously opened for her from the inside by a white-whiskered shopwalker in a stiff white collar and a morning coat. He bent slightly towards her and asked if he could help her. She told him that she needed at least two dresses, and would like to be served by an older assistant.

'Yes, indeed, Madam. Gowns and Mantles, Madam. Come this way.'

It was early and the shop was not very busy. She noticed that all the young women dusting or arranging their displays wore skirts like she did, but the older ones looked quite fashionable in garments with fitted waists, modified bustles and an apronlike drapery at the front; such dresses were not going to offer much disguise for her present condition, she decided with some trepidation. They passed through a department selling scarves and handkerchiefs, and she was suddenly charmed by a tree of hankies being created by a young woman standing on a stepladder. She shook out each hanky and poked it into a metal frame. To Wallace Helena, the result was like a pine tree of white and pastel colours, and her tight lips curved in a little smile.

Haberdashery was the only department that was so busy that the assistants could obviously hardly deal with the rush. All the customers were very young women, with swatches of material clutched in their hands. The shopwalker had paused, to make a way for her through the throng. 'Who are these young women?' Wallace Helena whispered.

The old man smiled. 'Dressmakers' apprentices, Ma'am. Not well-mannered at all, Ma'am. They're matching cottons and buttons and bindings for their employers.' Faced with the back of a struggling girl, he said, 'Now, Miss, make way,' and with a scared look on her pale face, the girl stepped back, and Wallace Helena swept after her escort.

He handed her over to a middle-aged lady neatly gowned in rusty black and with a velvet pincushion shiny with pins buttoned to her left wrist.

Since Wallace Helena was not known to the shop she stated frankly that she was expecting and wanted some dresses to disguise the fact for as long as possible.

The woman bowed slightly. 'Of course, Madam. Madam will not wish to remain indoors longer than necessary. May I ask your name, Madam?'

'M – Mrs Harding.'

'Ah, yes.' She wrote the name down on a pad hanging with its attendant pencil from her waistband. To her, Wallace Helena did not look very prosperous, so she said, 'We have a number of dresses made up, or partially made up – requiring only fitting and finishing. Our dressmaker can adjust anything to suit you. Or we can arrange for any pattern to be made up for you, in any material you desire?'

Amused by the formality, but feeling pressed for time, Wallace Helena said she would try on some of the ready-made ones. 'Suitable for everyday wear and for walking out,' she added, fearing suddenly the arrival of dinner gowns.

The woman was a genius, Wallace Helena thankfully decided. After measuring her customer, she found her a plain grey wool dress with a softly defined waistline. It had a loose overjacket with long grey velvet lapels that closed with a single button below the waist. A white fichu tumbled in frills to fill the neckline of the jacket. Though it made the expectant mother look stouter than she was, it would disguise an expanding waistline for a little while. It was the nicest frock Wallace Helena had ever owned.

She also bought a black cashmere costume, with a loose, fringed wrap and two different black bodices; the latter, though cut out, had to be made up. 'We cut them quite generously,' the shop assistant assured her; she had been temporarily joined by an elderly cutter and fitter, attended by a shrimp of an apprentice who gazed pop-eyed at Wallace Helena. The two new arrivals circled round their customer with a polite, 'Pardon me, Madam,' as the apprentice passed pieces to the cutter and that lady draped them on Wallace Helena and stuck pins in strategic places.

Once the fitting was completed, the shop assistant stepped forward again, and said, 'You will be surprised how well it will look, Madam, and it will certainly hide your little secret for a few months longer.'

The small apprentice had been picking up dropped pins. At the assistant's remark, she glanced up in surprise. The fitter saw the glance, as she was taking the pinned bodice off Wallace Helena, and she scowled at the girl and told her to get back to the workroom; apprentices should not stare at a customer – it might disconcert a lady.

Wallace Helena smiled at the shop assistant, and before she knew where she was, she had also been sold a grey silk dress, which had obviously been designed for the portly older woman. It had a drape of silk from one shoulder which swirled gently across her small chest and then round her waist. The result was a suggestion of the apronlike drapery which many women seemed to be wearing, but without a tight waistline. 'For best occasions,' the shop assistant said firmly, and the cutter murmured that Madam looked charming.

Feeling greatly cheered up and quite pleased with herself, Wallace Helena asked when the bodices would be ready.

'In two days' time, Madam. We can send them up to your house. The other slight adjustments can be done in twenty-four hours.'

Wallace Helena was alarmed. She said hastily, 'I'll come in – I enjoy coming to town. And you can see them on me – and make sure that everything is just so.'

Pleased by the implied compliment, the assistant agreed to this, and then asked cautiously, 'Madam has an account here?'

'No. I'm a visitor. I'll pay for the dresses now, and for the costume when I come for the clothes.'

As the assistant wrote out the bill, she inquired politely, 'Madam is from America?'

Wallace Helena froze slightly. She did not want to be identified. After a second, she said, 'Yes. From Chicago.'

'I trust Madam is enjoying her visit?' The assistant pushed Wallace Helena's sovereigns into a little brass tube, screwed it into a container hanging above her head, pulled a handle and, to Wallace Helena's delight, the whole contraption shot across the store, to be fielded by a prim gentleman seated in a tiny glass-enclosed office. Her change came back the same way.

It had been a most entertaining hour and she felt much better; the dresses should buy her a couple of extra months.

In the workroom, the small apprentice, Lena Grant, was bursting to tell her friend, Bettina, who sat next to her, that a lady whom she knew to be a Miss had a *little secret*, and she had just bought three dresses to cover it up. She dared not open her mouth, however, while the dressmakers were sitting nearby and constantly calling for cotton or tapes or bindings or even their heavy dress forms.

She worked until seven-thirty that night and forgot about her piece of gossip until she got home.

Her grandfather, Georgie Grant, had preceded her and was eating his tea at the bare wooden table in the tiny living-room. Her widowed mother was sitting opposite him, her youngest son in her lap. Lena had passed her other two brothers, who had been playing in the street.

''lo, Mam. 'lo, Grandpa,' she greeted them, as she took off her hat and hung it on the back of the door. 'Guess what I saw today. Your Miss Hardin', Grandpa.'

'You did?' He stuffed some more bread into his mouth and pushed his cup across to her mother to have it refilled.

The girl pulled out a stool and sat down at the table. She snatched up a piece of bread from the wooden board in the centre of the table, and began to eat. 'Oh, aye, and you know something, Mam? She's expectin'.'

Georgie Grant swallowed and then put down his piece of bread and the spoon with which he had been eating stew. He looked at his granddaughter in stunned amazement. Then he warned, 'Be careful what you say, you stupid judy. You probably got the wrong woman. You don't know Miss Hardin'.'

Lena tossed her head, and said, 'Everybody round here knows her. We see her walkin' over to the works from The Cockle Hole – that's where she lives, int it?'

Seeing fury slowly mount in Georgie's reddening face, her mother said anxiously, 'Now, Dad!'

Georgie half-rose from his seat. He shook his spoon in his granddaughter's face and roared at her. 'You mind your own business, you busy lizzie! What the gentry does int none of your business. You keep your bleedin' mouth shut or you'll soon be out of a job – and I'm not goin' to feed you, if you go on like that.'

Lena cringed away from the old man. 'I didn't mean nothin', Grandpa.'

He leaned forward and hit her with his tin spoon. She yelped with the pain, and he shouted, 'That's nothin' to what I'll give yez if you so much as open your mouth again about Miss Hardin'. First, it's a bleedin' lie and, second, if it int, all the more reason to keep your gob shut.'

He plunked himself back in his seat and his daughter handed him his refilled cup. Lena began to whimper and then leaned towards her mother. 'I didn't mean nothin', Mam!' she howled miserably.

'Jaysus Mary!' the old man swore and got up from the table. 'Shut up, will yez.' He picked up his cap from the mantelpiece and slammed it onto his head. 'I'm goin' for a jar,' he said, and swung out of the tiny house.

As he walked angrily down to his favourite pub, he muttered to himself, 'Our Mr Benji's jumped the gun, I suppose. The stupid bugger! Couldn't wait to ring the bell. The kid must've heard her say *somethin'* – Lena don't lie.'

Chapter Forty-Four

Back in her dusty office, Wallace Helena found that Mr Helliwell had opened the mail and put it on her desk.

'I gave two complaints direct to Mr Benjamin, Miss Harding – and an order to Mr Bobsworth. I believed you'd wish them attended to immediately.'

'Very sensible, Mr Helliwell. I forgot last night to ask Mr Al-Khoury to give me some time today. There are all the papers handed to me by Mr Benson yesterday to go through. See if he could arrange to spend the afternoon with me.'

Mr Helliwell bowed and was about to leave the room, when she called after him, 'And ask Alfie to get me something to smoke. Here's a florin.' She slapped a silver coin onto the end of her desk.

Rather shaken, Mr Helliwell turned quickly round, his mouth open as if to say something. He was forestalled by Wallace Helena who assured him with a twinkle in her eye that she was not going to smoke in the office.

He ventured to smile back at her and went off quite jauntily to find Benji. The old girl was much more herself this morning, thank goodness.

Wallace Helena skimmed quickly through the pile of letters on her desk and then knocked them into a neat pile again ready for Benji. She got up from her chair and unhooked her reticule from the coat-stand near the door. She opened it to take out Dr Biggs's medicine and a spoon. Then she took the prescribed dose, and made a face as she went over to the tiny sink in the corner of the office to rinse the spoon. In the excitement of going to Frisby, Dyke's, she had forgotten to take the medicine after breakfast and had snatched up the bottle as she left the house.

As she dried her hands on a small towel, she began to pace up and down the narrow room, methodically sorting out in her mind, first, where the child was to be born and, second, whether to put the Lady Lavender on the market. She kept coming back to what Joe would think about the child.

Then she began to worry about her employees. She did not want to sell the company only to see it almost immediately closed down. It was small in comparison with other companies making soap; yet it had the potential for growth. A bigger company might very well buy it to get rid of the competition.

Into this rumination intruded the idea that she could leave Benji to manage the firm for a few months, until the child was born; then, perhaps, keep the baby outside the city with a wet nurse.

It would not solve the matter, she decided almost immediately. The baby would still be as illegitimate as Benji, and that, added to its colour, would leave it terribly disadvantaged, no matter how well she endeavoured to educate it and provide for it.

And could she really desert Joe, for the sake of a comfortable life? She stopped dead in the middle of the dull brown linoleum of her uncle's office, as she faced the question squarely.

Through the open window, she heard the yard foreman shouting at his labourers, and the thud of boxes being loaded on a cart. A horse neighed and jingled its harness. Beyond these noises, it was as if she heard a door slowly close, as she answered, 'No.'

With no one watching her, her face saddened and, if Joe had been there, he would have recognized the resigned despair which he had seen on the scratched face of a fourteen-year-old girl riding towards him on a borrowed horse, so many years ago.

She must go back to Fort Edmonton; and trust that, when Joe saw the child, he would be convinced it was his.

She heaved a great sigh, and wanted suddenly to go home soon, to get it over with, to pick up the threads of her settler's life before the winter really set in, and plan with Aunt Theresa how best to deliver the baby. She smiled wryly. It wouldn't be the first child to be received into a fresh rabbit skin, instead of a blue crocheted blanket.

Perhaps the sedation of the cough medicine had lowered her

resistance a little, because she sat down suddenly, and began to cry slow, hot tears, not because of her current predicament, but for all the intense effort she had made since the terrible day when her father had lowered her from the roof of her home, while fire from other homes made a thick haze round them. She had stayed alive, she told herself, as she took out her handkerchief, but it seemed as if she was never to be allowed to crawl onto a plateau where she could rest – and *enjoy* life.

When Benji came in to say that he had asked Helliwell to get both of them some lunch, so that they could gain more time that afternoon, he found her sitting quietly, her head bent, her handkerchief clutched tightly in her hand.

She looked up at him and he saw the empty hopelessness in her wet eyes. She seemed to have aged suddenly. She nodded agreement to working and lunching with him at the same time. Then, she grinned at him unexpectedly, and ordered, 'Tell Helliwell to bring a pot of hot, very strong tea. I need it.'

He was relieved to see her smile, and he asked, 'Would you like a bottle of wine? He's not yet gone to get the lunch – he could bring one in.'

'Yes,' she agreed slowly. 'I'm not sure what it does to babies, but I would like a glass.'

Benji laughed. 'I'm sure the little tyke can stand a glass or two. I'll tell Helliwell.'

As she sipped a rather raw Italian wine from a teacup, Benji was thankful to see some animation return to her.

She proposed a toast to the longevity of the Lady Lavender, and they drank it with gusto; it cheered him up. After hearing that she was in the family way, he had worried about his own future. Now, at least she seemed to think the firm would survive; otherwise, why had she toasted it?

She brought out the papers she had received from Mr Benson. They went through the various financial statements, so that it was clear to him that the firm was in a sound position. Then she told him about the box of gold sovereigns. 'It was in the bank strong-room – a dead weight – and three locks.'

He whistled. 'No wonder he wouldn't part with a halfpenny if he could help it.'

'I'm sure he intended to plough the money into the company, as he seems to have done before, at times.'

'Yes, he did. I can remember a couple of times when he went on a spree of buying for the firm.'

'It seems to me, Benji, that he intended to bring the firm right into the 1880s; and I think his first moves were to recruit Mr Turner and Mr Ferguson.'

'I wouldn't be surprised.'

'Well, I'm having the sovereigns transferred to a special Capital Account, so that if all goes well it can be used to mechanize production, or start a new line – when we're ready. I shall keep it in such a way that, if I have to sell, that account remains with me.'

Benji sighed, and she said to him robustly, 'Now stop worrying. I have an idea in mind, but I want first to see Mr Benson and possibly talk to the bank people again. All you have to do is to keep the place going for me, and in a couple of days or so it should all be sorted out.'

'Have you heard from your partner, then?'

'Not yet.'

He waited for her to say more, but she seemed satisfied that they had completed what she wanted to do, so he took out his pocket watch, and said, 'It's still quite early, so I'll get back to my desk.'

She nodded agreement, and he unfolded his big, rumpled body from his chair and tucked his pencil into his breast pocket. He took up the notes he had been making and folded them into a neat square. 'See you later,' he said, and moved towards the door.

'And Benji,' she called to him, as he was about to turn the handle.

'Yes?'

'You're a sweetheart.'

He grinned in sheepish surprise, and left her.

She put her head down on the desk and burst into weary tears. Now, she had the difficult job of convincing Mr Benson about what she had decided to do, without telling him that she was pregnant.

Chapter Forty-Five

Mr Benson was unable to see her for two days, so in the meantime she collected her new dresses from Frisby, Dyke's. The enterprising shop assistant led her over to the Millinery Department and persuaded her to buy a new autumn hat which went with both the daytime dresses. She failed to sell her a pretty little veiled straw hat with a bunch of white feathers at the side to wear with the grey silk, for tea parties. 'Enough is enough,' said Wallace Helena grimly. The shop assistant wondered suddenly, when she saw Wallace Helena's forbidding expression, who her client really was; her rather shabby old-fashioned clothes had suggested someone of neither wealth nor eminence. Now, when Wallace Helena was shown out of the store by the shopwalker, she was not so sure.

That morning, Wallace Helena had received a letter from Joe, in response to one of hers in which she had first hinted at the idea of his coming to Liverpool and making a new life with her in the city. In four lines, he told her to hurry up with selling the soapery and come home. Did she realize she had already been away two months?

And now it's over three months, Wallace Helena considered irritably; Dr Biggs had made her acutely aware of the calendar.

The following morning, she walked through the soap works dressed in her new black skirt, bodice and carefully draped shawl. She looked round the stables and commended the stableman on their cleanliness, peeped into the carpentry and wheelwright's area and nodded good morning; she noticed that it was well swept – Benji had obviously followed up on her complaint about the plant's housekeeping. As she crossed the yard, she noted that it had been washed down and sanded. She spent a friendly half hour with Mr Tasker and suggested that they try again to get an apprentice or two for his department. He sucked his teeth over this, while he watched one of his men check the contents of a boiler and, at the same time, considered her suggestion.

Satisfied, he stepped down again and apologized for interrupting her. 'What with the silicate of soda and the boilin' of the soap, the framin', the crutchin', and checkin' of supplies, I've got me hands full. There's no end to it all.' He rubbed his hands down his thighs, and moved a little away from his assistants, to say quietly to her, 'I need a real bright youngster to train. These lads are all right, but they'll never be soap masters.'

Wallace Helena smiled, though she took his remarks very seriously. She assured him that she and Mr Al-Khoury were discussing a better organization of the work throughout the plant and he would certainly be consulted. Meantime, he should consider a good apprentice, or even a journeyman who had already some experience in soap-making; perhaps there was someone he knew who would like the job.

Within herself, she was saying goodbye to all her employees. With their tremendous humour, their eccentricities and their obvious interest in the Lady Lavender as an entity, they had enriched her life; and she wondered how she was going to bear her isolation when she returned home.

As she was crossing the yard to the Power House, she saw Georgie Grant. He was waiting to unload a wagon of barrels of fat. The carter was backing the horse to manoeuvre the wagon into a more convenient position.

'Good morning, Mr Grant.'

George straightened his bent shoulders a little, his wickedly shrewd blue eyes staring as he took in the obviously new dress; he could smell the newness of the material. So young Lena had not made a mistake.

'Mornin', Miss,' he said, smiling kindly, his few ugly teeth well displayed. 'Nice mornin'.'

'It is indeed, Mr Grant,' she replied, and passed on.

He watched her as she went up the steps of the Power House, and weighed her up carefully. Then he turned back to the wagon to unhitch the tailgate. He suspected that Lena had been right about there being a bun in the oven. Mr Benji had better get a move on and get the banns called.

Being received by Mr Ferguson was a bit like being received by a prince in his palace, Wallace Helena thought with amusement. Mr Ferguson belonged to the new wave of skilled mechanics, and he knew it.

After a few pleasantries, she asked him if there was any spare capacity in his installations – if she wanted to put new machinery into the plant which would need additional power.

'For sure, Miss. Much of what you see is fairly new; the Ould – I mean, Mr James Al-Khoury, had in mind to expand – and when he engaged me and the present power plant was built, we made plenty of provision.' He hooked his thumbs into the braces that held up the bib of his overalls, and continued, 'I told 'im to allow for expansion – and he done it.' While she digested this information, he took off his peaked cap, which he regarded as a badge of status, and scratched his balding head. Then he said, 'I reckon he were dead set on expansion, Miss. And put a lot of what he made back in the business. And very good he was at driving a bargain.' He grinned at her, his ruddy face shining in a shaft of sunlight. 'And so is Mr Benji; he learned 'im!'

She surprised him by holding her hand out to him when she was leaving. He took it shyly and shook it. 'Thank you, Mr Ferguson, for being so helpful,' she said, as she withdrew her hand, and he saw that, though she stood as straight as a guardsman and that her lips smiled, the expression of her eyes and the lines of her face were those of someone who had endured considerable grief. He wondered how old she was. Younger than he was, he reckoned. He longed to ask her if she was going to manage the company, but felt he had been forward enough; no doubt Mr Benji would tell him soon.

Her lips trembling, Wallace Helena made her way back to her office. A few minutes later, Mr Helliwell brought in her mid-morning cup of tea, and found her leaning back in her chair, her eyes half-closed, the lustrous lashes failing to disguise the fact that she had been crying.

At his entry, she straightened up quickly and he mentally

kicked himself for having forgotten to knock at the door before entering.

She thanked him, and he asked, with some anxiety, if there was anything more he could do.

'No, thank you,' she replied. 'Mr Al-Khoury can deal with the letters. You know I have an appointment with Mr Benson for this afternoon. Perhaps you had better order a hackney for me for a quarter to two.' She made no effort to wipe her face.

Though he remained as calm as a good butler, Mr Helliwell was shocked. Something was definitely wrong; she had not really been herself for several days, though her cough seemed to have diminished, thank heavens.

He promised to order the carriage, and withdrew to his own small cubbyhole next door. He prided himself on being aware of everything that went on in the works, but he could not think of anything which would reduce Miss Harding to tears. Rage, yes; but not tears.

Benji breezed in, with a list of items he wished to discuss with Wallace Helena. 'Is she free?' he inquired, nodding his head towards his cousin's door.

Mr Helliwell replied in an uneasy whisper. 'She is – but she seems very upset about something. Perhaps you should leave her for a few minutes.'

'In a temper?' Benji had known Mr Helliwell since the man had first started work with them at the age of thirteen, as an office boy; there was real affection between them.

Mr Helliwell screwed up his lips. 'Far from it,' he responded, again in a whisper. 'She's upset – like a woman.'

Benji restrained a grin. Apparently Helliwell did not think that, normally, Wallace Helena belonged to the feminine gender. 'I'll chance it,' he said, and went to knock on her door. An unexpectedly firm voice bade him come in.

He stood over her, big and clumsy-looking, his list in his hand. He saw immediately that she had been crying; she had the wide-eyed, heavy, exhausted look his mother sometimes had after a spate of tears.

'What's up?' he asked, without preamble. He himself was feeling good. The fact that she was, indeed, leaving the general management of the soap works to him had restored some of his customary optimism. To add to it, his mother had remarked, only a few evenings back, that if she was a Lebanese as good as his father she would never do anything to harm him – he was all the family she had.

Until now, he thought suddenly, and felt a twinge of jealousy about the coming child.

In answer to his question, she replied, 'Have a seat. Nothing's really happened. I got a letter from Joe in response to one of mine some time back. He wants me home, as I thought he would. I'd hinted that he should consider coming here, but he's ignored it. I've written since, of course, telling him about the baby, but it'll be weeks before I get a reply – and, frankly, I don't think it's worth waiting for one.'

'Don't cry,' he comforted. 'Things'll work out.' He wondered if he should again ask her to marry him. Not yet, he told himself. Let Joe Black make a move.

He went on, 'You know, you shouldn't have to bear all this alone; you should tell Mother; she can be as silent as a tomb – but she could be a comfort to you.'

Wallace Helena nodded. Eleanor was indeed very kind. 'Will she be home tonight?'

'Yes,' he replied, with relief.

'I'll come about eight, if that's all right. Now, what've you got on that list?'

Chapter Forty-Six

When Wallace Helena called on Eleanor Al-Khoury that evening, she found her alone.

'Our Benji hasn't come home yet. He said he'd be late – he sent me a little note by that coloured lad what works in the Lady Lavvie, so as I'd know you was coming. How are you, love? You're lookin' a bit peaky.' She took Wallace Helena's hat and shawl from her, and ushered her into the front parlour. 'All me gents are out tonight, so we can have a nice little get-together in here. Haven't seen you in ages.'

Wallace Helena kissed her and asked how *she* was.

Eleanor heaved a deep sigh. 'I'm not so bad, all things considered.' She moved towards the fireplace in which a small blaze gave cheerfulness to the room. As she bent down to put a black kettle on a hob and turn it over the fire to heat, she said, 'Sit down by the fire, love. Aren't the nights drawin' in? I made a fire 'cos it seems to be a bit chilly.'

Wallace Helena obeyed, and asked, 'What's making Benji late?'

'Well, he said the other day you gave him all the files in his dad's private drawer to read – so he thought he'd do it when he wouldn't be interrupted. I've saved him a bit of dinner for when he comes.'

Wallace Helena nodded. She decided Benji was probably making the reading of the files an excuse to give her time alone with his mother. Aloud, she said, 'I felt that, as Manager, he'd better know everything about the company – his father's private negotiations with suppliers, anything there was about the staff. I've read them, and they do contain good background information.' She bent towards the fire and rubbed her hands to warm them; she had not bothered to put gloves on.

They chatted desultorily about the weather, and agreed that they had both enjoyed an organ concert to which Benji had taken them about three weeks earlier. 'Aye. Mr Best's a lovely organist – there somethin' about organ music, int there?'

Wallace Helena agreed there was, and wondered how to bring up the question of her pregnancy. She helped Eleanor to lift a small tea table closer to the fire and, while Eleanor poured boiling water into the brown teapot, she mentioned that her landlady, Elsie Fitzpatrick, had had a lovely baby boy, and that her mother lived in Dublin and could not come to her.

'I expect the neighbours came in,' Eleanor responded placidly. 'Everybody loves a baby.' She stirred the pot vigorously, and put a teacosy over it while the tea mashed.

'I suppose,' Wallace Helena replied. She stared into the dancing flames of the fire, and then she said, 'Eleanor, Benji suggested I should come to see you tonight – because, quite flatly, you're the only woman who might care about me or mine!'

Eleanor had just lifted the milk jug in order to pour milk into the teacups – her best ones. Now she put it slowly back on the tray.

'What's to do, love?'

'I'm in the family way myself, Eleanor.'

'And it's our Benji's?'

Wallace Helena laughed suddenly. 'No, no. I'm much too old for Benji – though, when I told him about it, he did offer to marry me – to protect me, so to speak. Bless him.'

'You mean you're not married?'

'Right.'

'Well I never.' She was quiet, while she poured out two cups of tea. Then she said gently, 'Not to worry, love. If our Benji wants to marry you, and don't mind being a papa to your baby, you haven't got nothin' to worry about. There's a few people at the Lady Lavvie as would be thankful if you was married to each other.' She smiled warmly at Wallace Helena, and continued, 'And I can think of lots worse to have as a daughter-in-law. I know you're older, but you don't act like it. Benji'd be fine with you.'

'You're very kind, Eleanor,' Wallace Helena replied, with

genuine gratitude. She went on to explain that, even if she loved Benji to distraction, she would not dream of marrying him, because the child would not match up. 'Literally, it won't,' she assured a puzzled Eleanor. 'It'll be too dark.'

'Too dark? Well, who is its dad? Will he marry you?'

'Its father's my partner in Canada. He's half-Cree, half-negro, so his baby's going to be dark. He's a fine person, and I'd be happy to marry him. But, Eleanor, I'm in a terrible jam.' She stopped, and Eleanor waited, wondering what on earth was to come. 'You see, Eleanor, I must've conceived in the last day or two of my time in the Territories. He might not believe it's his. I'm terribly afraid, Eleanor.' The last words came out in a rush.

The other woman took a moment to assess this, then she said, with a laugh, 'He'll believe it when he sees it. There int many Blackies round these parts – and you'd never meet any, anyways.' She put some more sugar in her tea and then stirred it. She added, with dry humour, 'Rub the kid over with boot polish, to make sure!'

Despite the strain she was under, Wallace Helena began to gurgle with laughter. It set Eleanor laughing, and soon they were rolling in their chairs with mirth. It finished when Wallace Helena had a fit of coughing.

'Really, Eleanor! You're dreadful.'

When they had sobered a little and had mopped up the tea they had spilled, Eleanor asked, 'Will you be going home?'

'I'll have to. For a while, I had a hope that I might persuade Joe to settle here – the last few winters have bothered him; we get such bad ones. But thinking it over, I know he'd never be happy here. So I'll go home. I want the baby to have a father.'

'Oh, aye. That's important.' Eleanor's face was suddenly very sad, and Wallace Helena ventured to ask, 'Why didn't you and Uncle get married?'

'Me hubby's still alive,' answered Eleanor, her voice dull and hopeless.

Wallace Helena's mouth dropped open in complete surprise. 'I didn't dream you'd been married. I don't think Benji knows, does he?'

Eleanor looked at her suspiciously, wondering how much

Benji had talked about her with his cousin. She sighed, and said, 'I don't think nobody knows by now. It were a long time ago.'

'Couldn't you have divorced him?'

'I couldn't – being Catholic, like. Anyways, what for? He's mental, you see.'

'You poor woman!' Wallace Helena forgot her own problems. 'How did it happen?'

Eleanor swallowed, and looked round her rather helplessly. 'It were really me dad's fault,' she said. ''Cos I were so young – and proper innocent; with no brothers or sisters so I could see the difference between boys and girls – or guess where they come from. I didn't know what marrying was all about.' She twisted her arms into her apron, as if to protect herself from something, and then she went on, 'You know me dad left me this house?'

'Yes.'

'Well, he and me mam run a boot and shoe shop for years. Me dad were much older 'n me mam; but she were killed in a fall from the stepladder in the shop, when I were ten. And me dad couldn't stand the shop after she were gone, so he sold it when his auntie died and left him this house; and we started doing bed and breakfasts. We had some as was waiting for a boat and some as come on holiday to see relatives, or somethin', and not a few commercial travellin' gentlemen on their rounds.' She sighed gustily. 'I used to make the breakfasts and see to the washin' and all.'

'That's a lot for a ten-year-old.'

'Me dad helped with the cleaning and that, and he'd carry some of the trays. And it were better'n working twelve hours a day in a shop or being in service.'

'So, how did you meet your husband?'

'Well, when I were about sixteen, he come here with his mam and dad. He must've been about eighteen. They'd come from Cardiff on a visit, they said, and they was ever so friendly. They stayed about ten days, going out and about all over the place. We supposed they was on a holiday, but it come out afterwards they come to show the boy, Hughie, to a specialist.'

'Did he look mad?'

'No. Just a bit stupid, like some youths do. He didn't talk much,

302

and he did whatever his dad told him – and I realized afterwards that him or his mam told him every step of the way. He weren't too bad-looking – dark hair and blue eyes, like a smiling china doll. I was never alone with him for a minute – his mam or dad saw to that. Dad watched out for me pretty well, too, seeing as men were always coming and going in the house; but mostly much older men – being sales reps, like.'

She sniffed, as if to dismiss salesmen as not being worthy of much notice. 'Anyways, his parents made up to me dad like anything, and, two months later, they come back for another stay. They said as Hughie's uncle had got him a job, here in the docks. He were a big, heavy boy, so it sounded likely. And it seemed no time at all before his pa was saying to Dad what about a match between us.'

'Didn't your father see that he wasn't all there?'

'No. If you weren't expecting it, it weren't too obvious. When his mam said to kiss me, he wouldn't, and she said he were a proper shy lad. When he was alone with me, he'd be a lion, she said – and I remember her laughing.'

'Doesn't sound as if there was much to laugh about,' Wallace Helena said. 'What happened then?'

'Well, me dad hadn't been well for some time, and I think he were worried about me being left alone; and here were a decent family with a son with a job, a quiet enough boy who didn't drink – none of the family did. So he said it would be all right. And I were sixteen and thought, like most young girls do, that married life would be less work than being single; and me dad was going to buy me a new dress. I felt that important!

'So Mr Jones goes with Hughie to get a special licence – 'cos they've got to get back to their business in Cardiff. No time for calling guests or anything, and the next thing I know I'm in church being married, and Hughie being whispered to by his dad as to what he's to do and what fun it will be.' She paused reflectively. 'And that frightened me. We got back to the house, and I'd baked a cake and decorated it, so we had tea and cake. And Hughie was laughin' like an ape and eating half the cake. Then Mr Jones brought down their luggage, when a hackney come for 'em. He says goodbye, Hughie. They canter down them front steps as if the devil was after them, and away they go, leaving Hughie standing gaping in the hall. Me dad shuts the front door, and Hughie nearly goes berserk. He smashes the glass in the inner door, and out he goes, with his hand bleeding, screaming, "Mam!" after the carriage.

'Me dad went down the steps after him, wondering what had bitten him. Hughie turns round and hits me dad to the ground and comes back up the steps. I ran upstairs, I was so frightened. And I could hear him smashing the tea things on the table and then a big crash as he threw something through the sitting-room window here. He was a big lad and he made such a noise, a neighbour come out. Dad shouted to him to call the constable. Dad come in and couldn't see me; only Hughie tearing everything apart in an absolute little-boy paddywack, kicking and screamin'.

'I called Dad from upstairs, and he shouted back to stay where I was. It took the constable and me dad and the neighbour to arrest him.'

'How awful!'

Eleanor nodded. 'I were that scared, I thought I'd never come round,' she admitted.

'Whatever did you do?' asked Wallace Helena.

'Well, both me dad and me was terribly upset, as you can imagine. When Hughie were brought before the Magistrate, Dad went down to the Court. He told them he thought the man was mad, and told how he come into our house. The Magistrate agreed with him and the poor constable did, too. So they sent him to a hospital to be examined, and then they put him in a loony-bin.'

'And is he still there?'

'Not in that one. They finally traced 'is parents – they'd given us a wrong address, 'cos what they was doing was dumping him on us – getting rid of him, never wanting to see him again, like. He were like a little kid in his mind, and he acted like one when he realized his mam was leaving him with strangers.

'Me dad was heartbroken that he'd been had like that. All he wanted was a respectable fella to live in the house with me and bring a bit in. He died himself not too long after.'

'But it was considered a legal marriage?'

'Well, a long time after I heard that the Church could annul it. You see, being Catholic, as I said, I couldn't divorce him. It's a big job to get an annulment – and it costs. And the priests ask you such terrible private questions. And I were still young – I hardly knew what normally happened after the church service – working in the house all the time, I didn't have a close girl friend to talk to, like other girls have.'

'Did you talk to your priest?'

'I went once,' she said sulkily, 'and he read me a penny lecture about having to stay married even if your husband was sick. In them days, I was scared of God and the priests, so I took their word for it. I wasn't going to get married again, anyway – not after that basinful.'

Wallace Helena leaned forward and caught her hand. 'You poor girl,' she said.

Eleanor smiled dimly at the kindly gesture, and said, 'Then, years and years later, your Uncle Jamie come along.' A slow tear ran down her cheek.

'Did Uncle James know what had happened to you?'

'He did later. After Benji were coming, he wanted to marry me. But, you know, I couldn't apply for an annulment without the whole neighbourhood knowing. And as long as I kept quiet I doubt there was anyone around who knew the marriage had taken place, except the priest. Our next-door neighbour took it for granted that Dad had just had a spot of bother with a lodger.' She leaned towards Wallace Helena confidentially. 'And if I let it be known – or the Church did – that I'd been married to a loony, they could likely think that I were without me wits, too. And that would be proper awful for me – and for Benji. It'd only need a bit of a rumour.'

'Would they really be that stupid?'

'Oh, aye. They're more afraid of lunacy than anything else round here. Once they feel it's in a family – goodbye!'

'So you and Uncle James stayed quietly together?'

'Yes. It were a bit rough on Benji, but better than it going round that, maybe, he were me husband's kid and, therefore, tainted.' She sighed again, 'And I believed Jamie when he said he'd never leave me. Nor he never did. He were took, poor dear.'

She bowed her head and wept.

Wallace Helena hastily left her chair and eased her way round the tea table to comfort her. With her head against Wallace Helena's skirt Eleanor cried heartily.

'And now,' she sobbed, 'you got to go home, so the Lady Lavvie'll have to be sold – and what are we goin' to do, I'd like to know?'

'You've nothing to worry about there,' Wallace Helena assured her, as she took out her own grubby hanky to wipe Eleanor's face. 'Everything's going to work out just fine – as long as Benji agrees.'

There was the sound of a key in the front door lock. 'That'll be Benji,' his mother said, and hastily wiped her eyes with her hands. 'What was you sayin'?'

'I said everything's going to be all right. Just wait till Benji's here, and I'll tell you.'

As a very tired Benji came into the room, she straightened up and forced herself to smile. Behind it, she felt as weary as he looked. She had had to give comfort, when she had hoped to receive it.

Chapter Forty-Seven

That afternoon, Wallace Helena had spent over two hours with Mr Benson.

As soon as she was seated in his private office, she had gone straight to the point.

She said, 'You will be pleased to hear that I have reached a decision about the Lady Lavender.'

Mr Benson nodded, and drew a notepad towards him. 'What are you going to do?' he asked, with real interest.

'I'm going back to Canada,' she told him. 'But I don't want to sell the Lady Lavender.'

'Oh, really?' he queried, in some surprise.

'Yes, really. I want you to draw up an agreement between Mr Benjamin Al-Khoury and myself, which will make him a full partner in the enterprise. So that we share the company half-and-half. He'd run it – he'd have full responsibility for it.'

The lawyer looked at her in some perplexity. 'That would be very generous, Miss Harding. You do realize that you'll be sacrificing a considerable capital sum – which you'd get if you sold the property?'

'I know,' she replied, a little irritated because she was tired. 'But I believe I'll get a steady income out of my share of it for many years – and Benji – Mr Al-Khoury – has to be considered.'

'Does he know about this plan?'

He was surprised when she answered in the negative. He had imagined that young Benji had sold her the idea. She said, 'I'm buying his expertise with a partnership. If I leave him as Manager, he could be easily tempted to go to another soap company for higher pay – and I would not trust a new man. Then I would *have* to sell.'

'I see.' He sat quietly for a minute, while he thought the matter over, and she wondered if she could possibly explain to him the closeness which had grown up between her and her cousin. Would a lawyer understand such closeness? Or did he, as a family solicitor, have to negotiate, too often, between factions warring over Wills?

Finally, she said, 'As far as we know, Benjamin and I are the sole survivors of our family; we have no roots, except what lie in each other. Because of this and because I think he's an extraordinarily capable young man, I'm going to give him the chance of making a good living. He can draw a salary as Manager, and then whatever we make we share. Simple as that!'

'You have thought this over – and you're certain this is what you want to do?'

'Yes.'

'Well, frankly, I'm delighted for Mr Al-Khoury's sake. I've felt a great pity for him, ever since his father died. Mr James Al-Khoury always said that he could not have a better son.'

'He couldn't have had a more capable one,' Wallace Helena said.

They hammered out the details of the agreement, and Mr Benson promised to have a draft ready for her and for Benji to consider within a week. She reluctantly agreed to this. She wanted to be gone. The winter was coming.

It was the content of this interview that she unveiled to Benji and his mother, as they sat round the kitchen table while he ate his warmed-up dinner.

When she said flatly that she was arranging with Mr Benson that he should have a full partnership with her, he leaned back, fork and knife still in hand, and stared at her dumbfoundedly, and his mother, who was not quite certain what the partnership implied, looked anxiously at her son.

Then as it sank in, he swallowed hard. 'I don't know what to say!' he blurted out.

'Don't you like the idea?'

'Wallace Helena, it's wonderful! I never dreamed of such a thing.'

Wallace Helena heard Eleanor let out her breath as she

relaxed. She leaned across the table to pat her hand absently, as she watched Benji. He put down his knife and fork, pushed himself away from the table and came round to her. He put his arm round her shoulder, and said, his voice thick, 'I won't fail you. It's going to be tough, but I believe I can make something out of the Lady Lavender.'

'What do you mean? Tough?'

'The competition's very keen.'

'Tush! We're tougher. As I once said, "We live in interesting times!"'

He squeezed her shoulder and went back to his dinner. 'When do I start?' he asked, an eager light in his eyes.

'In about two weeks' time.'

Eleanor had seen the same expression on his father's face, the face of a man accepting a challenge. There's a lot of Jamie in our Benji, she thought happily.

'Are you ready for your puddin', luv?' she asked.

Chapter Forty-Eight

Joe had fumed and fretted for weeks over Wallace Helena's prolonged visit to Britain. Admittedly, she wrote regularly to him, keeping him informed of what she was doing. He did not reply to all she wrote; he was hard-pressed in her absence, first with the harvests of barley, hay and vegetables – and what little was left of the oats after a hailstorm, and then with the preparations for winter.

He had sometimes used Emily to help him and Simon Wounded, because the two hired hands were not very reliable and they had a fair herd of cattle to watch this year. Aunt Theresa complained when Emily was borrowed from her; she wanted her in the kitchen, to help to make pemmican and preserve vegetables.

As long as she did not have to go near the hired men, Emily never complained; she was easily frightened by any strange male, and she clung to Aunt Theresa as if she were still a child clinging to the nuns. It was as if she had suffered so much as a little girl that her mind and her normal responses to other human beings had been frozen. Joe did not think of her very much; she was simply another person to be fed and clothed in return for her work. Emily's real love, however, was for the hens that she fed and kept clean; they roosted in the barn and would come fluttering down from the beams, when she called them to be fed in winter. In summer, they fended for themselves and she clipped their wing feathers, so that they could not stray very far. During Wallace Helena's absence, she had set two clutches of eggs under broody hens, and she now had a goodly number of pullets scratching round the yard. She was anxious to show Wallace Helena how the flock had increased, before some of her

310

feathered friends had to have their throats slit; the flock was thinned severely every year, once the weather became bad, because they could rarely spare enough grain to feed a large number of birds until spring. She ventured to ask Joe one night over supper when he thought Wallace Helena would be home.

Joe had become more and more taciturn as the summer passed. He fought a growing fear that she would never return. He sensed that she had been seduced by the city – she was originally a city girl, wasn't she? He hoped that one of the fancy men around her had not also seduced her. Aunt Theresa had told him not to worry; but if Wallace Helena, without him, felt anything like he did without her, the temptation to seek consolation would be very great.

In answer to Emily's question, he grunted, 'Dunno.'

'Maybe there'll be a letter when you go down tomorrow,' Aunt Theresa suggested, as she ladled beans onto his tin plate. She spoke in Cree.

It took precious time to fetch the mail from the village which was growing up round the Fort; yet he knew he would go, because his longing for something of her was so great.

There was a letter. As was his custom, he slipped it into his jacket pocket; he would read it while on the trail riding home. Though a few more people now used the trail, it was still no more than a muddy lane, and ice from an early frost crackled under his boots as he dismounted to open the letter.

He was stunned by its content. A baby? How did he feel about becoming a proud father at his age? At her age? At first he grinned sheepishly. Then the idea hit him that it wasn't his – she said it was due in March.

It was as if he had been unexpectedly struck by a friend. The hurt in him felt worse than the pain he had suffered when he had caught the smallpox. Here she was, making smart little jokes that he would have to go out and shoot a rabbit so that there would be a warm skin to wrap it in – and yet how could it be his child?

By mutual agreement, they had always followed her mother's regime, so that they would have no children in such a harsh environment; he himself was easy about it because the tribe from which his mother came was either dead or scattered; his children would not have any particular group to belong to, and Wallace Helena had nobody, except her newfound cousin in Liverpool.

His attention had been so completely caught by her news of the baby that he hardly took in the information that she had divided the soap works between herself and her cousin; and that, given ordinary luck, there would be a remittance each year from her share, some of which could be used to help them out at the homestead.

His face was grey as he remounted and rode towards home.

As the sun sank lower, a cold wind arose in the north. It freshened him, and he tried to order his chaotic thinking and decide how he would deal with the situation.

She had said in her letter that she would probably be sailing across the Atlantic before the letter reached him; that meant she could be in Calgary within a week or two. What should he do?

When he rode into the yard and dismounted, he still felt so distraught that he thought he would vomit. Emily had just shooed the last of the hens into the barn for the night, and he asked her if she would stable the horse and rub it down for him. She took one look at his stony face, and nodded. She patted the animal and it went with her. His hunting dog, Bessie, heavy with puppies almost ready to drop, trotted over to him and nuzzled his hand. He ignored her, and she slunk away.

As he opened the heavy, wooden door into the cabin, Aunt Theresa looked up from the hearth; she was making bannock for supper. The cabin was still redolent with the smell of the dried meat, fat and berries of the pemmican she had made earlier in the month. Most of the work had been done outside, but she had finished the pounding of it indoors, because, she said, the wind had been so keen that it had made her old bones ache. Now, the smell was mixed with that of bannock, and to Joe it felt welcoming and homely.

He pulled out a chair and thankfully sat down. Aunt Theresa noticed, as he took off his felt hat and laid it on the table, that he was shivering slightly. He put his hand into his shirt pocket, took

312

out Wallace Helena's letter and flipped it onto the table beside the hat.

Aunt Theresa got up slowly from her squatting position and, in the silence, Joe heard her knees crack as she straightened them. The door also creaked, and he looked up. He had forgotten to shut it properly, and Bessie, his dog, nosed her way in. Half looking at Aunt Theresa, she slid almost on her stomach towards the fire. Aunt Theresa did not like dogs in the house, but Emily had accidentally shut her out of the barn, where she had found a warm corner in which to deliver her pups, and she knew her time was very near.

Aunt Theresa ignored her. She was far too concerned about her nephew. 'You ill?' she asked. She looked down at the letter and feared, suddenly, what it might contain. At no point had she thoroughly understood why Wallace Helena had had to go to Liverpool; the concepts involved were too far removed from her own experience.

Joe sighed. 'No, I'm not ill,' he said.

Aunt Theresa bent down and expertly turned over the bannock cooking on the hot stone in the hearth. 'What does she say?' she asked suspiciously, pointing to the letter.

'She's coming home - home within the month, I'd think.'

'You don't sound too happy about it.'

'She's going to have a baby.'

Aunt Theresa's normally immobile face broke into a suggestion of a smile. 'Well, that'll be good - we're all getting too stuck in our ways; there *should* be youngsters around.'

'How do I know it's my kid? We never had any before,' he snarled.

Aunt Theresa had turned back to her cooking. Now she froze where she stood. She was outraged.

When she found her voice, she was almost snarling herself. 'Joe Black! You've no reason to doubt her. She's never been flighty; if she had been, she'd have found a way to do it long since.'

'If it's not mine, I don't want it.'

'This is her home - and yours. If she wants to have it here, she'll have it here.'

313

'It don't mean I've got to stay here. I can go anywhere and make a living.'

Aunt Theresa clenched her teeth. She bent and took the last bannock to cook off the stone and wrapped it with the others in a cloth. Then she came round the table, to face her nephew. She had no children of her own, and he was the nearest thing to a son to her.

She said softly to him, 'We've all been together in this cabin for a long time; we know each other – and we've learned to trust each other. She's always shared what she had with us, good times and bad times. And she saved your life, when you had the smallpox, remember? If the child is yours, it's great to have a kid, especially if it's a boy; if it's not yours, then she'll need all our help very badly – she wouldn't be coming home if that weren't true.'

He did not respond. After she had waited for a moment, she touched the crouching dog's flank with her moccasined toe. 'You're not turning Bessie out because she's come home with a belly full of pups; are you going to turn away from Wallace Helena when she needs a place for her baby?'

He swallowed, and said, 'It'd be hard to be father to another man's brat.'

'Bah! It wouldn't be the first time a man's found a good kid by taking in a foundling. Anyway, she'd tell you straight if it wasn't yours – she's not afraid of anyone.' She put a comforting hand on his shoulder. The wrinkles on her face rippled as if, suddenly, she was trying to control a smile, and then she asked him, 'Are all Englishmen white?'

He looked sharply up at her in surprise. 'Sure,' he said. 'I've never seen a black one.'

'Well,' responded Aunt Theresa, with a flicker of triumph in her expression, 'where's she going to get a brown baby from in England? Any kid of yours she has is going to be easily recognizable.'

He stared blankly at her for a moment, and then he began to laugh, almost hysterically.

She did not let him see the triumph in her eyes. She merely said, in her usual gentle way, 'Now you get your stuff off the table

so that we can have supper. Simon and Emily'll be in soon -
starving, as usual.' She busied herself round the fire, and then
remarked, 'I know I'll be thankful when Wallace Helena's back -
there's too much work without her. And if we're going to have a
little kid round the place, I'll enjoy it, I know that.'

Joe nodded, and slowly took off his boots and jacket. He went
to the water barrel and took out a pannikin of water to wash his
hands. Aunt Theresa spread tin plates round the bare table.

'You know, Joe,' she said to him, 'lately I've wondered who
would look after you and Wallace Helena when you grow old.
Our tribe's scattered, your uncles and cousins are dead, except
for one - and he's in gaol in Montana. There are no young men to
take a lead in bringing the tribe together again. I reckon you need
a kid more than you need anything in the world.' She slapped
spoons down by the plates. 'It'd be someone to continue here,
after all the work you and Tom have put into this place - and
Wallace Helena.'

He bit his lower lip and did not answer her while he wiped his
face with a bit of towelling. She had brought up a subject which
he had never before considered. He and Wallace Helena had
always been smart enough to plan ahead for the homestead; but
he himself had rarely thought about his old age. When he had
thought of death it had always been because of an immediate
threat - epidemics like scarlet fever, diphtheria, tuberculosis, a
dozen scourges to which prairie dwellers had been subject. He
remembered his terror the day he had been cut off by a forest fire
- that would have been a fast but painful death. And out on the
trapline, alone, a small accident could incapacitate a man and
leave him to freeze to death. There had been for years the hovering fear of starvation. That he and Wallace Helena might grow
old and weak, in need of the help of others, had never occurred
to him.

As he sat down at the table, he shuddered at the idea of being
dependent upon others; but that was why his old grandfather
had had a number of wives - to breed sons to protect the tribe
and their hunting grounds when he was too old to do it, the best
man amongst them to take his place when he died.

He never said a word throughout supper. Afterwards, he went

315

over to the hired men's bunkhouse to have a word with Simon Wounded about the work for the next day. Then, though the temperature was dropping fast, he sat on the fence and again thought about becoming old.

Amongst the surviving Cree and Blackfoot, he had a number of friends and even distant relatives; he also considered some of the Metis who had settled round the Fort to be his friends, though Wallace Helena would have little to do with them; she had, in her youth, been too often insulted by them. Some of them already looked older than he himself did!

Partly because he had left his grandfather's lodge so young and partly because of the decimation of normal Indian life by the intrusion of white people – even the first settlements thousands of miles away in the east had had a ripple effect across the country – he had considered himself a loner, perfectly capable of looking after himself. He had never considered that he might need care from someone else.

Even as a young man, he had realized that the traditional Indian way of life was coming to an end, and he had seen the wisdom of joining up with friendly, easy-going Tom Harding in an endeavour to wrest a living from the land. That decision had been a wise one, which had brought Wallace Helena into his life as a wonderful, additional gift.

He was lucky, he reflected, as he struck a match to light another cheroot, that he had a large homestead – half a large one, he corrected himself – which was flourishing very well. And now Aunt Theresa had suddenly knocked his feet from under him, by telling him he needed a child because he was going to grow as old as some of the toothless gaffers sitting on the bench outside Ross's Hotel on a warm summer day. And who do they live with? he asked himself suddenly. The reply came equally fast – with their sons or daughters!

So, for his own sake, Aunt Theresa had advised him to welcome Wallace Helena's baby, foundling or not.

He did not like the way his thoughts had led, and he jumped off the fence, to walk up and down the frozen yard. He was getting stiff with cold, he realized.

He was reminded of Wallace Helena sitting with him on the

fence, evening after evening, and it was with deep longing that he considered her imminent return. Suppose Aunt Theresa was right and that the yellow bastard who was her cousin had not touched her; that by some fluke the child was his own? How did he feel about that?

Could the kid have been conceived in Calgary? That had been quite a wild night. He had always trusted her to tell him when they should not make love – he never bothered to count; his days were always so busy he was lucky if he knew whether it was Monday or Friday.

She'd been afraid that night, afraid of the long journey and of meeting a whole bunch of strangers, the first time he had seen her really nervous for years. He had tried to comfort her and she had cuddled into him, maybe thinking she'd get away with it, for once. Maybe she hadn't.

He slowly began to grin. He stopped walking to look at the moon shining through slowly falling ice crystals. He took a quick pull on his cheroot, dropped the butt and ground it under his heel. That, he decided, would be something else.

Chapter Forty-Nine

Wallace Helena sat silent and withdrawn beside the driver of a Red River cart, as it bumped its way along the familiar trail from Fort Edmonton to her home. The path was already covered by a light fall of snow and the trees that lined it were leafless; only a few spruce amongst them stood straight and proud, their ever-green branches holding a sprinkling of snow. Except for the piercing shriek of the ungreased wheels of the cart, there seemed to be no other noise. She had forgotten how still the countryside could be in winter; her ears had become attuned to the constant rumble of heavy horse-drawn traffic on city streets.

The five-day journey by stagecoach from Calgary had drained her strength to such a degree that she wondered if she would manage this last five miles without fainting; bearing a child cer-tainly took all one's stamina, she decided ruefully, her hands clasped across the base of her stomach to ease the jolting of the cart.

In view of her condition, Benji had insisted that she should travel second class on the boat, rather than steerage, which to save money she had been prepared to do.

'You're not that poor,' he had told her with a laugh. 'In any case, I won't hear of it; somebody's got to take care of you – and you'll have more care second class.'

Parting from Benji had been much harder than she had expected. Once he knew about the baby and then about the part-nership, he had cared for her as if she was something infinitely precious. He showered affection on her, as did his mother. Once again, he offered to marry her, saying he would do his utmost to help the baby.

It would have been so easy, she meditated, to be cosseted at home and be the soap mistress in public. And Benji loved her, she felt, even if he were not in love. Young and vigorous, he would have given her another child inside twelve months.

And yet, she could not imagine life without Joe. It was no good. Without him she felt she barely existed. And it was his child. So here she was going back to the day-in-day-out battle of being a settler.

'You're as crazy as a coot,' she told herself, but she grinned with anticipation of the end of the journey.

It was as well that Benji had insisted on a more comfortable sea journey, because she had been so seasick that she had feared she would miscarry. The steward had finally suggested that she would be better up on deck in the fresh air, and she had dressed and crawled up, to sit in a deck chair. The man had brought her a few precious apples to eat.

He had been right, and on the third day the seasickness had abated. Wrapped in a heavy winter shawl, a farewell gift from Eleanor, she was soon walking unsteadily round the deck.

In the fresh sea breeze, she felt suddenly happy to be going home. Her longings for Lebanon had slowly declined in the friendly atmosphere of Liverpool. When she had been tired or depressed, it had been to Joe that her thoughts had turned, or sometimes simply to the sunlit, snow-covered landscape and the keen, clean winds of Alberta. Lebanon, with its lovely scents, orchards, wines and silks, its wondrous mountains and tumbling rivers, its cosmopolitan, sophisticated people, had receded, had become an unattainable Garden of Eden, to which there was no return.

Perhaps, by the time her baby was grown, Lebanon would have thrown off the Turkish yoke and be at peace, and he could visit it, to see from what great beauty his mother had sprung. A sweetness from it would remain with her always, like the delicious after-taste of a good lemon sherbet; but she sensed that she would never see it again.

In her womb, feeling very uncomfortable with the bumping of the cart, lay a child whose roots lay in the history of the Northwest Territories. She smiled a little ironically when she thought about it. Its father would teach it to farm and trap, and she would teach it all the languages she knew, especially Arabic. Perhaps, by the time it was old enough, it could journey east to Upper or Lower Canada to have better schooling than the nuns and the priests in the Territories could give it.

When she and Joe were gone, it would own the biggest farm in the immediate neighbourhood and half of a soap factory in Liverpool; with luck, it would have friendly cousins in that city whom it could visit. It would have its niche in the world.

She began to think about the farm. After much debate with retailers, she had not brought any agricultural implements with her; instead, she had brought a number of catalogues from them for Joe to see.

When staying in the house of her grandfather's frail old friend, Mr Nasrullah, for one night after landing from the boat at Montreal, she had again mentioned to him her continuing interest in new farming practices. He had assured her that one of his sons, who lived with him, had already been asked to obtain any papers or magazines he could from eastern Canadian sources, for her. 'He knows everybody worth knowing,' the old man assured her, his dark eyes twinkling. 'He says there's a lot of research being done in Upper Canada, and with the postal system so improved because of the railway, he'll put you in touch with the right people.'

She had been very comforted at realizing that there was at least one more family in Canada which spoke Arabic, though the old man complained that his grandsons spoke only French, and to be assured that the Northwest Territories were not nearly so isolated as they had been. It was with a certain amount of hope that she sat in the train for over two days and watched the hundreds of miles of forest and silent lakes past which the train chugged. It disturbed huge flocks of birds, but very few other living things, except for an occasional tiny settlement. Winnipeg had been a turmoil of people, mostly men; other than that there was little to suggest that human life existed.

She had been bitterly disappointed that Joe had not been at Calgary to meet her, though it was probable that he had not yet received her letter giving the likely time of arrival.

Because the weekly stagecoach up to Edmonton would not

leave until the following day, she stayed the night at the same hotel in which she and Joe had stopped on her outward journey. The public rooms seemed full of male rowdies, so she prevailed on a hurrying young man in a white apron to bring her up a plate of dinner, and to obtain for her a basket of bread and cheese to sustain her on her journey north. The following morning, the same youngster helped her down with her luggage and onto the stagecoach.

She and a sturdy-looking Scottish youth were the only travellers; the driver said he thought some people had been deterred by the threat of snow.

In an accent which was difficult for Wallace Helena to follow, the boy confided that his name was Alex McLeod and that he had come from Glasgow to be a clerk with the Hudson's Bay Company. He was most impressed when she told him that she had farmed near the Fort since 1862, and he was further impressed when she slipped effortlessly into French to speak to the Metis driver.

Her attitude to the young Scot was very different from that which she would have exhibited had she met him before her visit to England. Though in Britain men had sometimes patronized her unmercifully, she had met with a lot of friendliness in Liverpool, and she had responded to it. Added to this had come the realization that, though she and Joe had lived their lives in comparative isolation, her baby would need friends. Her instinct to protect the child and smooth its path had become intense, and the lonely, rather scared young clerk was the first to experience her change of heart.

The driver knew who she was and her reputation for arrogance; he was surprised that she bothered to speak French to him and was pleased at her straightforward friendliness. They became quite a merry party.

The journey was bitterly cold, as if the wind was coming through snow. They were grateful for the four stops they made en route, where they could rest for a while, the horses were changed and the calls of nature dealt with. By the time they left Red Deer Crossing and were on their way to Battle River, Wallace Helena had become so fatigued she wondered if she would survive the remaining hundred miles. She was fortunate that snow did not hit them until they were on the last part from Peace Hills to Edmonton; it came down in short, sharp flurries, which made it difficult for the driver to follow the trail. It also seeped through the inadequate canvas roofing of the stagecoach and accumulated in a caked mass on the robes covering the passengers.

When they finally drove down the hill to John Walter's ferry and could see the Fort on the other side of the river, Wallace Helena was truly thankful; and young McLeod, though forewarned what to expect, wondered what on earth he had come to. They descended while the coach was loaded onto the ferry and they crossed the river, and they finally parted at Mr Ross's Hotel, McLeod to report to the Fort, Wallace Helena to seek rest and a meal in the hotel.

She felt better once she was thoroughly warmed and fed, and she was able to arrange for a carrier with a Red River cart to take her out to the homestead.

Now, as she was driven along the home trail, on top of her fatigue was the anxiety regarding the reception she would get from Joe. Perhaps he had not come down to Calgary to meet her because he was furious with her? Did not believe the child was his?

It was Aunt Theresa's sharp ears that first heard the squeak of the Red River cart and then the creak of the yard gate opening; it was Emily who ran out to hug her as she descended. Old Simon Wounded came limping out of the barn which he had been mucking out; he reeked of manure, but, with tears in her eyes at how he had aged in her absence, Wallace Helena flung her arms round him. He simpered shyly. Aunt Theresa met her at the cabin door to welcome her with her familiar gentle smile.

She stumbled into her home and sat down immediately on the nearest chair. Slowly she looked round her.

It was very untidy, she noted with a faint grimace, and it needed cleaning; but it had the same homely simplicity as Elsie's house down by the Mersey River; everything in it was there for a purpose.

While Aunt Theresa invited the driver in to have something to eat before he returned, Wallace Helena unpinned her hat. Emily promptly took it from her to examine it. She had never seen such an interesting bit of headgear before, and she giggled at it.

Wallace Helena closed her eyes; she was swaying on her chair with a fatigue deeper than she had felt for many years. Yet it felt so good to be home. Until she had arrived at Edmonton, she had not realized how well she understood her surroundings in Canada; everything was perfectly familiar to her. It was a harsh world that had helped to make her what she was and she knew how to cope with it. Except for Joe. At the moment, she was not too sure how to cope with him.

'Where's Joe?' she asked carefully.

Simon Wounded answered her. 'He's up checking the windbreaks – for the steers. We both reckon heavy snow is coming in. I thought he'd have heard you coming.'

'Wind's in the wrong direction,' Aunt Theresa told him absently as she brought out her coffee mugs.

'I'll go up and get him,' Simon Wounded offered.

'No. Don't bother him. Let him come when he's finished. I won't have coffee, thanks, Aunt Theresa. I need to lie down for a while. It's been a long journey. Could you bring my luggage in, Simon, when you've finished your coffee?'

She got up and lurched to her bedroom. The bed was a tumble of feather-filled covers, which had replaced the buffalo robes of long ago. She took off her boots, coat, skirt and bodice and, in her petticoats, lay thankfully down and pulled a quilt over her and slept.

She was still dead-asleep when, in the late afternoon, Joe came into the room. He stood looking down at her, and then he grinned. He was in his stockinged feet and now he threw off his jacket and very quietly crawled in beside her. She stirred and murmured, 'Joe, you old devil,' and took him in her arms.

Three weeks later, Joseph Black, bachelor, and Wallace Helena Al-Khoury Harding, spinster, were married in the little wooden church of St Joachim, in the hamlet of Edmonton. It was a small gathering attended by only a few Roman Catholic Crees, a few

Metis friends of the bridegroom and their wives and children, and a young Scottish lad, Alex McLeod, recently come to serve the Company.

Leila Helena Black was born on 10th March, 1887, to astonished, adoring parents. She was helped into the world by wise old Aunt Theresa and another knowledgeable old Cree lady friend.

'A girl!' Joe exclaimed. He began to laugh. Already besotted, he touched the tiny scrap of humanity's dark cheek with a tenderness surprising in so big a man. 'I can't teach a girl to trap, or – or castrate a bull!'

Wallace Helena turned her head on the pillow. 'Why not?' she demanded. 'Women can do absolutely anything, if they set their minds to it!'

He bent to kiss her, and said, with mock resignation, 'I guess if they're your kids they probably can.'

SELECT BIBLIOGRAPHY

Anonymous *Liverpool and Slavery*. A. Bowker and Son. Liverpool, 1884

Bibby, John P. *The Bibbys of Conder Mill and Their Descendants*. J. P. Bibby. Liverpool, 1979

Bibby, J. B. and C. L. *A Miller's Tale*. J. Bibby and Sons. Liverpool, 1978

Becker, Horst J. *Gateway Guide to Jordan, Lebanon, Syria*. Methuen. London, 1967

Cotton, E. J. *Buffalo Bud*. Hancock House Publishers. North Vancouver, 1981

Dempsey, Hugh A. *Big Bear – The End of Freedom*. Douglas and McIntyre. Vancouver, 1984

Dempsey, Hugh A. *Indian Tribes of Alberta*. Glenbow Museum. Calgary, 1988

Fawcett, Raymond, Ed. *Soap – Where Does It Come From?* Gawthorn. London, 1949

Gell, Robert. *Liverpool's Railway Stations 1830–1985*. Heyday. Crosby, 1985

Hitti, Philip K. *The Near East in History*. D. Van Nostrand Co., Inc. Princeton, 1961

Horne, J. B., and Maund, T. B. *Liverpool Transport Vol. 1*. The Light Railway Transport League. London, 1985.

Jackel, Susan. *A Flannel Shirt and Liberty*. University of British Columbia Press. Vancouver, 1982.

Jarvis, Anthea. *Liverpool Fashion, The Dressmaking Trade in Liverpool, 1830–1940*. Merseyside County Museums. Liverpool, 1981.

Leonard, David. *Richard Secord*. Richard Secord. Edmonton, 1981

Loren, W. *Black People Who Made the Old West*. Thos. Y. Crowell. New York, 1977.

Macdonald, George Heath. *Edmonton – Fort – House – Factory*. Douglas Print Co. Edmonton, 1959

MacGregor, James G. *A History of Alberta*. Hurtig. Edmonton, 1972

MacGregor, James G. *Edmonton, A History*. Hurtig. Edmonton, 1967

325

Metcalfe, V. *Journey Fantastic.* McGraw-Hill Ryerson. Toronto, 1970

Mohr, Merilyn. *The Art of Soapmaking.* Camden House Publishing, Ltd. Camden East, 1979

Nevitt, R. B. *A Winter at Fort McLeod.* McClelland and Stewart. Toronto, 1974

Pears, A. and F., Ltd. *The Story of Pears' Transparent Soap.* Pears. London, undated

Scott, Dixon. *Liverpool.* Adam and Charles Black. London, 1907

Thubron, Colin. *The Hills of Adonis.* William Heinemann, Ltd. London, 1968

Williams, Edmund. *The Story of Sunlight.* Unilever PLC. London, 1984

Wright, T. W. *Overlanders 1858 – Gold.* Western Producer Prairie Books. Saskatoon, 1985

326